Every Chance

With You

Every Chance With You

New York Times Bestselling Author
LEXI RYAN

Ebook ISBN: 9781940832326

Print ISBN: 978-1-940832-33-3

Created with Vellum

For Audrey, because she loves me more than she hates love triangles—thank you for being an amazing friend and cheerleader!

ACKNOWLEDGMENTS

This book is dedicated to my friend Audrey Carlan, who speaks about the sisterhood and lives it unlike anyone else. I am so grateful to have met you in France all those years ago and to call you a friend. You never fail to lift me up when I'm down and to inspire me with your passion and heart.

To everyone who provided me feedback on this story along the way—especially Tina Allen, Larissa Cardozo, Heather Carver, Thorunn Kristjansdottir, Aimz Woodz, Carissa Robins—you're all awesome. Lauren Clarke at Creating Ink, thank you for the insightful line and content edits. You push me to be a better writer and make my stories the best they can be. Thanks to Arran McNicol at Editing720 and Virginia Carey for proofreading. Thank you to Wander Aguiar, who took the gorgeous cover photo and to Hang Le for the cover design. I'm grateful for this team!

To all of the bloggers, bookstagrammers, readers, and reviewers who help spread the word about my books, I am humbled by the time you take out of your busy lives for my stories. I can't thank you enough. You're the best.

To my agent, Dan Mandel, for believing in me and staying by my side. Let's keep making exciting things happen!

As always, a big thank-you to my fans. Because of you, I live my dream every day. I couldn't do it without you, and I don't take one second for granted. You're the coolest, smartest, best readers in the world. I appreciate each and every one of you!

I owe this book to my family and friends, who helped me through one of the hardest seasons of my life. Thank you to Brian, who remains my safe haven through all life's storms, and to my children, who remind me that even the hard times are full of so much goodness. To my mom and siblings, thank you for all of your help over the past year. I love you all so much!

~LEXI

ABOUT THIS BOOK

From #1 *New York Times* bestseller Lexi Ryan comes a sexy love triangle about secrets, family bonds, and the kind of mistakes that haunt us.

When I met Alec Hayes in Vegas, I thought I'd stumbled into a love affair with the man of my dreams. Alec's sexy, confident, and charming. Our night together was full of laughter and the kind of toe-curling kisses that tempted me to believe in fate for the first time in years.

Until I flew out to LA to surprise Alec and ran into the unnamed half-brother he'd admitted to despising.

But I know Oliver Rhett as soon as I see him.

Oliver's the reason I stopped believing in destiny. He was my first love and my first heartbreak. And now he's the reason I can't be with Alec.

It's not fair to give one man the scraps of my heart when Oliver would always be right there to remind me he still holds the rest.

But when Alec needs a favor, I can't turn my back on

him. Even if it means falling a little more for his gentle charm every day. Even if it means facing Oliver and remembering exactly how brazenly he stole my heart.

My plan is to walk away. I can't make this family feud worse. But I didn't realize just how hard a broken heart can fall.

Every Chance With You *is the fourth novel in the Orchid Valley series. These books can all be read as standalones, but you'll enjoy reading them as a series!*

PROLOGUE

SAVVY

Some might say that showing up on a man's doorstep in nothing but a scrap of lace and a trench coat makes me a walking cliché. I, however, like to think of this moment as an homage to the night I met Alec Hayes.

It was Vegas, and we were both looking for a good time. The night went exactly how you would expect it to—a blur of dancing, drinking, and hot, stolen kisses. The even blurrier moments—the ones just beyond my grasp—were the ones in his suite. All I have from the end of that night are bits and pieces: his lips skimming down the sides of my neck, his big hands gripping my thighs before sliding around to cup my ass, and the delicious weight of his body on mine.

That wasn't a total blackout night for me, but I still wish I could remember it with more clarity. Which brings me here, to the doorstep of his fancy L.A. mansion. I'm ninety percent sure that it's not nerves but excitement that has my hands shaking as I extend a finger to press the doorbell.

I hold my breath as the heavy footsteps inside make their way toward the door. I grip the ties on my coat, ready to give Alec a show the moment I see his face.

But when the door flies open, I freeze.

Time and space fall away. I don't just question if I'm at the right house, but if the last five years ever happened. Because the man looking back at me is not Alec Hayes at all. The man looking back at me is straight out of my past. I haven't seen him since I was twenty-one years old and he broke my heart.

A smile stretches across Oliver Rhett's face, and he slowly scrapes his gaze down the front of my trench coat, as if he knows exactly what I'm wearing—or *not* wearing—beneath it.

"Savannah Downing," he says, his voice a gravelly rumble. "Holy shit. You're as beautiful as you were the last time I saw you."

I could say the same for him. His gray eyes are like the sea before a storm. His dark hair is neatly trimmed but swept back as if he's been dragging frustrated hands through it. And that body? I might only be able to remember snippets from my night with Alec, but I remember *exactly* how Oliver's body felt—the way his hips pressed into mine, the way he'd hold my wrists and my gaze as he slid inside me, how it felt to hear him whisper my name like a prayer before he surrendered to his own pleasure.

I never thought I'd see him again.

My gaze flies to the house number and back to the door, but I double- and triple-checked the address. I *know* I'm at the right place. "What are you doing here?"

He folds his arms and leans one shoulder against the doorframe, his smile turning crooked. "That's *my* line." He's silent a beat, then cocks his head to the side. "But from the look on your face, I'm guessing you're not here looking for me? Do you know Rose?"

Who's Rose? Is that his wife? Why does the idea of him being married feel like a dull blade in the center of my chest?

"This isn't your house." The words are strangled. Too desperate.

"You're right. I'm here visiting my sister."

I am a *confident, self-assured* woman. I won't let Oliver turn me into a mess again just because this moment makes no sense. How could I come to surprise Alec and find myself looking Oliver in the eye? *It doesn't matter. He hasn't mattered since he broke your heart and disappeared from your life.* I'm here for a man I know would never do that. "I'm looking for Alec Hayes."

Oliver straightens and drops his arms. All the warm amusement in his expression drains away and he turns as cold as his steely eyes. "I see. And how do you know my brother?"

Brother. Bullshit. There's no way Oliver could be

Alec's brother. Oliver is hardened and calculating, while Alec is sweet and thoughtful and possesses all the goodness I long ago stopped expecting from men. Never mind that they don't even share a last name. There's nothing remotely similar about these two.

Except their jaw lines. Except their smiles.

Fate couldn't be so cruel, could it? And anyway, wouldn't Alec have mentioned Oliver? We talked about our families in Vegas. We talked about—

I take a step back. Alec *did* tell me about a half-brother he can't stand. Did he ever say his name? Why didn't I ask?

And Oliver . . . well, Oliver never told me shit about his family when we were together. Because we were never really a couple. That was just my overly naïve perception of a fucked-up situation.

"Is this your idea of revenge?" Oliver asks. "Seems a little petty. And after all this time."

"What? This has nothing to do with you."

Stepping forward, Oliver trails a finger across my exposed collarbone. He tips his head to the side. "You're fucking my brother just weeks after you called me out of the blue, but I'm supposed to think this has nothing to do with me? That I'll throw myself at your feet to keep you from dressing like"—his eyes blaze as he scrapes his gaze over me again—"like *this* for Alec?"

Whore.

The word he didn't say howls through my head like a siren. His father thought I was a whore, and Oliver defended me. But then the truth came out, and any reasonable person could see I'd been fooling myself by believing I was anything more to Oliver than a means to an end. Love will do that do you.

I hate him. I hate him. I hate him. I hate him.

So why does my heart ache so much at the sight of those haunting eyes? And why did I make that drunken phone call just days after meeting Alec? Oliver didn't answer. I left a message. That night is pretty fuzzy, but I think I told him I didn't ever want to see him again and that I was moving on—though the fact that I'd made the call at all after all these years begs to differ.

"My relationship with Alec has *nothing* to do with you. If I had known that—"

"You *are* fucking him." His mouth curls in a sneer. "Hell, Savvy, if you were that hard up, you should've just said so in your message. You know I'm always here to take care of your needs."

Take care of me. Not *love* me. Not *be with me*. Fuck me. Get me off.

But my traitorous body thinks letting him take care of those needs is a great idea. The part of me that remembers just how good it was between us practically purrs at the possibility of going there again. Not that I would—not as long as I have a shred of dignity left in my body.

Oliver slides his cell from his pocket. "I'll drop my brother a text and let him know you're here."

"Don't," I blurt.

He cocks a brow. "Don't text the guy you flew across the country to see?"

I give a shaky nod. "Just forget it. Forget you saw me."

Whatever Alec and I had, whatever that single night in Vegas started between us, it ended the second Oliver opened that door.

Part One

PRESENT DAY

Two and a half years later

CHAPTER ONE

SAVVY

I'm late.

I hate being late. But the news I got this morning has left me off my game all day.

I slam my car door shut and jog across the street to Smithy's bar, where I'm meeting my friends.

"Savvy!" someone calls before I reach the door.

I turn and see the bar's owner, Smithy, coming up the sidewalk, hands tucked in pockets. "Hey, bud," I say. "What's up?"

"Just running in to check on the new bartender. What about you? How's my beautiful future wife?"

I roll my eyes and smile. "Not much. How's my future ex-husband?"

He chuckles, low and raspy, like he's laughed so much his vocal cords have worn out from it. "You know it, hot stuff. You and me would be like an explosion—short, but *so hot* and *so worth it*."

"No doubt." I grin and nod toward the bar, where I already know Abbi, Brinley, and Stella are waiting for me. "I'd better head in. I'm meeting the girls."

"For real?" He presses his palm to his chest. "Are you telling me my girls are reuniting after . . . what? A decade apart?"

"A *slight* exaggeration," I say.

"Barely."

I know what he means. It sure feels like forever since we've all been able to get together. I can't even blame the girls all having men in their lives now. My schedule is just as crazy. There comes a point in your life where you either need to make your peace with the status quo or start to hustle for something bigger. I've been hustling.

Smithy pulls the door open and gestures for me to head in. "After you, beautiful."

I wink at him, adjust my purse on my shoulder, and head to a booth at the back of the bar where the girls are already sipping their drinks.

"She's here!" Brinley crows, putting down her glass and clapping her hands. She slides out of the booth and wraps me into a big hug, as if we didn't just see each other at work this morning.

I squeeze her back. "Good to see you outside the office for once," I say, pulling away.

"I know. I've been working too much, but I was just telling the girls that I'm restructuring at The Orchid so I can slow down a little."

"Well, good for you!"

"It's about time, right?" Abbi says.

I nod. "For sure."

We take our spots in the booth across from Abbi and Stella, and Stella leans across the table and narrows her eyes at me. "Why are you late, bitch?"

"Don't call her a bitch," Abbi chides.

Stella rolls her eyes. "She knows I mean it lovingly."

"I was stuck at work," I say, and when Brinley's face creases with that worried-boss look, I add, "With a client."

"Someone else who works too much," she says. "When are you going to let me hire another full-time trainer to help you back there?"

I shake my head. "Not until I find the right person. Anyway, you know I'm a control freak. This way I get to make all the rules."

"Preach," says Abbi. She just opened her own bakery, but even when she ran the kitchen at The Orchid, she was known for being a hard-ass with her employees. No one runs a cleaner kitchen than Abbi.

"So, what's that look?" Stella asks.

I frown. "What look?"

She waves her pointer finger between my eyes. "That wrinkle only pops up when you're stressing about something. What's up?"

"It's nothing. I'm fine. I just didn't get a lot of sleep last night."

Brinley turns and narrows her eyes at me. "Stella's right. You *do* have that look. It's obviously *not* nothing."

"You know you can talk to us, right?" Abbi asks.

I sigh and do my best to relax my face. I'm sure I fail.

"Spill," the girls chorus.

"I had this stupid dream of being one of The Rage Fitness premier instructors."

"Why is that a stupid dream?" Abbi asks, cocking her head to the side. And that's what I love about Abbi. She might have her own issues with her body and her confidence, but she never projects that onto me. She never judges me for being a gym rat or for counting my macros to make sure I can get as strong as I want. And I know she won't judge me for this either. Honestly, I doubt any of them will.

"What's The Rage?" Stella asks.

"The fitness streaming app," Brinley says. "Marston said it's offered by a lot of the higher-end hotels they stay with when they travel."

"In hotels and in millions of homes across America," I say. "Every quarter, The Rage picks up a new fitness instructor and lets them create their own program for their streaming platform. The instructor gets to give guidance on everything from lifestyle to meditation to nutrition *and* stream a new live workout five days a week." I take a deep breath and clutch my hands in my lap. "Well, I applied, like I do every year, and they want to interview me in L.A. next week."

"That's awesome!" Abbi says.

"Congratulations!" Brinley adds.

Stella frowns. "What's the catch?" She knows me too

well. She *knows* I'd be all excitement and zero dread if I hadn't screwed this up. Well, minimal dread at least.

I look away, focusing on Smithy's servers hustling behind the bar for a few beats. I'm embarrassed about this part. "In my audition tape, I might have implied I was planning a wedding."

"Why would you do that?" Brinley's brow wrinkles.

"Is that the angle that you're going for?" Abbi asks. "Targeting women trying to fit into wedding dresses? Tightening tummies and sculpting arms and all that?"

Stella folds her arms. "Really? What happened to your mantra? *Work out to get stronger, not smaller*?"

I bobble my head from side to side. "I mean I might have tried to imply that? But the truth is I wanted the CEO to think I was planning a wedding so that she'd assume there was a man involved in my business."

Abbi wrinkles her nose like she smells something bad, and Stella's RBF holds strong. Brinley just looks confused.

I sigh. "It's disgusting and I'm not proud that I was willing to play the game."

"It's so out of character for you," Brinley says. "You're so independent. You don't need a man to—"

"I know I don't! But this woman? She's got internalized misogyny like you wouldn't believe. Everyone knows that if you get a meeting with her and she realizes you don't have a man on your team or programming your workouts or making your business decisions, she dismisses you."

Abbi mimes gagging over her shoulder, Stella looks like she's ready to cut a bitch, and Brinley says, "Yuck."

"I know. But this opportunity is bigger than that. We're talking about the ability to reach millions of women and teach them that heavy weights aren't just for men, showing them how good it feels to be strong and powerful in their own skin, teaching them to love their bodies and all they can do." I drag a hand down my face. "I thought it might be worth playing the game for this opportunity, but now she wants my fiancé to come to dinner and explain his role in my business."

Stella shudders as if she just discovered spiders crawling all over her. "This woman is despicable."

"Agreed! I know. So now I don't know what to do." I swallow hard. "I mean, obviously I need to admit I lied. Or tell her the wedding's off or . . . I don't know. I don't want to lose this opportunity. There's no other platform that would allow me to reach so many women."

"You reach *a lot* of women now," Abbi says. "How many followers do you have on Instagram? You're, like, the biggest influencer I know."

I make a face. I hate the word *influencer.* I get it, but I hate it. "First of all, I'm the *only* influencer you know. And it's not the same. I want to be . . ." I shake my head. "It doesn't matter. If I show up to that meeting without a fiancé, I already know what will happen."

Stella passes me her lemon-drop martini.

"Why not have someone pretend to be your fiancé?" Brinley asks.

I freeze with Stella's glass halfway to my lips. "What?"

"Hear me out," she says. "I'm not saying you should get married or anything. Just show up to the meeting with a friend. Have him pretend to be your fiancé and pretend he plays an active role in planning your program. It's icky, but you're right. The ends justify the means."

"The only guys I'm close enough to for that are attached to my best friends, and I'd rather not find myself in an awkward there's-only-one-bed scenario with Marston, Dean, or Kace." I shudder. "No offense. And the only other person I can think to ask is Smithy. Can you imagine him playing that role?"

Abbi snorts. "Oh God. Please do. And film it for me."

"I'm all about *sculpting dat ass*," Stella says in her best Smithy impression.

We laugh, and for a minute, my worries fall away. I've missed time with my girls.

"What about Alec?" Brinley asks. "He could do this for you."

I look down at my hands. "No. I can't ask him."

"Why not?" Stella asks. "You two are 'friends,' right?"

"Why the air quotes?" When she doesn't bother to bite back her grin, I roll my eyes. "It would feel like using him."

She waggles her brows. "From what Brinley's said, I get the impression he would very much like to be *used* by you. And then you'd have someone you could really enjoy that one-bed scenario with."

I put my head on the table and focus on the clinking glasses and laughter at the tables around us.

"Worried you might like it?" Abbi asks.

"Staaahp," I whimper.

"Alec is coming into town tonight," Brinley says, and I can feel all their eyes on me.

I bite my bottom lip. Alec Hayes still haunts my dreams in the very best way. Only it's not so great because I can't have him. "That's nice. It'll be good to see him."

Stella grins. "Good to see him like *hey, old friend,* or good to see him like *I'm ready to quit being stupid about this amazing guy who wants me in his life.*"

I shift awkwardly, wishing our server would hurry over and supply me with a vat of liquor. "Um . . . the first one?"

Brinley shakes her head. "My point is, you might as well run it by him. I'm sure he'd be thrilled to help."

Abbi stares at me so hard I'm convinced she's trying to peer into my brain. "I don't understand you. Alec is still head over heels for you. Do you realize that?"

"I'm sorry, but he is *so fucking hot,*" Stella says, biting her bottom lip. "Tell me again why you aren't climbing him like a tree?"

Abbi arches a brow. "I don't think my brother would like hearing you say that about another guy."

Stella scoffs. "As if that man has anything to worry about. He knows he owns me heart and soul, and there's *nobody* who does it for me like he does in the bedroom."

Abbi cringes. "I retract my objection. Please stop."

Brinley bites back a laugh. "I think what Stella was trying to say is that we know you're attracted to him, so what gives?"

"There's more to relationships than how hot someone is," I object.

"Yeah," Abbi says, swirling her martini. "Like how kind they are and how wanted and loved they make you feel."

Brinley hides her smile behind her hand, but it doesn't mute the sound of her giggle.

"Hardworking and successful are qualities that also don't suck," Stella says before snagging her martini back and taking a sip.

"You guys, shut up. It's just not gonna happen with me and Alec, and I'm not going to use him to get a job."

The girls hum in unison, an agreement to drop it for now, but I know this isn't the last I'll hear about it. I just need to figure out a better solution, because if I can't give Alec the relationship he wants with me, I'm not going to ask him to do me a favor this big.

ALEC

"Good to see you, brother," Marston says when he greets me at his front door. He wraps me in a big hug and slaps me on the back.

"You too," I say, returning his embrace.

He waves me in and leads the way to his and Brinley's family room. With a vaulted wood-beamed ceiling and warm colors, it's simultaneously grand and inviting. A *home.* Marston deserves this more than anyone I know, but that doesn't stop envy from twisting my gut.

"How was the flight?" he asks.

"Who knows? I slept the whole way. We could've flown through a tsunami, and I wouldn't have known."

Marston chuckles. "Can I get you a drink?"

"I'm good. I'm going to do some work when I get back to my hotel."

He shakes his head. "Why the fuck are you still staying in a hotel when you come to town? You know we have plenty of room."

"I know." I don't want to interfere. Marston and Brinley are finally getting all the time together they deserve, but after all the years they spent apart, it still feels too precious to intrude on.

I look around the room and realize it's quieter than usual. "Where are Brinley and the kiddo?"

"Cami is with her dad for the weekend, and Brinley's at girls' night," he says.

My stomach folds itself into a knot at the thought of her friends gathered around a table at Smithy's, laughing and smiling. Looking beautiful as hell. Well, it's only *one* of Brinley's friends who gets me all tied up.

"Ah," Marston says. "I get it."

"Get what?"

"You won't stay here because you're hoping you'll convince Savvy to come back to your room with you some night."

I cough out a laugh. "Seems pretty unlikely."

He cocks his head to the side and studies me for a beat. "You're still hung up on her, aren't you?"

I wish I weren't. "If she wanted anything to do with me, I'd be there in a heartbeat, but she's made her feelings on the matter clear." Except I catch her watching me when we're in the same room and find her leaning into me anytime we stand close.

He studies me for a beat, and I can tell he's trying to decide whether to say more.

It's not like I haven't tried to get over Savvy. Over the last couple of years, I've dated around, even had a couple connections I thought might go somewhere. But for some reason, she's still it for me. Even after all this time.

Marston sighs and shakes his head, clearly choosing to let it go. "When's the crew arriving?"

I grimace at the thought of my family descending on Orchid Valley. "Tomorrow afternoon. Lord save us all. Are you sure Brinley is prepared to work with my mother?"

Marston chuckles. "Trust me, she's worked with worse."

The sound of the garage door pulls our attention from each other and down the hall. Seconds later, the sharp tap of heels is headed our way.

Grinning, Marston leaves me to greet his wife. "Hey, beautiful," he says when she enters the living room. He wraps his arms around her waist before letting his hands drift to her ass. I pretend not to see. "You have a good night?"

"Sure did. We need to do that more often," she says.

"The timing was serendipitous. Savvy was dealing with some stuff, and it's the first time in too long she's talked to us about her stressors."

My ears perk at her name. "What's going on with Savvy?"

With a sigh, Brinley steps out of Marston's arms and drags a hand over her face. "Someone wants to give her an interview, but she doesn't think they'll give her the job if she's not married or at least engaged. I don't really understand the whole thing, but she feels like a great opportunity is about to slip through her fingers, and it sucks for her."

"The Rage?" I ask, remembering our conversation from Vegas. "The streaming service?"

The night we met, one of the first things we talked about was our careers. She told me she was a fitness instructor then cringed like she was embarrassed.

"I know what it looks like," she said. "I'm this blond girl who likes to work out, and who makes a living getting others to work out. It seems so surface. But for me, the aesthetics are just a bonus. I love helping women be strong and teaching them how to be comfortable in their own skin. Everywhere you look, our culture is trying to make us feel bad about ourselves. We're told we should want this part of ourselves gone or smaller, or these parts to be lifted or bigger or flatter or smoother. There's just nothing quite like knowing what your body is capable of to make you learn to love it. After I figured out how much I liked being strong, I realized I wanted to help other women be strong too."

I think that was the moment I fell in love with her. She laughed at herself for "sounding corny."

Brinley nudges me with her elbow, bringing me back to the present. She's beaming at me like I'm a student who just answered a difficult question. "How'd you know about The Rage?"

Because I make it my business to know all of Savvy's dreams. "She said she applies every year. They're offering her an interview?"

"Yeah, but she implied she was engaged on her audition tape, hoping that would make them consider her, and now the owner wants her to bring her fiancé to the interview. Since she doesn't have one, obviously, she's regretting her lie."

"But if she hadn't lied, she wouldn't have this opportunity," I point out.

"From the sounds of it." Brinley comes over and gives me a quick hug. "Are you gonna stay with us this time?"

Marston shoves his hands in his pockets and rocks back on his heels. "He got a hotel room. Again."

She props her hands on her hips and frowns. "You know you're welcome here, right?"

"I appreciate it, but it's nice to have my own space. Especially when my whole family is going to be in town." I pause for a beat before pulling the conversation back to Savvy. "Did she say when this interview was?"

Brinley chews on her bottom lip. "I don't remember. Next week, maybe?"

"Listen, don't tell her I know about all this. I think I

can help her, but if I know Savvy, she'll only take my help if she's helping me in return."

"Are you going to play fiancé?" Brinley asks. "Because I already suggested that, and she knocked me down."

"I'll convince her," I say. If I know anything about Savvy, it's that she has a good heart. It just so happens that I could use a favor over the next few weeks—a favor I wouldn't have been selfish enough to ask for before. If this might be path to helping Savvy pursue her dreams, I won't hesitate. "Leave it to me."

CHAPTER TWO

SAVVY

"Tell me more about these pole-dancing classes," my client says. He wipes the sweat from his face and scans the schedule posted over the free weights.

"Sorry, Justin. Those are only for women."

"Not a problem. I just want to watch." He winks. "Especially if *you'll* be demonstrating the moves. What's the point of all that hard work when there's no one there to appreciate it?"

Ugh. Men. "Fun. Empowerment." I force a smile, working to keep my tone light. "Believe it or not, women want to feel beautiful even when no men are watching."

"Okay, okay, I get it." He drapes his towel behind his neck and turns to look me over. "But I only have a few days left in town. Tell me I get to spend at least one of them with you."

I bite my lip and wrinkle my nose, hoping he'll backpedal before I have to say anything.

Why do so many guys think hitting on their trainers is okay? It makes me feel like they were working with me in exchange for sex and not my extensive exercise science background.

Be grateful, Savvy. At least my schedule is full.

When it's clear Justin is waiting for a response, I do my best to look regretful. "I don't date clients. I'm sorry."

Justin turns up his palms. "That's the beauty, isn't it? That was our last session and I'm not a client anymore."

"You're a really nice guy, but those are my rules."

He glances down to my naked ring finger then cocks his head to the side as he brings his gaze back up to meet mine. "You're too beautiful to be single."

I resist the urge to roll my eyes. He says it like *single* is some sort of terminal condition when it applies to a woman. I've dated assholes before, and I know full well that no relationship beats a bad relationship every day of the week. "Well, that's very kind, but how do you know I'm not seeing someone?" I wink in a conspiratorial way.

"He must not be very good to you if you're still working here. I wouldn't want my woman flirting with other men all day long. Touching them."

Those words pull the plug on my patience. Maybe I'm a flirt. I've been accused of worse. But he says "touching" like I'm doing something dirty when he's referring to me spotting him on the bench press and doing assisted stretches with him. And the idea that a man being good to me would mean leaving a job I enjoy? Gross.

"But I'm not you," a familiar voice says behind me, and I swing around to see Alec Hayes standing by the locker room, his hands tucked into the pockets of his tailored pants. He arches a brow at Justin before strolling to my side. "Savvy likes her job, and I'm secure enough that I don't need to worry that what she does with her clients is sexual in nature. Most of them get that too. You're a smart guy, so I'm sure you do."

Justin straightens. "Of course." His mouth draws into a flat line as he looks at me then back to Alec. "Funny she never mentioned you."

Alec shrugs. "If it makes you feel any better, she never mentioned you either. Unless . . ." He turns to me and cocks a brow. "Is this the creepy guy you were telling me about?"

I shoot Alec a hard look. It's one thing to step in and be the hero, but I don't want him to alienate my client. "That was someone else," I say.

Justin's jaw goes tight, but he forces a smile. "Well, thanks for the training," he says awkwardly. He gives Alec a curt nod before striding past us to the locker room.

I close my eyes for a beat. "You didn't have to do that."

"Do what?"

"Pretend to be my boyfriend. Put Justin in his place. All of it."

Alec searches my face. "Maybe it was just wishful thinking."

I stiffen and step away. "Alec . . ."

"Sorry."

My stomach flip-flops and my heart tumbles awkwardly. It's not like I don't like the idea of Alec being more than a friend to me. This man is amazing, and the concept holds a lot of appeal. But the day I showed up on his doorstep and realized Oliver was his brother, I had to stop my relationship with Alec dead in its tracks. That was two and a half years ago. Ever since, we've been *friends*—a civilized alternative to being lovers or maybe even more, but one that leaves me empty.

I grab a spray bottle and wipe down Justin's equipment, aware of Alec's eyes on me. I'm too much of a coward to face him. Every time I see him, I panic that Oliver has told him the truth about me. About us. About the past.

I swallow hard, hoping to push my heart out of my throat and back where it belongs. "What brings you to The Orchid today?"

"Actually, I need to ask you a favor."

"What's that?" Alec's richer than God, so he's certainly not here to ask for money, and it's not like I have any decent business advice to shell out. Not that he'd need it. Alec and Marston's consulting firm is incredibly successful.

"I think we can help each other. I heard you need a temporary fiancé for a meeting with The Rage CEO?"

"Brinley told you, didn't she?" Tipping my head back, I sigh. "She means well, but I'm sorry she dragged you into this. I made the mess, and I'll clean it up."

"Why not let me help? And in exchange, you could help me?"

"How?"

"My sister is getting married."

I grin. I've never met Alec's sister, but the night we met in Vegas, he sang her praises. "That's incredible. Pass on my congrats."

"Of course." He pauses a beat then clears his throat. "The problem is, she's decided on a destination wedding. Mother's a maniac with stuff like this, and Rose doesn't want a huge ordeal. So she's getting married in Orchid Valley to limit the guest list."

"If she's looking at The Orchid for her venue, you're talking to the wrong girl. You need to hit up Brinley."

"Already done," he says. "Wedding's in two weeks, and she'll be here tomorrow to iron out the details."

I toss my towel into the dirty bin and tuck the spray bottle back under the counter where it belongs. "Sounds like you don't need me at all."

He grimaces. "That's just it. My mother is coming as well, and she's planning to meet my girlfriend while she's here."

I freeze. "Oh." I'm not allowed to be jealous of the women Alec dates. That's not fair to anyone—not when I'm the one who insisted we couldn't have a relationship. Not when I'm the one who doesn't deserve him. But that doesn't help with the ache in my chest at the thought of him with someone other than me. And worse, a local? I swallow back my nausea at the thought of seeing them around town together.

"Do I know her? I didn't realize you were dating anyone."

Alec closes his eyes and sighs heavily. "I'm not. My mother has been trying to set me up with her best friend's daughter for years. Recently, Portentia ended a long-term relationship, so Mom's returned to her regular schemes and pushing the issue." He rubs the back of his neck. "I may have lied to get her off my back. Since Marston lives here, it was believable enough that I'd have met someone special in Orchid Valley. The family's all coming down to plan for the wedding, though, and I'm afraid they'll discover my lie."

His *whole* family? Oliver too? My head spins and I white-knuckle the counter. "Why would you lie to them? Why not just tell them you're not interested in this girl?"

"You don't understand. It's not that simple in my family." He shakes his head like it's not worth explaining. "Mistake or not, I have to think about how this plays out. If I admit that I lied, then suddenly my mom's going to insist that Portentia come to the wedding."

"And you don't like this Portentia?"

"She's a nice girl," he says, but something about the way he cuts his gaze away makes me think he doesn't actually believe that. "I've done my best to keep her feelings in mind through all this, but I also have to consider my little sister. Coming clean now will put the focus on me when it's supposed to be Rose's time."

"Understand what you're saying, but . . ." *But I couldn't possibly meet your family. But you would hate me if you knew my history with Oliver. Or, at the very least, think less of me.* "Surely there's someone better for this job."

"All I'm asking is for a few days now, and then a few more when we're all here for the wedding. In exchange, I'll go with you to the meeting and pretend to be your adoring fiancé."

Sighing, I take a seat on the nearest bench and grab my bottle of water. "The whole fake-dating thing might look easy in the movies, but I'm pretty sure it's a recipe for disaster in real life."

"I feel like we could pull it off okay." His eyes are so tender, and . . . *Gah. My heart.*

It's such a small favor. Honestly, I wouldn't hesitate . . . if it weren't for Oliver. "Just tell them your girlfriend is out of town."

Alec tucks his hands in his pockets and frowns. "May I ask if I did something to offend you?"

"What? No. Of course not."

"Is it that even *pretending* to be my girlfriend for a few days would be that distasteful to you? So distasteful that you wouldn't even do it to land your dream job?"

"Alec . . ." My shoulders sag. "Is your whole family coming down? I mean, how many people would I be pretending for?" Oh God, this is awkward, but even if I'm not Alec's fake girlfriend, I have to know if I'll be facing Oliver. Maybe I *will* leave town.

"The whole family will come. There will be about five of us this weekend, and then probably thirty the weekend of the wedding—plus everyone on Rose's fiancé's side. I guess I don't know for sure, but Mom will expect all the aunts and uncles to make the trip. The only one she won't guilt into coming is Oliver. He hasn't been in the same room as her since Dad's funeral, and I don't think either of them want that to change now."

Swallowing, I hold his gaze as I ask, "Oliver?" Can one word, said like a question, be a lie? Because this feels like one. Acting like I don't know who Oliver is feels unforgivably misleading.

Irritation colors Alec's features. Not irritation with me, but with— "My brother. *Half*-brother."

"And why wouldn't he want to be in the same room as your mom?"

"Because he's fucking ungrateful. My mother opened her home to him when his mom died, and in return, he treats her like a pariah." He shakes his head as if to shed any ill will he has toward Oliver. "It doesn't matter. He won't be here. Thank God for small mercies."

I focus all my energy on keeping the relief off my face. Maybe if Oliver won't be around . . . "What about Portentia? Will she be coming?"

"Not if I have a girlfriend. My mother won't invite her if I have a date. It would be too *embarrassing*." He rocks back on his heels. "I know it's all so petty and ridiculous, and I don't expect you to understand the politics of my family. In fact, I couldn't blame you if you saw me differently after all this, but I hope you won't. I want to do this for my sister. Rose deserves her day to be about her—not about my mother's plans to see me married off to someone she deems suitable."

"Can I think about it?" I ask softly.

"Of course." He studies my face before dropping his eyes to my mouth.

My skin heats at the memories his hot gaze evokes. *Hot lips skimming over my bare shoulder, rough hands gripping my hips.* I take a half step back, not fully trusting myself. "This can't be real, Alec." I couldn't forgive myself if I didn't make that clear. If he ended up hurt.

"I know where you stand," he says.

I blow out a heavy breath. "Then I'll let you know in the morning."

I want to do this favor for Alec—and God knows it would probably benefit me more than him—but I'm a coward, and I don't want him knowing my secrets.

I like to go to bed early so I can be up by five, but tonight I've been tossing and turning.

After an hour, I give up and grab my phone. Screens are the worst thing for my insomnia, but sometimes I just need to stop thinking about how I can't sleep.

I scroll through Instagram, tapping like on kind and encouraging comments on my posts and ignoring the more suggestive and straight-up repulsive ones. I show my body on my Instagram because it's good business. What it can do, how it makes me feel, and—whether I like it or not—how it looks. It's all part of my brand, and I make the best of it. Unfortunately, there are men who think that because I post pictures of myself in sports bras and workout shorts, they're entitled to me. I delete and block the worst of them and ignore the others.

I screenshot a couple of posts that are getting the best traction to send to my sponsors and then turn to my messages and message requests. The second is the place where messages go if I'm not otherwise connected to the person on Instagram. I used to ignore that space entirely, since it's mostly home to notes and disturbing requests from weirdos, pervs, and creeps, but more and more companies have started reaching out to influencers through DMs rather than email. This little, hellish corner of social media sometimes hides opportunities I can't afford to miss.

Because I'm procrastinating my second attempt at sleep, I scroll down farther than I have since I started checking over here. There are dozens of unread messages. Most are innocuous, in the vein of "How many crunches do I need to do each day to see my abs?" and "No matter how much weight I lose, the cellulite won't budge. Help?" Many are sales pitches for magic pills and shit I'd never suggest to my clients, and some are straight-up vile. I'm about to close out the rest of the unread messages before a familiar name catches my eye. *Oliver Rhett.*

The message was sent over two years ago—not too long after our ill-fated reunion in L.A.

My hands shake as I tap it open.

Oliver_Rhett: I always said you could be strong, and fucking look at you now. I won't pretend I'm not proud. Been thinking about you since you showed up at my sister's place. Don't be a stranger.

Butterflies make my stomach flip-flop. They've apparently forgotten that Oliver broke my heart.

For years, I've forbidden myself from looking him up. Cyberstalking an ex might be harmless for some, but I was always afraid of what keeping up with him would do to me. Afraid I might turn pathetic and forget how he used me. But now, when I need to decide if I can do this favor for Alec? Now I need to know for sure what he's doing and where he is. I need to make sure saying yes won't end up hurting Alec.

I click through to Oliver's profile, relieved when I see it's public.

His bio says he's an agent and lists a couple of big-name UFC fighters he represents, along with some other athletes I don't recognize. I had no idea that he'd gotten to pursue his dream career after all—but of course I didn't. He skipped town and never came back.

I scroll down. The most recent post went up yesterday, and it's a picture of him and some Formula One driver in Monte Carlo. *Beautiful morning for breakfast in my favorite city! Two months until race day!*

I'm relieved that I don't have to worry Oliver might show up this weekend, but on the tail end of that relief is . . . something else. A bittersweet ache. How is it possible to miss someone so desperately when they hurt you so much?

Part Two

EIGHT YEARS AGO

CHAPTER THREE

SAVVY

I don't completely trust my judgment in this moment, but I'm ninety percent sure that rooms aren't supposed to tilt to the side like this when you walk. And the little spinning thing that happens when I move my eyes too fast doesn't seem normal either.

Five minutes ago, drunkenness was fun. It was the solution to all that ailed me.

Classes start on Monday? Bring it on!

My boyfriend's an asshole? Who cares?

Can't break up with him because I can't risk messing with his head before the big fight? Tomorrow's problem!

My brother has some guys with face tattoos looking for him, saying he owes them money? Hey, they might be nice guys when you get to know them.

But happy, don't-give-a-shit drunk faded to feel-sick drunk way too fast once my friend Julie cut me off, and now I just want to leave. The party is crowded and too damn loud, and this floor keeps shifting beneath my feet like this is a carnival fun house.

"Not-so-fun house," I mutter, catching myself on the wall as I stumble down the hall.

I couldn't find Julie anywhere downstairs, but someone said they saw her and a guy come up here.

Lucky Julie, hooking up with her boyfriend in the middle of a party. But not me. *Noooo.* I make bad decisions and have shit taste in men, so I'm just gonna be celibate as a freaking nun until after Chuck's fight. And even then . . . I shudder slightly and my stomach heaves, reminding me why schnapps is always a bad idea. And, yeah, when you're this hard up but the idea of sex with your boyfriend makes you shudder, it might be time to move on.

"Just as soon as he wins that fight," I mumble, leaning my shoulder into the wall as I move down the hall. "Julie? Where are you?"

I hit something and my shoulder aches. Trim. A door.

Right. Because if she came here to hook up, she's probably doing it behind a door. I smile, proud of my brain for still working at some level.

"We are smart," I sing. "S-M-R-T."

I turn the knob. The door flies open, and I stumble into the room where, yes, Julie is indeed mid-hookup, her blond head bobbing over the crotch of a dark-haired guy

I don't recognize. A bearded guy that's *definitely* not her boyfriend.

"So sorry," I slur, turning my back to them in a stumble. I grip the doorframe to steady myself.

"I think you're lost," a deep, rumbling voice says behind me.

"Yeah." I cringe. "I'm here for . . . uh, her." I glance over my shoulder to nod toward my friend, but Julie just keeps doing her thing, totally unaware of my entrance. Or maybe she's into an audience. I wouldn't judge, but I hope it's not because she's drunk. She's my DD and I really want to leave. Also, last I knew, she was really into her guy, and I'd hate for her to ruin that.

In my peripheral vision, I see the guy cup Julie's face and gently pull her up. "Sweetheart, we have company."

Julie whips her head around, scowling at me as her guy pulls his pants back up. His shirt is unbuttoned all the way, revealing the most impressive six-pack I've ever seen. The schnapps must be eating away at my brain because I can't tear my gaze from that body, those strong hands.

"Holy hell. Way to go, Julie." No wonder she forgot about her boyfriend. This guy is as hot as an Atlanta summer. The kind of hot that turns smart girls dumb.

"Who the fuck are you?" the blonde snaps. The blonde who is definitely not Julie.

Oops. "Oh. Sorry. I'm looking for . . . my friend?"

"Does it look like she's here?" She stands, and I realize only as she pulls it up that the top of her dress was around her waist. I'm so glad I'm drunk right now, because this whole thing is fucking awkward. What's the appropriate etiquette for interrupting a blowjob? If only Mom had found the money to send me to that finishing school she always threatened me with.

Footsteps sound in the hall and a short Black guy pokes his head in the open door. "Crissy, your ride's out front."

"Dammit."

"Hey." Mr. Chiseled Abs grabs her hand and gives it a gentle squeeze. "You okay?"

She plops in his lap and wraps both arms behind his neck. "I don't want to leave yet," she whines.

He kisses her neck gently. "So stay. I'll take you back to the house."

"Can't. Those bitches are serious about curfew until I'm off academic probation."

"Ah. Well, be safe," he says as she pulls herself off him.

"You'll call me?"

He shrugs. "Maybe sometime. I have to focus on my classes this term, though. Lots of hoops to jump through if I want to get out of here in December. You know how it is."

I snort out a laugh. The girl just had his dick down her throat and he's giving her the brush-off. *Real nice.*

Crissy glares hard at me. Yes, *I'm* the bad guy here. Obviously. "I've gotta bounce," she snaps, then heads out, knocking into my shoulder unnecessarily on the way. I stumble back. The floor does another tilty thing, and I fail to catch myself before I hit the ground.

The girl—what was her name again? Not-Julie laughs as she jogs down the hall.

I try to stand but can't quite manage it. I stumble and only make it to my knees. Mr. Chiseled Abs unfolds himself from the blowjob chair to help me up, and I find my eyes right in line with the hard ridge in his jeans. A dark, wild thought springs to mind, and before I can push it away, my tongue darts out to wet my lips. How pathetic and sex-deprived am I that I still find him so attractive after what I just witnessed?

So pathetic. So sex-deprived.

And so *drunk.*

He offers me his hand. "Unless you had other plans for your time down there."

I haven't given Chuck a blowjob in three months, which might be fine if his whole sex-fast didn't also include his not touching me. Not that it matters. Once I found out my brother, Nathan, placed that bet, any remaining sexual attraction I felt for Chuck went out the window, but I still think his sex-deprivation-for-increased-testosterone theories are bogus. "It's unnatural," I mutter.

Mr. Chiseled Abs releases a dry laugh as he helps me to my feet. "Blowjobs, unnatural? I beg to differ."

I recoil then adjust my stance so I don't lose my balance again. "No." Jesus. Do I look like some kind of prude?

Going without sex just for a fight is unnatural. And now, apparently, I'm a fucking voyeur. That's how bad things have gotten. I really miss sex. But I might not miss it enough to have it with Chuck again . . . which is gonna be a problem.

"What's that?"

How much of that did I say out loud?

Hot guy shakes his head. "Never mind. I don't want to know."

I smile, an idea occurring to me. I can't break up with Chuck right before his big fight—not when Nathan has so much riding on it—but if Chuck breaks up with me, that wouldn't be my fault, and maybe he'd still win just to prove that I lost my chance with a winner.

"What if I went home smelling like you? He'd be pissed. He doesn't look at me half the time, but he's possessive, and if I smelled like you, he'd probably be jealous." I put one hand to that bare chest as if I can pick up the masculine scent of him with a single touch. "And even if it doesn't work, at least you smell good, and you —" I bite my lip to keep my drunk ass from finishing that sentence. I'm rambling, but I don't want to stop. I'm afraid if I stop talking, he'll button up that shirt or something. Or just leave. "You do smell good."

His expression shifts from irritated to amused. "Baby girl, typically I'd be happy to let you do whatever it is you think you want to do to me—especially since I'm going to have a roaring case of blue balls thanks to your little interruption—but you're drunk as hell, and drunk chicks aren't my thing."

He starts to step around me, but I grab his wrist. "Please." I'm not even sure what I'm asking for—only that I need his help to get it. "You don't understand how awful it is. No sex. Grumpiness. And worst of all, he's all buddy-buddy with my brother, who's, like, the *worst.*"

He glances down to where my hand's wrapped around his wrist. "I don't know what you want from me."

Sex, my lizard brain cries. But that part of my brain doesn't understand STIs or stranger danger, so I muzzle her and think about his question. What *do* I want from him?

I blink and look around the room. Why did I come in here? Hot guy, yeah, but that was a happy surprise. I came in here— "I'm looking for my friend. She's supposed to take me home."

He releases a breath and stares at the ceiling, muttering something, but the only words I make out are *fucking frat parties.*

"I don't like parties either," I say. "I used to, but then I got a boyfriend and he's no fun, so I stay home and pretend I care about the dumb shit he does, but tonight, Julie made me come because she said I'm going to get high blood pressure at a young age if I don't let loose a little, but honestly, if she knew my family, she'd understand." I look around the room. "Why did I come in here?"

"Julie?" the hot guy says. Does he know her? "Never heard of her," he says, making me realize I must've asked the question out loud.

Right. Julie. I turn toward the hall, but he grabs my shoulders and stops me from behind.

"At this point, you're a danger to yourself and others,

and I can't in good conscience let you return to that party."

The room tilts again, but less severely this time. I step sideways and lean against the wall. Maybe if I just close my eyes for a minute, I'll feel better.

"Nope." His hands are on my shoulders again, drawing me away from the wall and making me stand on my own. "Don't pass out on me. Let's find your friend. Where's your phone?"

I reluctantly search my pockets. I start to shake my head before I remember I tucked it into my bra. Hot guy's eyes go wide as I delve into my shirt to retrieve it. "Here," I say triumphantly.

"Do you always keep your phone in your bra?"

"Phone, ID, keys." I shrug. "These girls can conceal quite a bit inside a padded cup, but jeans this tight? Not so much."

His gaze skips down over my legs for a beat. "I noticed."

I want to revel in those eyes on me, and I don't know if it's because I'm truly that hard up or because I'm so damn lonely. But he doesn't give me a chance to revel in anything before he snags my phone.

"What's your passcode?" he asks.

"Like I'd tell you."

"I'd have you do it, but you'd stop halfway through to complain about your sex life again."

Shit. I really need to sober up. "I did that?"

"Yeah," he mutters. "A few times." He holds up the phone, screen toward me, and I tap in the passcode.

"I should find Julie and go home," I say, my eyes floating shut again. "Otherwise, I'll end up in bed with you, and then Chuck will be pissed and lose his fight and Nathan will be fucked, which means *I'll* be fucked. He says Chuck's a sure thing, but why would they have him fighting this guy if there was no real competition?"

He looks up from my phone. "Chuck Kruger, the fighter? That's your boyfriend?"

I hold a finger to my lips. "Shh. The fighting's a secret."

He grunts. "Not much of one." He passes my phone back to me. "Looks like Julie was looking for you about an hour ago, and since you told her to leave without you if Chuck showed up, she did."

I frown, feeling more dread than hope. "Chuck's here?" I'm not up for dealing with his *moods.*

He shakes his head. "Nope. The last text he sent said he couldn't find you. He headed home to hang with your brother."

Chuck's place is like three miles from here. I do so much walking that three miles isn't necessarily a deal breaker—but it's the middle of the night, and these heels were meant for making my ass look good, not for a midnight stroll.

"I take it this means you need a ride home?" he asks.

"Home." I huff. "I don't have one of those." Ugh. *Will the real Drunk Savvy please shut up?*

"Where are you staying?" he asks gently, like he understands my drunken ramblings more than he wants to.

"With Chuck. But I don't want to go there if my brother's around. I'll just stay here for a while and head back later."

He holds my gaze for a long moment before muttering something and shaking his head. "That seems like a bad idea." He offers me a hand, palm up. "Come on. I'm taking you somewhere to sober up."

CHAPTER FOUR

OLIVER

Savvy—that's her name, judging by the messages on her phone. It suits her. Pretty, flirty, casual. Typically, I want nothing to do with strange, drunk women who look at me like starved sex kittens. Especially considering she interrupted the first blowjob I've gotten in months. Only, as skilled as Crissy was with her mouth and tongue, as much as she checked all the boxes in the random hookup list I was looking for, the whole experience was missing something. It wasn't until Savvy walked in the room with her tight jeans and hungry eyes that I felt much of anything at all. And *that* is messed up, even for me.

I can't believe she's dating Chuck fucking Kruger. Now *there's* a piece of work.

And what is this shit about him abstaining from sex?

I pull in front of my favorite twenty-four-hour diner and park the car. When I turn to Savvy, her eyes are closed and her head's slumped to the side.

Great. I was so lost in my thoughts I let the drunk girl pass out.

"Savvy?" I stroke her bare shoulder gently. Her skin is cool and soft under my fingertips.

She jerks awake and blinks at me, scanning the car like she's not sure how she got here.

"We're gonna go in and get some coffee and food," I say before she can decide to panic. "Water too. I'll take you home after you sober up."

Her gaze drops to my mouth and she licks her lips—I fucking wish she'd quit doing that. My dick still remembers that Crissy didn't get to finish what she started, and while no part of me is into drunk girls, it's pretty obvious all parts of me are into this one—drunk or sober. The fact that she's Chuck's just adds another level of fucked-up to this whole situation. I hate him just enough that I'd really enjoy giving his girl everything she's not getting from him.

"What's your name?" she asks.

Right. Because I never told her. She never told me hers either, but she's too drunk to remember that. "Oliver Rhett."

She coughs out a laugh. "Of course it is." I'm not sure what that's supposed to mean, but before I can ask, she says, "Nice ride, Oliver."

Normally, I'm ridiculously cocky about my Viper, but something about her tone makes me feel more mocked than flattered. "Thanks."

She climbs out of the car, and I follow her. Her stride is steadier and more confident than it was when we left the party—as if the car ride and a little fresh air were all it took to sober her up. That might mean I'll have to take her back to Chuck sooner than I wanted to. If she's already sober on our way into the diner, I won't have an excuse to keep her there. Disappointment tugs at me.

"Oliver!" Cindy, the night-shift waitress, calls when I follow Savvy inside. Her gravelly smoker's voice makes her sound a couple decades older than her fifty-some years. "Your booth is open. Coffee?"

I hold up two fingers, and her eyes go wide as she looks back and forth between me and Savvy.

"Two coffees, coming right up," she says, winking.

I lightly place a hand on Savvy's back and usher her toward "my" booth in the rear corner.

"You come here a lot?" Savvy asks when she slides into the cushioned vinyl seat across from me.

"I'm not a great sleeper." Understatement of the century.

I settle back to study her. I was right. She looks a hell of a lot more sober now. Her hazel eyes are clearer, and she rubs them as she looks around the diner, leaving smudges of eye makeup behind.

"Feeling a little better?"

She huffs then bites her bottom lip. "I'm not a great drinker."

"I noticed."

"Two coffees," Cindy says, sliding the mugs on the table. "Any cream?"

"Yes, please," Savvy says.

Cindy scoops a handful of individual creamers from her apron and dumps them on the table between our mugs before turning her full attention on Savvy. "We don't have a cook back there this time of night, so we're on a limited menu while I pull double duty, but I'll whip up some pancakes for a friend of Oliver."

"That's so sweet," Savvy says, "but you don't have to."

"Pancakes sound great, Cindy," I say. Savvy might be on her way to sobriety, but she should eat something if she wants a better chance at not hating life in the morning.

"Got it." Cindy studies Savvy for a beat, smiling. "Well, you're certainly pretty enough to explain the sudden change in his behavior."

Savvy's brow wrinkles. "I'm sorry?"

"I usually come here alone," I say before Cindy can launch into her favorite speech about how I need a "good girl" in my life.

"We're just friends," Savvy offers.

"Mm-hmm," Cindy says before walking away.

I bite back a smile.

Savvy snatches a creamer off the table and dumps it into her coffee. "Are you laughing at me?"

"What? I would never. I'm glad to know I've made a new *friend*."

She squeezes her eyes shut. "I said something to you, didn't I? Something incriminating?"

"Not unless being the sex-deprived girlfriend of an asshole and wanting me to help make him think you cheated on him would be considered incriminating."

She drags a hand over her face. "Why do people like getting drunk? I enjoy drinking, don't get me wrong, but drunk is just stupid."

I nod. "Usually."

She chews on her bottom lip. "I'm sorry about earlier. Your girlfriend probably—"

"She's not my girlfriend."

She arches a brow. "Right. What a stud. Am I supposed to be impressed that you can get head anywhere you go?"

I cough out a laugh. "I didn't say that, but I'm flattered that you think so."

She scrapes her gaze down my chest and slowly back up to my face. My shirt is buttoned now, but it's all too easy to remember how she looked at me when it wasn't. "Yeah, well, I'm drunk, not blind."

Not completely *sober, then.* Or maybe she's always this forward.

"Does your boyfriend know you talk about your sex life with complete strangers?"

She wrinkles her nose, and—Christ. I can handle the tight jeans and great ass. But she's not just hot. She's *cute.* I never realized the combination was my kryptonite.

"I would worry about that, but since there are no details to share . . ." She shrugs.

"You should talk to him about that. Communication

is important." Honestly, though? I'm not sure Chuck Kruger knows how to communicate without his fists.

She shakes her head. "It's so dumb, but I'm not supposed to complain about his tactics because I *don't know what it's like to be a dude*." She says the last part in a mocking, low, dude-bro voice.

"Well, I happen to know a little bit about it if you want to bounce anything off me."

Sighing, she stares into her coffee and shakes her head. "Nah. I've said too much already."

"Ah, so it *was* the booze making you overshare."

She lifts her gaze to meet mine for a beat before dropping it back to her coffee and shrugging.

"Okay, let me guess, then. He believes he's more powerful and aggressive going into a fight if he deprives himself of sex and orgasms beforehand?"

She wrinkles her nose again. "So this is a *normal* thing?"

I bark out a laugh and lean back in the booth. "I don't know if I'd call it normal, but I've definitely heard of it before." I've heard of it a *lot* among fighters, but I've never been a believer myself. Chuck's probably feeling cocky as hell if his girlfriend is bent out of shape over a few days without sex. "But I'm sorry you're, er, suffering. For what it's worth."

She sips her coffee and scans the diner. The place was built in the '80s and is pretty run-down. I'm pretty sure the booths are original, and the linoleum floors have seen better days, but it's clean and—most importantly—open during hours when nothing else decent on this godforsaken campus is.

Savvy's avoiding my gaze, and I take advantage of the opportunity to look at her. I admire the smooth skin of her neck and the freckles on her bare shoulders. This girl definitely does it for me, and that's a problem. Despite our unconventional meeting, I would put money on her being a relationship kind of girl, and I'm not a relationship kind of guy. There are some mistakes you only make once.

"Here ya go," Cindy says, sliding two plates stacked with pancakes onto the table. She plops a bottle of syrup between them. "Anything else?"

Savvy blinks at the food as if she forgot why she was here. "No. Thank you."

"Thanks, Cindy," I say, nodding at her before she turns away.

Savvy and I both dig into our food, but after a couple bites she sets her fork down, licks her perfect pink lips, and pushes her plate away.

"You don't like them?" I ask.

She screws up her face. "I love them. They're delicious. But they're all carbs, and . . ."

I arch a brow, waiting, and when she doesn't finish her sentence, I jokingly say, "And you're trying to make weight for *your* fight?"

She rolls her eyes, pink blossoming into her cheeks. "I probably had enough carbs with the booze tonight." She shudders slightly and meets my gaze. "Ever drink a mix of SunnyD and 99 Bananas?"

I feel myself blanch. "Why would *anyone* ever do that?"

She laughs. "It was tasty, but . . ." She shakes her head. "Schnapps are always a bad idea. They hit different, and not in a good way."

I tap the end of my fork handle to her plate. "You should eat. Carbs be damned."

"Easy for you to say. You're not the one who'll have to snuggle up to my fluffy ass when they catch up with me."

I'm pretty sure she's parroting Chuck's words there, and the realization makes rage simmer in my blood. That sonofabitch doesn't deserve shit, let alone a beautiful woman like this. "Yeah, unfortunately for me, I'm not," I say before I can think better of it.

She straightens and holds my gaze for a long time. The silence stretches between us, and I can almost feel the weight of her unhappiness bearing down on it.

"Why are you with him?" There are a dozen questions I have no business asking, and that one's at the top of the list. I'm not sorry for putting it out there, though.

"I don't know what you mean."

Lie. She knows exactly what I mean, but she's embarrassed now and doesn't want to share. I put down my fork. "You're gorgeous, Savvy, and from what I can tell, you have a great sense of humor. You're obviously unhappy. Why stay with an ass who makes you feel like shit? Why stay with a guy who makes you not want to go home at night?"

She shoves out of the booth. "I should go."

Fuck.

She digs in her bra—Lord help me—and comes up with her phone and her ID before cursing. “I don’t have any cash, but tomorrow I’ll drop some money at the frat house to pay you back for my food.”

I grunt. There are so many things wrong with what she just said. “One, I don’t want your money. You didn’t even eat. Two, if you leave money there, it will never get to me. I’m not involved with Lambda Chi—wasn’t even when I *was* an undergrad. I was at the party with a friend tonight, not because I’m a *brother* or whatever.”

She bites the corner of her lip. I swear blue balls have fucked with my brain, because this is *not* the moment to wonder how her mouth tastes. Not the moment to contemplate how she’d respond to the scrape of teeth on her lips and neck.

“Where can I leave money?”

I shake my head and climb out of the booth myself. Cindy’s pancakes are the best, and it’s a shame, but I’ve been so distracted by Savvy that I wasn’t really tasting them anyway. I throw some cash on the table. “You don’t need to pay me back, and I’m taking you home. Come on.” I don’t give her a chance to shoot me down before I head out the door in front of her.

The night’s still hot, but some of the humidity has slipped away with the sun and the sky is clear, with a few stars twinkling overhead. I can’t get over the stars in Crossport. They don’t stand a chance to shine against the lights of Manhattan.

“I live close,” she says, not looking at me. “I’m fine walking.”

"I need to stretch my legs." I could add that it's too fucking late for her to be walking alone, but I'm getting the impression that she'd only be more stubborn in the face of that argument.

She studies me for a beat before giving a curt nod. "Okay. I'm over on Sixth and Crawford."

I already knew that, having had the dubious pleasure of visiting Chuck a time or two. "Cool."

The scuff of our steps on the sidewalk mingles with the rustle of the wind through the trees.

She tilts her face up to the sky and sighs. "It's a beautiful night," she says, echoing my thoughts from moments ago.

We stroll slowly toward Crawford, and I get the impression that despite leaving the diner in a rush, she isn't in any hurry to get home. "I was just thinking the same thing."

She flashes me a tentative smile. Maybe I didn't totally screw up in there after all. "Thanks for everything tonight."

"There's nothing to thank me for."

She turns her head and studies me for a beat before turning her gaze back to the sidewalk. "I'm not sure why you're being so nice to me. Especially after I ruined your night the way I did."

"You didn't, though."

She coughs out a laugh. "If that's true, I can say you're the first guy I ever met who wouldn't mind being interrupted mid-BJ."

"I didn't say I didn't mind. I said it didn't ruin my

night," I say. She cuts her eyes to me, her expression cautious, so I change the subject. "Are you from around here?"

"Nah. I grew up south of Atlanta."

I nod. I noticed an occasional Southern lilt to her voice, but not enough to make me guess Georgia. "You don't have much of an accent."

"I worked really hard on that," she says with a smile. "But really, Atlanta's not too bad. It's enough of a melting pot that not a lot of people have the stereotypical drawl."

"A shame, really."

She smirks. "You have a thing for Southern accents?"

"Not necessarily." I shrug. "I have a thing for diversity."

She arches a brow. "And you came to rural Pennsylvania for grad school? Bad call."

I grunt. "No kidding. Mistakes were made." The ring of her laughter into the dark night pulls a smile onto my lips. "I'm saying, I hope we never turn into a world where we all sound the same."

Her expression softens. "My Gram lived in southern Alabama, and when I spent weeks with her during the summers, I'd find my words getting thick like molasses. I loved her accent, but my mom thought . . ."

"What?"

She shakes her head. "Never mind. What about you? You from around here?"

"Nope. I'm a transplant like you. I grew up in Brooklyn."

"Well, that explains a lot. You like it there?"

I nod. "Not as much as I like Manhattan—that's where I was born—but Mom believed a boy should have a backyard to play in, and since she didn't think Central Park qualified, we got a place in Brooklyn."

"She still there?"

I swallow the unexpected lump of emotion rising in my throat. "She died when I was in high school."

"Oh my gosh. I'm so sorry." She wraps soft fingers around my wrist, and we slow our steps. "Shit, Oliver. I'm really so sorry."

"It happens."

"I didn't mean to bring up a difficult subject."

"I miss her." My voice is a little too rough, and I find myself wishing she weren't sober enough to hear the truth of my grief beneath it. "I hate that she died so young, but I can talk about her."

She bites her bottom lip. She's still holding my wrist. "What was she like?"

I tilt my face to the sky again and shake my head. "Fierce. When it came to me, at least. She would have done anything for her kid."

"The best parents are like that. Was she a stay-at-home mom?"

I shake my head. "She was a nurse, but never defined by her job. She loved photography and scrapbooking and spoiling me. And journaling. She was always writing in a journal. I'd do just about anything to have those back."

"Where are they?" she asks.

I have to swallow down the bile that rage forces into my throat. "After she died, my father took them away as a punishment. And when I lashed out, he told me he threw them into the fireplace."

"Oh my God. I'm so sorry."

I shrug. "It's life."

"But your mom—she sounds great."

I scratch the back of my neck. "What sucks is that I lost her when I was in my asshole teen years. It's not like my last words to her were cruel or anything dramatic like that, but I'd like to think I wouldn't have given her such a hard time if I'd known I'd lose her."

She trails her fingers from my wrist down to my hand and gives it a quick squeeze before pulling away. I liked her touching me, or maybe I liked the fact that she understood I needed that connection when talking about my mom—something I haven't done this openly since arriving in Crossport two years ago.

"So, it's just you and your dad?" she asks.

I cough out a shocked laugh before I can stop myself. Oh well. In for a penny, in for a pound. "Fuck no."

"No love lost there?" She steps off the sidewalk and leans her hip against a bench.

"Nope." I glance across the street then back to her. She's stopped walking half a block from Chuck's, but I'm not going to call her on it. "He wasn't around much when I was a kid. Turns out, I preferred it that way."

"I hear you on that." She tucks her hands into her pockets and looks down at her heels. We've only walked a few blocks, but her feet have to be killing her. "My dad was around way too much for my liking."

I want to ask questions, but I recognize the hurt in

her eyes. If she's anything like me, she won't want to get into details.

"Do you live in grad student housing?" she asks.

"Nah. I'm that way about five blocks," I say, nodding to our left.

"Off-campus, then."

"Yep. I did the whole dorm thing in undergrad, but it was never a good fit for me. I need my space."

"I felt the same way about the dorms." She frowns.

Does living with Chuck make her feel smothered?

"How long have you lived with the boyfriend?"

She draws in a shaky breath. "We moved in together at the end of spring semester."

I hate that this turn in the conversation has taken the joy from her eyes, so I take a step forward. "Let me hear it."

"What?"

"Your best southern Alabama drawl. I wanna hear you talk like Gram."

"It's hotta than the hinges on the gates ah Hell," she says, running the words together like they're all sticky. *Molasses, indeed.*

I feel my face split into a grin so wide it feels foreign. "That's impressive."

"If she could hear me now, she'd make me go pull weeds for mocking her."

The wind blows a strand of her hair across her lips. I brush it behind her ear without thinking, and her breath catches. Her gaze settles on my mouth, and I trail my fingers down the side of her neck.

Slowly, I dip my head, watching her lips part subtly. I can smell her shampoo.

Her hands slide up my chest, and the hunger in her eyes ticks up another notch.

Just as her eyes start to drift closed, she shoves me away. "Stop." She jumps behind the bench, gripping the back of it like it's a fucking shield.

I stutter, step back, and press my lips together. They're still buzzing in anticipation for a kiss that isn't coming. For a kiss I have no business taking. "Sorry."

"I just . . ." Her eyes dart toward her building then back to me. "I can't."

But you want to. "Why'd you move in with him?"

She looks away and thinks a long time before answering. "It was time for me to move out of the dorms, and he invited me to live with him. It seemed like a good idea at the time."

"Regrets?" I ask.

She shoots me a look. "I don't think I should talk to you about this."

"Why not?"

She wrinkles her nose. "It feels wrong. Like if anyone's going to know how I feel about living with Chuck, Chuck deserves to know first."

"I respect that." Or I would if the man in question were anyone but Chuck. Chuck doesn't deserve shit. Certainly not this girl. But her reply confirms what's seemed so obvious all night: she definitely has regrets when it comes to her asshole boyfriend.

She gives me a sad smile. "I'm sorry I walked away from perfectly good pancakes earlier."

I roll my shoulders back. "I crossed a line. Your relationship is your business." I force a smile and tilt my head toward Chuck's building. "Let's get you home."

"I do want to pay you back," she says, hurrying after me. "Come to The Naked Bean tomorrow and ask for Savannah Downing. I'm working four to close."

"Downing? Like, the family whose name is all over this campus? The old department store?"

She groans. "Unfortunately."

"Any relation?"

"Yes." She cuts her eyes to me, weary. "That was a long time ago. There's a reason you don't see Downings in shopping malls anymore."

I laugh softly and slow my steps before the entrance to Chuck's building. "I'm not after your money, Savvy."

"Sorry. People just get the wrong idea."

I nod then glance between the door and her. "You okay to go in there?"

She nods. "You'll come see me? So I can pay you back?"

I look her over one last time. "We'll see," I say, then I walk away.

CHAPTER FIVE

SAVVY

"Where the fuck have you been?" Chuck slurs when I walk in the door. He's on the couch, gaming remote in hand, looking sullen as hell.

Fantastic. He's drunk.

"Excuse me?" I'm so sick of the animosity that's been bubbling between us lately, but I just walked in the door and he's already pissing me off.

"Sorry, your majesty. Where *the heck* have you been?"

I roll my eyes. Chuck's body is a temple—except when it comes to boozing with the bros. Then it's all about the vodka or sometimes gin. Tonight it was the latter. I can smell him from here. "I told you I was going to that party with Julie."

I dig my ID out of my bra and toss it and my phone

onto the counter before turning toward the bathroom to get ready for bed.

I'm halfway down the dark hall when he grabs me from behind. His hands slide around to my belly, and he pulls me against him. It's honestly the most physical contact I've had in weeks, and despite my recent disillusionment with my boyfriend, I catch myself melting into him. This summer I learned just how lonely it is to live with someone who ignores me. I never felt lonely when I lived alone.

He sniffs my neck.

"What are you doing?"

"Just making sure you haven't been stepping out on me." He sniffs again.

I wriggle from his grasp. "What are you, a dog? Stop smelling me." I stride into the bathroom, but he grabs the door before I can shut it behind me.

Ignoring him, I grab my toothbrush and turn on the water.

"My buddy Tim saw you leave that frat party with Oliver Rhett."

I spit out my mouth full of toothpaste. "You know Oliver?"

"He's a fucking rich prick. Of course I know him. Everyone knows him."

"Well, I didn't before tonight." I resume my brushing, refusing to give any credence to his jealousy.

"But you do now?"

I shrug, meeting his eyes in the mirror. "I guess," I say around my toothbrush. "He bought me pancakes."

I'm not trying to poke the bear, but I don't see the point in lying.

Chuck's nostrils flare and his neck turns dark red. "Motherfucking asshole."

I rinse out my mouth then turn the water hot to wash my face. "If you say so." Nothing about Oliver struck me as asshole-ish. Chuck in this moment, however? That's a different story.

"You liked that?" he asks.

"Liked what? The pancakes?" I face him while I scrub my face.

"Him feeding you. Acting like he likes that fat ass."

I flinch before I can stop myself. Intellectually, I know there's nothing wrong with my body. All bodies are good bodies, et cetera, et cetera. But I grew up with an image-obsessed mother who could never come to terms with her own above-average size. As a result, puberty was hell. She hounded me day in and day out about every bite that went into my mouth and every ounce I gained.

I just want to make sure you're only gaining it in the right places.

I'm starting to see it in your thighs.

Your period is no excuse to consume empty calories.

Chuck grunts. "You do like it. You liked him feeding you. You want to tell yourself that he wouldn't care if you got fat. But I'm here to tell you the hard truth. Oliver Rhett isn't going to sweep you off your feet."

I toss my washcloth in the sink. "I said he bought me pancakes, not a fucking engagement ring. Chill out."

He sighs then pulls me into his arms. "I'm chill, okay? Sorry. I'm just all wound up about this fight."

I close my eyes and rest my head against his chest. "I know. Things have been tense lately, though." I take a breath and confess the thought that's been haunting me all summer. "I'm wondering if me moving in was a bad idea." *I wanted another guy to kiss me tonight. Wanted it almost badly enough to make the move myself. Isn't that a bad sign?*

"Nah." When he releases me, I step back, grateful to get away from his boozy stench. "After Wednesday, this will all be over." He smacks my ass. "Just don't go getting fat between now and then." He strides out of the bathroom muttering, "Fucking pancakes."

"Who gives an assignment this big during the first week of classes?" Miranda whines on our walk to The Naked Bean after class.

"It's not that big, really," I say, then soften my words with a smile. Miranda's a freshman and my friend Julie's little sister. When Julie found out we were in the same women's studies lecture, she warned me that Miranda was a bit coddled through school and that she would lean heavily on me. "You'll get used to it."

I remember my first days of class on this campus—how strange it felt to be in such a quiet town after growing up in the constant bustle of Atlanta, how uncomfortable it was to be surrounded by strangers, how nervous I was about being able to meet the expectations of my professors.

We turn into The Naked Bean and plop our bags on a table just inside the door.

"Easy for you to say," Miranda whines. "You get to live off-campus with that hot fighter. I'm stuck in the library trying to get my work done, and the only tens I meet are already taken."

Yeah. Lucky me. But I flinch the second I register the thought. I'm not being fair.

This morning, I woke up to a note on the counter with a couple hundred-dollar bills on top.

Sorry I've been in a mood. I fucking love you so much it makes me crazy sometimes. Keep your Friday night free for me. I want to take you out. Thought you might want to use this to get yourself something sexy to wear for the occasion.

My first thought was that I would be long gone by Friday. Then I felt guilty. Chuck's not perfect, but he can be sweet.

"You'll find a relationship eventually," I say. "You're young. Don't rush it."

"I don't want a *relationship.* I want a good time. I thought college was supposed to be fun," she says, digging some cash from her backpack. "All I'm going to get to do is read and go to study tables. Ugh!" As if someone flipped a switch, all the whiny bitchiness falls off her face and is replaced by a smile. "Well, hello," she says to someone over my shoulder.

I turn to find the guy from last weekend standing not two feet from me—Oliver of the pretty eyes and sexy laugh. He's dressed in dark-wash jeans and a white T-shirt that strains across his chest and biceps—the kind of shirt that's cut to show off a guy's muscles. And his tattoos. *Damn.*

"Savvy, we meet again," he says, ignoring Miranda and offering his hand to me.

"Oh, hey." I dig in my backpack for my wallet. "How's the first week of classes been?"

He shoves his hands into his pockets. "Fine. It's my last semester, so I'm just doing my capstone."

Miranda bats her lashes. "What's your major?"

His lifted-brow expression suggests this is none of her business, but he says, "I'm finishing my MBA." He shifts his gaze back to me so swiftly that even Miranda seems to pick up on the dismissal.

"I'll see you Thursday," she says to me, flipping her dark hair over her shoulder and giving us her back.

"Text me if you need anything," I call, but she just waves and continues to the line at the register, utterly disgusted at Oliver's lack of interest in her.

His eyes seem to catalogue every inch of me, and I ignore the flip-flopping, nervous mess that makes of my insides. *Nothing happened. Nothing is going to happen.*

I pluck a twenty from my wallet and shove it at him. "Here. For the pancakes."

He pulls back like I just offered him a pile of steaming dog poo. "I already told you I don't want your money."

I frown, pulling my Naked Bean apron from my backpack. "Then why are you here?"

"I have a proposition for you. Can I take you out after work? Or tomorrow between classes?"

The word *proposition* sends all sorts of inappropriate scenarios running through my head. What is it about this guy? I give him my best quizzical WTF face. "I have a boyfriend, remember?"

"So you're not allowed to eat lunch or dinner with a friend?"

I loop my apron behind my neck and position the ties at my waist. "I didn't say that."

"Then come out with me. Everyone needs to eat."

Not me. I'm going to have to spend the whole week making up for the extra calories in all those ill-advised drinks I had at the party. "It's not a good idea."

"Because you almost kissed me?"

That question makes my insides freeze. I snap my head up, gaping at him before looking around to make sure no one heard. The café is bustling, as it always is this time of day, with a line that nearly reaches to the door, but no one is paying us any attention. "Seriously?" I ask in a harsh whisper. "That's not what happened. *You* almost kissed *me.* I stopped you."

He grins, his gray eyes dancing. "Is that what you told your boyfriend?"

"I didn't tell my boyfriend anything."

"Is that so?" That grin twitches into a cocky smirk. "Okay. I'm cool with being your dirty secret if that's how you want to play this."

"You're incorrigible."

"I think the word you're looking for is *irresistible*." His eyes scan my face. "Look me in the eye and tell me you haven't thought about me in the last two days."

I can't do that. I've thought about Oliver way more than I want to admit. I've thought about the things he said about his childhood, about how easy it was to talk to him, and about how when he bent to kiss me, I felt a pull to him that I've read about but never thought was real.

Maybe if things were different, I'd have let it happen —let his lips sweep over mine, reminded myself what it was like to be touched by someone who doesn't spend half their time trying to convince me I'm repulsive. Maybe in that same world, I'd let Oliver take me out tonight, maybe even go home with him after. But instead of living in that world, I live in one where I've promised my idiot brother I won't break up with my idiot boyfriend until after the big fight.

Which is tomorrow night, a little voice whispers. I'm pretty sure that voice belongs to the same hussy who almost let me kiss Oliver on Saturday. My promise to my brother might be over after the fight, but I'm counting on Nathan making good on *his* promises before I walk away from Chuck. Namely, paying me back the cash he borrowed two weeks ago. Without it, I won't have the deposit I need to live on my own.

Oliver must take my silence as an answer, because he gives me a soft smile that I'm sure makes all the girls' knees go weak. "It's okay. I won't make you admit it," he says, his voice lower now.

"I have to clock in."

He nods gravely. "See you tomorrow, then."

I frown. Didn't we just cover that he *won't*? "Because you're stalking me now?"

He chuckles. "The big event at ten p.m.? I assume you'll be there to cheer on your boyfriend?"

The underground fighting circuit on campus isn't exactly the best kept secret, but it's one most people don't talk about in public. Myself included.

I shrug. "Maybe."

He nods and drags his eyes over me with such heat my insides turn molten. I half expect my clothes to turn to ash. "Looking forward to it."

I spin around and walk away from Oliver as fast as I can. He's *looking forward to it*, and now, fuckity fuck, so am I.

CHAPTER SIX

SAVVY

I think I'm gonna puke, and somehow I don't think the pretty brunette in front of me would appreciate that.

Cheers echo off the concrete walls, and people all around me bounce on their toes to get a better view of the fighters in the ring. We're packed in like sardines. Everyone's been buzzing about this fight.

"Come on!" Nathan screams, his face red with rage. "Hit the sonofabitch, fucking loser!"

He's screaming at Chuck, and the anger on his face matches the horror eating away at my gut. Chuck was supposed to win this fight. "Easy money," my brother's been saying for weeks now. *Easy money.* I know there's no such thing, and I know better than to give my brother money I can't spare. Yet here I am, wishing I hadn't had a cup of the spiked red punch before coming down to the secret underground fighting ring beneath Crossport U. If I can't calm my stomach, the brunette's tight white tank top is going to gain a splash of color.

Chuck's opponent swings right, and Chuck dodges at the last second and lands a punch to the guy's shoulder, but the guy isn't fazed.

"Come on, Chuck," I whisper. "Please." But I might as well be praying to Santa Claus, because I know what the people around me couldn't.

Chuck isn't *trying*.

I stare at the ring, but all I can see is the greedy smile he flashed me when he realized he'd talked Nathan into betting on him. "Must be nice to have so much cash," he said, giggling manically.

I didn't correct him. Everyone at this school thinks my family's rich because the stadium and liberal arts buildings carry my name. My *grandfather's* name. People assume my father couldn't possibly have been stupid enough to lose all our family money in the two decades since Grandpa died. *People* are naïve.

And so am I.

Did Chuck plan this? Did he set Nathan up?

The other guy in the ring dodges a weak punch then pivots with an uppercut right under Chuck's jaw. Chuck stumbles back. The guy sees his opening and attacks.

I feel every swing and kick to my heart, my pride, and my future. I almost envy Chuck when he collapses, his body surrendering to unconsciousness.

"Fuck this!" Nathan roars, then he spins on his heel and shoves through the crowd and toward the exit.

I'm pushed side to side, front to back, as people around me shove their way in opposite directions—some trying to get to the ring to meet the new champ, and some trying to follow Nathan out. I don't go anywhere. I just let the crowd jostle me around.

The unofficial medics attend to Chuck, and when he finally sits up and blinks his eyes open, I should feel relieved. *I don't.* We were played. Nathan was played.

Because he's an easy target. And so are you.

"Are you okay?"

I tear my gaze off the ring and try to focus on the girl standing in front of me, her head cocked to the side in concern. My brain isn't functioning quite right and the only thought that registers is the first thing that comes out of my mouth. "I have nowhere to go."

Because Nathan's gone and so is my money. Because I know what Chuck did, and I won't be staying with him.

The girl bites her lip. "That was ugly." She blows out a breath and glances over her shoulder. "He's a little messed up, but he'll be okay."

"I hope I'm wrong. I better be wrong." I flinch. I need to get control of my freaking mouth.

"What?"

I shake my head. "Nothing."

I'm dragged away from the girl when someone yanks on my arm. I don't know him, but I recognize him from the last time Nathan owed a bookie money. Hard to forget those face tattoos. "Where the fuck's your brother?"

My numbness retreats, but my nausea returns like a smack in the face. It's so freaking hot in here and that punch doesn't want to stay in my stomach. "What do you want?"

"Your brother owes my boss money. Be a good little thing and tell me where he ran off to."

I try to pull my arm from the guy's grasp but fail. I can feel bruises forming beneath the pads of his fingers. "You're hurting me!"

"This is nothing compared to what we'll do if he doesn't pay."

"He doesn't owe you shit. I gave him the money to place that stupid bet."

"That was just a down payment. A deposit. Now my boss needs the rest." The guy's grip goes tighter. "Where the fuck is he?"

"I don't know. I'm not his keeper."

My gaze darts again to the ring, where Chuck is stumbling to his feet. I want him to come over here and tell me I'm wrong. I want him to say something—anything—to make these awful thoughts go away. Maybe I haven't felt close to him in weeks. Maybe I knew this wouldn't work between us and was already planning my exit, but he wouldn't con my brother into betting on him in a fight he planned to throw. Would he?

In the ring, Chuck catches my eye and winks. He *winks*.

"Will you fucking listen when I'm talking to you?" the bookie says.

I try to turn my focus back to him, but at the same moment, I lose the battle with the contents of my stomach and throw up red punch right onto the guy's white shoes.

He scrambles back. "Bitch! What the fuck?"

I wipe at the back of my mouth, torn between horror and the next wave of nausea. "Oh my G—"

The hand that strikes my cheek cuts me off before I can finish my apology, and I stagger back as if I'm doing a comical replay of Chuck in the ring.

I shake my head. "I don't know where he is, but I'm sure he's going to pay you."

It's a lie. Nathan doesn't have the money. He doesn't have anything. We were conned out of money we don't even have.

I wish this were a nightmare, but the smell of my own vomit makes it all too real.

Chuck uses that moment to remember my existence. "It's fine." He limps as he comes toward me. "Savvy's family is loaded. Her brother is good for it."

I spin on him. "You did this on purpose!"

The crowd's cleared out. Only a few groups of people remain in this dingy, cavernous space, and they gasp as they hear my accusation.

"Excuse me?" Chuck rocks back on his heels and folds his arms. "You think I *enjoyed* that?"

I don't even try to hide my sneer. You don't have to enjoy something to profit from it. "You don't understand what you did. Nathan doesn't have any money."

"I'm sure he can ask your daddy for it," Chuck says.

A few minutes ago, I hoped to never see another fist connect with Chuck's jaw, but I've changed my mind. Now, I would relish the sight. And I'd like the fist to be my own. "He *doesn't have it*."

"Your girlfriend's lucky. I'm willing to let her work off her brother's debts," the bookie says. "Otherwise she wouldn't have a brother anymore."

Chuck huffs. "Yeah, right." He smacks my arm playfully. "Quit acting like you don't have any money, Savannah. Call your parents."

"No," I growl, stepping away from him. If I doubted it before, now I'm sure. Chuck did this on purpose. He set up Nathan to make a big bet on this fight.

This is what you get for pretending to have money. You become a target. If they knew my family was living on borrowed money and the power of my grandfather's name, they never would've bothered.

"What'll it be?" the bookie asks.

"Fuck off."

Chuck gapes at me. "*Call. Your. Parents.* Jesus, Sav, these people aren't playing."

"My parents are *broke*," I shout, and I swear the word echoes so loudly it makes my eardrums ache. If this gets back to my mother, she'll disown me. If my parents worked half as hard at making money as they do trying to pretend they never lost Dad's inheritance, we'd be fine. Maybe we wouldn't be millionaires, but at least Nathan wouldn't be running around making dumbass bets on illegal fights with money he doesn't have.

Maybe Chuck got punched in the head too many times tonight, or maybe it just takes him that long to register that I'm serious, but he finally gasps. He pales and whispers, "Fuck. *Shit.* Your brother's gotta find a way to pay these guys, Sav. This is serious shit."

I grab his arm. "Then help him." If I'm right and he threw this fight, he didn't do it for free. "Help him pay them!"

"I'm not the one who placed a bet with money I don't have. Fuck that." He worms away from my grasp and backs up a step before shaking his head and turning to the exit.

A redhead with her hair in fucking pigtails grabs on to his arm on the way out. "Come back to my place and I'll clean you up," she says. She sneers at me over her shoulder, and I think I'm supposed to be jealous, but I'm not.

If literal death glares were a thing, Chuck wouldn't make it out the door, but my rage has no real power. Because he and Miss Pigtails disappear.

The bookie chuckles, and when I swing my attention back to him, he cocks his head to the side. "Do you know what we do to people who fuck us over, little thing? And how long we take to do it?"

It was a rhetorical question, but I'm stupidly shaking my head anyway. Nathan's not new to gambling, and I've seen him bloodied by a bookie in the past. Somehow, I know this is going to be much worse.

"I guess you'll find out, then." The bookie turns around and strides toward the exit.

The remaining crowd is silent as they watch our exchange, and my words echo off the concrete walls when I shout, "Wait!"

The bookie's face is full of satisfaction as he turns back to me. "Yes?"

"Where are you going?"

"To find your brother and make sure he knows how serious this is."

I swallow hard. "What would I have to do—to pay off the debt?" I'm not naïve enough to think it's washing dishes or folding his laundry, but surely it can't be as bad as I think. This is real life, not the movies.

The bookie relaxes a little and strides back to me. "Come with me and we'll talk about it, 'kay?" Before I can refuse, he wraps his rough hand around my upper arm and pulls me toward the exit opposite where Chuck disappeared.

"Let her go."

My head snaps up, and I meet a pair of familiar gray eyes. *Oliver.*

"Mind your business," the bookie says.

"It is my business," Oliver says. He nods to the bookie's side just as the phone there begins to ring.

The bookie releases my arm and answers the call. "Yeah?" He gives Oliver a withering look, but Oliver only lifts his chin. "Got it." The bookie ends the call and flashes me a bitter grin. "All's well that ends well, right?"

I look back and forth between him and Oliver as the

bookie walks down the dark hall. Only once the echo of his steps fades do I dare breathe again.

"You okay?" Oliver asks, stepping closer.

I open my mouth to lie then shake my head. "No. I'm not." *Chuck conned me. And my brother left me to cover for him.* I blink up at Oliver. "What just happened?"

Oliver glances in the direction that the bookie disappeared. "His boss told him to let you go."

"Why? What about my brother? Are they going after him?"

"He's safe."

"How?"

He shrugs. "I know people. I called in some favors." He looks me over slowly and cringes at the red vomit splattered on my white jeans. "Wanna get out of here?"

"What—why?"

"Because it smells like a dumpster down here and you've had a rough night?"

"Why did you call in favors?" *Why did you come to my rescue?*

"Because I need a favor from *you*. And anyway, I hate to see the assholes win."

He offers me his hand, palm up, and I take it.

Part Three

PRESENT DAY

CHAPTER SEVEN

SAVVY

I'm surprised to see Alec after my six a.m. spin class the next morning. He's sitting at a table on the restaurant's patio with Marston. They're both staring at their laptops with cups of coffee steaming beside them.

The second my feet hit the flagstone, Alec tears his gaze off his laptop and grins at me. "Morning, beautiful."

Something inside of me tugs hard, as if it's saying, *There. Go there. Give him your heart,* but I don't know if it's my heart or my loneliness, so I stand strong and give nothing but a polite smile. "How are you this morning? Did you sleep well?"

"I did, and it's a good thing, too, because this one had me up and running before dawn," he says, nodding to

Marston. He gestures to the seat beside him. "Do you have time to join us for a cup of coffee?"

I swallow. "I was hoping we could talk in my office."

"Sure." He pushes out of his chair, leaving his laptop behind but taking his coffee, and I lead the way back into the building and to my small office tucked between the group workout room and the gym. "Marston knows what's going on," he says, pulling the door closed behind him.

"Good." If Marston knows the truth, that means I don't have to lie to Brinley. "I don't want to have to lie to my friends."

Alec turns up the wattage on his grin. "Are you saying . . .?"

"I'll do it." I swallow. "As long as this won't change our friendship, if this is going to help you out, then I can do it."

Alec beams. I haven't seen him smile like that since the morning we separated in Vegas. We were both sad to say goodbye, and then I told him I'd come see him in L.A. In that moment, we both believed we stood a chance—despite the distance, despite any mistakes that haunted either of us. He smiled at me because he believed in *us*, and for a few short weeks, I did too.

He deserves so much better than me and my secrets.

"Thank you, Savvy. I know your time is valuable, and . . ." He shoves his hands in his pockets, as if he's not sure what to do with them. After a long silence, he says, "I appreciate it."

"It doesn't need to be a big deal, right?"

"Right," he says softly. "And with any luck, I'll be able to help you get that position with The Rage."

I bite my lip. "Only if you're comfortable with that. In your business, you might travel in the same circles as the CEO, so I don't want you to feel like—"

"It would be my pleasure. Don't give it another thought."

My heart races. I want this job so badly, but I'm terrified that using lies to get it—even with good reason—is going to bite me in the ass. "Thank you."

"My family will be arriving in town this afternoon. What's your schedule for the day?"

"My last class is at five, so I can be out of here by six."

"Perfect. We're doing dinner on The Patio at seven. Will you join us?"

I nod, afraid the fear will be too obvious in my voice if I speak.

"I'll pick you up at about a quarter till?"

I laugh. "I can meet you here. I'm pretty familiar with the place."

He cocks his head with a sly smile. "What kind of man would I be if I made my date drive herself?" He winks at me and backs toward the door. "See you tonight."

ALEC

Savvy looks *stunning*, and for a moment after she opens the door, I can't remember how to breathe. Can't remember, honestly, why I even need to breathe.

Her long blond hair is down around her shoulders, sleek and smooth. I know exactly what it would feel like to slide my hands into that hair while I took her mouth. I'm haunted by the way her eyes flashed with heat when I wrapped those locks around my fist as she—

"You're early."

I swallow back my inappropriate thoughts. *Just friends.* That's her rule. "Sorry. Did you need more time? You look . . . amazing." I shove my hands into my pockets to keep them from reaching for her.

She cocks her head to the side. "Are you nervous?" She wrinkles her nose. "Is it me? Are you afraid I'm going to embarrass you?"

I scoff. "Not even a little." My nerves have nothing to do with worrying about how she might act and everything to do with worrying about how *I* might.

When I asked Brinley if she knew why Savvy pulled away from me, she said Savvy had a rough breakup in college. She said she didn't know the details, but she knew it'd been the root of a lot of her trust issues with men. I decided then that I just needed to earn her trust. To prove I'm not going to hurt her like her ex. But that's been hard to do when I never get time with her.

I need this time with Savvy. The last thing I want is to scare her away.

"Are you ready?"

"I think?" She fingers the simple pendant pearl necklace at her throat. She's *shaking*, and I'm once again overwhelmed by the urge to touch her. To show her with my hands just how beautiful she looks.

"Just be yourself, Savvy. That would win anyone over."

She lifts her eyes to mine for a beat before nodding. "Thank you. Just let me—" She waves toward the back of the apartment. "I need to grab my shoes and I'll be ready."

SAVVY

Breathe, Savvy. It's just dinner.

I might be hiding in my bedroom, shoes in hand. I might be panicking—as one does when one is playing with fire.

But I would do anything for Alec, and rationally, I know Oliver won't show up. He's in Monaco, and he can't stand this side of his family. I knew that even before I knew Alec was part of it.

"Are you about ready?" Alec calls from the foyer.

Suck it up, buttercup. "Yep," I say with more enthusiasm than I feel. I slip on my shoes and join him at the front of the apartment. "Sorry. I couldn't find my shoes." *More lies. Lies upon lies.*

My stomach knots. He would see me differently if he knew the truth, but maybe I should tell him anyway. *Hey, remember when your brother was finishing his MBA and your dad had to buy him a new car out of the blue? Yeah. That was my fault.*

"We should go. My mother can't abide tardiness." He smiles while he says this, but I get the impression it's also true.

He opens the door and turns his palm up toward the Lexus parked out front. The truth about Oliver can wait. Revealing that ugliness before tonight would be wrong anyway. I should let Alec enjoy the evening with his family without having to process my history with his estranged brother.

Alec opens the door for me and waits for me to settle into the passenger seat before he walks around to his side of the car. His strong hands grip the leather steering wheel as he pulls out of my apartment complex. I have to pull my gaze away before my thoughts drift to memories of those hands on me. That night. The chemistry between us.

"Any questions before we get there?" he asks, navigating toward The Orchid.

I worry my bottom lip between my teeth. "What have you told them about your girlfriend?"

He cuts his gaze to me for a beat before bringing it back to the road. "What do you mean?"

"I mean, who am I supposed to be tonight?"

One corner of his mouth hitches up in amusement. "Just be you, Sav. That's all you need to do. This doesn't have to be complicated."

Oh, Alec. You have no idea. "Is it okay if I talk about what I do?"

He narrows his eyes. "Why wouldn't it be?"

"I mean, are you okay with your family knowing?" *Will you be embarrassed if your fancy family knows your supposed girlfriend is a personal trainer?* I know my family would be. If I still spoke with them.

"I don't understand."

I blow out a breath. "Alec, you're a big deal in the business community, and your family has money. Jobs like mine aren't glamourous."

"But you're about to interview to be a premier instructor for The Rage. That's a big fucking deal."

"And it's little more than a shot in the dark. They have hundreds of applicants—probably thousands. Right now, I'm just a personal trainer and fitness instructor."

He furrows his brow. "When we were in Vegas and you told me about what you do, you didn't make it sound like *just* anything. Your job matters. You empower women."

His words are a warm hug around my heart. *He gets it.* "I love that you heard me when I explained, but not everyone does."

"Brinley told me you don't feel comfortable around money. Is that what this is about?"

I open my mouth to argue but snap it shut. Growing up a Downing taught me how to step into a room with the richest people in America and act like I belonged. I give zero shits if the people around me have money, but what Brinley likely picked up on was my discomfort around those who are always chasing more. "I can handle it. I'm thinking of you. Of how what I do and don't say about myself can make this better for you."

"I don't care what my family thinks about what you do," he says. "I think you're amazing. I want you to be yourself."

I swallow. "I appreciate that." I hesitate a beat. "Who all will be there tonight?" I ask. If there are a hundred ways to get reassurance that Oliver isn't going to show up, I will try one hundred and two. But it's more than that. I'm also nervous about meeting Alec's family because regardless of my history with his half-brother, Alec means a lot to me. For better or worse, I want his family to like me.

Alec's family. *Oliver's* family. It's not like I ever met them, and Oliver made it perfectly clear that he didn't share the details of his personal life with them, but what if that's changed? What if somehow someone here recognizes me and tells Alec about my history with his brother? What if Alec thinks I'm the whore his father accused me of being?

He turns toward downtown and hums, thinking. "Obviously my sister, Rose, and her fiancé, Jared. My mom and Jared's mother. And I think Rose's maid of honor, Caroline, was also going to make it to town."

I blow out a long breath. "Okay. I can handle that."

"Listen, my mother . . ." He takes his eyes off the road to glance at me. "She's pretty protective of me."

"Aren't all mothers protective of their sons?"

"She's had a complicated life, and she's not an easy

person to deal with. Just don't take it personally if she comes off as abrasive tonight. We're actively crushing her dreams of marrying into the Mayhue family."

I nod. "I deal with difficult women all the time. I'm sure I can handle her."

Alec parks the car and reaches across the console to take my hand. "You're shaking."

I close my eyes. I hadn't realized the quivering in my stomach had invaded my limbs. "I'm nervous," I admit.

Alec lifts my hand to his mouth. As he kisses each of my knuckles, I remind myself that this is not what friends do, but his gesture is too comforting to stop.

"You have nothing to worry about," he says. "They will love you."

I bite my bottom lip. "Is this a mistake? Lying to them? What if they . . ."

"Figure us out?" He drops his gaze and studies his thumb as it strokes across the back of my hand. "It'll be okay. I've talked about you enough that it won't be a huge surprise to have you here as my date."

I take a deep breath. *Just do this, Savvy. If tonight goes smoothly, the wedding weekend won't be as scary.* "We better get in there, then."

CHAPTER EIGHT

SAVVY

I'm lucky that dinner is at The Orchid, since I consider this my turf. As soon as we step onto the outdoor dining space that overlooks Lake Blackledge, my shoulders drop and my lungs allow just a little more air in than they did before.

"Welcome!" squeals a pale brunette who has Alec's ice-blue eyes.

Alec grins. "Savvy, this is our bride-to-be, my sister, Rose."

I offer Rose my hand, but she ignores it and pulls me into a hug. "I'm so happy to finally meet you," she squeals.

I meet Alec's gaze over her shoulder. *Finally?*

He shrugs, tinges of pink appearing on his cheeks.

A regal-looking woman with ivory skin crosses to us

from near the doors that connect the indoor and outdoor sections of the restaurant. She's tall and lovely in a dark blue dress. Her dark hair is swept off her face in a twist at the back of her head, and diamond earrings glint in her ears.

I smile at her, but her gaze sweeps over me like I'm a roach she's found under her shoe. My smile falls away.

"Mom," Alec says, "this is Savvy, who I've told you so much about. Savvy, this is our mother, Cheryl."

"Yes. I've been told about you."

"Alec, you have to see this!" a dark-skinned man calls, waving Alec over to the bar.

"I'm being summoned," Alec says. "Are you okay here?"

"Of course she is," Rose says, nudging him away with her elbow. "Get out of here."

With an indulgent grin, Alec kisses my cheek then strides away.

His mother clears her throat.

Right. Introductions. I offer my hand, and she takes it by my fingertips, shaking it limply and releasing it quickly.

After one more beat of staring into my soul, she turns her gaze toward the guys gathered at the bar. "You got lucky with my son. He's absolutely incredible."

Something about her tone implies *unlike you*, but he *is* incredible, so I say, "Oh, I know."

"I would hope," she says, and I decide that she is the exact opposite of her daughter. Rose fills a room with her joy, doling it out to everyone, and Cheryl smothers it.

"Ignore her," Rose says. "She married my brother off in her head when he was twenty and has been ignoring everything he's said about you for months."

"How was I supposed to know they were serious?" Cheryl asks. "He hasn't brought her out to L.A. even once."

Wow. How can I be so offended when she hasn't said anything that isn't true?

"Mom," Rose says under her breath, "please play nice. For me?"

The smile Cheryl pastes on would make a snake's gaping maw look inviting. "This is incredibly unexpected, is all," she says. "I hear you work at a gym. Is that right?"

"Yeah. I'm a personal trainer and group fitness instructor."

"My friend's daughter did something similar for spending money while she was in dental school."

I am too stubborn to let my smile waver, but the implication is clear. My job isn't respectable as a profession. I wish I could say I didn't see this coming. "Good for her."

She eyes my shoulders. "You shouldn't work your upper body so much, dear. All that muscle can make you look rather masculine."

Oh, yay. One of those. *You're doing this for Alec. Just keep smiling.*

"Mom!" Rose groans.

"Excuse me," Cheryl says. "I need to talk to the servers about circulating with the appetizers." She disappears into the restaurant, and I hope she stays there.

When I turn back to Rose, she looks me over. "Don't listen to her. You are stunning. I checked out your Insta, but you're even more beautiful in person." She hugs me again, and a weird tangle of guilt and gratitude pulls my insides in opposite directions.

"You're too sweet."

"And your shoulders are to die for! Can you write me a program to get more definition in my shoulders? I will totally pay you, but—"

I laugh. I don't know if she means it or if she's trying to smooth over her mother's faux pas, but I appreciate her words either way. "I would be happy to. You don't have to pay me. Just drop me a DM with info about where you work out and the kind of equipment you have available."

She claps and bounces on her toes. "You are so awesome. Come on. I want to introduce you to my best friend and maid of honor."

I let her pull me away from Alec and toward her friend. Rose grabs a glass off a passing waiter's tray along the way and shoves it into my free hand. "Trust me," she says, her voice too low to carry. "If you're going to spend the evening around my mother, you'll want this. But you probably figured that out already."

When I glance over my shoulder toward the bar, Alec winks at me. I take a sip of champagne.

Rose pulls me to a cocktail table near the lake and slings her arm around a petite Asian woman with streaks of white in her dark hair. "Caroline," Rose says, "this is Alec's Savvy."

Alec's Savvy. I wish I didn't like the sound of that so much.

"I'm so excited to finally meet you," Caroline says. "I was there the day Alec came home from Vegas. He couldn't stop talking about you."

Again with the stomach flipping. I want to dig for more information, but it doesn't seem right. "It's so nice to meet you."

"I see you survived your introduction to Cruella de Vil," Caroline says with a smirk. "On a scale of one to ten, how Wicked Witch of the West was she today?"

Rose coughs like she's choking on a stifled laugh. "She was a solid five."

"That was only a five?" I blurt before I can stop myself, and both girls burst into loud giggles that make everyone else on the patio turn and stare.

"Oh, yeah." Caroline lowers her voice further. "I like to call her Cruella, but we think she might actually be Satan."

Rose fights a smile, but it wins. "Alec is pretty protective of her, though."

"Of course he is. He's Alec," Caroline says. "He sees the best in people."

"Most of the time," Rose says.

Caroline peeks over my shoulder to study the man in question. "He's, like, the most eligible bachelor in our parents' circles, and it's totally warranted. Not only is he hot and successful, he's a complete teddy bear."

"Caroline has known Alec since high school," Rose explains. "He's three years older than me, and I had to figure out the hard way that the girls always wanted to come over when they knew he'd be home."

I have to laugh. "I can totally see all the high school girls falling head over heels for Alec."

"Not as badly as we fell for *Oliver*," Caroline croons.

I stiffen at his name. I wondered if he'd come up tonight and tried to brace myself for it, but it still feels like two very different worlds colliding.

"Don't remind me," Rose says. She turns to me. "Ever walked onto a beach carrying a basket of fries and found yourself surrounded by begging seagulls? That's how it felt to have my friends over when Oliver was around."

Caroline waves a finger at her. "Until your mom convinced all our moms that their daughters couldn't be trusted around him, and then we were *forbidden* from sleepovers until he left for college. I swear, Cheryl had our moms convinced he'd somehow impregnate us all."

I flinch. "That's awful."

Rose rolls her eyes. "It is, but that's very on brand for Cheryl."

"Especially when it comes to Oliver," Caroline says.

"And anyway," Rose says, "she was wrong. Oliver didn't want anything to do with the girls in L.A. He was counting down the days until he could get out of there."

"How often does he come back?" I ask, one foot testing the ice. *Shut up, shut up, shut up!*

"When he was in college, you couldn't drag him home," Rose says. "But since Mom's moved out of Grandmother's house, he'll come a couple times a year to visit with me."

"Don't worry," Caroline says, as if reading the distress on my face. "Oliver won't be showing up to the wedding and making waves. He loves Rose too much to bring any drama to her special day."

Rose frowns. "He's not the one who'd bring the drama," she mutters, cutting her eyes to the back of the patio where her mother has reappeared and seems to be arguing with a server.

"Yeah, but what are you going to do?" Caroline says with a sigh. "Disinvite your mom to your own wedding just so your brother can be there?"

Rose tilts her head from side to side with an expression that says she'd consider it, and both girls erupt into more laughter.

"What's so funny over here?" someone asks, stepping up behind Rose and sliding his arms around her waist. It's the guy who pulled Alec away earlier. The groom. He's at least a foot taller than Rose, with eyes that light up when he looks at his bride. He presses a kiss to the crook of her neck, and Rose smiles.

"Savvy, this is my fiancé, Jared. Jared, this is Alec's girlfriend, Savvy."

He releases his fiancée to offer me a hand. "It's a pleasure to meet you. Rose said Alec was bringing his mystery girl."

"That's me," I say, and there's an underlying squeak to my voice. I am a terrible liar.

"We were just talking about why Oliver won't be at the wedding," Rose tells her fiancé.

Jared frowns and sighs. "It sucks, but what family doesn't have its complications, right?"

"Oliver invited us for a weekend on his boat after the honeymoon," Rose says. "We'll celebrate with him then." She's smiling, but again, I feel like her light's been dimmed.

"So, Oliver and Alec don't get along?" I ask. *Oh my God. Will someone please shut me up before I dig myself a hole?* It's not like I don't already know the answer to this question, but I'm hungry for as many details as I can get. I need intel to keep this thing from blowing up in our faces.

Or maybe you miss Oliver and want to know everything you can about him.

Caroline coughs out a laugh. "That's like asking if Batman and the Joker are buddies."

"It was hard for them," Rose says. "After Oliver's mom died, Dad just moved Oliver to L.A. and demanded we all act like some big, happy family. It was messed up. Oliver was so fucking bitter about being there. He hated us all."

Caroline shakes her head. "Cheryl didn't make it any easier. She hated having Oliver there and made sure he knew it."

"Poor guy," I whisper. Oliver had his flaws, but I never doubted that he had trauma to match. After only a few minutes in Alec's mom's presence, I'm beginning to imagine what those years might have been like for him.

"Ugh." Rose shudders. "He would *hate* knowing we're

all standing here gossiping about him. Let's change the subject, please."

Jared nods in agreement and shifts his attention to me. "So, tell us about yourself, Savvy. Did you grow up in Orchid Valley? It's a beautiful little town."

"No. I'm a transplant. I moved here when I took the job as the fitness director at The Orchid," I say, waving to the building that houses my office.

"She's interviewing to be an instructor for The Rage," Rose says. When I shoot her a questioning look, she giggles. "Alec told me. He might be a little proud of you."

"That's great," Jared says.

"Just don't let Kyle hear you say that," Caroline says. She turns to me. "His business partner was one of the major investors that got Diva Studios off the ground."

"That's incredible," I say. Diva Studios isn't as well known as The Rage, but it's one of its competitors and definitely an up-and-comer.

Jared nods. "It's Kyle's sister's passion project. It's been awesome to see it flourish in a relatively short time."

"If things don't work out with The Rage, maybe you should make some introductions," Rose tells her fiancé.

I force a smile. If things between Alec and I were real, I would jump on that opportunity. But they're not, and I won't drag this out longer than I need to and risk his getting hurt.

The evening was a whirlwind. I was introduced to the groom's mother when she arrived, and even a couple cousins from one side or the other—I lost track somehow, probably because my wine glass was never empty, despite my sipping at it all night.

Only once dinner was served was I returned to Alec's side, but by that point I was too tipsy to feel frazzled.

"I knew you'd love Rose," Alec says, walking me to my door at the end of the night.

"She's like a walking ray of sunshine," I say.

Alec blinks at me then nods. "Yeah." He swallows. "That's perfect. I can't think of a better way to describe her."

I pull my keys from my purse. "So you think tonight went okay? I played the girlfriend acceptably?"

"I think you were perfect." He shoves his hands into his pockets. "I fly out early tomorrow, so I won't see you until you land in L.A. next weekend. Just text me when you have details."

I nod, but my gaze drops to his mouth. It would be so easy to let him kiss me right now. So easy to kiss him. The wine in my system makes it hard to remember why that's a bad idea. "I don't think I made a very good impression on your mother."

He grimaces. "She can be difficult. Don't take it personally."

Nodding, I look down at my keys. Staring at his mouth will send all the wrong signals.

He gently takes my wrist in his hand and strokes. I

feel my pulse accelerate beneath his touch. "I mean it. You were great tonight. You have no idea what it means to me."

I lift my gaze back to his. "It was nothing."

He steps back toward his car but doesn't release my wrist until the last moment.

When I get inside, I lean back against the door and close my eyes, willing my racing heart to slow.

CHAPTER NINE

ALEC

I sit in my car for ten minutes after she goes inside, waiting for her to come back out, waiting for her to ask for what I know she wanted when we stood at her door.

A kiss. Maybe more.

She's afraid of something, and I wish I knew what it was. Maybe Brinley's right and this is all rooted in her past with the guy who hurt her. Maybe my family's money scares her too much. People like my mother can make others acutely aware of the divide between haves and have-nots. But I hope Rose helped. I'd like to think she did. I could almost see Savvy letting down her guard every minute she chatted with my sister.

I'm about to drive away when my phone buzzes. I

scoop it up fast, hoping it's Savvy, but instead I see a message from Rose.

Rose: I love her. And I totally see why you've been so into her all this time.

I quickly tap out a reply.

Alec: Thank you for being so friendly with her tonight. I don't think Mom made her feel welcome.

Rose: That woman could turn a golden retriever into an introvert. Tell Savvy it has nothing to do with her!

Alec: I did.

Rose: Shit. Is she right there? You're probably staying at her place tonight.

I'm sure I would be if we were a real couple.

Sighing, I scrub a hand over my face. I want to tell Rose the truth, but part of the reason I'm doing this is to remove the possibility of my drama affecting her day. It will have to wait.

Alec: Hotel for me. Heading to the airport before dawn.

Rose: Drive safely. Thanks for coming tonight.

Alec: Of course.

The dots bounce, indicating she's typing. They stop then bounce again, and finally a message comes through.

Rose: I need to ask you something.

Alec: Anything.

Rose: I was talking to Savvy tonight, and I realized maybe I'm giving Mom too much control over my special day.

Alec: I thought that was why you were doing it here?

Rose: Yes, but not just the location. I mean the guest list. I mean Oliver.

I sigh. I've never understood my sister's affection for our half-brother. It seems to me like he's never been anything more than an ungrateful ass to our family, but I know she sees something in him that I never did and never could. Rose gives love to everyone, even when they don't deserve it.

Alec: Do you think he would come if you asked?

Rose: You mean do I think he'd be willing to endure an evening in the same room as Cheryl? Yeah. He'd do it for me.

Alec: It's up to you. You have to decide if you want that kind of tension at your wedding.

Rose: I know. I have to think about it. I just wanted to make sure YOU were okay with it.

Alec: I'll support whatever you want.

Rose: Thank you, Alec. You're the best.

SAVVY

I can never sleep well when I've had more than one drink, so I'm not surprised that I'm wide awake at two a.m. after meeting Alec's family.

I grab my phone from the bedside table and scroll through my Instagram messages.

The thread with Oliver is bolded again, meaning there's a new message, and unlike the one I found last night, this can't be more than a few hours old.

My stomach knots in anticipation. My heart rate kicks into a different gear.

Why does he still affect me this much after all this time?

I tell myself it's better to know, so I click and read his message.

Oliver_Rhett: You looked beautiful tonight. Hope my brother is treating you well.

The message is sent with the link to a post, and when I click through, I'm directed to Rose's Instagram profile and see a picture of myself on Alec's arm. I'm smiling up at him like he's hung the moon and stars.

"Strategic error," I mutter to myself. How did I think I could do this and keep it truly disconnected from Oliver? Of course Rose is going to post pictures of the events leading up to the wedding and the wedding itself.

Maybe I'm feeling feisty, because I head back into my messages to reply. I need some reassurance that this isn't all going to blow up in my face.

SeeSavvyLift: Are you going to come to the wedding?

After I send the message, I pull up my text thread with Alec. I should just tell him. This is torture.

Savvy: Are you still awake?

A notification lights up from Instagram. Oliver has already replied, but since I've officially replied to one of his messages, he's in my primary inbox now.

Oliver_Rhett: That depends. Do you want me to?

My phone vibrates with a text.

Alec: Yeah. What's up?

Savvy: I need to tell you something.

Alec: You can tell me anything.

I stare at the screen. I should've thought this through.

How would that go, exactly? Would he ask how we met and I'd explain Oliver *bought* me? Then say that I fell in love with him anyway? I already feel far too low-class for these people. That would only make me feel lower.

The dots bounce. Alec is typing again.

Instagram gives me another new message notification.

Oliver_Rhett: Is he there? Are you chatting with me while he sleeps beside you? That's a little cold, don't you think?

Oliver_Rhett: Then again, maybe you need to think about me to be interested in being in bed with him.

SeeSavvyLift: You are still so fucking cocky. If he were in bed with me, do you think I'd be thinking about you?

Oliver_Rhett: Do you really want me to answer that?

SeeSavvyLift: Get over yourself.

Oliver_Rhett: Either way, he's not in bed with you and you ARE thinking about me. I'm okay with that, Savvy.

SeeSavvyLift: I wasn't thinking about you. I just couldn't sleep.

A new text notification pops up on my screen, covering Oliver's message.

Alec: I know my mom is a lot to take. She'll warm up to you. Just give it time.

Guilt scrapes through me. My relationship with Alec might be fake, yet chatting with Oliver still feels like cheating somehow. I should tell Alec the truth, but I hate the idea of his looking at me differently. The least I can do for Alec is get through this wedding and save him from some attempt at an arranged marriage on his mother's part.

I'll tell him, but *after* the wedding.

Savvy: It's not her. I'm still worried about leading you on.

Alec: You've made it very clear where you stand. I'm a big boy. I can handle it.

He texts again before I can think of how to reply.

Alec: Sleep well. I'll see you next weekend.

Savvy: Thank you. You too.

When I close out our text thread, Oliver's most recent message is on the screen waiting for me.

Oliver_Rhett: If you need help relaxing, just close your eyes and remember that time I found you in the campus library. I know thinking about that night always helps me wind down.

His hands under my skirt, his breath in my ear as he told me to be quiet, the cool metal shelf against my palms as I arched back into him. The memory swamps me, and my entire body clenches in response—needy and wanting. I press my head into the pillow and try to block out all the heat pooling in my center, willing me to do just as he's suggesting. It would be so easy to lose myself in all my favorite details from that night and so many others from the short weeks when we finally gave in to the chemistry between us.

Instead, I type out a reply.

SeeSavvyLift: Don't hurt Alec. You two might not get along, but he doesn't deserve you rubbing our past in his face.

Oliver_Rhett: You still haven't told him? Interesting.

But I get it. Alec would hate knowing I had you first. He'd make himself crazy with it.

Any heat I felt from the library memory is snapped away like a blanket at those words.

Oliver_Rhett: It'll make him even crazier when he realizes how long you've kept the truth from him, but that's okay. I don't mind being your dirty little secret. I'm actually pretty good at it . . . among other things.

SeeSavvyLift: A little hypocritical of you to have any opinions about me keeping you a secret from your family, since you kept ME a secret from them.

Oliver_Rhett: Can you blame me? I can only assume you've met my stepmother by now. I did you a favor by never subjecting you to that bitch.

SeeSavvyLift: I see nothing's changed with you.

Oliver_Rhett: Nope. I'm the same cocky asshole who could never get enough of you.

Until you did. I bite my bottom lip, cursing the twist in my chest. I don't want his words to affect me. I don't like that I would torture myself just to get answers.

SeeSavvyLift: Still breadcrumbing me, eight years later.

Oliver_Rhett: I can't breadcrumb a woman who's committed to her boyfriend. Which begs the question . . .

SeeSavvyLift: Goodnight, Oliver.

I turn off my phone before he can respond. It would be too easy to talk to him all night. And too dangerous.

Part Four

EIGHT YEARS AGO

CHAPTER TEN

SAVVY

I don't understand what just happened, but my head is swimming, and between the heat in this room and the smell of vomit in the air, I want to leave more than I want almost anything. I followed Chuck down through the tunnels, and I'm too afraid of getting lost on the way back out if I try it alone.

I look at Oliver's offered hand and wrap my arms around myself. "Okay." He gets my message. I'll go with him, but we're not leaving *together*.

Oliver nods and turns to one of the exits I've never used before. I follow.

Crossport U was expanding during the Cold War and decided it would be a good idea to create bunkers around campus. The tunnels connecting them have been closed to students for a couple decades, but since this side of campus was sold to a developer who covered it in high-end student housing, "closed" suddenly meant "monitored by people who could be paid to look the other way." Now, there's a whole underground world on this side of campus that's just as seedy as it sounds. It's home to illegal fights, gambling, and the wildest parties I've ever seen—not that I've seen many of them. I try to stay far away from the tunnels and only came tonight for Chuck.

Oliver pulls out his phone and turns its flashlight toward a dark stairwell in the corner of the room.

I stay close until we emerge in a dark alley between a dorm and a sorority house.

"Are you okay?" Oliver asks.

"No, but I will be." Just as soon as I figure out where I'm going and how I'm going to move out of Chuck's with a ten-dollar balance in my checking account. "I appreciate you saying whatever you did to buy Nathan some time, but I think I've taken advantage of your kindness enough for one night."

"It was nothing," he says. He scans our surroundings. It's quiet out here except for a few people smoking by the building's back entrance. "It's late, and I'm not going to just leave you in a dark alley alone. Where to?"

There's no fucking way I'm going back to Chuck's. I fumble in my purse for my phone. Maybe Julie will let me crash in her dorm room tonight.

I tap on her contact and wait as it rings. And rings. And rings.

"Hey, you've reached Julie! Leave a message or, better yet, text me!"

"Hey, Jules, this is Savvy. I'm in a pinch. Could you call me as soon as you get this?" I sigh and hang up. *Shit.*

"She's probably in the shower or something," I say, but in truth, I have no idea. "I'll just go to her dorm and wait until she calls me back."

"Aren't the dorms locked after ten?"

I wince. This is not my night.

"Come on," he says. "You can get cleaned up at my place while you wait for her to get back to you."

"Are you sure?" I need to scrub off the stench of vomit and the tunnels. My adrenaline's crashing, and the only thing that sounds better than a hot shower is a week of sleep. But part of me also hopes that one of Chuck's friends sees me go home with Oliver. Or better yet, Chuck himself. Because *fuck him*.

"It's just a shower, Savvy. It's not a big deal."

I follow him a few blocks to a building off-campus known for high-end lofts. "I thought only professors lived here," I say as he uses his key to open the door to the lobby.

Oliver chuckles. "That's not exactly true, but I wouldn't mind if it were. The last thing I want when I leave campus at the end of the day is to be surrounded by a bunch of partying undergrads."

I follow him into the elevator, where he slides his key card before pressing the button for the third floor. My limbs feel heavier with every step. How long can I stay awake waiting for Julie to get back to me?

A shower will wake me up.

When the doors slide open, Oliver leads the way out of the elevator and into a small vestibule with only one door. He unlocks it and leads me into an apartment. A *huge* apartment.

"Holy shit."

He shrugs. "It's a little over the top, but like I said, I wanted to get away from party zones."

I knew these apartments were high-end, but I didn't realize they were this big. The space has industrial-style décor, with exposed brick walls, wood ceiling beams, and wide-plank hardwood floors. The kitchen is to the left, with dark walnut cabinets, creamy white countertops, and a giant island with four stools. On the other side of the room, a sectional faces a stone fireplace with a TV mounted above it. The wall across from the entrance is made of floor-to-ceiling windows that overlook downtown Crossport.

"How do you afford this place?" I blurt, cringing when I realize how invasive that question is.

Another shrug. "Asshole father is generous when it suits him. He wanted me to get an MBA, so he paid for this."

I wander in, wide-eyed. "Damn. That's a total different kind of asshole than mine." Though in truth, my parents would love me to be in a place like this—but only if everyone could know about it. Their favorite way to spend money is ostentatiously.

Oliver chuckles and tosses his keys onto the island.

"The bathroom's right there." He points over my shoulder. "Let me grab you a clean shirt."

Before I can object, he disappears down the hall. When he reappears, he hands me a soft black T-shirt and gray sweatpants.

"They'll probably be a little big, but at least they're clean."

Showering at his place, wearing his shirt . . . it all seems so *intimate.* Maybe that should scare me, but I've never felt as scared and alone as I did watching that fight tonight. I need a little tenderness. "Thanks."

"Towels are in the cabinet to the left of the sink. Can I get you anything else? Maybe make you some food while you're in the shower?"

"You don't have to do that. I'm fine."

"How about I order a pizza?"

Trying to feed me again. Does he think I'm drunk? I guess I can't blame him after Saturday and then the whole vomiting thing tonight. "I only had one glass of punch. I'm just . . ." Where to start? Disgusted by Chuck's betrayal? Sick that my brother lost my savings? Worried that he'll only dig himself deeper trying to pay those guys back?

"You just need a shower and some time to clear your head," Oliver finishes for me.

I nod gratefully and turn that way.

"Use whatever you need," he calls after me. "There's shampoo and stuff in the shower, and even a new toothbrush in the cabinet."

I cough out a laugh and glance back at him. "I smell

that bad, huh?"

He wrinkles his nose and looks me over. "I've yet to meet someone who wears vomit well."

I can't quite manage a laugh, but I find myself smiling for the first time all night.

OLIVER

I distract myself from thoughts of Savannah in my shower by ordering food.

I've never been good with emotional breakdowns—and I can see hers coming from a mile away—but I can manage to feed her. What I can't seem to manage is imagining Savannah under the hot spray of my showerhead, water sluicing down her breasts, her soapy hands roaming over every inch of her skin.

My phone buzzes, pulling me from X-rated thoughts of joining her. X-rated thoughts of just how much I want to help her forget her asshole boyfriend.

I need her, but if this is going to work, I'm going to have to keep my hands to myself. No matter how much I'd like to indulge in this attraction.

I pull my phone from my pocket to see who's texting me.

Eddie: The Viper? Seriously?

Oliver: Getting that much cash so quickly was too

complicated. This was easier.

Eddie: But I fucking love that car. I was hoping you'd bequeath it to me or some shit.

Oliver: You were hoping I'd die so you could have my car?

Eddie: We both would've remembered you fondly.

Oliver: Ass.

Eddie: Hope it's worth it, man.

Me too, Eddie. Me too. Instead of replying, I dial the only pizza place on campus open this late. They keep hot pizzas ready to go, so at least I know they'll be here quickly. I order a pizza, breadsticks, and add half a dozen of their fresh chocolate-chip cookies to the delivery on a whim. My sister says chocolate is medicine for broken hearts, so maybe it will help Savvy.

Either the delivery guy is really fast or Savvy's shower is really long, because by the time I hear the shower turn off, I'm putting the food on the island. When I turn around to tell her what I ordered, I freeze and all my words fall away.

My T-shirt is too big on her, and it's already wet at the shoulders from her long hair. She's rolled the sweatpants at the waist, which is too big for her, yet they still fit snug at her hips and ass.

Fuck. What is it about the sight of a woman in my clothes, fresh out of the shower?

When she meets my gaze, I see nothing but vulnerability in those hazel eyes. A surge of protectiveness fills my chest and is followed quickly by a tidal wave of guilt. *She trusts me.*

"Food's here," I say, jerking myself out of my stupor and waving to the counter.

She gives a tentative smile. "Seems like you're always feeding me. Taking care of me."

Guilt lodges in my throat. "I'm sorry to give you the wrong impression. The truth is, I'm a selfish asshole. Stick around long enough and you'll see."

"If you say so." She pads toward the island nevertheless. Her feet are bare, her toenails painted a pretty pink. "No one's tried to feed me in a long time. Before you did last weekend, I mean." She looks a little sad as she says it, and it makes me wonder about her childhood and if maybe her parents weren't around much.

I clear my throat. "I am a pro at ordering pizza, so anytime."

"Still." She slides onto a stool and opens the pizza box, closing her eyes and breathing in through her nose. She moans softly.

"Would you and the pizza like to be alone?"

She coughs out a laugh and shakes her head. "Sorry. Tonight, I am officially reuniting with carbs without any booze to blame for it." She sighs. "This could get a little intense."

I chuckle. "Good to know. So does this mean you and

Chuck . . ."

Her gaze flicks to mine. "I think he threw the fight. No. I *know* he did."

Well, shit. "He told you?"

"No. He denied it, but I've seen him fight a dozen times before, and . . . tonight was different." She stares at the pizza box, but I know she's not seeing it. "He knew my brother bet on him—hell, he's the one who convinced Nathan to make the bet. He'd been trying to get me to put money on him for months, and then he met my brother and left me alone about it because Nathan is the gambler in the family. And now I think he played us." She shakes her head. "Who does that?"

Dirty assholes with no integrity.

She wrinkles her nose. "You probably think I'm crazy, but I could see it in his eyes. Chuck hates losing anything. We can't even play fucking Monopoly together because he turns into a dick any time I start to win. But tonight, I didn't see that in his eyes. Tonight, losing made him believe he was winning. I saw it."

"I don't think you're crazy." I grab a slice of pizza from the box, lean my hip against the counter, and take a bite to keep myself from saying more.

She's lost in her thoughts anyway, and despite her warnings about an intense reunion with carbs, I'm pretty sure she's working on autopilot and not tasting a thing as she eats her pizza. "And now I have nowhere to live," she mutters. "What a fucking mess."

In the time it takes her to finish a slice, I've eaten three. "Another?" I ask, opening the box again.

"No, thank you." She casts a longing glance toward the cookies but doesn't touch them. "Sorry. I should be finding a place to stay." She grabs a napkin to wipe her hands and then retrieves her phone from her purse. She frowns at it. "Shit."

"No word?"

She shakes her head. "She must be asleep already. It's okay, I'll . . . I'll call someone else."

"Savvy?" I wait until she looks at me. "You know you can crash on my couch, right?"

"No, I couldn't."

I laugh. "Or I can take the couch and you could use the bedroom—if you're worried I'm a creeper and you need a locked door between us."

She rolls her eyes. "I already know you're not a creeper."

"Good. The couch or bed? Lady's choice."

"Couch is fine." She glances around the living room and shakes her head slowly. "Thank you, Oliver," she says, her words thick with emotion. "You have no idea how much I needed your kindness tonight—how much I needed a soft place to land." When she focuses on me again, she's smiling but her eyes are bright with unshed tears.

I want to pull her into my chest and tell her everything's going to be okay. To promise that I'll always be that for her. But I have no right to pretend I'm a saint and am in no position to make promises, so I swallow back all my words and leave her alone and teary-eyed in my kitchen while I get her blankets.

CHAPTER ELEVEN

SAVVY

The sun coming in through the balcony doors pulls me from sleep before I'm ready. I burrow beneath the blankets, reviewing everything from last night.

Chuck fucked my brother over and fucked *me* over in the process. I've seen him fight too many times to doubt it, and I've watched Nathan get screwed too many times to be surprised.

The only difference is that this time I was part of the problem too. And it's not even about my money anymore. I have to figure out a way for him to pay back this debt. *At least Oliver bought us some time*.

When I pick up my phone, I see I have missed messages. Three from Chuck. One from Julie. Nothing from my brother.

I open Julie's first. She's apologizing for sleeping through my call and wanting to know if I'm okay. I'm tempted to admit I stayed with Oliver, but she'll read more into it than is there, so I just say I'm good and that I'll catch up with her later. Then I take a deep breath and open the texts from Chuck.

Chuck: Where are you?

Chuck: Sorry I had to bounce. I can't be associated with those guys.

Chuck: You don't have to give me the silent treatment like a little bitch.

He's such a dick. I feel like someone just yanked film from my eyes. I knew he wasn't awesome to me, knew I needed to end things and get out of there, but suddenly I can see so clearly just how bad it got.

Savvy: You lost on purpose.

He must be messing around on his phone because his reply comes almost instantly.

Chuck: I don't know what you're talking about.

Savvy: Bullshit.

Chuck: You know I worked my ass off to prepare for this fight.

Savvy: But you didn't so much as try once you got in the ring.

Chuck: Would you stop with that shit? Fighting pays my bills, but it won't if you talk like that.

Savvy: Then when you realized my family isn't rich—like I've been telling you this whole time—you ran away.

Chuck: They're saying you went home with Oliver. Is that true?

Fresh anger pumps through my blood. Seriously? That's what he cares about right now?

At least Oliver did something to help us, I type, but then I delete it. I know Oliver called in favors, but I'm not sure that's public knowledge.

Savvy: Why are you pretending you care? You're the one who convinced Nathan to take that bet. How could you do that to him?

Chuck: I told you I don't know what you're talking about. I got beat. It happens.

Savvy: You're a lying asshole. I'll send Julie to come get

> *my shit. This is over. I don't want to talk to you anymore.*

I jab *send* then immediately block his number.

Chuck doesn't deserve my tears, so I wipe my cheeks dry and take a deep breath. My grandmother would call this situation a blessing in disguise. I'm out of a bad situation. And Nathan . . . well, Nathan will have to figure out a way to pay off his debts.

I throw back the covers and roll off the couch. The hardwood floor is cool beneath my feet as I follow the smell of coffee to the kitchen.

There's a note on the island in clean, blocky print with a plastic key card and a key on top.

Had to run. The key's yours. The doorman knows you're staying for a while. I'll be home later. He's scribbled his number at the bottom of the note and signed it *O*.

My heart does a little tumble as I trace that *O* with my index finger. There's a big difference between letting me crash on his couch for the night and letting me "stay awhile." Does he realize how much I need this? How screwed I am until I save enough money for a deposit on a place of my own? I feel like he knows. And I feel like he did it this way to save me from having to try to decline a favor I desperately need.

I should admit it to myself now—I'm crushing hard on Oliver Rhett.

I leave the key where it is and pour myself a cup of coffee. I was such a headcase last night I couldn't really take this place in, but it's gorgeous. Immaculate. The kind of apartment you'd expect a rich guy to live in. Someone who trades stocks during office hours or some shit.

Beyond the picture windows that line the living space is a balcony that overlooks downtown, now bustling with what passes for traffic in Crossport.

I sip on my coffee as I wander room to room, noting all the details that don't quite fit Oliver. Floral paintings above the oversize white sectional, the glass coffee table, the bookcases staged with more knickknacks than books.

I wander down the hall, passing the bathroom where I showered last night and carefully opening the door opposite it. The smell of him hits me the moment I step inside. A light cologne or maybe an aftershave. Woodsy and clean.

The bedroom is as neat as the living area, but something about it seems to suit Oliver better. Maybe not the quilted headboard, but the gray bedspread that matches his eyes and the pile of books on his nightstand. There's a big TV on the wall opposite the bed and a large bookshelf packed with everything from murder mysteries to biographies to books about finance. On the other side of the TV is an open door that leads to another bathroom. This one is even larger than the one I showered in last night. A soaking tub sits under a frosted window, and the shower has more spray nozzles than my high school locker room.

Opposite the tub, his closet is open. I step in, unable to resist running my fingertips along the shirts hanging there. Who is this guy? Why does some city kid rich enough to have his own high-end loft hang out at underground fights?

"Need something to wear?"

I jump then spin around to see Oliver smirking at me. He's all sweaty, like he just got back from a run.

I should apologize for snooping, but I'm too stubborn. "Why'd you sneak up on me like that?"

He cocks a brow. "I didn't realize I was sneaking. This *is* my closet." With a shrug he crosses his arms, grabbing the hem of his shirt with both hands. He pulls it off over his head, revealing more muscles than I've ever seen on one guy. Chuck is muscular, but he's nothing compared to Oliver.

There's a smattering of hair on his chest and a dark path running from his navel past the waistband of his low-slung athletic shorts. My eyes latch on to that trail like it's the path to salvation.

"Your clothes from last night are sitting on the dryer if that's what you're looking for."

"You washed them?"

"Yeah." He rakes his gaze over me. "Figured you'd need something to wear to class."

"Thanks. That was . . . really thoughtful." Just like the key and everything else last night.

He tosses his shirt into the hamper. "You're welcome to watch, but I *am* planning to take off the rest of these sweaty clothes."

With a squeak, I come to my senses and skirt around him—out of the closet and then out of his room.

The sound of his low chuckle follows me into the hallway.

"Cocky asshole," I mutter, biting back my smile.

Oliver's place is quiet when I get back from my classes. It feels weird to be here without him—like I'm doing something wrong—but I use my key as if I do this every day and drop my bag on a kitchen chair.

I turn to the couch to grab the bag of clothes Julie brought me from Chuck's this morning. It's not there. Neither is the romance novel she lent me. I have forty-five minutes to decompress before work, and all I want to do is change quickly so I have time to curl up with a book and forget my problems for a minute.

Instead of the bag of my belongings, there's a fresh pile of pillows and blankets on one end of the couch. Oliver probably has a housekeeper.

"Must be nice," I mutter.

I head to the bedroom, figuring the housekeeper has put my things in there. I stop in the doorway when I spot my book on the bedside table by Oliver's big bed, like it's been there all along. Was *this* the housekeeper, or does Oliver think I'm sleeping with him tonight?

Oh well. We'll figure it out when I get home from work. Honestly, I wouldn't object to a night in his bed—God knows there's chemistry between us—but after Chuck, I don't trust my judgment. If I'm smart, I'll steer clear of men altogether and focus on my classes.

I strip out of the jeans I wore to classes, dig a fresh work shirt out of my bag, and toss it on the bed. It's hot as hell outside, and it feels good to be in nothing but a tank and underwear.

When I head to the bathroom in the hall to freshen my makeup, I swing the door open and find Oliver is standing in front of the sink in nothing but a towel. His hair is wet and there are beads of water on his shoulders, like he's just climbed out of the shower. He finishes a stroke with the razor before turning to me with an arched brow. "Can I help you?"

"I . . . You . . ." It's final. His body should be etched in bronze and shown off in a museum. "Sorry. I didn't know you were here," I finally manage, though my gaze is stuck like glue to the trail of hair that disappears into his towel. Who knew a smattering of soft hair could be my new obsession, but here we are.

"Savvy, if you keep looking at me like that, my body's natural reaction will seriously compromise the security of this towel."

"Oh . . ." I tear my gaze off his abs and chest and meet his eyes. "Sorry. I thought there was a bathroom connected to your bedroom?" Great, Savvy. Tell the man where he can and can't shower in his own home.

He shrugs and turns back to the sink, resuming his shave. "I'm giving you the bedroom, so I thought it made sense to give you the en suite bath as well."

"You're giving . . ." Why can't I put a sentence together? Am I so feeble-minded that the sight of this mostly naked, beautiful man has fried my brain? I want to blame it on sex deprivation, but I've gone a few months without sex plenty times before.

"You didn't sleep well on the couch," he says, as if that explains everything.

"You're, like, twice my size. How are *you* going to sleep there?"

He swipes away the last of the shaving cream with a final pass of the razor then turns on the water. "I can sleep anywhere."

"Okay." I bite my lip. "But why? Why are you doing any of this for me?"

"Maybe I'm trying to balance out my karmic debt." He splashes water on his face, dries his hands on a small white towel, then turns toward me, stepping close. "Or maybe I want to be able to get home as late as I need to without waking you." He tilts my chin up and studies my face. "How are you holding up today? Miss your boyfriend yet?"

I cough out a laugh. "*No*. He can go fuck himself. And he's not my boyfriend."

He grins. "That's my girl."

My girl.

I swallow, but he suddenly drops his hand and steps back as if realizing what he just said.

"Oliver, I'm kind of in a mess right now. It's nice of you to offer me a place to crash, but I gave my brother what was left in my savings, and it's going to take me a while to save up enough to get my own place."

He shrugs. "Stay as long as you need. It's not a problem."

"It seems like too much."

"It's not. Stay as long as you want. We'll talk tonight about how you can repay me."

"I'll do your housekeeping or something."

"I already have a housekeeper." His gaze skips down my body for the first time since I stepped into the bathroom. "Nice panties."

He steps around me and out of the bathroom, and I'm left trying to put out the fire in my cheeks.

CHAPTER TWELVE

SAVVY

We're slammed at The Naked Bean from the moment I arrive for my shift until the moment we lock up at the end of the night. Maybe if it had been a slow night, I would've recognized the smirks on my coworkers' faces hours ago, but I was too busy serving lattes and blending frappes to worry too much about it.

Once the doors are locked, though, their snickers are impossible to miss, and annoyance boils in my blood.

Julie steps up to my side and gives me a sympathetic smile. "They're just jealous." She looks over her shoulder. Across the room, the two other baristas are laughing behind the counter. "It doesn't matter what they think."

My frown deepens. "Think about what?"

Julie unties her apron and hangs it on the wall. "About Oliver and everything," she says, not looking at me.

"They know about Oliver?"

She coughs out a laugh. "Everyone knows about Oliver." She bites her bottom lip and presses her hand to the center of her chest. "That man is *so* fine. If *I* had a few hours alone with him . . ."

"I'm sorry to interrupt whatever fantasy is happening in your mind right now, but I don't know what you're talking about."

She winces. "Chuck has pretty much told everyone."

That he threw the fight? I almost say the words but catch myself just in time. I might not like my ex very much right now, but I'm not vindictive enough to let everyone know he plays dirty.

The girls laugh again. Louder this time.

I finally can't take it anymore, so I snap my head to them and glare. "What are you staring at?"

One girl hides her laughter behind her hand and the other smirks. "Bunch of nothing," the first says.

I roll my eyes and turn back to sweeping the lobby.

"Just not every day you get to see a whore in the wild," the smirking one says.

That's it. "What did you just call me?" I carefully set my broom against the wall before skulking toward them. I've had enough of their snickering and whispering, and now the name calling?

"I called you a whore," she says, all wide-eyed innocence.

"Cheyenne," her friend says. "That's enough."

"No, no," I say. "I'd love to hear more of what Cheyenne has to say." One thing I learned about bullies while growing up is that very few of them have the backbone to stand behind their taunts. "Why am I a whore?"

She rolls her eyes and scoffs. "Because that's what we call women who've been bought and paid for."

What the—

"And everyone knows that Oliver bought you to pay off your brother's gambling debts. And you let him. And now you're fucking him. Ipso facto, you are a whore."

I feel like I've been punched in the gut. "You don't know what you're talking about. He didn't . . ." Each word out of my mouth gets softer and weaker as her words set in.

He bought me. Is that what he thinks? Is that what he's telling people?

I look to Julie, and she shakes her head and says softly, "Chuck's telling everyone that you sold yourself to Oliver to pay your brother's debt."

I blink. Oliver stepped in. He helped me.

Stay as long as you want. We'll talk tonight about how you can repay me.

"No. He just called in a favor to give Nathan more time."

"Fifty grand? How did you figure your brother would ever get that kind of money?" Julie's smile is full of pity. "It's okay. No one blames you. They *really* would've killed your brother if you hadn't made the deal with Oliver."

"I didn't . . ."

She squeezes my wrist gently. "It doesn't matter what

those bitches think. We all do what we have to in order to protect the people we love."

"Oliver doesn't love me, though. He barely knows me." Which means . . . he really did *buy* me. And now everyone knows it.

Anger surges through me when Oliver walks through the door—no, *struts* through the door. He's cocky and full of authority. A man who knows what he wants and gets it.

And now he thinks he bought you.

Fuck him for being so sexy by wearing that so well.

I spring off the couch and stride toward him.

Oliver drops his keys on the counter and turns to me. "Hey," he says. "Are you okay?"

"You *bought* me?" And *God*, why does that hurt? It makes way more sense than what I thought happened. That he helped. That he *cared.* "And you *told them* you bought me?"

His brows jump up. "What are you—"

Dropping to my knees, I look up at him through my lashes as I release the button on his jeans. I slowly drag down the zipper, never letting my eyes stray from his.

His nostrils flare. "What the fuck do you think you're doing?" There's a rough edge to his voice that sends a thrill through me. Maybe I don't have money. Maybe I don't have shit in this town. But he wants me, and even if it shouldn't, even if it's fucked up, that makes me feel good. *Powerful.*

I tuck my fingers into his waistband, ready to expose the length of him already swelling behind his zipper. But before I can, Oliver drops to the floor in front of me.

We're both on our knees, face to face, and when those sinful gray eyes roam over my features, I don't feel so powerful anymore. I feel like maybe he can see exactly how broken and lonely I am. How lonely I've been for years.

"Don't you dare." He cups my jaw, stroking my cheek gently before he slides his rough fingers into my hair and tugs me against him.

He smells like heaven. Clean and warm. He presses his mouth to my ear, and the heat of his breath sends a shiver through me.

"Don't you dare use what I did as an excuse." He draws in a long breath and runs the bridge of his nose up and down my neck.

I shiver. "I don't know what you're talking about."

"If you want something from me, Savvy . . ." He snakes his free hand under my shirt, stroking his thumb over my ribs before sneaking beneath my waistband. "You want something? Have the fucking courage to tell me." He flicks my earlobe with his tongue then sucks hard, drawing it between his teeth and making me shudder in his arms. "What *do* you want? My hands?" The hand on my side shifts up and skims the underside of my breast through my bra. Once. Twice. "Maybe here? Or maybe . . ." His hand dips, and his fingertips invade beyond the waistband of my shorts. His knuckles brush the front of my panties. "What would I find if I touched you here? Would I be right?"

"Right about *what*?" I try to sound defiant. Try to lift my chin. But I find myself swaying toward him, desperate for that hand between my legs to give me more.

"Would this tell me your secrets? Would this tell me the truth? The real reason you dropped to your knees when I walked in this room? Not because you're pissed, but because you want me inside of you however you can get me?"

"I'm not the one who—"

"Who what? Saved your ass?" He withdraws his hand, and I have to bite back a whimper. His warm breath on my ear is the most delicious kind of torture. "I could spread you out on that kitchen island. I'd make a fucking *meal* of you, Savvy. I'd taste you and touch you until the downstairs neighbors knew from the sound of your cries just how badly you wanted to come."

Please. I have to swallow back the word. Remind myself why I'm here. "Fuck you," I breathe.

He smirks and cocks his head to the side. "Or I could take you to my bed. Strip you bare and play with those tits. Suck on those perfect nipples until you wanted me so badly you could feel it between your legs."

I press my palms into his chest and shove. "Why didn't you tell me?"

"Because I need you to trust me."

I do. That's the problem. I do and I shouldn't. "That's the most ridiculous thing I've ever heard."

"Do you think this is how I get girls? You think I go around and give away cars in exchange for sexual favors?"

"I don't know," I whisper. "No one's ever given up anything for me before."

Something flashes in his eyes—there and gone before I can name it. "You can put away your scowl. I'm not going to ask you to get me off."

A sound slips from my throat that's half like a laugh and half like a cry. "What a relief. You'll seduce me before I start paying off my debt—is that it?"

"Have you ever *heard* the words *thank you*? You have no idea what kind of shit you were in last night. I'm not the asshole here."

"Explain this to me, then. No one just *gives* their car to someone without expecting anything in return."

He sighs. "I never said I didn't expect anything, but I don't pay for sex." He pauses a beat, as if he's once again waiting for gratitude, then shakes his head and stands, offering a hand to help me up.

I ignore it and stand on my own, folding my arms. "Tell me what you want from me."

"Wait here," he says, turning away and disappearing down the hall.

"I thought you weren't going to order me around?"

"Can you get the fifteenth off work?" Oliver calls. "Three weeks from today?"

I frown. "Probably. Why?"

"We're driving to New York," he says.

"In what car?" I don't have one, and Oliver sold his.

"My buddy is loaning me his until I can arrange for

another. It's no Viper, but it's reliable. You want to pay me back, and this is how we start."

"Do I get to know what this favor is, or do you intend to keep me in suspense?"

"It's simple." When he reappears in the kitchen, his hands are full of shopping bags. He holds them out for me. "You'll wear these things, sit at the bar at a fancy restaurant, enjoy an overpriced martini, and make meaningful eye contact with the guy at the bar."

"Any guy?"

"No. A very specific guy."

"How do you know he'll be there?"

"Because he's obsessive about routine. When he's in New York, he goes to Clementine's at nine every night, where he drinks a double of his favorite bourbon."

"Seriously? That predictable?"

"Like clockwork."

I stare at Oliver. My gut says I can trust him, but intellectually, I realize this is all too good to be true. "Who is he?"

"A businessman who has something of mine. You're going to help me get it back."

With a skeptical frown, I take the bags, gaping when I register the logo on each. The biggest bags are from Louis Vuitton and Louboutin. The smallest bag is from Tiffany, and the bag in between is from Bergdorf. "These are for me?"

"Yes. For next week."

"How did you know my sizes?"

He shrugs. "Your stuff is here. It was easy enough to find out."

I can't bring myself to be annoyed with him over that because I'm sick to my stomach at the thought of how much money is hanging from my fingertips. Even though I've never worn anything so expensive—at least not in my adult life—my mother is obsessed with appearing wealthy and scours the internet for affordable second-hand high-end brands. I know how much this is worth.

"You should probably try it all on so I can arrange for replacements if anything doesn't work on you," Oliver says.

I finally tear my gaze off the bags and meet his eyes. "Why the fancy clothes?"

"Anything else and he won't come near you. He'll recognize the value of everything in those bags, and it will put him at ease." He jams his hands into his pockets, and his jaw tightens. "He's the kind of man who is too jaded to interact with a woman beneath his social status."

"Because if I go in there in my own clothes and . . . *make eye contact*, he'll think I'm a gold digger."

"Something like that."

My skin goes cold. *It's not what you thought. It's worse.* "I'm not fucking a stranger, so if you—"

"Savvy. That's not what this is." He holds my gaze for a long time, sending my heart racing faster and faster with each second. "I promise he won't lay a finger on you. That's not what he's looking for. But I'll be watching from the bar across the street to make sure you're safe every moment."

"So that's all?"

He blows out a breath. "I want you to stay here too. I'm only in town until early December. I want you to stay here until I move out." He folds his arms. "And before you give me that look, I'm asking you to live in my loft, not to be my sex toy."

"Why?"

"Because I want certain people on this campus to know you're not available." He shoves his hands in his pockets. "Actually, consider it part of the deal."

"You want me to wear fancy clothes and drink at a bar to attract the attention of some guy, and you want me to live here? And in exchange, my brother's debt to you is paid?"

"Yeah. Is that going to be a problem?"

I study the bags again. "I don't understand."

"You don't need to." He nods toward the bedroom. "Now go get some sleep. You had a hard day."

I bite my bottom lip. "I'm sorry that I thought . . ." God. I'm mortified. What did I think I was doing? Was I really going to give him a blowjob just to prove a point? "I'm sorry."

I head down the hall and reach for the bedroom door.

"Savvy?"

I turn. "Yeah?"

"When I let you get on your knees for me, we'll *both* know you want to be there. Got it?"

I don't reply, just shove into the bedroom and shut the door behind me, but not even the silence of his bedroom can calm my racing heart.

Part Five

PRESENT DAY

CHAPTER THIRTEEN

SAVVY

"What do you think?" I lift my arms out to my sides. "Does this look okay?"

Alec sweeps his tongue across his bottom lip as he looks me over. "I think I need you to turn around. You know, so I can do a full inspection."

Little butterflies shimmy in my stomach. I bite back my grin and do a slow turn. We didn't talk all week except for a few texts solidifying our plans for this weekend. He offered to let me stay at his place—*Plenty of bedrooms. This isn't a proposition.*—but I passed. Taking him up on that offer seemed too intimate, and I'm trying to keep my boundaries clear for both of us. But then I got to the hotel and the lady at the front desk said someone had bought me a massage so I could relax before my big night. So much for boundaries, but isn't that just like him? Too sweet and caring to worry about rejection.

Why do you have to be such a good guy?

I finish my slow turn, and when I face Alec again, the playfulness has fled from his expression. "What?" I ask, meeting his too-serious gaze.

"You're stunning," he says, his voice gruff. "Simply stunning."

My heart tugs for what could've been. In a different life, under different circumstances, Alec would have no connection to Oliver, and I could be with him without the guilt and the constant reminders of old heartache. Without the shame and the hurt.

"Thank you," I say softly before looking away.

"Hey." He catches my chin in his big hand and turns my head until my gaze meets his again. "Don't freak out on me, okay?" He sweeps his thumb over my bottom lip. "I'm not going to hide how I feel about you. I don't have it in me. But not once since that night in Vegas have you pretended to want more from me than friendship. You've made it very clear where you stand."

"I'm sorry. I—"

He shakes his head. "I'm saying you can relax. I'm not gonna spend these days with you and then get angry when you don't want more from me. That's not who I am."

Swallowing, I nod. "Thank you. That means a lot." I reach for my purse and sling it onto my shoulder before realizing he's still watching me.

He tucks his hands into his pockets. "I do have one thing to ask you, though."

"What's that?"

"Tell me if you ever change your mind." He shrugs. "And until then, I'll assume all this is just a function of our friendship."

The words *I'll take what I can get* seem to hang in the air between us. *Don't hang your heart on me, Alec. You deserve so much better.*

He leans against the doorjamb and looks me over. "Nervous?"

"I can't decide if I'm going to vomit or run a 5K. So . . . I guess?"

He chuckles and strolls into the bathroom. "You look amazing. That dress . . ." He licks his lips. I wish he'd quit doing that. It makes my mind go to places I have decided it's not allowed to go. "But you're missing something."

I look down at the white cocktail dress. "What's that?"

"Well, you're supposed to be engaged, right? That's what you said in your audition video?"

Another wave of nausea crashes over me. Was I high when I recorded that? Lying is never a good idea, and now I'm in this mess where I'm dealing with that lie while juggling a lie of omission. I cringe. "Yeah."

Prowling toward me, Alec looks me over again. Slower this time. "And tonight, you're supposed to be *my* fiancée, right?"

"Have you changed your mind?"

"Not at all." He takes my left hand from my side and

squeezes it in his. "But anyone who knows me wouldn't believe my fiancée would go to a fancy dinner without her diamond."

Before I realize what he means, he slides a ring onto my finger. I hold up my hand between us and gasp. "Alec, where did you get this?" I blink at it, and my chest goes tight. "Oh my God. This isn't—"

"Not the exact one," he says, tilting his head from side to side as he studies it on my finger. "But as close as I could manage on short notice."

When we were in Vegas, drunk on insta-love, we saw a ring like this in a shop window, and I told him I wanted something like that for my engagement ring.

I can't even identify all the emotions tangling in my chest right now, but there are so many I can feel them crawling up my throat and choking me. "It was supposed to be a joke. We were playing." I shake my head. "I never meant . . ." Except I had. That night I was loose and happy and unburdened by the mistakes in my past. *Part* of me had been buying into happily-ever-after. Part of me had been buying into the fairy tale.

"Savvy?"

I blink up at him.

"Relax. I have a good friend who owns a jewelry store on Rodeo Drive. It's a loan. I wanted you to be able to wear a ring I knew you would've picked if this weren't pretend."

My eyes fill with tears. "Alec . . ." I shake my head. "I don't deserve you. I don't deserve any of this."

He cups my face in his big hand and tilts it up to his. "You deserve everything."

His mouth is so close to mine, his words so sweet, that it feels natural to roll to my toes and press my lips to his. He slides his hand into my hair and exhales, as if he's been holding his breath this whole time. *Waiting.*

I know better than to let myself deepen the kiss, but I linger, uninterested in returning to a reality where I can't have him.

In the end, it's Alec who steps back and breaks the contact. His gaze searches mine for a long breath before he smiles. "Just as sweet as I remember." I wish I could believe his carefree tone, but there's pain in his eyes.

I swallow, my cheeks hot. "Thank you—for borrowing this for me, I mean."

He nods. "It was truly my pleasure." He points over his shoulder and backs out of the bathroom. "I'll wait out here and let you finish getting ready."

"We're here to meet Mrs. McCoy," I say, squeezing Alec's hand tighter.

The host smiles. "Yes. She's waiting for you. Right this way."

The restaurant glitters with low light and candles, but I barely process it as I focus on putting one foot in front of the other and heading to the table.

Our hostess doesn't stand when we arrive, but extends her hand. "Ms. Downing," she says, and despite her lower position, she manages to look down her nose at me. "Thank you for meeting us."

I take her hand. "It's my pleasure."

"This is my husband, Derek," she says, motioning to the much older gentleman to her right.

I offer him my hand, and he kisses the back of it instead of offering a handshake. His thumb grazes the underside of my wrist in a suggestive way that makes me feel slimy. I pull my hand away at the first second it wouldn't appear rude. "So nice to meet you. This is Alec Hayes, my"—I almost choke on the lie but push it out anyway—"fiancé."

"It's a pleasure to meet you both," Alec says, shaking their hands. He pulls my chair out for me before taking his own seat. He looks so natural in this setting. The money. The glitz. The business meeting. All of it.

"I appreciate you both coming to this meeting," Mrs. McCoy says. "We realize it's considered a little old-fashioned, but the beauty of having our own company is in getting to maintain our values."

Puke. I force a smile. "I'd love to hear more about those values," I say, and at least that's not a lie. I'm already uncomfortable with the innate misogyny of how she runs her business. Before I sign over my intellectual property, I want to make sure this compromise is worth it.

"Of course," Derek says, signaling to the waiter. "But first let's have some wine and get to know each other."

Fuck. I was hoping we could skip the elbow rubbing and get right down to business.

"Tell us how you met," Mrs. McCoy says. "And when is the wedding?"

Derek's gaze drifts to my hands where they're folded on the table in front of me. "That's quite a ring. Please, tell us everything."

Alec drapes his arm across the back of my chair and leans in with the grin of a man in love. "Believe it or not, we met in Vegas."

Derek arches a brow and looks me over, reassessing. "You were working there?"

The implication is clear. That I picked up Alec when I was working as a showgirl. Or a sex worker. Nothing is wrong with either of those jobs, but the assumption rankles.

I swallow my annoyance and laugh, hoping they can't tell how forced it sounds. "No. I was there celebrating my best friend's birthday, and somehow we found ourselves in the same club as Alec and his business partner Marston, who happens to be my best friend's first love."

Derek's eyes light up. "Oh, the drama!"

"Only in the best way," I say, sharing a knowing smile with Alec. "Brinley and Marston were meant to be together, and they're happily married now."

"What a stunning coincidence that you found them that night!" Mrs. McCoy says.

Alec looks at me, and his eyes soften. "It felt like fate from the very first moment."

"I cannot thank you enough for doing that," I tell Alec later that night as his driver opens the back door to a shiny town car.

Dinner was a combination of awkward and exciting. It was easier than I expected to pretend Alec and I were a couple planning their wedding. Although I'm still not sure about the McCoys and whether they'll be asking for more information about my program, at least I'm walking away knowing I did everything that I could to make the most of this opportunity.

"It was my pleasure." Alec slides in beside me and pulls the door shut.

"I don't just mean for the fiancé thing, either." I pull off my heels and sigh in relief. "It was just good to have you there."

"What are friends for?"

"Where to?" the driver asks.

Alec studies me for a beat. "One of my favorite martini bars is just down the street. Good drinks, nice atmosphere. Could I talk you into a stop there before I take you back to your hotel?"

I'm simultaneously exhausted and wound up. I know I won't sleep if I go straight back to my room, and I'm not in any hurry to say goodnight to Alec. For better or worse, I like being around him. I always have. "I would love that."

He leans forward and murmurs something to the driver before settling back in the seat. When he takes my hand, thumb stroking the inside of my palm, I don't pull away.

Maybe it's the wine we had at dinner or the relief of knowing I made it over one more major hurdle with The Rage, but I'm more relaxed than I have been in months, and I want to revel in this feeling.

Our destination, however, is so close that, despite traffic, the driver announces our arrival a few minutes later.

Alec climbs out and offers his hand to me as I step onto the sidewalk. When he doesn't let go but threads his fingers through mine, it feels so natural that I don't pull away.

"Savvy!" someone squeals, and I turn to see Rose running down the sidewalk on sky-high heels. "Alec didn't tell me you were coming to town!"

Alec and I exchange a glance. I feel like I've been caught in a lie, but the truth is this helps us maintain the image for Rose's wedding.

"It's just a short visit," I say. "For business."

She slaps her brother on the shoulder. "You wanted to have her all to yourself. You can admit it!" She looks me over. "God damn, you look incredible in that dress! I hope that . . ." Her jaw unhinges and her gaze lingers on my hand.

This time when I meet Alec's gaze, I know my eyes are wide. *The ring.*

"You didn't tell me you were going to propose." She throws a hand over her mouth, and tears fill her blue eyes.

My gaze darts back and forth between the siblings—Rose looking like sunshine spilling over, and Alec with that deer-in-the-headlights look about him. I take a deep breath. "Listen, Rose—"

"I'm so happy!" she squeals, throwing her arms around me. "I get it. You two didn't want your engagement to overshadow my wedding, but I swear, I am *not* that bride. I *love* this news."

When I meet Alec's gaze over Rose's shoulder, there's an apology in his eyes. Our little lie just got a whole lot messier.

Rose steps back and takes my left hand, tilting it this way and that as she studies the ring in the light of the streetlamps. "Good job, brother." She flashes Alec a grin. "It's just stunning."

He nods. "It suits her."

"You've told Mom, though, right?" She barely waits a breath before her eyes go wide with horror. "Alec, you *have to* tell her. Like, ASAP. She'll go apeshit if she thinks you intentionally kept this from her."

"We weren't ready to share the news yet," he says, and it comes out smoothly. He must've recovered from the shock of this encounter.

At least one of us has.

Rose turns back to me, and her smile turns into a grimace. "Mom is a *shark* when it comes to this one. When you met her last weekend she was on her best behavior, but when she feels slighted, you have to watch out." She finally releases my hand and props her fists on her hips. "You're playing with fire, brother.

She's got it in her head that you and Portentia will get back—"

"That's never happening." Alec folds his arms and shakes his head at his sister, fondness written all over his amused expression. "And if you don't tell Mom before I do, we won't have a problem, will we?"

Rose presses a hand to her chest, showing off her own beautiful ring. "I would never narc, you turd!"

He flicks her nose then steps to my side to slide his arm around me and pull me close. "It's going to be okay."

Rose bites her bottom lip and studies my ring one more time before giving a sharp nod. "Okay. You always handle her better than the rest of us, so I'll take your word for it that you have a plan."

"Thank you," he says, pulling me tighter into his side. Maybe he can tell that I'm two seconds away from blurting out the truth.

"Oh, look at me, keeping you on the street when you're out celebrating. I need to get back to my friends anyway." She waves to a trio of women chatting together at the end of the block. "Go. Drink, dance, be happy. I am so thrilled for you both." She claps her hands together.

I really like her. So much that part of me wishes this moment were real. I would've loved having a sister-in-law like Rose.

"I'll see you at home," Alec says.

Rose gapes at him. "Oh, hell no! I'm staying with Jared tonight. You two need the house to yourselves to celebrate *properly*."

Alec's blush is the most adorable thing I've seen all year. "Thanks, Rose."

She winks, blows me a kiss, turns on her very high heels, and walks away.

I sag against Alec. "Holy shit."

He presses a kiss to the top of my head. "It'll be okay."

"I hate lying to her." I turn into him and bury my face in his chest to muffle my scream of frustration, and he chuckles.

"Come on. This place has the best drinks in town, and I don't know about you, but I need that about now."

CHAPTER FOURTEEN

ALEC

The first time I laid eyes on Savannah Downing, I felt like I'd been punched in the chest. Was it her beauty? That silky blond hair spilling down her back, the long legs showcased in the kind of tight, short skirt that would look out of place anywhere but a nightclub in Vegas, or the bright eyes and easy smile? I was instantly aware of all those things, but I've seen beautiful women before, taken more than a few to my bed. Maybe it was the way she looked at me—with a predatory glint in her eye that said she'd spotted something delicious and planned to keep it all for herself—or maybe it was the way she softened a few moments later when she sat in my lap and asked if I was going to break her heart.

"Never." I scanned her face as I breathed the promise, cataloguing every detail.

I think part of me already knew that I'd get one night with Savannah and nothing more.

When she introduced me to her best friend as the future father of her children, she'd known me for all of ten minutes. As crazy as it was, I could picture it. Almost like a memory. Instead of being spooked by that feeling, I relished it—and relished the moments I knew would be fleeting.

I wish I was surprised when she texted months later to tell me we should just be friends. We both knew her excuse about distance and avoiding inevitable heartbreak was just that, but I didn't push, didn't argue, didn't declare my premature love or promise to move to rural Georgia to make it work between us. I hoped I might win her back someday, hoped that time would prove there was something about me that made it worth risking whatever she was so afraid of.

Tonight, I feel like a thief—stealing moments in time with a woman I know I can't keep. I'm not sorry for it. I can't be.

Little Black Book is a martini lounge and one of my favorite places in town. The best part about it is the cushy semicircle booths bathed in shadows at the back, and I'm sure to slip the maître d' a handsome tip to make sure he gives one to us.

"This place is gorgeous," Savvy says after we're seated. Our booth faces the dance floor and is catty-corner to the stage where a jazz trio plays a low, sexy riff. She scans the digital menu on the small tabletop screen. "Think

Smithy would die of jealousy if I ordered a lemon-drop martini at someone else's bar?"

I chuckle. I don't know the owner of her favorite bar well, but he seems way too laid-back for jealousy. "If you want something sweet, try their chocolate martini. It's one of Rose's favorite drinks ever because it's made with ganache."

She moans, and the sound rumbles through me like nails down my back. "I'm in." She taps her selection before handing the screen to me. "What will you get?"

"One of their bourbons, probably." I scroll through the selections while resisting the urge to pull her tightly against me again.

"Do I even want to know what the best bourbon at a place like this costs?"

I shrug and tap on the ten-year Rip Van Winkle before sending in our order. "Life is short." I want to tell her that if she were with me, she wouldn't have to worry about money. If she were with me, I'd take care of everything. But money seems to be a tricky subject for her. As much as she seems to crave financial stability, maybe the idea of being with someone who can offer it scares her. I'm beginning to suspect that money's been a tool used to manipulate her more than once—that was certainly an issue for Brinley and Marston—so I'm careful never to do or offer anything that might come off that way.

Savvy settles back with a sigh. "I can't believe your sister thinks we're engaged."

Right. *That.* "Is it that different than her thinking we're seriously dating?" She narrows her eyes, and I bark out a laugh. "Okay, so it is. But Rose is awesome, and we can trust her."

"Trust her enough that we could tell her the whole truth?"

Something snags in my chest at that request, but I swallow it down. "If that's what you want."

She scoots closer to me and leans her head on my shoulder. "I want to do this however *you* want to do it. This is your thing too, and I trust you to know what's best."

I inhale deeply through my nose, breathing in the clean, floral scent of her perfume. "Thank you for that."

"But I really do like your sister, and I don't want her to hate me when this is all over."

Under the table, I find her hand and thread my fingers with hers. I love holding her hand. Love when she lets me. "I'll make sure she doesn't."

"I don't want you to hate me either," she whispers, and it kills me to hear how small her voice sounds admitting it.

"I don't think I could, Savannah."

She lifts her gaze to mine and holds it for a long time, like she's trying to communicate her darkest secrets through eye contact alone. It's only broken when the server appears with our drinks.

"Thanks," Savvy says, and the server just nods and steps back into the darkness.

She takes the first sip of hers and flicks her tongue over the melted chocolate smeared across her lips. "Oh my. That's not a drink; it's an *experience*."

I chuckle. "So I hear."

Sighing, she settles back into the booth. "So, Rose lives with you?"

"In a manner of speaking. We live in my late grandmother's house."

"Oh. That explains why . . ." She drops her gaze to her untouched drink. I hate that the low lights make it difficult to read her expression.

"Why what?"

She clears her throat. "Why you said you'd see her at home."

"By technicality, it belongs to Rose as much as it belongs to me, but she'll move in with Jared when they get married."

"Not living together before the wedding, huh? Rose didn't strike me as the old-fashioned type."

"She's not, really. It was a stipulation of my father's estate that she not live with her future husband before the wedding." I shrug. "Once Rose and Jared got serious, she moved in with me rather than signing a new lease on an apartment of her own. She knew she'd spend most nights with Jared and wanted to save the money."

"The loophole," Savvy says, grinning.

I huff out a laugh and smile at her. "Yeah. And no one really cares because it was obvious Dad was doing his regular controlling bullshit from beyond the grave. She'll get her inheritance by technicality, and that's good enough."

"Any other family ever live there with you?"

"Not since Mom remarried."

"And before?"

"It's where we grew up, so we all lived there at one point—even Oliver for about a year and a half. But he hated it there as much as Mom hated him being there."

She cocks her head to the side. "Why did he live there, then?"

My sharp breath is audible even over the low drone of the club around us.

Savvy cringes. "I'm sorry. I'm not trying to pry."

"Don't be. I want to share with you." I drag a hand through my hair. "The whole thing with Oliver was complicated. It was so embarrassing when my family found out about him, but when he came to town, he was so fucking cocky. Like he was proud of it. Proud of the damage he'd done to my family when the truth came out."

She scans my face, as if she's trying to see my past through every little detail there. I love how close she is. How intimate this setting feels. I'm not ashamed to admit it was a calculated choice on my part.

"And what's the truth?" she asks.

"Before I was born, Mom and Dad were separated for a while, and that's when my brother happened." I sigh. "Mom and Dad reconciled when she got pregnant with me, but instead of telling anyone he had gotten his mistress pregnant while he was living in New York, Dad just sent Oliver's mom money. For years. Then Oliver's mom died and Dad was like, 'So you have a brother and he's coming to live with us.' I swear, I'd never seen my mom lose her temper more times in my whole life than she did in those eighteen months Oliver lived with us."

"But if you think about it, that must have been really awful for him. I mean, he lost his mom—his only family—and then suddenly he was thrown in with this family that didn't want him."

"Trust me, he didn't do anything to win us over. The opposite, in fact."

She winces. "I mean, it just seems like there might've been a reason he was a difficult kid."

"It's not that I don't feel for him." I take one sip of my bourbon. Then another. "He was awful, Savvy. To me. To my mother. Defied my father at every turn. I think Rose was the only one he gave a shit about. My father would pit us against each other—like he thought the only way either of us would be successful was to spite the other."

"I'm so sorry."

"Don't be. I just want you to understand that I'm not some asshole who hated his brother for the fun of it."

She swallows down a large gulp of her martini. "I would never think that."

"Tell me something about your family. I bet they make mine look like a mess."

She throws her head back and laughs, exposing the long, creamy skin of her neck. I can't help but smile. Her laugh is infectious. The most beautiful thing in this whole damn sparkling lounge. The whole city.

"No. Not at all. I'm not really close to anyone in my family anymore, actually. I have a brother, but . . ." She sighs. "He's always into something self-destructive. I had to step out of his life years ago to protect myself—otherwise I'd end up crashing and burning right along with him."

"Hell, Savvy. I'm sorry."

She shakes her head. "I'm not. He's . . . difficult. And, really, as sad as it sounds, I'm better off without him."

"When was the last time you talked to him?"

She finishes the little that's left in her glass. "A couple years ago? He needed some money. That's always what gets him to come around again."

I wince. "Ah. One of those." I lift my hand and wipe away the smudge of chocolate she missed on her bottom lip.

She watches me as I pull my hand away, hunger in her eyes.

I glance toward the sparsely populated dance floor then back to her. "Would you dance with me?"

Her lips part, indecision in her eyes, and I'm bracing myself for an excuse when she smiles. "I'd love to."

I stand and take her hand, slowly drawing her from our booth and leading her to the dance floor.

"You look beautiful tonight," I murmur, dipping my head to brush my lips over her bare shoulder.

She shivers in my arms but doesn't pull away. "Thank you. You don't look so bad yourself."

I skim my fingers along the back of her dress, letting them skate the line where the fabric touches her skin. She's soft and warm, and my nose is full of the vanilla and rosewater scent of her. "Do you remember our night together?" The question comes out so husky I barely recognize my own voice.

"The early hours, yes. The later ones are just snippets. Flashes. I don't do well with the quantity of alcohol we consumed." She pulls back and looks up at me through her lashes. My gut clenches. "Do you?"

"Same. I just wish . . ." I probably shouldn't say it. *I wish I could remember. If I only get that one night, I want it all.* "I can't decide if not remembering makes it better or worse."

She lies her head on my shoulder. "I've wondered that too."

"Tell me one thing you remember."

Her breath hitches. "I remember you over me, your face in my neck and your hand . . ."

"My hand between your legs," I finish. I remember that too. The feel of her on my fingers, the way her lips parted when I slid them inside her.

She closes her eyes, as if she's recalling these details at the exact moment as me. "This is torture."

"I can stop."

She shakes her head. "I don't want you to."

Good. "I still remember how you taste." I use two fingers to touch her lips. "Here." Her neck. "Here." Then down between her breasts. "Here." With my other hand, I follow her zipper down her back and to the curve of her ass then slowly back up. "I rolled you onto your stomach and kissed my way down your spine. When I scraped my teeth over the curve of your ass, you made the sexiest sounds."

She shudders. “I wish we could have a redo.”

I swallow hard. “Who says we can’t?”

She buries her face in my chest, hiding her eyes from me. “Alec . . .”

“Come home with me, Savvy,” I say, my voice low. “I want you in my bed.”

When she lifts her head, there’s so much heat in her eyes it nearly knocks me over. I haven’t been fooling myself. This connection between us is real.

“Can we really have one night without it messing with our friendship?” She tugs her bottom lip between her teeth. “I’m not going to pretend I don’t want it, but I know you want more than—”

I put my thumb against her lips. I can’t handle hearing her talk herself out of this. “We’ve already been together once. Denying ourselves tonight won’t change that.” I stroke her lip. “It won’t change how much we want it.”

“And tomorrow?” she asks.

My heart is racing, tripping over how much I want this and how much I want more. But at the end of the day, this is Savvy. If tonight’s all I can have, I’m going to take it. “Tomorrow can be whatever you want it to be.”

Part Six

EIGHT YEARS AGO

CHAPTER FIFTEEN

SAVVY

I prefer to close up at The Naked Bean. Not only are the late-night tips usually better when students come for coffee after drinking, but I like the quiet satisfaction of cleaning up at the end of the night. After a shift of running around, the solitude gives me a chance to decompress before I head home.

The walk is my favorite part. I used to draw it out, reluctant to return to Chuck and his bullshit, but that's changed since I started staying at Oliver's two weeks ago. Tonight, I lock the deadbolts on the back door and walk home at a steady clip, with no need to delay my arrival. My stomach flutters at the thought of him waiting there for me, and I do my best to tamp down my subconscious enthusiasm.

He's not my boyfriend.

But my brain keeps forgetting that.

"Hey!" someone calls from the alley.

I stiffen and keep walking. In my experience, if you act confident and like you have nothing to fear, people will assume it's true.

Hurried footsteps sound behind me. "Slow down, Savannah."

My steps falter at the sound of Chuck's voice, and seconds later, rough fingers wrap around my upper arm.

"Now you're too good to stop and talk to me for a minute?" His hot breath is foul, but I make myself look at him. I'm all too familiar with the glaze in those heavy eyes. Chuck is drunk.

"Leave me alone." I try to yank my arm away, but he holds tight.

"I just wanna talk."

I yank back again. This time I come free. "Well, I don't."

"Oliver Rhett isn't the only guy in this town who has money, you know. I could take care of you. Just come home."

"Not. Interested." I fumble in my purse, trying to slide my work keys between my fingers just in case I need to defend myself, but they fall from my hand to the ground.

He scoops them up. "Just talk to me a minute."

"Give those back." My manager will kill me if I lose those.

"You think Oliver's some big hero, don't you?" He

chuckles. "Does he tell you everything, though? Or maybe you like being his whore."

"Chuck, you are *drunk*, and I'm not talking to you like this." Maybe I don't need my keys. Maybe I can get back to Oliver's and figure out how to replace them all.

I take a step back and then another, but he prowls after me, and I can't bring myself to turn my back on him. He grabs my shirt and hauls me against his chest. "You know he's just trying to get me back, right?" he asks, stutter-stepping to catch his balance. "He was so mad I broke his bitchy sister's heart that he's been dying for a way to make me pay, and I fucking fell for it."

I'm so stiff I feel my body shatter to dust, as if someone has knocked me over. He's too big and too drunk. "I said, back off."

"Shh. I've missed you." He trails a knuckle across my cheek. My keys jingle with the movement, and I jerk away.

A figure emerges from the darkness and grabs Chuck by the back of his shirt. "She said *back off*," Oliver growls, throwing him to the ground. The keys slide across the pavement, and Oliver scoops them up.

Chuck calmly returns to his feet and wipes his palms on his jeans before lifting his hands in surrender. "I'm not trying to hurt anyone. Just trying to talk to my girl."

"Fuck you," Oliver spits, putting his body in front of mine. "Savannah isn't yours, and if I hear about you so much as looking at her too long, I will fucking come after you. Don't test me."

"Whatever," Chuck says. "Enjoy your whore." Then he has the gall to wink at me. "See you around, Savvy."

"The fuck you will," Oliver growls. The threat is too low for the man to hear it, but I know Oliver means it.

Only once Chuck is out of sight does Oliver turn to me. He tucks the keys into my purse then puts both hands on my shoulders and looks me over. "You okay?"

I swallow hard. "He wouldn't have hurt me," I say, but I'm not sure I believe it.

"He's a creep," Oliver says. "But I swear I'll make sure he knows there are consequences if he messes with you again. He doesn't want that."

"Thank you," I whisper. "Is that true? What he said about your sister?"

He scowls in the direction Chuck disappeared, as if he might still find him there. "It's true that he fucked around with her and then fucked her over."

I swallow. Maybe all this with Oliver makes a little more sense now. "And that's why you did what you did? Paying the debt? Getting me to live with you? So Chuck would think I left him for you?"

"Not completely. I consider pissing off Chuck an added bonus." He takes my hand and threads his fingers through mine before giving a reassuring squeeze. "Come on. Let's get home."

We're quiet on the walk back to his place. I can feel the rage radiating off Oliver, but I'm too twisted up in my own thoughts to analyze it. My chest aches with every step, and I start shaking a little. Then a lot. Then shivering violently.

Once we step into Oliver's loft, I just stand there and stare to make sure he turns the deadbolt.

"Want to get a shower?" he asks, turning to me. "I can get you some food."

"You don't have to do that." My thoughts are spiraling. What if Oliver hadn't shown up? What would have happened? I thought I loved Chuck once—thought he loved me—but he always scared me a little when he drank too much. Tonight, he scared me a lot.

"Savvy." Oliver clasps both of my hands between his. They're warm and rough, and they make me wish he'd wrap me up next to him and hold me close. "You're shaking."

I look down at my hands as if they belong to someone else. He's right. I'm trembling.

"You don't have to worry about Chuck. I won't let him bother you again."

"How?"

He shrugs. "I know things. And I can be pretty mean when I want to be." He smirks. "Sometimes it's nice to have an asshole like me on your side."

"How'd you do it?" I swallow the bile surging up my throat. "Knock him down like that?"

He laughs softly. "If you weren't so shaken up, I'd be offended by that question."

I blink at him. "You fight too?"

He shrugs. "More in undergrad. Not so much these days. Gotta keep my face pretty for all these internship interviews."

Oliver fights too. I'm not sure how I feel about that.

When I was with Chuck, I hated it. But with Oliver . . . "Teach me how. I want to know how to do that."

He sighs. "It's not as simple as knowing the moves. You have to have the strength too."

"But I've seen it on TV—women my size learning to overpower an attacker. I want to learn."

He nods. "Sure. And I'm not saying you can't. I'm saying you need some strength." He squeezes my shoulders. "You're not afraid of some weightlifting, are you?"

"I lift weights sometimes."

He scoffs softly then gives me a gentle smile. "I'm not talking about twenty-rep sets with three-pound dumbbells. I'm talking *heavy* weights. So heavy you can only lift it a few times. *Power.* I'll teach you if you want."

"I do." I don't bother trying to hide how eager I am. I've always wanted to be stronger. And now? Now it feels necessary. "Can we start tomorrow?"

"Sure." He cups my face in one hand and strokes his thumb across my cheek. "You could be so fucking strong. Just wait and see."

OLIVER

After one session at the gym with Savannah, it's obvious that training her was a terrible idea. She fucking *loves* weights, and the way she smiles at me when I show her that she's already stronger than she thinks? I'm pretty sure I could move mountains.

Add having my hands on her sweaty skin to her infectious joy and I'm screwed. I know I'm screwed.

But I'll be fucking damned if I'm going to let anyone else do this.

It's a dangerous thought, but one I can't let go.

CHAPTER SIXTEEN

OLIVER

I hurry home after my meeting with my advisor on Monday. I shouldn't be this anxious to see Savvy. Shouldn't keep running back home any time I think she might be there. Shouldn't keep reliving the rage I felt when I saw Chuck with his hands on her.

This whole arrangement isn't supposed to involve all these fucking inconvenient things I feel when she's around. I love her smile and how nice it is to know she'll be curled up reading a romance novel if I get home late. I never knew it could be so much fucking *fun* to talk about your day with someone. Even studying with her is better. She makes these little comments about her classes that always leave me grinning. And the attraction? Fuck yes.

It's been two weeks since the night she dropped to her knees and unbuttoned my pants. Two weeks, and I still haven't stopped thinking about it. I knew she was pissed. I knew something was very wrong, but it still took everything in me to stop her. Because *fuck*. That mouth? Those big eyes looking up at me? It's an image I'll never get out of my brain. One I've spent every shower since playing out in a much different way.

She's not mine, and I didn't pull her into my life to change that. I'm annoyed with myself every step of the way home, but all that annoyance fades the second I walk in the door. She's standing in my kitchen, chopping lettuce on a big cutting board.

"Whatcha doing?" I ask, tossing my keys on the table by the door. She doesn't seem to hear me, so I step into the kitchen and brush her arm with the back of my hand. "Savannah?"

She startles and pulls out an earbud. "I didn't hear you come in." She tucks the headphones back into the case, and a voice starts coming from her phone.

"*Arturo's hands were rough against her thighs as he spread them, his mouth hard and hungry on the—*"

"Oh my God!" She stabs at her phone until the voice stops.

I bite back a smile. "Audiobook or sex hotline?"

"Shut up." Her cheeks are pink. Fuck, she's cute when she's embarrassed. "There's nothing wrong with enjoying a little romantic literature."

"Never said there was."

She narrows her eyes at me as if she's waiting for me to make a joke, then closes out the library's audiobook app. "I was just making dinner. I hope you don't mind."

"Of course not." I told her to make herself at home, and I'm glad to see she finally is. Despite her declaration that she was reuniting with carbs, I'm not sure I've seen her eat more than egg whites and an occasional apple since she got here. I don't know if that's because she doesn't eat much or because she feels weird making herself food at my place.

I rub my hands together. "And anyway, I'm starving. How can I help?"

She glances around and shrugs. "Sure, but there's not much to do. I'm just making some chicken breast for a salad."

I step behind her and frown at the ingredients she has laid out. "Where's the rest?"

"What?"

I arch a brow. "I see chicken breast and I see lettuce. Where's the rest? The goodies? The stuff that makes a salad worth eating?"

She laughs. "I just ran into the store to grab stuff for a quick dinner. I didn't buy anything to make it fancy."

"I'm not talking fancy. I'm talking delicious. I bet I have some stuff." I dig into the fridge and pull out cheese, cucumbers, tomatoes, and more cheese. Then in the pantry I find tortilla strips, a can of corn, and a can of beans, and slide them onto the counter. "How about a Santa Fe-style chicken salad?" She nods, but the look in her eyes has me hesitating. "Or are you still counting carbs and shit?"

She glances down at the pile of ingredients I've added to the island. "I guess it's just an old habit at this point."

"Can I ask why?" I turn to the sink to wash my hands. "Why with the dieting? Do you have a health condition or something?"

She coughs out a laugh. "No. It's just . . ." She sighs. "My mom was always on me about watching it when I was growing up, and Chuck had this thing about how a man should be able to pick up his woman."

I grunt. Savvy could binge on pizza and donuts for two months and I'd still be able to pick her up. Easily. However, I don't think this is a good time to flex, so I keep that to myself.

"I tend to get a little heavy in the butt and hips," she says, cringing. "And since he was cutting weight for the fights . . ."

"He couldn't pick you up, so that was something *you* needed to fix?" I ask. Fuck staying quiet. Chuck is such trash. I suspected that before my sister got tangled up with him, but afterward, he left no doubt.

Savvy drops her gaze to the counter and shakes her head. "It's stupid, I guess."

"Hey." I wait until she meets my eyes. She's so fucking gorgeous. I love those hazel eyes—how much she always seems to have going on in them, like she never stops thinking. "It's your choice how you want to eat. And if you want to do the whole low-carb thing or live on plain lettuce and dry chicken breast, I'll shut my mouth. But don't do it for him. He's not fucking worth it."

She swallows. "Yeah. I know that." She folds her arms over her chest and looks away. "Like I said, old habits."

I can't wait to feed this girl. Heavy in the hips and

ass? Chuck's an idiot. She's incredibly petite, but no amount of dieting can give a woman the hips of a ten-year-old boy. I don't get why so many women think that's the goal. Savvy's hips and ass are the reason I practically have to sit on my hands when she's near me. And while they might not be the *only* reason I want to touch her so badly, they're sure as hell a contributing factor. But I won't. She doesn't need to get herself wrapped up with a guy like me.

We make dinner together, working side by side, and then eat at the table. I love watching her enjoy food, and I'm planning all the ways I can get away with feeding her.

When we're both finished, I grab our plates before she can stand and load them into the dishwasher.

"You should let me do that," she says when I start filling the sink to scrub the skillet.

Let me guess—Chuck made her do all the cleaning too? *Human garbage.* "I'm perfectly capable of washing a couple of dishes."

"I can't pay you back for the car," she says.

I still, then turn to face her. "I know. I thought we covered this."

"So this is about your sister? It can't just be about the trip to New York."

I shrug. "Like I said, it doesn't hurt. Chuck's a dick, and I enjoy him thinking I took you from him."

"When did she date him?"

"A year ago. She lived with me for the summer and came to a couple fights. She met Chuck and decided to date him despite my every objection."

Savvy worries her bottom lip between her teeth. "I'm sorry."

"Yeah. Well, I guess it was a lesson she needed to learn the hard way. Have you tried the stuff on for Thursday?" I ask, mostly to remind myself of my goals. God. I wish I could be there to see the look in the old man's eyes when he finds out she's a Downing.

She shakes her head. "I was afraid I might accidentally ruin something, so I put it off. Then I forgot."

I wave toward the bedroom. "Do you mind putting it all on before you head to work?"

She holds my gaze for a long time, the hazel of her eyes pulling me under, hypnotizing me.

I can't fall for this girl, but sometimes I'm not sure if I'm protecting her or myself.

SAVVY

Oliver's mood has changed from relaxed and fun to hard and cold in the span of the last thirty seconds. "You're acting weird. Are you pissy with me, or . . ." I cock my head to the side. "Who is this guy to you?"

Oliver huffs. "Like I said. He's a rich asshole who has something of mine."

I nod slowly. There's more he's not telling me, but what's new? Oliver isn't exactly an open book. "Fine."

I scoot around him and head to the bedroom to try on what I know has to be thousands of dollars' worth of merchandise. Taking a deep breath, I open the Bergdorf bag first. Inside is a small black cocktail dress and . . . a matching black panty set. "Seriously?" I yell, loud enough to be heard through the door and down the hall. "Why do I need new underwear for this? Because I fucking swear, if you think I'm going to let him see me in it—"

"Calm down. The girl who did the shopping for me said the dress needed a special bra. She asked what you had, and I didn't know, so she included one that would work."

I hold up the scrap of lace wrapped neatly in the same bag. "And the *thong*? How do you explain that?"

This time when he speaks, his voice is lower and closer, like he's moved to the door. "Panty lines, sweetheart."

"You really didn't think I owned a single pair of panties that would work with this dress?"

"I didn't think you'd want me searching through them to see for myself."

"You didn't hesitate to go through them to figure out my size." The only sound from the other side of the door is his laughter, and it's a relief. Whoever this guy is, it's obvious Oliver gets out of sorts just thinking about him. "Well, she could've gotten cheap underwear. It's not like he's gonna know if I have boring Target panties on beneath this overpriced dress."

"There's nothing boring about your panties, Savvy."

I snap my attention to the door, as if I might be able to see his face through the solid wood panels. *Welcome back, Mr. Mixed Signals.*

"How's it look?" he asks.

With a sigh, I strip out of my clothes. "Give me a minute." The undergarments are silky smooth and fit like a glove. Even the lace panel on the panties is soft. I catch a glimpse of myself in the mirror and bite my bottom lip. The panty set is classic and sexy. I can't help but wonder if Oliver had other reasons for buying it for me. Like maybe he liked the idea of me in it. Like maybe he wanted to be the only man who would know the most intimate part of this outfit he bought me.

If I were someone different, I might open that door and ask if he approved. If I were bolder, I'd do it just to see the heat in his eyes. Would he finally touch me then? Would he investigate the texture of the lace between my thighs or study the swell of my breasts in the plunging push-up bra?

I close my eyes as the fantasy washes over me. I imagine how the scruff of his stubble would feel against my neck. Would he be quiet as he explored my body with his hands, or would he whisper dirty thoughts in my ear?

"Need help?" he asks, tearing me from the fantasy.

I shake my head to send the images from my mind, but my cheeks are still hot. "I'm trying not to damage anything," I say. Yes, let's pretend *that's* the problem. I flip over the tag on the dress, and my heart stutters. "Holy fuck. Do people really spend this much on a single item of clothing?"

"You're stalling," he says. "Do you hate it?"

I unzip the dress and carefully step into it.

It's longer than I expected, reaching my knees, but

his shopper was right about the undergarments, because this dress fits like a glove and the fine black fabric will show any lump or bump beneath it. Reaching behind myself, I get the zipper halfway up before I'm stuck. The dress is too tight for me to zip it by myself if I don't want to risk popping a seam.

"I'll need help zipping it the rest of the way."

"No problem," he says tersely.

"Are you sure?" I ask, trying to bring that smile back to his voice. "Have you ever zipped *up* a woman's dress before?"

"Pretty sure I can manage," he mutters.

Okay. So we're back to Grumpy Oliver. I pull out the shoes. Classic black, but with the telltale red sole to make sure the world knows I'm wearing thousand-dollar heels. They fit perfectly and are surprisingly comfortable for the height. "Do you want me to put on the jewelry?" I ask.

"Do you typically have trouble fitting into earrings?" he asks.

I roll my eyes. Fine. We'll skip the jewelry. Turning, I look myself over in the mirror and imagine a little sparkle at my neck and ears, my makeup done, my hair . . . up, I think? I'll ask Oliver, since he's so sure he knows what Mr. Businessman is into. I pull the bedroom door open and find him leaning against the opposite wall, arms folded.

He straightens and twirls his finger in the air, indicating I should spin around. Obediently, I give him my back. His fingers brush the bare skin between my shoulder blades as he closes the zipper, and I shiver softly.

When I face him again, he's already sweeping his gaze over me.

"Good. Be ready to leave at four Thursday. I've gotten a room so you can change when we get there."

He turns away and heads back to the kitchen, and I swallow down a burn of . . . not rejection. He didn't buy this for himself. And yet I thought he might take a moment to appreciate it.

Then his words click in my mind. "Wait. A room? Are we spending the night?" *In a hotel room. Together?*

Oliver stops at the end of the hall, and his shoulders rise and fall. "I'm not Prince Charming and this isn't a fairy tale, Savannah. So quit imagining this might turn into something you can enjoy."

I'm grateful he has his back to me, because I don't want him to see the embarrassment that's making my cheeks flame. "I didn't mean to imply . . ."

He glances over his shoulder and arches a brow. *Fucking asshole.* "This is work, not one of your books."

"And what kind of *work* will I be doing with this man by talking to him?"

"Leave the details to me."

I bite back a frustrated growl. "Got it." I stride into the bedroom and slam the door behind me only to realize I can't unzip this dress by myself. "Oliver!" I call. "Get back here and help me out of this dress."

I open the door to find him already standing on the other side, cocky smile in place.

"Maybe you could learn something from those books of yours," he says.

"What?"

"I bet the heroine in your audiobook at least said please when she asked *Arturo* to undress her."

"I knew you wouldn't be able to forget you heard that."

His gray eyes dance. God, he's even sexier when he's laughing. "Never said I would."

CHAPTER SEVENTEEN

OLIVER

Beautiful. Fucking rip-my-heart-out beautiful.

That's how Savannah looks in that dress. Those heels. Even the fucking *earrings* are sexy on her—a tiny string of diamonds that emphasizes the smooth length of her neck.

"You're going to return these, right?" she asked when she put them on.

I shrugged. "Probably not. You'll wear them again when we come back."

The day has finally come, and I hate everything about it. Everything except that I know it will work. Her beauty, her age, her *name.* She's perfect, and he'll see that right away. In the end, I'll have what I need. And then I'll be free. *Finally.*

She's bent forward slightly, looking in the full-length

mirror inside our hotel room as she applies a second coat of red lipstick, and it takes everything in me to resist the urge to step close behind her and settle my hands at her hips. I have little doubt her ass would feel perfect nestled against my groin, and even less that she'd like my hands on her.

Instead, I keep my back pressed against the door, fearing that lingering too close to the bed might put ideas in my head.

I paid for this room for the night—it's not exactly the kind of place that rents by the hour—and part of me wants to forget our plan and keep her here. Strip her out of that sinful fucking dress and replace that clinging fabric with the touch of my roaming hands.

The drive up here was misery. When I got back from class, she was fresh out of the shower in a white T-shirt and a pair of jean shorts, her face clean, her hair blown smooth, and she left her window down for the drive, letting the wind whip her hair around her face.

I didn't say much, and she picked up on my mood and left me to brood. But then she popped in her earbuds and used the ride to listen to her book.

I wanted to ask what Arturo was up to. To know what was happening when she shifted in her seat and glanced over at me like she wanted to make sure I couldn't hear. I've never had much of an opinion one way or another about romance novels, but they are suddenly my favorite genre. Not to read myself. But to know she's reading.

I have a plan, and I need to stick with it. Savvy

doesn't see me for who I am—an asshole looking out for his own best interests. She sees me as some sort of hero. She wouldn't have dropped to her knees in front of me like she did if she thought otherwise. She knew I wouldn't let her do it. Maybe I should have. Just so she hated me and kept her distance.

I keep catching myself doing shit to match that skewed perception she has of me. Giving her the bedroom. Cooking her dinner. Telling Rose to buy her lingerie to go with the dress when I knew damn well she didn't need it. I need to fucking stop. I'm making everything complicated, and there's no reason this shouldn't be simple.

Savvy straightens and caps the lipstick, then tucks it into her purse. When she turns to me, those big eyes emphasized with dark liner, my gut clenches.

"What?" she asks. "You look worried. What is it?" She looks down at herself and skims her hands over her dress.

"I'm not worried." He'll take one look at her, at these clothes, and she'll be a candidate. Then, once he finds out she's a Downing, he'll zero in. That's all it will take.

"Are you having second thoughts?" she asks.

Yes. "No. Come on." I open the door and hold it for her as she strides down the hall toward the elevator.

When I asked Rose to find a dress for Savvy, she asked what feature I wanted to emphasize.

"What do you mean?" I asked.

"Every body is different, and dresses should accentuate our assets. Is she busty? Petite? Graceful?"

"She has an ass like J.Lo and tries to hide it."

Rose *cackled.* "I know just the dress," she said, and fuck. She's hit a home run. It emphasizes that ass and makes my hands itch to touch. To take. To claim like I'm the fucking hero Arturo and not the asshole Oliver Rhett.

I can't have Savvy, but there's nothing stopping me from taking in the view as she strides to the elevator, her hips swishing with every step.

She presses the button, showing off her freshly manicured nails. They're a bold red that matches her lipstick. And those red lips are putting some bad ideas in my head.

The doors slide open with a *ding* and she steps inside, clutching her purse in front of her like a shield. When the doors close and the elevator starts to descend, she flashes me a worried look.

"I'm surprised you're going with me. Won't he suspect something if he sees me walk in with you?"

I look at my watch. "He won't see me. I'll point him out from the hotel's lobby bar and wait for you here while you go across the street and drink your martini."

"But what if he—"

"Like I said, he's predictable."

She bites her bottom lip, her teeth sinking into the red and making me think of another time, another place I'd like to see her do that. Like under me. Like in my bed. Like when I'm inside her.

"Don't do that," I say gruffly, staring at her mouth.

"Oh." She brings two fingertips to her lips and stops before touching them. "Did I ruin it?"

"No."

Her shoulders sag. "Good."

"But you need him to be interested in who you are—not determined to get those pretty lips on his cock before he can be intrigued by more than your body."

She flushes, but her moment of embarrassment is followed quickly by angry-eyed indignation. "What the fuck are you getting me into, Oliver? I told you I'm not getting on my knees for—"

I close the space between us and look down at her. At those lips. "Not for anyone but me," I say against my better judgment. "Not as long as I have anything to say about it."

She draws in a shaky breath, her eyes going back and forth between mine. "I don't understand what you want from me."

I step back, and the elevator doors slide open. "It doesn't matter what I want. Only what I plan to take."

~

SAVVY

"It doesn't matter what I want. Only what I plan to take."

What are: infuriatingly vague and suggestive statements made by Oliver Rhett that lead nowhere?

My stomach is a fluttery mess by the time we enter the restaurant bar in our hotel lobby, but for the first time today, that has nothing to do with nerves about tonight's assignment. Oliver rattles me. One minute I think he hates me, and the next I think he wants to strip me bare and make me moan.

I suppose it could be both.

"So you just want me to go to that restaurant across the street, sit at the bar, and make eye contact with the silver fox with the jacket?" If I sound skeptical, it's because I am.

"That's all—this time."

I fold my arms. "*This time*? And what happens next time?"

"If I told you, you wouldn't be able to act natural."

I glance out the lobby windows and try to get a good look at the man I'm here to "make eye contact" with. All I can tell from here is that he's wearing a suit and has more silver than black in his hair. "Who is he, anyway?"

"Just another rich asshole."

I shoot Oliver a look.

He sighs. "Listen, the less you know, the better." My stomach knots, and he must see the distress on my face because he takes my chin in his hand and leans forward. "I will not let anything happen to you. You have my word."

I take a breath and glance toward the exit. Oliver saved my ass and Nathan's, and he's asking almost nothing of me in return. I've never been a coward, and I'm not going to start now.

I roll back my shoulders and strut my way across the street and into the restaurant. I ask the bartender for a martini and take the stool three down from the silver fox. When I glance his way, he's already looking at me. I don't have to work to make eye contact. He does the work for me. I hold it for a beat, give a subtle half-smile, then look down at my hands as I wait for the martini.

He says something to the bartender, who gives a low laugh in response before glancing my way, leaving no room for misinterpretation. They're talking about me.

Pigs.

The bartender delivers my drink with a napkin. "The gentleman at the end of the bar has asked for the privilege of buying this for you."

What the actual fuck? Because of ten seconds of eye contact? Does he buy drinks for every young woman who happens to sit near him at the bar? Or did Oliver just know his type that well?

Time to play the game, though—that's why I'm here. I flash the gentleman a small, grateful smile and sip my drink. His glance turns my way only a few times, and when it does, it's not fleeting. This guy watches me sip vodka like it's a performance and he's paid the price of admission. And maybe I should be freaked, but there's something about him. He's . . . nonthreatening.

I'm careful not to let my gaze stray to the windows, even if I'm dying to know if Oliver is watching from his spot across the street.

The guy finishes his bourbon before my martini is gone. He stands, shrugs his jacket on, and slides a bill across the bar to the bartender. Just when I think he's going to leave without looking my way again, he winks at me then walks out the door.

Is that it? Am I done? Did I screw this up?

My phone buzzes in my handbag, and I reach for it.

Oliver: Well done.

I frown at my phone.

Savvy: How do you know? We didn't sit together or even talk.

Oliver: Exactly. But he'll remember you.

Savvy: I still feel like you're pimping me out.

Oliver: Stay and finish your drink. I'll go get your stuff and check out of the room. I'll text on my way to get the car so you can pay your bill and meet me out front.

I roll my eyes. *Way to avoid my objection.* But what's the point of bringing it up now?

Savvy: No bill. Silver Fox picked up the tab.

Oliver: Must you keep calling him that?

Savvy: Does it bother you that I find the guy you're pimping me out to objectively good-looking?

Oliver: Yes.

Savvy: And why's that?

Oliver: Whatever. Just don't ever let him hear you say that.

I frown. If we're trying to get this guy interested in me, wouldn't a compliment be a *good* thing? Or maybe this is a timeline thing, like why Oliver didn't want me biting my lip in front of him.

"I'm not getting on my knees for—"

"Not for anyone but me. Not as long as I have anything to say about it."

Oliver may be an asshole half the time, but there's no denying those words will play on repeat in my head for the next week. Maybe the next month.

"Can I get you anything else?" the bartender asks.

I blink at my martini and realize I drained it while texting with Oliver. "No, thank you." I pull a twenty from my purse and slide it across the counter. "That's for you. Thank you."

He smiles. "My pleasure."

I keep my seat but apply a fresh coat of lipstick while I wait. If Oliver is going to work so hard to be infuriating then I might just spend the whole ride home biting my bottom lip and getting under his skin.

Part Seven

PRESENT

CHAPTER EIGHTEEN

SAVVY

I'm going home with Alec. Going to be with Alec. It's a terrible gamble. A sort of masochism to have him tonight and then cut myself off from any possibility of a future. I can't decide if it was weakness or strength that had me agreeing. Lust or courage.

His town car is waiting for us when we exit the bar, and Alec doesn't let go of my hand as he opens the door and guides me inside.

"Where can I take you, Mr. Hayes?" the driver asks.

"Home," Alec says, pulling the door shut as he slides in beside me.

"Yes, sir." Maybe he always does it for longer drives or maybe he can sense the sexual tension vibrating between us, but without our asking, the driver closes the privacy screen.

Just like that, we're alone. The darkly tinted windows shield us from prying eyes on the busy sidewalk. Alec pulls me onto his lap, and I turn to straddle him even as his hands shove my dress up high on my hips.

I take my time lowering my mouth to his, and he lets me, resting his hands patiently at the hem of my dress, waiting for my signal. When our lips touch, it's like exhaling for the first time all night. My body unwinds from the tension of resisting only to slowly coil up into the ache of *wanting*.

Our lips skim and part. We suck gently. Taking our time. Easing into the kiss before we let it take over, before our mouths and tongues and lust take over.

His hands slip under the hem of my dress, and his fingertips skim over the lace of my panties. He groans against my mouth. "Lie to me and tell me these are for me."

I shift my hips until I can feel the hard length of his cock through his pants. "But it wouldn't be a lie."

"You knew this would happen?" He opens his mouth against my neck and sucks lightly before scraping his teeth over the same spot.

I gasp. "No. Just wanted to imagine that it might. I imagine it a lot."

His grip on my hips tightens. "Fuck. You're killing me."

"You've thought about me too?" I know he has. He's never pretended otherwise, but I want to hear him say it.

"Every fucking day. Can't get you out of my head." He kisses his way across my shoulders. I lean back to give his mouth better access to my bare skin, and he rewards me by trailing kisses across my collarbone and over the swell of my breasts.

I writhe against him, fumbling between our bodies to find the button on his pants. I need him now.

He grabs both my wrists in one big hand and squeezes gently. "Patience, baby. I won't be taking you in the back of this car. I've waited for this way too long to let you rush me."

I bury my face in his neck and release a sound that is half whimper, half laugh. "I'm dying here."

He chuckles against my hair before gripping my thighs and nudging me back. "Look at me."

I lift my head and meet his dark, hungry gaze.

He cups me between my legs and strokes, teasing the lace against my clit until my eyes float closed again.

"More." I'm shameless. *Desperate.*

Alec yanks the lace to the side and plunges two fingers inside me, turning his hand to give me the pressure of his palm against my clit. Instinctively, I rise onto my knees and rock against the delicious pleasure winding through my core.

My head falls back and my body takes over, moving against his hand and into his touch, letting pleasure wind me tighter.

Alec's breath is warm and sweet against my neck, a sharp contrast to his words. *Like that. Love the way you move. So wet. Fucking dreamed of this.*

His strokes seem to go on and on, and I love every second, want more and more and more. I lose myself in the pleasure of his fingers and his mouth, the erotic anticipation of knowing there's more to come.

He latches on to my neck and sucks gently, and I feel that pull everywhere. Sharp and hot. With a helpless cry, I come on his hand.

"Fuck," he groans. "So beautiful."

I collapse against his chest, trapping his hand between our bodies. "Sorry," I whisper, pulling back.

"About what?" He grabs my hips, his fingers gentle but firm as he holds me close.

"I'm smashing you."

He grins. "I like it."

I glance out the window, but I have no idea where we are or how much longer it will be before we pull up to his house. "Do we have time?" I slide my hand between our bodies and stroke his erection through his pants.

"We have all night," he says, just as the driver makes a turn that brings us into a big, circular drive.

The sight of this huge house steals my smile. I want to be confident enough that Alec's world doesn't faze me, but I'm not. Big money ruined my family. Ruined my brother. It terrifies me.

I slide off Alec's lap and situate myself on the seat next to him, pulling down my dress as the car comes to a stop.

When the driver opens the door, I step out onto the stone pavers. The sight of the front door sends my heart racing as I remember the last time I was here.

The trench coat. The way Oliver looked at me. The nightmare feeling of realizing that the troublemaker half-brother Alec couldn't stand was also the man who once stole my heart.

"Why do you look like you're about to enter a house of horrors?" Alec asks behind me.

I force out a laugh. Paste on a smile. "It's a little intimidating."

"It's just where I live. Don't read too much into it."

It's more than that, and we both know it. It's a sign of the differences between us, proof that we live in different worlds. But he sweeps my hair to the side and presses a kiss to my neck, and I tell myself to forget all that. Just for tonight.

ALEC

This isn't the first time I've wished I could sell my grandmother's home, but tonight, as I lead Savvy in through the massive front doors, I'm feeling it more acutely.

Savannah, so hot and needy in the car, went cold the second she saw the house. How can I explain that this isn't who I am? That I live here because none of us can bring ourselves to sell the house a sweet old lady loved so much?

"Do you want the tour, or . . .?"

She scans the foyer, eyeing the oversize curved staircase and the custom marble floors. I can feel her freezing up on me, all the heat from the car sliding away as she pulls into herself.

"Hey." I turn her to face me and slide a hand into her hair. "Don't let this place fool you. This is where I live on the increasingly rare occasions that I'm in town. It's not who I am."

She lets her eyes drift close, and I stroke her cheek with my thumb. "It's just a reminder that this is a mistake. That we don't work."

I study her for a beat, my heart aching with how much I want her. Not just tonight, but always. "Do you still want this? To be with me?"

"Yes. But that doesn't—"

I put a finger to her lips. "Close your eyes." She obeys, and I quickly loosen my tie and slide it out from under my collar. "Do you trust me?"

"Yes." The word shakes enough to communicate how hard that is for her. I want to understand that. To know everything that's made her who she is. Everything that scares her and everything that makes her feel brave.

I place the middle of the tie over her eyes and secure it behind her head.

"Is this what I think it is?" she asks. Her smile is back, and the sight of it pulls some of this incessant weight from my shoulders.

"That depends. Do you think it's a blindfold meant to distract you from this ostentatious fortress parading as a home so I can keep you focused on what matters?"

She laughs softly. Not all the way unwound, but closer. "What matters, huh?" She presses a hand to my chest and lazily skims it down my body. "And what's that?"

I kiss the corner of her mouth then the edge of her jaw before cupping her breast through her dress. "Wait and see," I whisper against her ear.

She shivers in my arms. "Have I ever told you that you're full of good ideas?"

I hoist her into my arms, and she squeals. "I'm just getting started."

SAVVY

I wrap my arms around Alec's neck as he carries me into the house, and I will my mind to go quiet. I shove aside my guilt and shame and focus on tonight. On *us*.

Even if I tell him the truth—an *if* that's beginning to feel a lot more like *when*—Alec and I don't get forever. It would be too complicated and hurtful for everyone involved. But I've made my boundaries very clear, and he's giving me tonight anyway. I won't let anything ruin this gift.

I hear the soft thud of a door closing, then Alec slowly slides me down his body.

When my feet are on the floor, I reach for the blindfold, but he stops me with the brush of his fingertips against the back of my hand.

"Leave it?" he asks. The heat of him moves closer, then soft lips brush against mine. "Just for a little bit."

"Okay." Chills of anticipation race up my spine. His fingers dance across my rib cage then fabric slides down my arms and back, and cool air tightens my nipples through the thin lace of my bra.

"You are the most beautiful woman."

Lips against my ear then my neck. The heat of his palm against my breast. His thumb circling one pebbled nipple through the whisper of fabric.

"I've thought about touching you again every day since the night we met."

Same. I don't let myself say it. It seems too cruel to admit the extent of my feelings. Of my craving for him.

His mouth captures mine in a rough kiss that seems to say more than either of us can. Tongues and teeth clash while our hands greedily explore each other.

I fist his shirt in both hands and tug it from his pants before blindly searching for buttons. Our mouths are fused, and I fumble between our bodies. I want the heat of his skin under my palms.

He chuckles, breaking the kiss. I whimper in protest as he pulls away.

"I'm hurrying," he murmurs. Then his hands are there again, cupping my ass, pulling me close.

His chest is bare—warm and solid against my breasts. His pants are rough against the sensitive skin of my thighs, and his erection presses insistently against my belly.

I cup him through his pants, and he growls an unintelligible curse.

"You're gonna be the death of me." He takes my wrist

then finds the other and holds them both behind my back in one gentle hand. "Look at you."

Hot kisses trail down my neck, rougher this time. His teeth scrape against my sensitive skin, and his tongue soothes.

I sink into the sensation of his mouth traveling across my collarbone and down to my breasts. All I can do is let him touch and taste and suck. He tugs down the shell of my bra, then his mouth is there—kissing, exploring, playing. He draws my nipple into his mouth, and my knees buckle.

"Better than I remember," he says. "Fuck, I love the way your body responds."

I wiggle my hands free from the loose cuff of his hand, find his belt, and release the buckle before pulling it free and letting it drop to the floor.

I take my time to unbutton his pants. I relish the way he rocks into my touch. When I free him from his briefs and he rasps out a low "fuck," the muscles between my legs clench.

His hands are in my hair, tugging my mouth toward his for another kiss. Harder. Rougher. Hungrier. I love every bit of it.

But it's not his mouth I'm craving.

I drop to my knees and find his shaft with my hand and then my mouth.

"Hell yes." His hands are still in my hair, and his grip tightens roughly as I work over him. I have fuzzy memories of doing this the night we met, fuzzy memories of the noises he made and the way it felt to bring this man the kind of pleasure that cuts him loose. But no drunken memory can compare to the reality of his jagged breaths, the weight of him on my tongue, the feel of his hands in my hair, and the jerk of his hips when he loses his grip on his control.

I was already turned on—from the dance floor, from the car, from his whispered promises and teasing touches —but this takes my arousal to a new level. And to be blindfolded while doing this? Every sound he makes is amplified. My nerve endings are buzzing.

I've never done anything like this, and I know it's because I could never do this with someone I didn't trust. There's a kind of vulnerability when I'm on my knees and sightless while his fingers thread through my hair. I'm at his mercy, and instead of being unsettled by it, I'm *moved* by it. Because I know he won't hurt me. Because I know I can trust him.

I draw him deeper, and his knees buckle slightly.

"Christ. Come here." He steps away from my mouth, and the next thing I know, Alec pulls me to my feet and the tie blocking my vision is gone. "I want inside you too much to finish like this." He cups my face in both hands and takes my mouth with his. "Do you want that?"

I want it so badly the question is almost laughable. "Condom?" I rasp.

"Yeah. I have protection." He kisses me again, his hands busy pushing the panties from my hips. My bra is next, peeled from my arms before he tosses it across the room.

I back toward the big bed and lower myself onto it while looking up at him.

He doesn't come with me. His nostrils flare as he looks me over and he shakes his head slowly. "Tell me this isn't a dream."

"Does it matter?" I ask, though I know what he means. We've been circling each other all these months, and he's kept his distance because that's what I asked for, but that never made the *want* go away.

"It does to me." He grabs a condom from his nightstand drawer and rolls it on.

"Why?"

He shoves his pants down and steps out of them. "Because I've already dreamed this a million times." He comes onto the bed, supporting his weight on his elbows and hovering over me. "But the dreams always fade in the morning. And I never want to forget this."

I bite my bottom lip. *Don't fall. Don't fall. Don't fall.*

I thread my fingers through his hair and pull his mouth to mine—kissing him to hide how much his words mean, arching my body into his to keep myself from melting.

He drags his mouth to my ear as he slides into me, his voice raspy as he whispers, "Perfect. Why do you have to be so fucking perfect?"

I draw my knees up, meeting him stroke for stroke because—God, I've wanted this too. Even if I've wished I didn't. Even when I knew I shouldn't. I've wanted to know if the flashes of heat and lust from my booze-soaked memories were real. If the connection between us was real.

Alec turns his mouth to my neck, scraping his teeth across my collarbone and the swell of my breasts. Then one hand finds its way between my legs, and his thumb finds and strokes that spot in perfect rhythm.

I'm still slick and swollen from before, and pleasure coils tight and fast in my core. I scrape my nails down his back. "I want you to come with me. I want to feel you."

He groans in my ear. "You're so close. I feel you. Jesus. I feel you." His thumb stills, and I want to cry out, but then he pushes down on my clit with perfect pressure and picks up his pace. Half wild, I feel him swell, see the surrender on his face as he closes his eyes.

Then I close mine and we fall. Together.

CHAPTER NINETEEN

SAVVY

I'm sleeping in a cloud, wrapped in Alec's strong arms. I know I need to wake up, but I wish I could stay here all day.

"Good morning," Alec murmurs, his lips brushing the top of my head.

I roll to my back, and he props himself up on one elbow, his gaze following the sheet as it slips down to my waist. "Morning." I stretch, reaching toward the headboard I gripped last night. My cheeks heat, but when Alec rolls onto me and kisses his way down my body, that heat finds its way to other places.

I groan when his mouth latches on to my breast. "You're going to make me late for my flight." I sigh. It's so tempting to just stay here. "I need to get back to my room to shower and pack up."

His tongue flicks over my pebbled nipple. "I'm just making sure you remember why you want to come back."

All the morning-after bliss drains out of me, and I sit up stiffly in bed. "Alec . . ." My heart is stumbling into a run. I want to spend more time with Alec, but I also don't want to hurt him. Which leaves . . . *telling him.*

Alec shifts, unfazed, and presses his thumb to my lips. "Don't say anything yet. Go get your shower while I make us some coffee, then I'll take you back to your hotel."

I swallow hard. I don't deserve his patience.

He rolls out of bed, and I can't help taking in his body—the way his muscles move as he reaches for his boxers, the little dimples at the base of his spine, and the soft sprinkling of hair on his thighs.

When he turns back to me, he catches me looking and winks. "Find me in the kitchen when you're done."

I bite my tongue to keep myself from inviting him to join me in the shower. If I do that, we may never leave this bedroom.

Alec's bathroom is something out of a luxury hotel. There's a steam shower with heated floors and marble counters. I don't let myself think too much about how much money it must take to even maintain a place like this. I make my shower quick, helping myself to his body wash.

After, I dry myself off with a fluffy white towel and give last night's dress the side-eye. Is it still a walk of shame if you showered?

I wiggle into my panties but can't bring myself to put

on the rest. I pull open dresser drawers until I find a pair of black joggers and a T-shirt. I'm swimming in the shirt, and I have to cuff the joggers several times at the ankle to keep from tripping over them, but it still beats walking into my hotel in last night's clothes.

I follow the smell of coffee to the kitchen and find Alec leaning against the enormous center island, steaming mug of coffee in one hand, phone in the other. He's in nothing but his boxers, and it's all too easy to imagine this life with him. Mornings sharing coffee, him scrolling through emails and oblivious to my gawking at his bare chest.

I cut the fantasy off at the knees.

Alec might not want anything to do with me once he knows the truth. Maybe when I tell him about Oliver, I could explain how it all happened in a way that doesn't mortify me. Maybe . . .

He must sense me staring, because he puts his phone on the counter behind him and looks me over, his nostrils flaring.

"I hope you don't mind that I borrowed some clothes."

"Not at all." He crooks a finger at me, and I wander forward, stepping between his legs. He sets his coffee down next to his phone and loops his arms around me, palming my ass. "I like the way my clothes look on you."

I smile. "They're soft."

"Let me kiss you."

I tip my face up to meet his lips with mine and melt like sugar on his tongue.

He angles my head to deepen the kiss and hardens against me. I moan into his mouth, tangling my fingers in his hair.

Alec hoists me up onto the counter. The granite is cool under my ass, even through the pants, a sharp contrast to the heat of his bare chest at my front. I wrap my legs around his waist to pull him closer and feel his smile against my mouth.

"I wanted to make you breakfast." His hand snakes up my shirt, and his thumb seeks out my nipple. "But that's going to have to wait."

In a fluid motion, he frees himself from my clinging limbs and peels the joggers and panties from my hips, dropping them onto the kitchen floor.

He dips his head between my legs. His mouth is hot and wet against my bare sex. He licks and sucks, kissing me like he's been starved for this. Starved for *me*.

I brace my palms on the counter and watch him from under heavy lids. He looks up and meets my eyes as he licks, and a shiver of pleasure shoots down my spine.

When he hooks my legs over his shoulders to hold me in place, I let my head fall back. I'm tender from last night, but I don't even care. The things he's doing with his mouth and tongue feel too good, and when he slides a finger inside me—

"Alec!" My body arches and clenches tight, pulsing and releasing in time with the waves of pleasure coursing through me.

He stays there, sweeping tender kisses against my inner thighs, as I come down.

When he straightens, his mouth is red and glistening. *From me.*

He grins. "I've been waiting to do that again since the first time I tasted you."

I hook my legs around his waist a second time and pull him forward. "You have something . . ." I sweep my thumb across his lips. "There."

He snags it in his teeth and pulls it into his mouth, sucking gently. "Change your flight. Stay the weekend."

"I have work."

"And a boss who's totally rooting for me." He winks.

I swallow hard. I've been a coward. I didn't want him knowing about my history with Oliver because I know how bad it sounds. I know what his father called me. *Your whore.*

I need to be brave. Alec deserves it, and if he still wants me to stay after I tell him the truth, I will. "How about you make me some breakfast and we talk about it."

His grin stretches across his face like he's a kid at Christmas. Guilt is a bag of sand on my chest. I know how he feels about his brother. When I tell him the truth, he might never smile that way at me again. When I tell him, he might never see me the same.

I take his face in both hands and kiss him deeply. Just in case this is the last time. Before I know it, my hand is on his chest, trailing down to his waistband.

He stops me with a hand on my wrist. "Breakfast. Talking. Remember?"

"You need me to take care of you." I want to. But I

also want to avoid the conversation we need to have. *Coward.*

"You know I do. But if waiting means I get you all weekend instead of all morning, I can handle it." He steps back and winks at me before he turns to the fridge.

I always get a weird sense of *déjà vu* when Alec winks at me. It has to be because of Oliver. I don't remember Oliver ever *winking*, but they are brothers, so of course one is bound to remind me of the other occasionally.

My heart is racing, but I know this is the right choice, and right alongside my panic, a tendril of hope blooms.

Alec pulls eggs from the fridge. "I have an appointment for a massage this afternoon, but if you stay, I'll have her work on both of us."

I laugh. "Another massage? I think I'm set for a while after the one you surprised me with at the hotel."

"What do you mean?" He frowns. "I didn't get you a massage."

"Remember? You called ahead, and . . ."

Alec's face is blank.

Oliver. Shit. I should've known that "anonymous gift" had Oliver written all over it. How did he know where I was staying?

"Oh." I clear my throat. "I just assumed it was from you. Maybe it was a gift from The Rage."

He grins. "I wouldn't be surprised. They know they'd be lucky to have you. They should treat you like a queen."

"I sure hope so," I say weakly. "How can I help?"

"You can wait in the family room," he says, messing

with the coffee pot now. "I'll bring you a fresh cup of coffee and get breakfast on."

Under normal circumstances, I'd like to stand here and watch him work, but I can't be still right now, so I roam toward the cozy room just off the kitchen. Cream couches with fluffy cushions are arranged in a U around the massive stone fireplace. Unlike the foyer, which made me feel uncomfortable in its grandiosity, this space is all about warmth and comfort. I wander around, looking at the artwork on the walls and the knickknacks on the sofa table and wondering which pieces Alec picked out and which are remnants of his mother's and grandmother's style.

I'm just done admiring a bronze sculpture of a dancing woman when my gaze snags on a photo perched on the sofa table.

My lungs stop working. I'm not sure my heart is beating.

I recognize everyone in that photo. All four of them. Alec, Rose, Cheryl, and the man Oliver had me con.

"Savvy, are you okay?"

I blink toward Alec. He's bare-chested and smiling, walking toward me with a cup of coffee.

"Who's this?" I'm breathless, but I try to swallow back my panic. I point to the picture. Maybe he's a family friend. Maybe it's not a genetic resemblance but one of those things that happens after you spend a lot of time with a person. "This man standing by your mom?"

He cocks his head to the side, like this is an odd question, and my heart sinks. "That's my dad. Why?"

Oh God. Oh God. Oh God. Because I know him. Because I stole from him.

That wink. That's why Alec's wink seemed so familiar to me. I've met his father.

Alec's father. *Oliver's father.*

"Savvy, what's wrong?"

He lied to me. I didn't know. I bite my bottom lip and shake my head. "You look like him." It's true. I can't believe I didn't see it before now. But I haven't thought much about Charles in eight years.

"That happens when someone is responsible for half your DNA." He winks, and my stomach turns sour. *Don't do that. Please.*

"Were you close to him?" I ask. Why am I still talking? I need to get out of here.

"Yeah. Mostly. I think we would've been closer as adults, but we never got the chance." He extends a mug toward me.

I take it, but there's no way I can drink what's inside. Not when the contents of my stomach are pure acid and already threatening to crawl up my throat. "When . . . when exactly did you say he died?"

He stares into his coffee, either remembering or doing mental calculations. I can't be sure. "It was eight years ago." He glances toward the picture. "He'd gone to his New York office, and—" There's nothing but pain on his face, but he clears his throat and shakes it away. "He was sick, and like with everything else, he was determined to go out on his own terms. Don't say anything about it in front of Mom. We don't talk about that day. I think she could've forgiven him for giving up, for choosing not to fight the cancer, but that same day he died, he had a woman in the apartment with him. Grief and betrayal make for terrible bed partners."

"A woman? Like, a friend?" The hope in my voice is impossible to miss, and I need to shut up and get out of here before I vomit all my secrets on the floor.

Alec sighs. "You know my father wasn't the most faithful man. My half-brother is the most obvious evidence of that. But when my mother got pregnant with me and my father moved back home, he promised he wouldn't stray. Then one day, Mom's getting a call from the staff at his New York office telling her they found him at his desk unresponsive. We took the first flight we could and went straight to the hospital." He stares into his coffee, seemingly lost in his memories. I'm grateful he's not looking at me. I'm terrified that if he did, the truth would be written all over my face. "He'd had a massive pulmonary embolism—a complication from lung cancer. He didn't stand a chance."

My breath catches. He knew. Somehow he knew it was the end for him. "I had no idea." The words slip out before I think better of them.

"How could you know? We don't really talk about it."

I frown. "Why not? Was the cancer a secret?"

He shakes his head. "It wasn't his death so much as the circumstances around it that are so troubling. Mom went back to his apartment after leaving the hospital, and she said some of my dad's things were missing." He huffs. "Whoever she was, she didn't just sleep with a married man. She stole from him. And she didn't even bother to show up to the funeral."

"Maybe he wasn't cheating. Maybe she was a friend or . . ." *Maybe this is just a terrible dream.*

Alec lifts his gaze to meet mine. "My father was a very private man. Even his best friends in Manhattan never saw the inside of that place. Do you really think he had young women up to his apartment because they were *friends* of his?"

"It's possible."

Alec sets his mug on the sofa table then takes mine to place next to his. He pulls me into his arms and kisses the top of my head. "I love that you're trying to make me feel better about this, but I've made my peace with all of it."

I close my eyes and breathe in his scent. I want to pretend my past wasn't my past. I want to strip it off like an unwanted sweater and leave it behind so I can stay here with Alec. But I can't. The truth doesn't work that way.

"So," he murmurs into my hair, "how can I convince you to stay the weekend?"

I swallow hard. I was ready to tell him about my relationship with Oliver, but I can't tell him about my involvement with his father. And it's not just cowardice this time. I stole from that man, and to this day, I don't know what was in the chest I emptied for Oliver.

"I can't," I whisper. "I need to go home."

The gentle rise and fall of his chest stills beneath my cheek. One beat. Two. He steps back. "I thought we were going to talk about it? Can you tell me what changed in the last five minutes?" He blinks toward the photograph then back to me.

Does he see it on my face? Does he suspect?

"I'm not my father, Savannah. I would *never* be unfaithful. Not to you. Not to anyone."

My heart turns hollow in my chest then crumples like tissue paper. "It's not that."

"Is it my family? I know they're a lot, and my mother —I'll deal with my mother."

"Alec, don't." I just want to run. Can he see it in my eyes? This terror? This guilt? "This isn't about your mother, either."

"Then what's this about?" he asks. "Is it the money?"

"Nah, brother. I'm pretty sure it's me."

Alec's gaze whips toward the kitchen, and I follow it.

Oliver Rhett is leaning against the counter, the façade of amusement twisting his lips a sharp contrast to the anger in his eyes.

Part Eight

EIGHT YEARS AGO

CHAPTER TWENTY

SAVVY

I've always admired the women at the gym who worked with the barbells. I assumed that they were born strong and that was why they could lift so much. Assumed that the things they did were out of reach for me.

But now I'm one of them, and I feel like someone's opened a door to a whole new world.

I'm not very strong, and the girls I've admired since I started at Crossport U have more plates on their barbells than I do on mine, but I'm completely addicted to how lifting feels. Oliver told me I was stronger than I thought, and he was right. It's only been a few weeks of this, and I know real changes will take time, but I feel stronger after every session. I thought learning to fight would be my favorite part—I won't deny that I get a thrill from punching and kicking the pads Oliver holds up for me—but it turns out that the weights make me feel like I can take on the world.

"How are your quads?" he asks, squeezing one of his own with a big hand. "Still sore from Tuesday? Because we can just do back and biceps if—"

"No. I'm fine." I shake my head. "Not too bad. Sorry if I whined about it."

He grins. "You didn't. You whine less than most of the fighters I've trained with. Never doubt yourself. You're an absolute badass." He leads me over to the squat rack and adjusts the barbell height for me before loading it up. "Did you finish the warmup I wrote for you?"

I nod, and he gestures for me to get in place under the barbell. "How many?" I ask.

"Eight here, and then we'll go up."

I knock out eight with no problem, focusing on my form with each part of the movement, bracing my core and using my whole foot to ground myself like he taught me. "That wasn't bad," I say, re-racking the barbell.

He chuckles. "That was a warmup set." He adds more weight then has me do another set of eight.

Before long, the sets are short and the weights are feeling really heavy. But Oliver slides another ten-pound plate onto each side anyway.

I eye the new weight skeptically. "I don't know."

"Two reps. Just one at a time."

"What if I can't stand it up?"

"Then you can bail."

I shake my head. I've seen people do it, but it scares the shit out of me. "I'm afraid I'll panic."

"Then I'll spot you."

I get the barbell on my shoulders and step away from the rack. Oliver steps up behind me, keeping his body close to mine and his arms extended under the bar.

"Take a breath," he murmurs in my ear, "and brace your core."

I nod, focus, brace, and squat. The way back up is harder but less terrifying than the descent, and Oliver's in my ear the whole time.

"That's it. Easy does it."

I re-rack the bar and spin to him with my biggest smile. I'm *floating*.

Without thinking, I throw my arms around his neck and squeal in delight. "I did it!"

His body tenses against mine, then relaxes, and he sighs into my hair. "Of course you did."

When I pull back, our gazes stay tangled for a long time. "Thank you," I finally say.

"Don't thank me yet," he says, grabbing a pair of dumbbells and handing them to me. "We're doing lunges next."

"Look who's here," a familiar voice says from the other side of the gym.

I spin around and see Chuck strolling toward us. *Shit.* I haven't seen him since the night he grabbed me outside The Naked Bean, and I was hoping I wouldn't have to. At least he's not drunk this time.

"What do you think you're doing with those

weights?" he asks. His lips twitch and he shifts his gaze to Oliver. "She getting a little soft for you? Bringing her to the gym to work it off?"

It's so ridiculous. Only a few weeks away from Chuck and I see so clearly now what I somehow missed when we were together. I was never big, and never had more than a few pounds to lose, so his jabs about me needing to diet were never really about my size. They were about control. Sometime early on he realized I was insecure about my body, realized that my past made me hyper-fixate on fear of food and weight gain, and he used it to control me.

Oliver's gray eyes are harder than steel. "Nah, Chuck. 'Cause real men don't need to make their women as small as possible. Don't need to make them feel small, either."

"Whatever you need to tell yourself." Chuck coughs out a laugh. "Real men. Do real men hide from the ring too?"

I frown and look at Oliver. What does Chuck mean by that?

"You don't want me to accept your invitation, man," Oliver says. "You know you'd lose. It's not even a fair fight."

Chuck shrugs. "Then try me."

I look back and forth between them. Chuck wants Oliver to fight him. "No." I shake my head. "Don't do that."

"I don't have anything to prove," Oliver says, his gaze still locked with Chuck's.

"Nah. It's cool," Chuck says. "I'm sure you have your

reasons. Not like you have any secrets you need me to keep." He winks and backs away before finally looking at me again. "Don't forget your cardio, Pancakes."

OLIVER

I fucking hate Chuck. He's cruel and small-minded and despicable.

"I'm embarrassed I ever thought he loved me," Savvy says on our walk home. "God, why didn't I see him for who he was when it's so obvious now?"

"Because he made you question your own worth."

She makes a sour face. "But how stupid was I to let him?"

"With my sister, it was street smarts," I say. "Chuck would mock her for not being street smart. It hurt because she was afraid it was true. Her parents coddled her, so when he told her she knew nothing about the real world or said that she had no street smarts or that no one would ever want to hire a stupid bitch like her, she didn't think it was abuse. She thought he was stating facts."

Generally, I try not to waste my energy thinking about small people, but I hate that once, Savvy was his. I hate that he got to touch her and that he got to hold her. But mostly I hate that he made her feel insecure about her body.

I hate him, and I hate that he's the only one who knows something that could make *Savvy* hate *me.* His threat tonight was clear. Accept the invitation to fight him or he'll tell Savvy the truth.

I don't want to fight him—not only because I don't feel the need to fight anymore, but because I don't trust him to fight fair. I wouldn't put it past him to sneak in some brass knuckles or some shit.

"So you said you needed to talk to me about this weekend?" Savvy asks.

I shake myself free of my thoughts and pull the door for my building, holding it for her. "I'm sorry. What?"

She cocks her head to the side and smiles. Fuck, that smile lights up the whole city. I am so gone for this girl. "This weekend? New York? I assume Mr. Silver Fox will be in town?"

I grunt. I hate when she calls him that. "Yeah. Friday and maybe Saturday, depending on how it goes. We'll be staying in the city Friday night."

"I have a class Friday afternoon, but I could skip it. I haven't missed any yet."

I want her to skip class to spend a weekend away with me for real, not head to the city to deal with this bullshit. But I need to stay focused. I need to remember why I got involved with Savvy to begin with.

I jab the button for the elevator. "Email your professor Friday morning and let her know you're not feeling well."

"Oliver." She props her hands on her hips and glares.

"What?"

"You turn into a dick every time we discuss this *job* you're having me do for you."

"Nah. I'm always a dick." The doors slide open, and I wave her inside. "Any other impression you got is just a figment of your vivid imagination."

"You are so full of it," she mutters.

I cock a brow. "What's *Arturo* up to these days?"

She snorts. "You wish you knew." Then the elevator doors open to my floor and she's laughing and pushing her way into my loft, and I can't be pissy anymore. Even after Chuck's threats. Even knowing what tomorrow will bring.

CHAPTER TWENTY-ONE

OLIVER

I didn't like this last time, but I like it even less this time. Which just proves that I'm getting too attached, and I have no fucking business doing that.

"Another new panty set?" she calls from the bathroom, a flirty lilt to her voice.

I close my eyes, imagining her in the creamy white bra and panties my sister picked out. "Yeah." The word comes out scratchy, and I have to clear my throat. "My shopper said you can't wear black under this dress."

Savvy opens the bathroom door and sticks her head out. "You do know I actually own a variety of underwear, don't you?" She has a towel wrapped around her, and I take in her bare shoulders like an addict searching for even the smallest hit. I've barely let myself be around her in the last week because the temptation is too strong. To touch. To taste. To turn this arrangement of ours into something else altogether.

I could tell her the truth—that I like buying her things. That I like the idea of something she got from me being with her for a while after this is all over. That this is the only way I can give her gifts without her reading more into it than I can give.

But of course I have no intention of telling her any of that. "She's already shopping, so it's more efficient to have her grab anything you might need."

She grins. "I just think it's hilarious that you have a personal shopper."

And Rose would think it was hilarious if she knew I was calling her that, but telling Savvy that my sister is really the one doing the shopping would invite too many questions I don't want to answer. I like the way Savvy looks at me, and I'm not prepared to change that by telling her about my screwed-up family life.

Savvy disappears behind the door again and clicks it closed. I hate that fucking door between us. I *need* that fucking door between us.

I should've gotten us two rooms tonight, but I didn't. Because I'm a masochist? Probably. Or because I know I'm going to want her close after exposing her to him again? That too.

There are two beds, and we share my place every night, so this shouldn't be so different. Only it seems completely different. I'll be able to hear the sounds she makes in her sleep, and having the scent of her in my nose is bound to inspire some interesting dreams.

"So?"

I snap my head up to see Savvy in a formfitting white dress with a slit up the side of her thigh. My gut clenches.

I didn't even hear her come out of the bathroom, which is a shame because I could've used a moment to prepare myself. I can't get air into my lungs.

She cocks her head to the side. "Cat got your tongue?"

"He doesn't even deserve to look at you." The words are out before I realize I've said them out loud, and she blinks, some of the sass slipping from her expression.

"Are you ready to tell me what the end game is here?"

I swallow and blow out a breath. "You already know."

"Right. He has something of yours and you want it back. And him watching me drink cocktails will help how?"

"Slowly. Just like it's supposed to." I tilt my head toward the door. "Ready?"

Something flashes in her eyes. Confusion? Hurt? But she lifts her chin, snatches her handbag off the dresser, and heads for the door.

I follow her down the hall and into a waiting elevator that feels way too small. She won't look at me, but she scoots closer as the floors tick down, the back of her hand brushing my thigh. Is she nervous, or is this about torturing me?

When the doors slide open, she moves to step out, but I grab her hand to stop her. She doesn't face me, but she waits and lets the doors slide closed again.

"He won't touch you." My voice is serrated. Gravelly. "I wouldn't do this if I wasn't sure of that, but I need you to act naturally, and the more you know, the harder that will be. I can't afford for him to be even a little suspicious."

The elevator ascends.

Slowly, she turns and looks up at me through dark lashes. "Why do you care who touches me when you won't?"

The elevator dings softly as it passes each floor, and the air between us draws tighter and tighter with every second. I can't bring myself to lie. To tell her I don't care.

The doors slide open, and the woman waiting on the other side steps back at the sight of us. "Oh," she says. "Going down?"

I hold Savvy's gaze for a beat before she nods imperceptibly.

She turns to the woman and greets her with a smile. "Yep!"

"Do you two have special plans tonight?" the woman asks, stepping in to join us.

Savvy cuts her eyes to me then back to the woman. "Not so special."

"Well, you're certainly a lovely looking couple. I'm sure you'll have a good time no matter what's in store."

"For sure," Savvy says.

This time when the elevator doors open, she strides out before I have a chance to stop her. I expect her to wait for me in the lobby, but she keeps going right out the front doors.

"Oh," the woman squeaks again. "You better go catch up."

"We're not together." I don't know why I tell her. It doesn't matter what she thinks. Maybe I'm trying to convince myself.

The woman pats my arm gently. "Oh, honey. I saw the way you two were looking at each other. It's only a matter of time."

SAVVY

Oliver is the most maddening man I've ever met in my life.

I swear I can feel his gaze burning me from all the way across the street, but I refuse to look over my shoulder to check.

The host greets me at the front of the restaurant, and I motion toward the bar and stride past him. This time I don't sit at the end. This time I take Mr. Silver Fox's seat from last time and no one stops me. If he really is such a creature of habit, he probably takes the same spot every time.

"Good evening," the bartender says. "Would you like the wine list?"

"Just a vodka martini, please. Up. With extra olives."

"My pleasure."

While he busies himself making my drink, my phone buzzes. I pull it from my purse.

Oliver: Wrong seat. Move down. He's a creature of habit and you'll throw him off.

I darken the screen and slide it back into my purse, ignoring Oliver's instructions and taking the martini from the bartender. I don't understand what this is all about, but if I'm going to do it, I'm going to do it my way.

"Good evening, sir," the bartender says to someone behind me. "My apologies. We didn't know you were in town, or we would've saved your seat." He nervously looks back and forth between me and the person behind me.

I glance over my shoulder and give Mr. Silver Fox my best innocent smile. "Is this your seat?"

He pulls out the stool next to me and slides onto it. "Don't be silly. I can sit anywhere."

From the corner of my eye, I see the bartender visibly sag.

Mr. Silver Fox looks me over, pleased. "I wasn't sure I'd see you again. Do you live around here?"

I bite into an olive then lick the brine from my lips. "I'm in town visiting a friend."

"And yet here you are, drinking alone again. Is he too busy for you?"

"She." I look up at him through my lashes. "She's with her boyfriend tonight, and I don't mind drinking alone from time to time."

He extends a hand. "I'm Charles."

"Savannah Downing," I say, and his eyes light up. "It's

nice to meet you." I take his hand, ready to have every sixth sense in my body stand at alert and tell me he's a creep. But it doesn't. I'm getting nothing but *decent human* vibes from this guy.

"Any relation to the Downings' Department Stores?"

I force a laugh. "Not many people remember those days, but they were my grandfather's stores." *What are you up to, Oliver?*

"It's a shame, what happened to your grandfather. He was a good businessman and a better man. Had he lived to manage the store's shift into an online world, I believe his company would've flourished."

But he didn't live. And my father ran the business into the ground. "Did you know my grandfather?"

Charles shakes his head. "No, no. Nothing like that. I'm just a businessman who appreciates those who have a natural talent for it. I studied his business model back when I was in college."

The bartender slides a bourbon in front of Charles and quickly steps away, obviously trying to give us privacy.

"What about you?" I ask. "Do you live around here?"

"I have a place close by," he says.

A place. Interesting how he chooses his words. He doesn't indicate that it's a second home or that he doesn't live there full-time. He makes no effort to impress me with his obvious wealth. Then again, between the way Oliver has me dressed and Charles's impression of the Downing family empire, he doesn't have any reason to believe I don't possess wealth at some level, even if it's not at his.

"I love the city," I say dreamily, because it's true. "I came here often with my grandmother when I was a child."

"So not all that long ago," he says, winking.

I throw my head back and laugh. "Oh, is this where you tell me you're *so* much older than me?"

He settles into the high-backed stool and sips his bourbon. "Well, it's true."

I look him over. I don't know how old he is, but he wears his years well. "I'm not sure that kind of thing matters much."

Something in his expression goes guarded, and I realize I've pushed too much, too soon. This is why Oliver wanted me to take it so slow. This is a guy who's used to people trying to get whatever they can from him. Or maybe this isn't supposed to be about sexual attraction at all.

I'd know how to play this if Oliver would tell me *something.*

"I've always enjoyed talking to those who are older. The truth is," I say, pivoting, "I'm in my third year of college, and I'm still not sure what I want to do with myself. My father will be the first to tell you I have a lot of growing up to do, but it was my grandmother who always helped me find my way. I miss having that."

"What are your passions?"

I don't have to fake the sadness I'm sure comes into my expression with that question. "I don't even know.

I've spent my whole life being told who I'm supposed to be. Before I can find anything so intense as a passion, I need to figure out who I really am."

"As a father myself, I can tell you we drive our children hard because we love them," he says, swirling his drink in its glass. "And sometimes the pressure we put on them is less about trying to mold them into who we want them to be and more about wanting to make sure they have security once we're gone."

I wish I could believe that were true for my father, but I know better. Dad never cared about anything other than himself and his bank account. "That's a lovely way to look at it."

"I'd like to think I've gained a small amount of wisdom in my old age." He turns away and coughs into his elbow. "Tell me about yourself, Savannah."

With a smile, I do, and we talk as I make my way through my martini one sip at a time. Charles is charming and a great conversationalist. We talk about Crossport U and our favorite parts of the city. He tells me about his favorite memories from when his children were small—"before they realized that it wasn't cool to hang with Dad"—and I tell him about my gram and my summers in Alabama. Before I know it, an hour has passed.

"Oh, goodness. I need to go." I wave to the bartender. "Sorry. I'll cash out."

Charles shakes his head. "I'll take care of it." He pulls a business card and pen from his pocket. He scribbles something at the bottom before sliding it along to bar to me. "My contact information is on there. If you need anything while you're in the city, reach out."

I study him for a beat before tearing my gaze away. This isn't a man who is looking for a hot young thing to date, but I'm not sure what his end game is. He comes across as nothing but kind. "I really appreciate this."

"That includes a job," he says. "Should you decide you need an excuse to stay in the city while you figure out where your passions lie."

I tuck his card in my purse. "What kind of job?"

"One of my companies is always searching for sales reps, if working with people is in your wheelhouse. If not, you could start in admin."

I want to laugh and ask him how many companies he has, but I swallow back my amusement and the question, since I, too, am supposed to be wealthy. "I'll consider it."

CHAPTER TWENTY-TWO

SAVVY

"That man isn't interested in me, so are you going to tell me what your end game is here or not?"

We're back in the hotel room and Oliver is in a worse mood than he was before I met with Charles, if that's possible.

Sighing, he strips off his shirt and tosses it over the back of the chair. "I wasn't planning on it yet, no."

"What the fuck, Oliver?" I catch my gaze slipping to his broad chest and force it back up to his face, crossing my arms to remind myself I'm mad at him.

"I already told you. He reads people better than anyone I've ever met. The less you know, the more natural your reactions will be."

"Is he your dad? Is that why you're being so cloak and dagger about this?"

Oliver scoffs. "No. The only guy Charles is a *dad* to is a spoiled prick in L.A."

I dig Charles's business card from my pocket and toss it on the bed. The card reads, *Coast to Coast Equities and Investments*, and has a website and email address on it. At the bottom, in neat block print, he wrote *Charles* and a phone number in black pen. "Well, tonight he offered me a job and gave me his personal number to call if I ever 'need anything.'"

Oliver snatches the card up and grins. "Well done. I thought it would take at least two more meetings." He meets my gaze and taps the card. "You did it."

"That's what this was about? You getting his *phone* number?"

"No. It was about *you* getting it. Now we can intentionally not use it for a couple of weeks, and then next time he's back in the city, you'll call and tell him you think your ex is following you. He'll invite you over and let you stay until you feel safe."

"Why would he do that? He doesn't even know me."

"Because he's searching for a wife for his son."

"The spoiled prick?"

He nods and meets my eyes. "And you're the perfect goddamned candidate, Savvy. You're smart, sexy as hell, and have the name he wants for his spoiled-ass progeny."

"That's ridiculous. First of all, my family is broke as—"

"Doesn't matter."

Easy for him to say. "Second of all, how could you have known he'd be interested in marrying me off to his son just from looking at me?"

"Like I said, he's predictable. And I was right. If he gave you his card, he's already made his choice. He'll invite the fox into the henhouse, and while you're there, you'll get back what's mine."

My skin goes cold, and I sink onto the edge of the bed. "You want me to steal from him." Oliver isn't saying anything he hasn't already, but suddenly, what he's asking me to do feels very different.

"No. I want you to get back something that belongs to me." He sighs and softens his tone. "I've been telling you that since the beginning."

But that was before I met the guy. "He's not an awful man, Oliver. And I get the impression he has more money than God. Why would he steal from you?"

His expression cools. "You only think he's decent because you don't really know him. You're right about the money part, but this isn't about money. Again, the less you know, the better."

I throw up my hands. "That again? So, let me guess—I'm going to go in there and use my Spidey-Sense to figure out what I'm supposed to take from him and where it is? Or should I just take anything shiny that will fit in my purse?"

"Everything I want is in a decorative chest on his guestroom dresser. No Spidey-Sense required."

"A fucking treasure chest, then? Am I a pirate now? Sorry, I left my eye patch back home."

"You're hilarious."

"And you're crazy. I can't steal a *chest.* As if no one's going to notice me lugging that out of there?"

He folds his arms, and his pecs swell above them. "You'll take the contents and leave the chest. Everything in it will fit in that big purse of yours, and there's a good chance he'll never even realize anything's missing."

I frown. "I've never stolen a thing in my life. Maybe I could just ask him for it. If you tell me how he ended up with something of yours, I could explain it to him and convince him to give it back."

He cups my chin and tilts my face up until I'm looking at him. "I love that you believe you can use reason to get people to do the right thing." His gaze drops to my mouth, and my heart stumbles into a run.

He drops his hand and turns to the bathroom. "Enjoy the room tonight. Order room service, whatever you want. I'll be back late." He shuts the door, and the next thing I hear is the spray of the shower.

His phone buzzes on the bedside table, and I look at it without thinking. A preview of a text from someone named Peony pops up on the lock screen.

Are we still on for nine? I need to get . . .

Who's Peony? And what does she need to get?

I'm tempted to guess his passcode so I can read the rest of the message, but if he caught me, he'd never let me live it down. I collapse back on the bed. Leave it to me to fall for a guy who is so emotionally unavailable.

I stare at the ceiling until he emerges from the shower in nothing but a low-slung white towel. Then I only *try* to keep my eyes on the ceiling but keep watching him move around the room to gather his clothes.

He has a tan line at his hipbones. Does he spend his summer poolside or working shirtless in the sun? Or is that tan all from his morning runs?

Little drops of water cling to his muscles as if they're as obsessed with them as I am.

When he grabs his phone, I don't even pretend I'm not staring. "You got a message from Peony while you were in the shower."

He glances at me then back to the phone. "I see that."

He scans the screen and chuckles to himself before typing out a reply.

"Who is she?" I ask, because clearly subtlety isn't my forte.

"Does it matter?"

I push up onto my elbows and glare at him. "You think I don't see the way you look at me? You think I don't feel this chemistry between us?" I hop off the bed and rake my gaze over him. I'm so tempted to tear away that stupid towel. "It matters because I want to know why you're meeting Peony instead of staying in this room with me and taking what you already know I'd offer."

"And then what?" he asks. His jaw is hard but his gaze dips to my breasts, where they're nearly spilling out of my dress.

"Then we fucking *enjoy* each other, Oliver." Digging deep for a little more bravery, I slide a hand behind his neck and pull his mouth down to mine.

He's still at first, his lips warm against mine and his body hard, his wet skin dampening my dress. I suck his bottom lip between my teeth, and he releases a soft grunt and tilts his head, taking control of the kiss. Taking my mouth. My lips. My breath.

He grips my hips roughly, and I press closer. I want every inch of him pressed against me. I want this on the bed, his hips aligned with mine. I crave the feel of his weight pressing me into the mattress.

When he tears his mouth away, I hold his gaze. We're both breathing heavily.

"Stay," I whisper, toying with the hair at the base of his skull. "Be with me."

He blinks, his eyes going guarded. "You can't fix me, Savannah. I'm not fixable."

I feel like I've been slapped. "I'm not trying to *fix* you."

"Aren't you? Isn't that what all this is about? The nights you rush home to make me dinner, the heart-to-hearts you always want to have over coffee?" He releases my hips and steps back. "You want me to be like a hero in your fucking books, and I'm not. I've told you from the beginning that I'm not."

The next night, I find Julie in her boyfriend's basement doing shots. I take the seat next to her, pour one for myself, and throw it back.

Oliver and I stayed in Manhattan last night, but he

left to meet Peony and didn't get back until after one in the morning. At that point, he collapsed onto the empty bed and quickly fell asleep. We were both sullen and quiet on the drive back to Crossport.

I refill my shot glass.

"Whoa! What's gotten into you?" Julie asks.

What's wrong? Well, last night, Oliver kissed me like he'd found salvation and then left to meet another woman. This morning, he acted like nothing had changed between us.

Fine. Whatever.

But what's so great about *Peony*? Why isn't he worried that *she'll* think he's some sort of hero?

"I hate men today," I mutter. "Or I *wish* I hated them."

Julie chuckles. "Well, I hate them most days, so good for you." She nudges me playfully with her elbow. "Oliver in the doghouse or something?"

"Do you know if Oliver is dating someone? Or if he has an ex he was serious about?"

"He's known for being a no-strings kind of guy." She wrinkles her brow then spins around to face the other side of the room, where her boyfriend, Travis, and his buddy are playing the latest shoot-'em-up game. "Has Oliver ever had a serious girlfriend?"

Travis tears his gaze off the screen to look at his girlfriend for a beat before returning his attention to the game. "You mean Oliver Rhett?"

"No, Oliver Twist. Of course I mean Rhett. How many Olivers do you know?"

"He was dating that one girl," the guy beside him says without pulling his gaze off the screen. "You know, the little thing who was in all the musicals. She was crying one night over him. Apparently he had an ex in undergrad who screwed him over, and this girl was asking everyone for any information they had. Was trying to get any details she could because she wanted to track her down and go all god of wrath."

Travis frowns and shakes his head. "Damn."

"Not ringing a bell," Julie says.

"Blue eyes, tiny voice, big tits?" her boyfriend's buddy offers.

"Oh, yeah," Travis says. "Her name was Emily or something."

"You're both pigs," Julie says. "I hope you know that."

Her boyfriend winks at her. "Love you too."

She fights a smile as she spins back around on her stool. "So, Emily. Do we hate Emily?"

"Do you know a *Peony*?" I ask. "She was texting him, and I think he met up with her."

"What the fuck kind of name is that?" She spins back to the boys. "Know a Peony?"

"Woman, do I look like I have time to keep tabs on Rhett's romantic life?" Travis asks.

"Nah," his buddy says. "I remember Rhett answering a call from a Peony once. He had to leave class early to go get her or something."

"Does she go to school here?" Julie asks.

"No idea," Travis's buddy says.

Horrible screaming and rapid gunfire noises come

from the TV, and Travis tosses his remote. "Dammit, now I'm dead."

"Aww," Julie says with zero actual sympathy or remorse in her voice. "I'm so sorry I interrupted your game."

He lazily unfolds from the couch then saunters over to his girlfriend. "Why are you so interested in Oliver Rhett's former girlfriends all of the sudden?" he asks, sliding his hands around her hips. "Should I be worried?"

She laughs. "Savvy would knock my teeth out before letting me touch him, so I'm pretty sure you're good."

"What?" I squeak. "I would not."

She buries her face in Travis's chest, but it only muffles her laughter. "Whatever you need to tell yourself, girl."

I shake my head, but a not-so-little part of me knows she's right. I like Oliver—more than like him. I *want* him. He might not be mine in any official way, but the idea of him with another woman grates.

Part Nine

PRESENT

CHAPTER TWENTY-THREE

SAVVY

Oliver has my panties in his hand, the lace hanging between two fingers. "I think these are yours."

I want to close my eyes at the sound of that voice, to revel in the memories it sends washing over me. Like the finest melted chocolate—dark, delicious, and so damn tempting.

Dangerous, the rational part of my mind warns.

I stride into the kitchen and snatch them away. There are too many words clogging my throat and none can make their way out. *What are you playing at? How dare you? Why did you make me steal from your own* father?

And the worst—*Why does looking at you still hurt so much?*

Fuck Oliver. I owe him nothing. But Alec . . .

I spin around and Alec is exactly where I left him, his gaze bouncing between me and his brother. Slowly, he follows me into the kitchen and wraps one arm around my waist. I bow my head, unable to look either brother in the eye.

"Oliver," Alec says, "I thought you were in Monaco." He's holding me tightly, as if it wasn't his brother who just surprised us but a crazed, irrational criminal.

"I came back early. Our baby sister wants me at her wedding, and I couldn't let her down."

"Well, as you can see, Rose isn't here," Alec says. "And I don't know what you think you have to do with me and Savvy, but you can show yourself out."

Oliver smiles—wide and devious. "She didn't tell you?"

Alec sneers. "Tell me *what*?"

"Alec," I plead. I don't want to have this conversation. Not right now. Not like this. "Let me explain."

"Savannah and I lived together while I was finishing up my MBA." Oliver folds his arms. "I never thought I'd see her again until she showed up at the door with nothing but a trench coat on. Not much takes me by surprise, but *that* was a reunion I hadn't expected."

"You make it sound like something happened between us," I snap.

"Didn't it?" He looks me over slowly, and there's no way Alec misses the carnal knowledge in that gaze. "I remember a *lot* happening between us."

Alec drops his arm from around my waist and sidesteps—away from me. His gaze ping-pongs between me and Oliver.

"Alec," I whisper, shaking my head. "I haven't touched him since college. That day I showed up here looking for *you*, and—"

"It's true," Oliver says, and somehow his corroboration feels more damning than his implication did.

I force myself to meet his eyes so I can silently beg him to shut up. If Alec is going to know the truth, I want him to hear it from me. Oliver's gray eyes are hard and angry, fixated on his brother. "You're an ass," I hiss.

"What does he mean, Savvy?" Alec asks softly.

Oliver exaggerates a cringe. "Sorry. I was supposed to be your dirty little secret, wasn't I?"

"You know Oliver," Alec says, the words stilted like he doesn't quite understand them. As if he can't wrap his mind around how they could be true. "How?"

"Apparently in the same way she knows you," Oliver says, then gestures to the panties in my fist. His face, already twisted in cruelty, turns cold, and he blinks, his attention fixed on my hand.

No. On my ring. *Alec's ring.*

"Get out of my house," Alec says.

"It appears congratulations are in order." Oliver's gaze snaps back to mine. "You never told me the news when we chatted last week. If I'd known, I would've thrown in some extra services with the massage I got you yesterday."

He's making it sound like we've been *in touch.* Like

we've been messing around. I knew Oliver could be cruel, but I never thought that cruelty would extend to me.

Alec strides forward, going toe to toe with his brother. "You're not welcome here."

Oliver smirks. "It's Rose's house as much as it's yours, and she asked me to come over."

"She's not here," Alec says, face stony. "So you can leave."

Oliver's gaze returns to my hand again. To the ring. "I'll do that." He spins on his heel and strides from the kitchen toward the foyer. "Hit me up if you want to catch up before you leave town, Savvy. I'm staying at the Four Seasons, room 1204."

"Fuck off," I whisper.

When he slams the front door, the whole house shakes.

I can barely breathe. "Alec . . ."

He's silent for so long that I have to wonder if he's in shock or if this is all just some terrible hallucination. Only, he's not just silent. There's a chill in the air. An iciness that rolls off him. And he won't meet my eyes.

I step toward him. I have to explain. "It was a long time ago. I knew Oliver in college. When I met you, I didn't know you were his brother."

"But you figured it out," Alec says, voice cold. "Obviously you figured it out before today."

"A couple months after Vegas," I say softly.

Alec meets my gaze, and the hurt in his eyes is enough to cut me down. "That's why you called it off with me. Why you didn't want to try to make this work. Because of *him*."

I bow my head and stare at the floor.

"Instead of *telling me* that you know my half-brother, you kept it a secret. Hid it from me. You *asked questions* about him as if you'd never heard of him before."

"I couldn't tell you." I press my hand to my chest. "I didn't want you to know the truth."

"That's the problem, isn't it? You never want me to know shit about you. But he knows. Obviously you were okay with letting Oliver past those walls of yours."

I could almost laugh at the irony. How many times did Oliver and I fight about *his* walls? About not letting *me* in? And now Alec's accusing me of the same. "I'm so sorry. I didn't know how to tell you."

"Rose told me you were the one who made her realize she should invite Oliver to the wedding." He shakes his head. "Well done. Looks like you got the reunion you were hoping for."

"I never . . ." All those questions I asked at dinner. I was digging for information, and it made Rose rethink her decision about Oliver and the wedding. "It's not like that."

He scrubs his hands over his face. "Please spare me the lies."

"I'm not lying. This has been killing me. My history with Oliver is the reason I knew I had to end things with you before they really started."

"If you wanted to tell me, nothing was stopping you.

Don't insult me by pretending you didn't choose to keep this secret."

I steady myself on the kitchen table then sink into a chair. "It *was* a choice," I whisper, staring at my hands in my lap. "But it was a choice I made because I'm embarrassed by my past. By my mistakes."

My gaze drifts back to the picture in the family room. *His father. I tricked and stole from his father.*

Alec paces the length of the kitchen island and runs his hands through his hair. "So you chose to embarrass me instead."

"You don't understand. I had . . ." I swallow hard, shame still bearing down on me. "My brother placed a bet on a fight. A bet he couldn't cover because it was supposed to be a sure thing. Oliver bailed him out. We had a deal."

"What kind of deal?"

I lick my lips. "I moved in with him. I . . ." *I didn't know he was your father. I'm so sorry.*

"You want me to believe you just moved in with him? That living in his place was his price?" He clenches his jaw. "I know my brother. He doesn't do anything out of the kindness of his heart. If he wanted you, he had you."

I bite my bottom lip. "It wasn't like that."

His brows shoot up. "Wasn't it? Look me in the eye and tell me you never fucked him."

I drop my head. Memories flash through my mind. "When Oliver and I got physical—"

"No. Just stop. I don't want to know any of this.

You've known how I feel about Oliver from the night we met, and you never—"

"I knew you had a brother you hated, but I didn't know it was Oliver. I didn't know that until I flew across the country to surprise you and he answered the door."

He stops pacing and turns to stare at me. "When?"

"Not long after Vegas."

"You've known for over *two years*?"

"Don't you see? That was why I couldn't date you. That was why I couldn't let our relationship go beyond friendship."

"Is that what you've been telling yourself?"

Hot tears roll down my cheeks. As if each one is filled with the burn of my shame. "My past with Oliver is complicated."

He huffs out a dry laugh, but there's no humor in it, and it feels like a smack in my face. "No. It seems pretty simple."

"Please don't look at me like that," I beg. "Please just try to understand. I never wanted to hurt you."

"I would've given you anything, and you couldn't even give me the truth."

"I'm sorry." I pull off the ring and offer it to him in an extended palm.

He stares at it like it he finds it offensive. "Does he know this thing between us . . . does he know it's fake?"

I shake my head, causing more tears to spill down my cheeks. "No. The girls back home are the only ones who know."

He's quiet for a long time, staring at the ring. The

grandfather clock in the corner ticks through the seconds ominously until he finally speaks. "If you ever cared about me at all, you'll keep it that way. At least until after the wedding. I think I've been embarrassed enough."

I slide the ring back onto my finger, but this time it doesn't feel like a fun game. It feels like a shackle, tethering me to a too-heavy lie. "I should get back to my hotel so I can catch my plane."

He nods sharply, avoiding my eyes. "I'll let my driver know."

I stand to go upstairs and pull on my clothes but stop before I leave the kitchen. "I'm sorry, Alec."

"Not as sorry as I am."

CHAPTER TWENTY-FOUR

SAVVY

I knock on Oliver's door so hard my knuckles hurt.

I couldn't bring myself to ask Alec's driver to take me to Oliver, so I had him take me to my hotel, where I changed into my travel clothes and checked out before taking an Uber to Oliver.

When he opens the door, I fold my arms and glare. "What the fuck was that?"

He looks me over, no hint of that cocky smirk on his face. When his gaze lands on the ring again, he scowls and turns into the room, leaving the door open behind him. "Not sure what you mean."

I follow him inside and slam the door behind me. "You couldn't talk to me first? You had to rub it in his face? Make it sound like we've had something recently?

Make it so I couldn't even tell him about our relationship on my terms?"

"Relationship?" he says, and I flinch, regretting the word. "Is that what it was?"

My eyes fill with hot tears. "You're right. It wasn't anything like that. You used me. You *hurt* me."

For a split second, something softens in his face. Or maybe it's just my imagination, because I blink and his old, cocksure expression is back. "Want a drink?" he asks, hoisting a bottle of bourbon in the air.

"It's not even nine a.m."

He shrugs and uncaps the bottle, pouring two fingers into a glass. "Suit yourself."

"What are you *doing*?" I ask, my voice breaking. This is not the way I wanted Alec to find out, and I want to scream at Oliver for it, but deep down I know this mess is my fault. I'm the coward who couldn't own up to the truth.

"What do you mean what am I doing?" He takes a sip of his drink and looks me over slowly before stepping forward. He's so close that the scent of him fills my head and brings a hundred memories to the surface. "You show up at my sister's door. I see you for the first time in years . . ."

"And whose fault is that?"

He shakes his head. "I don't know, Savvy. Mine? Yours? Or maybe we should blame our parents, since they're the ones who fucked us up."

"*My fault*? Seriously? How do you figure, Oliver?"

His eyes go hard. "You left. You fucking *ran*."

"You made me a thief."

He laughs. "Made you? Is that how you remember this?"

"You didn't tell me he was your *father*. You didn't tell me I was stealing from your *family*."

"No. What I told you was that I'd changed my mind. I told you *not to do it* because I didn't want you involved anymore. But you did it anyway. On your own. So don't give me that *I made you* bullshit."

"What was in there? What was it that you needed so badly that you were willing to get me to steal it from your family? Surely not money. You've always had more of that than you needed."

"It doesn't matter anymore."

"Do you still have it? Have you considered giving it back to Alec's mom? The man's *wife*?"

His nostrils flare. "I would sooner die than let that bitch lay a finger on those things."

"Charles was your *father*! You lied to my face when I asked you."

"I never lied. You asked if he was my *dad*. Charles was never a *dad* to me. He was my sperm donor and my warden, and he used what he had of mine to control me."

Tears spill down my cheeks. He lied. I trusted him, and he *lied*. "And you never told me any of that. Never let me in."

"I've thought about you every day since you walked out my door. When you showed up on his doorstep, I wanted to believe whatever was happening between you two had something to do with me. Naïve of me, I realize, since you came all this way to make sure I wouldn't be ruining it for you."

I lose the beat at that admission, my steps stuttering at the unexpectedness of it. Oliver takes what he wants, but he rarely deigns to admit he wants it, and he certainly never admits to wanting something he can't have. "You just couldn't stand to lose what you bought and paid for."

Something flashes in his eyes. Hurt? Betrayal? Anger? "Is that what you think of me? After everything?"

It's what I *want* to think of him. What I *need* to think of him. That lie is the only thing that held me together after everything else around me fell apart.

"Was I supposed to act like seeing you didn't fuck me up?" he asks.

"That was over two years ago. It must've been really eating you up if it took you this long to say anything."

"I was trying to let you go," he growls. "To let you live your life."

"Well, good fucking job at that. You walked into that house this morning and dropped a bomb, and you knew it."

"I walked into that house and saw you half-naked, your fucking panties on the floor, and him looking at you like you were *his*. Apologies if my reaction was inconvenient for you."

I can't decide if I want to smack him or curl into his chest and beg him to hold me. Can't decide if I hate him or need him. "You didn't have to hurt Alec. Not like that."

"Was I supposed to be okay with my brother

touching you?" His gaze drops to my ring. "And now I'm supposed to be okay with you marrying him? Having his babies?"

I flinch at that word. *Babies.* For months after Oliver moved away, I wondered if things might've been different for both of us if I'd been pregnant. "I would've known he was your brother if you ever told me," I say, my voice softer now. "But you didn't. You didn't share your life or your family. You never wanted to let me that close."

His jaw twitches. "You wanted me to—what? Introduce you to the family that detests me? Take you home to the stepmom who wouldn't miss a beat before telling you all the reasons she thinks I'm a piece of shit?"

"You could've trusted me. Instead, you *hurt* me."

"I was honest with you from the start." He looks me over again, his gaze lingering on my jean-clad legs. Is he still seeing me as I was in Alec's kitchen this morning? Half-dressed and tousled from a night in Alec's bed. "I always knew you'd go your own way sooner or later. It was better that way."

Better for whom? Asking would hurt too much, so I choose a different question. "Are you going to tell him?" My heart is in a vise. Past and present pain are pressing in. "Are you going to tell him what I did?"

He flinches as if I slapped him. "That's why you're here." His throat bobs and his gaze dips to my ring finger again. "You came to my hotel because you're afraid I'm going to tell your precious fiancé your secret." He exhales heavily. "It wouldn't matter if I did. He's in love with you. I haven't seen him so protective of a woman in . . . Well, it's been a while. And when he's this far gone, he'll forgive anything."

I shake my head. "I'm not here because I'm worried about his forgiveness. I'm here because I'm afraid telling him the truth might hurt you, and for some goddamned reason, I still care."

"Well, that's where you've always gone wrong, isn't it?" He turns his back on me and adds more bourbon to the glass. "Tell him whatever you want, Savvy. Tell him all of it. I already got more of you than I ever deserved. I hope you have a nice life."

ALEC

I feel like my heart's been ripped out of my chest and then been left on the 405 freeway to be pulverized.

An hour ago, I was relishing the sight of Savannah in my shirt, in my house, and now I can't shake this feeling of betrayal. I'm a fool. *Again.*

Savvy has known the truth for years and not told me. And maybe I could forgive that, but knowing they've been talking during that time is a bigger gut punch than their history.

The doorbell rings, and I spring off the couch. Maybe Savvy changed her flight. Maybe she came back to . . . what? Beg for my forgiveness? Or end this for good and explain that, like Portentia, she too prefers Oliver?

I've wanted Savvy for so long. A week ago—a month

ago, a year ago—I would've done anything to have her show up unexpectedly at my home. But I don't think I can face her now.

When it rings again, I force myself to answer, but when I pull the door open, Savvy isn't standing there.

"Portentia." As if my day wasn't shitty enough. Now I have to look into the eyes of the first woman to break my heart. The first woman to betray me for my brother.

She blinks up at me, her big brown eyes wide. "Alec," she says. "I . . ." She looks me over, her gaze lingering on my bare chest and stomach before sweeping over the jeans I pulled on after Savvy left, and moving down to my bare feet. "I'm sorry. Your mom wanted me to meet her here?"

I drag a hand through my hair and sigh. Mother is always pulling these tricks. Getting Portentia over here and making her wait—always trying to get us back together. I've handled it with next-level avoidance for more than a decade. "Come on in," I say, waving her into the house.

She tugs her bottom lip through her teeth then nods and walks past me.

I follow her through the foyer and into the kitchen. She takes a seat at the table, stiff as can be, hands in her lap while she waits.

"You want some coffee?" I ask. The hope in her eyes slays me. Usually, I lock myself in my bedroom or office while she's here rather than have all the old memories dredged up to the surface, but after the start to this day, I guess I'm feeling masochistic.

"You don't have to make me anything," she says, her voice small. She licks her lips before snapping her gaze back to her hands. "I hear you have a girlfriend."

I sigh. "Yeah."

"I wasn't stalking—I saw pictures from last weekend's dinner with Rose. She's very pretty."

I huff out a laugh and take the chair beside her. Savvy is very pretty, but she looks a little like Portentia, if I'm honest with myself. "I guess I have a thing for beautiful blondes." *Beautiful blondes who want my brother.*

Portentia's gaze flickers back to mine. "I want you to be happy, Alec. I'm sorry that our mothers have kept us in each other's paths all these years. I know you want nothing to do with me, and I can tell having me here is upsetting you. I'll—"

"It's not that." I cut my gaze away and squeeze the back of my neck. "This morning I found out that Savvy and Oliver have a history she never told me about." I'm surprised to hear myself say it, yet I know Portentia will understand how this is tearing me up better than anyone else can.

"Oh, no. I'm so sorry."

I swallow hard. "I didn't take it well."

"But she's with you, right? She chose *you*."

My stomach twists hard at the memories. Portentia, almost eleven years ago, eyes puffy and nose red from crying. *"I made mistakes, and I regret them, but you're the one I want."* Part of me wishes I'd been able to believe her.

"It's never been that simple for me," I say.

"Because you've never been able to see your own value."

I scrub a hand over my face. "Can you tell me why you let him pull you away from me? What is it about him?"

Her eyes fill with tears. "Alec, it wasn't like that."

"But you cheated on me. With my brother. He got you pregnant, and I didn't even know until . . ." I should be over it by now, but the memory is always a gnawing ache in my gut. She wanted to take it slow, and so we did. I didn't even care. I was young and dumb, so sure we would have the rest of our lives to experience each other's pleasure the way I wanted to.

And then I found out Oliver had taken her to the hospital. Found out he'd been the one to hold my girlfriend's hand after she miscarried a baby. *His* baby.

"I did horrible things," she says now, "and I told so many lies trying to protect you from them. Maybe sometime we should talk about what happened." Those tears spill out of her eyes and down her cheeks. "About the mistakes I made."

The sound of the front door opening and closing is followed by the tap of heels through the foyer, and then my mother appears in the kitchen.

"Don't you two look cozy," she says, approval in her tone. Her smile falls away when she takes in Portentia's tears. "Oh. Should I go and give you time to talk?"

Portentia shakes her head and wipes her cheeks. "No, ma'am. I'm ready when you are."

Mother purses her lips in disapproval. "It's okay if you

need to cancel, Portentia dear. We can shop for dresses for the wedding another day. You look beautiful in everything, so finding something won't be an issue."

I frown. "The wedding?" I look to Portentia. "You're going to Rose's wedding?"

Cringing, she looks back and forth between my mother and me. "I thought everyone was okay with that?"

Mom gives me a hard look. "Of course we all are. Everyone wants you there. Isn't that right, Alec?"

Portentia and Oliver and my whole family at Rose's wedding. *What a fucking disaster.*

I force a smile. "Wouldn't be the same without you."

"Thank you," Portentia whispers, pushing out of her chair.

When I watch her walk away, the pain from Savvy's dishonesty still fresh, it's like I'm twenty all over again, finding out that the woman I love has been sleeping with my brother.

CHAPTER TWENTY-FIVE

OLIVER

"I'll take a mimosa, no OJ," Rose tells the server.

She pulls out the chair across from me on the shaded patio of our favorite brunch place, and I flick my gaze up to her. "The rest of us call it champagne, Peony."

"Eh. It's more socially acceptable to drink it in the morning if you call it a *mimosa.*" She winks, all light and joy, like always. But for once I'm spinning too much for her lightness to lift me out of my gloom. "I thought we were going to meet at the house?"

"Yeah." I swallow. My head's still spinning. When I walked into the kitchen of that place I was forced to call home for almost two years, I was prepared to potentially run into Alec. But I wasn't prepared to see him all cozy with Savannah in the living room. "You weren't there, and I didn't want to stay."

"Right. I was going to *meet you there*. So I could show you my *wedding dress*? You know, the big white thing I'm going to wear for the most important day of my life? Any of this ringing a bell?"

"But when I got there, Alec was in the family room with Savvy, and I didn't want to hang around."

Her smile cranks up a few more watts. "You met Savvy!" She bites her bottom lip. "Did you see the *ring*? That one took me by surprise. Last I knew, she was Alec's *one that got away*, and the next thing I know he's telling Mom he has a serious girlfriend who will be with him at my wedding. And now they're engaged? Can you believe Alec never ran it by Mom? I don't mean to be a fiend for drama, but I kind of wish I could be a fly on the wall when he tells her. I feel like she'll find a way to arrange some bride swap or something at the wedding and try to trick him into marrying Portentia."

I take a big swallow of my coffee, but this fucking lump in my throat stays put. "I saw the ring."

And I saw her bare legs and her discarded panties. I saw the way Alec was looking at her. And her panic at realizing who our father is.

"Isn't she amazing? I mean, I haven't spent that much time around her, but you know I have a sense for these things, and Alec has been crazy about her since the first night they met in Vegas. It all seems a little sudden, considering she was reluctant to make it official between them—probably because of the distance. Who can blame her? But now they're getting married, and I wonder if she's going to move to L.A. or if Alec and Marston will hand off management of the L.A. branch of the firm so Alec can move to Orchid Valley. If you ask me, that's what he should do, but . . . Why are you staring at me like that?"

"Alec is engaged to Savvy, Rose. Savannah Downing."

"Right. That's what I'm saying." She cocks her head to the side, studying me. "Did you know her or some—" Her eyes go wide, and I realize it's clicking into place for her. "Holy shit. No way."

"Yes way."

The server returns with her champagne, and my sister snags it from him before he can place it on the table. After downing it, she hands the glass back to the server. "One more, please."

The server nods and turns away without a word.

"Savannah," Rose says, testing the syllables on her tongue. "That Savannah is *your* Savvy?"

"She's not *my* anything." I drop my gaze back to the table. I can't handle the pity that's creeping into my sister's eyes. I think I preferred when she was rambling and I couldn't get a word in.

"Oliver!" she snaps. She sounds like a grumpy mother reprimanding her toddler.

"It's been eight years."

"But you never got over her. Wait. Did she know you and Alec were brothers? Jesus. That's fucked up. Do you think she was trying to get back at you for up and leaving her? I told you it was a dick move."

"First of all, *she* walked out on *me*. Secondly, she . . ." I drag a hand over my face. That fucking ring. And the way she looked at me. Like I'd just destroyed everything. Like what I asked her to do eight years ago had destroyed her chance at happiness.

Happiness with Alec.

"You're *killing me*, Oliver," Rose says, leaning forward. "Use your words."

I blow out a breath. "I knew she was seeing him. She showed up at the house a couple years ago, and when I answered the door, we were both a little rocked. At first, I thought she was there for me." I shake my head, the shock and embarrassment of the day flooding back. "Which makes no sense, but neither did her showing up, ready to seduce my fucking *brother*."

"Oh, damn." Rose leans back in her chair, and the server reappears with a fresh glass of bubbles. "I think we're gonna need a bottle," she says.

I arch a brow. "Shouldn't *I* be the one drinking my feelings right now?"

She turns up her palms. "By all means, join me, but this is a lot to process. The woman you fell head over heels for in grad school is the same one who is marrying Alec." She inhales sharply. "Shit. Does *Alec* know you two have a history?"

I study my coffee. "He does now."

"What does that mean?"

I don't look up.

"Oliver Rhett, you fucking drama queen. Did you see

them together this morning and decide *that* was the moment to make sure Alec knew what was going on?"

I lift my head, and the disappointment in her expression fades, replaced with pity. I have no doubt that the turmoil tightening everything in my chest is reflected in my eyes. "I didn't realize they were serious," I rasp. "After that day she showed up, I figured she cut ties with him rather than risk seeing me again."

Rose nods. "Because she still has feelings for you."

"Because she hates me. And I don't blame her for that." I swallow. No matter how hard I try, I can't forget that voicemail she left me weeks before she showed up at Alec's door. Her words were slightly slurred, like she'd been drinking. *I'm over you, Oliver. I've met someone, and I'm moving on. I hope I never see you again.*

"But she didn't cut ties. And now they're engaged."

My gut twists. Once upon a time, I let myself imagine what it would be like to put a ring on Savvy's finger. To plan a life with her. But I knew she deserved better than me, and then everything fell apart before she could make a choice she'd regret for the rest of her life. "I don't know what to do."

"Well, you start by apologizing for your asshat behavior, and then you tell her you still love her."

I blink at my sister. "Aren't you the one who just sat there crowing about how great it was that she was marrying Alec?"

"Obviously that was before I had all the information," she says.

"How many Savvys do you know? It didn't even cross your mind?"

She cocks her head to the side. "What are the chances that the woman you fell for in Pennsylvania eight years ago would be the same woman Alec fell into insta-love with in Vegas? *Why* would that cross my mind?"

"I wondered at first if he knew about our history. If this was all some effort to show me up."

"But you know better now? You underestimate Alec. He's not our father."

"I know, and he's shit at hiding his feelings," I say. "He couldn't have faked his reaction this morning."

The server returns with an ice bucket with a bottle of champagne and two fresh glasses. Rose beams at him as he settles it beside the table.

"We'll need a few minutes before we order food," she says. "Thanks so much."

Once he steps away again, she turns her attention back to me. "So if you aren't planning to grovel, what *are* you going to do?"

"Other than try to wake up from this nightmare? I guess it won't matter soon anyway. Once you move in with Jared, I won't have a reason to be at the house. I'll *avoid*, *avoid*, *avoid*, and let them live happily ever after." How can the twist of a metaphorical knife in the gut hurt so fucking much? When I press my hand to my stomach, I half expect to feel the sticky heat of blood.

"This is *your* Savvy." Rose leans across the table. "You need to tell her how you feel. At least let her make an informed decision."

"She's already wearing his ring. It's a little late for confessions of the heart." I shake my head, trying to chase away the hope my sister is trying to plant there. "Shouldn't you be looking out for Alec? Doesn't he love her too?" That's easy enough to admit to myself. Alec loves Savvy. Of course he does. She's so fucking easy to love.

But it's the other side of it that hurts too much to swallow. Savvy loves my brother. Loves him enough to marry him, *even knowing his connection to me.*

"It's different," Rose says softly. "Alec loves her, and if this were anyone else, I'd tell you to back off. But this isn't just anyone. This is *Savvy.* You loved her on another level. There are people we love and then there are the people who are stitched into our hearts. You left half of yours behind when you left her."

I snatch the champagne from the bucket and fill my glass.

Rose grins. "You really do still love her."

"What?"

"That terror that you're feeling? I call that love holding its breath. It's exactly how I felt when I realized I was actually falling for Jared when my life plans very clearly had me staying single until my forties."

"Love holding its breath, huh?" Sounds like something her therapist told her.

"Yes, and you can continue to deprive it oxygen or you can release it." She shrugs. "The question is whether you're willing to get hurt again for nothing but the chance to tell her how you really feel."

"I told her today when she ripped my head off for trying to fuck things up with Alec."

Rose arches a brow. "And by *told her* you mean you used your words and explained exactly how much she means to you? Explained that you left town and never even tried to apologize for your jackassery because you have more baggage than a 727? Explained that you never told her all your ugly truths because you didn't believe she could love you if she knew?"

I set my jaw and shoo away a pigeon looking for scraps at my feet. "I *mean* that I told her I hated imagining my brother's hands on her but that I knew she deserved better than me anyway."

Rose scoffs. "Really? I pulled all my strings to get you into the best therapist in New York, and you're still going to come at me with *I don't deserve her*? Nancy would drop your ass if she knew."

She's not wrong. It's something I've worked on a lot over the years. Rose talked me into it. She said I needed to be ready to "receive love" next time it came along. But most days, I think Savvy was it for me. I don't know how to move past feelings as big as those.

I blow out a breath. "I don't even know how to make her talk to me."

Rose studies me for a long time. "You could come to my wedding."

"You really want that drama there on your day?"

She rolls her eyes. "First of all, it was never going to be *my* day. Jared and I eloped last month—we had *our* day then."

I set down my glass. "Keeping secrets, sister?"

She scoffs. "I told you I was going to."

"I thought you were joking. Letting off steam because Cruella was ruining your wedding-planning fun."

"Nope. I was serious, and I'm glad we did it. This whole ceremony thing is for Mom. I'm not inviting you to make drama. No fighting with Alec and no public declarations of loving your brother's fiancée. I only mean that if you're there, you can find a moment to pull her aside. If this is your only chance to set the record straight with Savvy, you should take it."

I stare at the bubbles floating to the top of my glass. "What if I tell her how I feel and she still marries him?"

"Then at least you'll have avoided a much worse fate."

My stomach clenches. "What's worse than that?"

"Her marrying him without you ever telling her how you feel."

SAVVY

I'm a wreck on the way to the airport and all the way through security. Seeing Oliver again—and for more than a five-minute porch conversation—sent me back in time. It's been so long, and I don't understand how walking away can still hurt so much.

When they call my zone to board, I'm stopped by someone's hand on mine, and I catch a swath of short, dark hair out of the corner of my eye.

Oliver. My heart floats in my chest, but when I turn, it's not the man I expect.

"Alec, what are you doing here?"

He nods toward the boarding gate. "I'm flying back with you. We need to talk."

He looks upset, and my gut twists. I never should've slept with him last night. I never should have done any of this.

I follow him numbly onto the plane. When I get to my seat, he sweet-talks the woman in the coach seat next to mine into taking his spot in first class so he can sit by me.

When we settle into our spots, I draw in a ragged breath. "I'm sorry." I could say the words a hundred times and it wouldn't be enough. "I should've told you, and I shouldn't have let last night happen. But my history with Oliver is messy, and I didn't want you to see me differently, which you would if you knew the truth."

He swallows, his gaze focused on the flight attendant who's going through her preflight instructions at the front of coach. "When I asked you to leave this morning, I was so hurt. I assumed you knew everything—that Oliver told you everything—and I couldn't understand how you could keep the truth from me if you knew it all."

"Knew everything about what?" I ask.

He closes his eyes. "About the last time he came between me and the woman I love."

My stomach sinks. "Oliver was incredibly private about his past. There was very little that he shared with me."

"So he didn't tell you about Portentia?"

I frown. "The woman your mother wants you to marry? The reason you needed me to pretend to be your girlfriend?"

"Yeah." He studies his hands in his lap. "I guess you aren't the only one who had a past you were too embarrassed to share."

"What happened?"

"Mom introduced me to Portentia when we were teenagers, but we didn't start dating until we were in college. Our schools were a couple hours apart, but we still saw each other at least once a week, and we went to all our family functions together." He blows out a breath. "I thought I was going to marry her, just like our parents wanted. I *dreamed* of marrying her, and I thought that went both ways. It never occurred to me to worry about the fact that while I only saw her a handful of hours each week, she and Oliver were on the same campus and could see each other every day. But then one day, I got a call from her mom because Portentia was in the hospital. She'd suffered a miscarriage and was having some complications, and Oliver had to rush her there."

"I'm sorry, Alec. It must've been hard to know he was there for her when you couldn't be."

He shakes his head. "You don't understand. Portentia's family is very conservative. She said she didn't want to have sex until after marriage. I believed her. But somewhere along the line, while I was planning our future together, she'd started sleeping with my brother."

"Oh no." Was that why Charles was looking for a wife for Alec? Because Portentia broke his heart? "Alec . . ."

When he lifts his eyes to meet mine, they're full of pain. "You see what I mean? There are no rules that apply to Oliver. He takes whatever he wants, the rest of us be damned."

And then today when he found out Oliver and I knew each other, all those bad feelings came back. "I'm so sorry, Alec."

"You know what pissed me off the most? She obviously had feelings for him, but after she miscarried, Oliver just dropped her. It was like all he cared about was taking her from me, and once that was done . . ." He shrugs. "But it sounds like you already know how conniving he can be. He found a way to pay off your gambling debt so you'd have to give him whatever he wanted."

I open my mouth to defend Oliver and then snap it shut. How many times did I accuse Oliver of the same thing? But every favor he asked of me was a choice on some level. Yes, he used the gambling and the debt to get in with me, but he never treated me like I was bought and paid for. He just . . . took care of me. He made me feel safe and taught me how to be strong.

And I threw it all in his face.

I swallow hard. I could tell Alec about meeting his dad. About what I took. But I believe Oliver, believe that whatever was in that chest was rightfully his. I believed that even before I knew Charles was his father. Honestly, the connection makes more sense than Charles being a stranger. I won't tell Alec about it and risk Oliver losing whatever it was he was so desperate to get back.

"So, what now?" I ask.

Alec's gaze drops to my ring. "Now I know the truth. And I still want you. Now I want to know if you'll give me the chance you couldn't before."

I hate myself. All this time I was holding back because I didn't want Alec to know the truth, but I still can't give him the chance he deserves. And maybe that's for the best. The last thing Alec needs is to be in love with another woman he'll always fear secretly wants to be with his brother.

"I'll go to the wedding," I say as gently as possible. "I'll play your fiancée in front of your family, but I can't offer you more. It would never feel right. The lies and omissions would always be between us. Your issues with your brother and what my past with him makes you feel would always come between us."

The plane coasts along the runway, preparing for takeoff. I don't even care that I'm crying in public or that people are looking at us. I just want to be home in my bed, where I can forget this whole weekend.

Alec cups my face in one hand and wipes away my tears with his thumb. "Are you sure that's why? Are you sure you aren't pushing me away for another reason?"

"Like what?"

"Like you know if you're with me, you'll have to see him."

"That's what I'm saying. There's too much baggage. We'd be doomed from the start."

He shakes his head. "No, Savvy. This isn't about you and me. This is about you and Oliver. Do you still love him?"

I open my mouth to object then hang my head. My feelings for Oliver are a mess of anger and hurt and shame and regret. But Alec's right. There's part of me that loves Oliver even now. Part of me that never stopped. So I say the only thing I can. "I'm sorry."

He nods and looks away. "Maybe it's petty, but after everything that happened with Portentia, I can't handle being humiliated by him again."

My chest aches for him. "You won't be."

He cuts his gaze to me. "You're sure? You can continue on playing my fiancée—even with Oliver—just because I asked?"

"Yes." I squeeze his bicep. "Alec, I absolutely will. As long as you don't take it to heart. I don't want to say goodbye next weekend and feel like I led you on."

He holds my gaze for a long time. "I wish I'd met you first."

I want to wish for the same, but I can't. I wouldn't be the person I am today if it weren't for those months with Oliver. "We can't change the past."

Alec cringes and shakes his head. "Not that it would matter. He would've taken you away anyway. Just to prove he could."

Part Ten

EIGHT YEARS AGO

CHAPTER TWENTY-SIX

SAVVY

Where is Oliver when he's out this late? It's Wednesday night, and I've spent the last four hours sitting on his couch studying for next week's midterms and watching the door.

I hate the idea of him with another girl. The thought burns a hole somewhere deep in my gut.

He's not mine, despite what I may or may not owe him, but I hate the idea of another woman touching him.

I've never been like this about anyone. Sure, I didn't like when Chuck flirted with the women who came to watch him fight, but that was more of a pride thing for me than jealousy. It was embarrassing to be his girlfriend and watch him act like I didn't exist. It was embarrassing to have everyone see just how little he respected me. But actual jealousy? This *burning* at the idea of Oliver's hands on someone else? That's totally unfamiliar to me.

I've picked up my phone five times to start a text to him, but each time I've made myself put it back down and return to the book that's keeping me company. What would I even say? *Why aren't you home?*

He doesn't have to update me on his whereabouts. It's not like I'm his wife or even his girlfriend. He made that very clear last time we were in New York. I'm nothing but the girl currently making a mess of his life, the girl who cost him his car, and all I've done in return is wear some fancy clothes and drink a couple martinis. Oh, and live here. As if that's a hardship.

Oliver said he'll need me again, but the originally predicted two weeks has already come and gone. He blamed the delay on the fact that Charles hasn't been in the city as much as usual, but mostly he says nothing at all on the subject. He doesn't like to talk about Charles. Or about anything remotely personal, for that matter.

I pick at a bowl of ice cream and snuggle deeper into the nest of blankets I've made on the couch. I should go to bed, but I want to know when he gets home.

I want to see him.

So pathetic. I should be enjoying what's left of my evening with my book and the sound of the rain on the windows, but instead, I'm obsessing over the broody roommate who walked away after I threw myself at him.

I poke around at my ice cream some more, taking another bite and savoring the coldness on my tongue and the smoothness of it sliding down my throat.

I'm glad there's no scale here. I've probably gained five pounds since moving in, maybe more with all the strength training I've been doing. But truth be told, I don't mind. Chuck always pushed me to be thinner, but I was starting to feel scrawny and weak.

And Oliver doesn't seem to mind these extra pounds. I catch him looking at me, and I like it, but for once in my life I'm not choosing my food based on what someone else thinks my body should look like. I'm just feeding my body, sometimes to make it stronger and sometimes because food is *delicious.* It's so fucking liberating.

But that doesn't mean I don't enjoy Oliver's eyes on me when I come out for coffee in the mornings in nothing but a T-shirt and panties. I've been picking my pajamas based on how much ass they show. I never cared much before—any T-shirt would do—but now, the shorter the better. And tonight, I'm not hiding a damn thing below the waist. With the excuse of having the apartment to myself, I'm dressed in nothing but a skimpy cotton thong and a fitted tank top that barely grazes my navel.

I straighten at the sound of the elevator and put my bowl down on the coffee table. *He's finally home.*

"Don't panic," I hear him say from beyond the front door. "It will open. It just sticks sometimes."

He's talking to someone. Did he bring a woman home?

I look around, suddenly super regretful of this outfit choice. I glance toward the bedroom. Could I get in there before the door opens? Or maybe he was planning on using his bed tonight.

The door opens before I can make a decision, and Oliver stumbles in, his arm wrapped around a guy I've never seen before. They're both soaked from the rain.

His friend spots me on the couch and his eyes go wide. "You must be Savannah," he says, grinning.

I look back and forth between the stranger and Oliver.

"Savannah, meet Eddie. Eddie, Savannah," Oliver says.

I clear my throat, well aware that the polite thing to do in this moment would be to stand and shake the man's hand. Except this blanket is the only thing allowing me to hold on to my last shreds of dignity. *A thong and a tank top.* Why am I just full of brilliant ideas? "Hey, Eddie." I put my book to the side and flit my fingers in a pathetic wave.

"Your man here is pretty banged up after tonight," Eddie says.

"What happened?"

Eddie guides Oliver to a chair, and Oliver grimaces as he lowers himself into it, pressing his hand to his side.

When he turns to me and I see the other side of his face, I gasp. His cheek is swollen and his eye is puffy—discolored in a way that tells me it's going to be covered in a dark bruise by morning.

"What happened?"

He leans back, exposing his blood-soaked shirt. I jump off the couch, sending blankets falling to the floor, and run to the kitchen, where I open and close cabinets until I find a washcloth.

"Do you need to go to the hospital?"

"Nah," Oliver says. "It's just a cut."

Just a cut my ass. He looks like he was jumped.

I wet the cloth with hot water and am headed back to the living room before I realize both guys are staring at me. I stop in my tracks. Oliver, despite his condition, is *smirking.*

How can a smirk on a bloodied man still look so damn sexy?

"What?" I ask, though I already know. His eyes keep drifting down to my legs, reminding me of what I'm wearing and exactly why. Of course, I had no idea *Eddie* would be coming home with him.

"You know *what,*" Oliver says, leaning back and grimacing as he shifts in the chair. He sighs. "I'm sure Eddie appreciates the show as much as I do, but I'm going to have to punch him if he keeps gawking at you like that, so if you wanna put something on, you'd be doing us both a favor."

Eddie chuckles softly and shrugs as if to say, *Can you blame me?*

"Fucking close your eyes when she turns around, Gaines," Oliver grumbles.

Eddie puts a hand over his eyes. "I promise I won't look." He peeks at me between two fingers. "But, like, nice . . . shirt."

"Face the fucking wall," Oliver says, but there's a

lightness to his tone I wouldn't expect. One that tells me he doesn't feel threatened by Eddie.

"Thanks." I hand Oliver the warm washcloth, noting the way his eyes immediately drift closed. Exhaustion or pain? "Eddie, want to get this bloody shirt off him and I'll go get some pants on?"

"Sure thing." Eddie turns then seems to remember why he was facing the wall in the first place and gives us his back again.

I head toward the bedroom, but behind me I hear, "I fucking swear, if you don't get your eyes off her ass, I'll cut them out."

Eddie sounds unfazed. "Maybe I just want a good look at the first girl I've ever seen you twisted up over."

Oliver grunts and says something I can't make out.

"You heard the woman," Eddie says, once I'm in the bedroom. "Strip."

"What the fuck are you, my nurse?"

I shut the door behind me and wonder what Eddie means. Does Oliver talk about me? Or are Eddie's comments really just a reaction to whatever Oliver's been saying to explain my presence here? Are Oliver and I supposed to act like a couple that's living together, or does Eddie know what's up?

I step into a pair of Oliver's sweatpants because I don't have any of my own and don't feel like squeezing into my jeans right now.

When I return to the living room, Eddie's taken my spot on the couch and Oliver is patting his bloodied side with the rag. "Jesus," I say, surveying the damage.

"It looks worse than it is," Oliver says.

I drop to my knees in front of him, snag the cloth from his hands, and take over where he left off. "What happened to you?"

He's right; it's not that big of a cut and there's not as much blood as I thought. His rain-wet shirt made it look more gruesome than it really is.

"Someone doesn't like losing," Eddie says from the couch as he flips through the channels.

"Losing what?"

"Losing fights," he says. He stops on the History Channel and puts down the remote. "This ancient Egypt shit is so cool."

When I look up from cleaning his wound, Oliver's smiling down at me. "What?" I ask

He shakes his head. "Just didn't know you cared."

I glance over toward Eddie, who seems totally happy to keep his attention on the TV.

"I just don't want you bleeding out. I'm not an asshole," I say. "Who did this to you, anyway?"

"Doesn't matter."

"Chuck jumped him after the fight," Eddie says.

"Fucking hell, man," Oliver growls. "Don't bring her into it."

"What?" I jump to my feet. "Chuck did this?" I spin around in a circle, looking for my phone. "I'm going to call him and—"

"Chill, Cujo." Oliver hooks two fingers into the waistband of my sweats—*his* sweats. "Relax. I'll take care of it."

"*Why* did you fight him? I thought you didn't do that anymore. And why would you agree to that when you knew he was pissed about what happened with me?" I bite my bottom lip. "He did this because of me, didn't he?"

"He did this because he's a *dick,*" Oliver says. "He couldn't beat me in the ring, so he tried to jump me with a knife afterward. But he's not fast enough, and I'm *fine*."

"Oliver, I'm so sorry. I—"

"Hey." He tugs me toward him until I collapse into his lap. He searches my face, but his gaze snags on my mouth for a few too many beats, and I think he might be about to kiss me, and I want that kiss more than I should. More than I ever thought possible. "Relax," he murmurs. "I've got it handled."

I swallow hard. "You should call the police."

I try to stand, but he loops his arms around my waist and holds me still. "It's handled."

Eddie's phone buzzes, and he pulls it from his back pocket before scowling down at it. "Fuck. Again?"

Oliver chuckles then winces and grabs his side. "Roommate?"

"We had an agreement, but this is the third time this week," Eddie says. "It's getting ridiculous. I can't take another night on the lobby couch." Sighing, he runs a hand through his hair. "I'll get a room at the Holiday or something."

"Dude," Oliver says, "that's unnecessary. Just crash here."

Eddie looks back and forth between us. "You two really don't care?"

My eyes widen. I'm not sure I want to answer this question. If Eddie sleeps on the couch, where will Oliver sleep?

"It's totally cool," Oliver says. He glances at me. "I'll sleep in the chair."

"You're hurt," I object. "If anyone's going to sleep in the chair, it's going to be me."

"You think I'm going to have you sleep out here with Mr. Roaming Eyes just so I can sleep in a bed?" Oliver asks. "Woman, I'm *not* that soft."

I bite my lip.

"*I* can sleep in the chair," Eddie says. "It's totally cool if you two are, like . . . saving yourselves or something. Wouldn't want to be the one who put you in temptation's path." There's a question in his tone and his eyes that Oliver doesn't answer.

"It's fine," I say quickly. "We can share the bed."

Oliver smirks. "Try to keep your hands to yourself, Savvy." His gaze flicks to my book, where I left it on the middle of the couch. "Even if tonight's reading put ideas in your head."

"That won't be a problem."

Eddie chuckles. "I'm staying out of this one."

CHAPTER TWENTY-SEVEN

OLIVER

What a fucking night.

I'm exhausted on every level. The fight didn't go as well as I'd thought it would, and I barely eked out a win. And then Chuck? That motherfucker. I knew he had no principles, but I didn't think he had it in him.

Leaning back against the headboard, I close my eyes and listen to the sounds of Savvy getting ready for bed in the bathroom. I can't pretend I'm disappointed to be sleeping in my own room tonight. The couch isn't awful—it's some high-end shit my dad's decorator picked out—but nothing compares to a real mattress.

Yet somehow, despite how tired I am and how soft these sheets are, I already know sleep won't come easily. Not when she's so close.

When Savvy walks back into the room, she's still wearing my sweatpants. I'm not sure what's hotter—the way they stretch around her hips and or the fact that she's wearing *my* clothes. It would take the lightest tug to expose that sweet ass to me again.

What was she thinking, hanging out in my living room dressed like that? Was she hoping I'd come home and see her, or was it a coincidence?

My body aches so much I wouldn't think it would be possible to get hard, yet just the thought of her wearing that fucking thong for me has blood pumping south.

"You're sure you're good with this?" I ask, my voice more gravelly than I expected. Because hell, I'm not sure *I'm* good with this.

"If I had a problem with it, I could sleep on the floor." She hooks her thumbs in the waistband of the sweats and shoves them down. She steps out of them and climbs into bed, sliding those long legs beneath the covers.

Jesus fucking Christ.

I manage to bite back a groan. She's gonna kill me.

She rolls to her side and stifles a smile as she studies my face. "I don't know. Maybe I should go share the couch with Eddie."

"You're not funny." I scoot down the bed to lie down.

I turn away from her to click off the bedside lamp and barely hear her whisper, "I do, you know."

I roll to my side, wishing I hadn't turned off the light. Wishing I could see her face. Between the blackout curtains and dark walls, I can't even make out her silhouette. "You do what?"

"Care about you." Cool fingertips touch my face, graze over my stubble, along my jaw and to my ear, down my neck. "I tried not to, but you're kind of irresistible. For an asshole who is absolutely nothing like the sexy and heroic Arturo."

I cough out a laugh. "Right."

The low drone of the TV in the living room suddenly stops, and the only sound left is the hum of the fan and the soft hush of our breath.

I sense her moving toward me, and I don't move an inch. I'm afraid that she'll stop, and I want her close, even knowing she should stay away.

Since she kissed me two weeks ago, I've barely thought about anything else. When her lips find mine in the dark, it's like the answer to a prayer. She's soft and sweet and so fucking gentle. Like she's afraid she might break me. She should be worried that I'll break her.

I lick across the seam of her lips, and she parts them for me, sighing into my mouth as if she's been thinking about this as much as I have. She shifts closer, and I angle my head to kiss her more deeply, slide a hand into her hair. Christ, she's sweet. And I have no right to touch her.

She pulls away and straddles me, and I grunt as her knee catches my bruised side. "Shit," she says, sliding off before I can grab her. "I'm so sorry."

"I'm fine."

"You're not, though. You're beat to hell and . . . I'm sorry."

I reach for her in the darkness, finding her hand and grasping it between both of mine. "Don't apologize."

"Hey," she whispers. "Tell me something."

"What?"

She draws in a long, shaky breath. "Why did Chuck do this? He's lost before, but he's never attacked someone after. Not as far as I know."

"He's had it out for me for a long time."

"Why?"

I shrug even though she can't see it. "Because I'm better than him. Because I call him on his shit. Because I got my sister away from him before he could do more damage. Our hatred for each other has been building from the beginning."

"I'm still sorry," she says. "He's such a dick, but I had no idea he was this crazy."

I palm her hips. It's just so natural to hold her here. "Tell me about your night. Hot date with a book?"

"You make that sound like a bad thing."

"Not at all. I'm just wondering if that tattooed guy on the cover left you needing something." I swallow hard. "Maybe something you can't take care of yourself, since you're stuck with me tonight."

She releases a rough laugh. "Oh. My. God. Did you really just ask me that?"

I wish I could see her face. I find her wrist in the darkness, tracing up her arm with the gentlest touch of my fingertips. Her breath snags as I brush the inside of her elbow, and then again as I inch higher. I can't be what she deserves, but at least I could give her release. "Afraid to answer?" I brush the outside of her breast with my knuckles. "Because you can tell me. If there's something you need."

"Maybe," she breathes, arching into my touch. She rocks into me, finding the ridge of my erection with the juncture between her thighs. "Oliver. I—"

"Lie down for me." I don't want her to say more. I'm afraid she might confess something that will bring me to my senses before I get to touch her.

The air goes still between us, and then the rustle of sheets breaks the silence as she settles onto the bed beside me.

I return to my side, wincing a little at my bruised ribs.

"You don't have to do anything," she says. "You're hurt and you're . . ."

"I don't have to do shit, but I want to do this." I lean over and scrape my teeth across the shell of her ear. "Let me do this."

I trail my fingers down, between her breasts and over her stomach, feeling the heat of her skin through the thin cotton of her tank. I prop my head up on one hand. With the other, I trace the hem of her shirt.

I circle her navel before tracing the strip of skin just above the band of her panties.

She lifts her hips from the bed, as if she's chasing my touch.

I scoot closer until the heat of her side presses against my torso. Then I cup her between her legs. "Tell me you thought about me when you dressed this pussy in this sexy scrap of fabric." I shouldn't ask. I know better than to ask. Know better than to put ideas in her head. This is about release, not about me. But then she gasps out a little *yes*, and I can't regret it.

The slightest pressure against the cotton and I can feel she's already wet. "Relax and just let me . . ." I find her shoulder with my lips in the dark and follow the sweet path to her neck.

She slides a hand in my hair. "Please," she whispers, tugging gently.

"Please what?"

"I need . . ." She lifts her hips, urging my hand to slip farther between her legs. I tease her instead, circling her clit through the fabric before pulling her panties to the side to feel her. She's swollen and wet and ready for more than I can give her tonight. "I was right," I say, breathing her in.

"About what?"

"You're going to ruin me." I finally sink a finger inside her, and she gasps. "You smell so fucking good, and you feel even better." I add a second finger and open my mouth against that tender spot beneath her ear, sucking. She clenches tight around my finger, and my dick throbs.

"I thought about this," she says.

I withdraw, and she lifts her hips, chasing my fingers before I plunge them in again.

"Tell me." I don't recognize my own voice.

"When I'd lie here at night, smelling you on your pillow. I'd put my hand between my legs and imagine it was yours. Or I'd think about you walking in and watching me."

If she keeps this up, I'm going to come right here on my sheets like a fucking pubescent teen. Knowing she wants me is one thing, but imagining her touching herself and wishing it were me? Fuck. I'm done for. As much as tonight sucked, I might volunteer for a pummeling daily if it means I get Savvy in my bed, fucking my hand.

I lean over to skim my lips across her mouth. Her lips part and she kisses me, her hands roaming all over my bare back, making me think of sex and being inside her. She wraps her legs around my waist and digs her nails into my shoulders.

"So sexy," I murmur against her lips. "So hot."

She snags my bottom lip between her teeth and sucks. I groan into her mouth and rub my palm against her clit. She gasps, and I know she's close.

"I need you inside me when I come," she says.

I squeeze my eyes shut. She's going to be the death of me. "I'm not fucking you tonight."

She arches her back and moans. "Why not?"

"Because you're right. I'm not at my best right now, and I'm going to need to be at one hundred percent when I finally fuck you, Savvy."

Her breathing hitches, and she's quiet for a few beats. "Is that a promise?"

Drawing in a breath, I curl my fingers inside her, searching for the spot that will bring her to the brink. Because I can't make promises. Never before have I cared about breaking them, but I care with her.

"Oliver."

I've never loved the sound of my name more than in this moment—ragged and desperate, as if she's clinging to the edge and about to lose control.

"I've got you. Just take it. Take what you need."

She does, riding my hand. *Fuck.* She feels good. Hot and slick.

"Oliver. God . . ."

Then she's there. Arching. Crying out. I keep my fingers buried inside her, not letting her run from the pleasure. Guiding her to ride out every last wave.

"Jesus. That was . . ."

"You better now?" I ask. She can probably hear it in my voice—the lust, the ache. My cock is throbbing because she feels so fucking good.

I want her almost as much as I want better for her.

She laughs. "Yeah. You could say that."

I kiss her shoulder then roll to my back. "Goodnight, Savvy."

SAVVY

When I wake up, Oliver is already out of bed.

I smooth the sheets on his side and stretch happily. After weeks of tension between us, our chemistry was combustible last night.

I hear him in the kitchen, talking quietly. Eddie must

still be here. I roll out of bed and grab the joggers I was wearing last night, tugging them on.

"It's not really your business what I do with my car, is it?" Oliver says. "Well, the title was in my name. I had every right to sign it over."

I straighten. Are he and Eddie fighting? About the Viper?

His voice gets louder. "Call her a whore again and see what happens."

My stomach twists. Whoever he's talking to, I have no doubt they're talking about me.

"Fuck off, old man. You weren't around the first sixteen years of my life. I don't see why you need to be around now."

A door slams, and I flinch.

Swallowing, I step into the hall and peek down toward the living room. I don't see anyone inside, but Oliver is on the balcony, his back to me, his hands white-knuckling the rail.

I head that way, frowning when I see his phone in the middle of the living room floor—like it's been thrown there.

A door opens behind me, and I spin around to see Eddie emerge from the hallway bathroom. He glances worriedly toward Oliver. "Don't let him know you heard that," he says. "He's a private person, but when it comes to his father, he's irrationally so."

"That was his dad?"

His dad called me a whore?

"Don't let it bother you. He'll say anything to control Oliver."

"I understand," I say. But I don't understand, and I feel small. Smaller than I did the night the girls at work called me that.

"Cool. Listen, thanks for letting me have the couch last night."

"Of course." I swallow. *Call her a whore again and see what happens.* "I'm gonna go shower, but I'll see you around?"

"Yeah. I hope so. You're good for him."

I'm not sure what that means, but I force a smile and wave goodbye.

By the time I'm showered and dressed for my classes, Oliver is back in the living room. He's sitting on the couch and scowling at his phone.

I'm not Prince Charming, and this isn't a fairy tale.

"Hey," I say softly.

"Hey." He doesn't look up from his phone.

He's obviously upset about something, but if Eddie thinks I shouldn't bring up the phone call, I won't. "You okay?"

"Yeah. You?"

No. I'm not okay. You touched me last night but then didn't let me touch you. You said you wanted me and kissed me like I was your everything, but now you're back to pushing me away. "Are we going to talk about last night?"

He finally tears his gaze from his phone to look at me. He cocks a brow. "What's there to talk about? You asked me for something, and I gave it to you."

"Don't be crass. Don't try to make me feel dirty."

He stands and tosses his phone on the couch before prowling toward me. "I leave in five weeks. I'm not trying to hurt you, but I'm doing a shitty job of it. There's nothing about last night that should make you feel dirty." He's so close, and I keep expecting him to touch me. But he doesn't. "I wanted to make you feel good, and now I'm ruining it because I see the way you look at me. I don't know how to prove to you that I'm not the guy you think I am."

"Five weeks?" I ask.

He swallows hard and nods.

"Where will you go?"

"Hopefully L.A. I applied for a few internships with sports agencies."

I nod. Five weeks. That's all we have, and then he'll move across the country. He's trying to save me from heartache, but he doesn't realize it's too late for that.

His phone buzzes on the couch, and he grabs it. But not before I see the name on the screen. *Peony*.

Less than fifteen minutes later, he's heading out the door.

CHAPTER TWENTY-EIGHT

OLIVER

The house party is packed, and normally that would make me turn around and leave. I'm not in the mood to deal with these people or to pretend keg stands are the best entertainment in town. *Normally* I would leave, but normally I'm not all tangled up over a girl I should be keeping my distance from.

Eddie called me half an hour ago and told me Savvy was here. *"I know I should mind my own business, but she's in a mood, and I'm a little worried she's going to do something reckless."*

The *in a mood* part didn't surprise me. Savvy has been *in a mood* since we shared a bed two weeks ago. She's done her studying at the library instead of at home, cancelled our workouts, and picked up extra shifts to spend more time at the café. I've told myself it was a gift.

That it's easier to keep my distance if she's avoiding *me*. But mostly I've wanted to call her on it and make her tell me what's wrong.

Thankfully, Eddie had left his car at his place and told me to use it for the night.

"Oliver!" a female voice croons from a dark corner.

I glance over and see Melody—or was it Meredith? She's sitting on another girl's lap and crooking a finger at me. We hooked up once last year, and ever since she's acted like we had some long, drawn-out, kinky affair any time I see her.

"Come here," she says. "You look lost."

I cross to her. "Have you seen Savannah Downing?"

"Don't know her," Melody/Meredith says. "We're just partying, but we'd have more fun if you were with us."

Her friend winks at me then licks Melody/Meredith's neck while never tearing her gaze from mine.

Normally I wouldn't care, except that's the moment Savvy spots me. *Shit.*

Her eyes shift between me and the pair in the corner before going wide for a beat. She turns on her heel and strides out of the room.

I race to follow her. "Savvy!"

She keeps going. Past the kitchen, down the dark hall, and into a room at the end, closing the door. I grab it before she can lock me out, and I step into the darkness with her, pulling the door shut behind me.

"Jesus. Would you just talk to me for a minute?" I ask into the shadows. We must be in some kind of utility room. I can faintly make out some brooms on the far wall next to a big cylinder I'm guessing is a water heater.

"What's there to talk about?"

"Why are you avoiding me?"

"I'm not avoiding you. I was just letting you enjoy your friends. I didn't want to be in the way. Does *Peony* know about them?"

Peony is my nickname for my sister Rose, but I don't want to get into that right now. What I want is for Savvy to quit shutting me out. I want to see her face, to look into her eyes while I ask what's going on with her. But this room is pitch black, and when I search the walls for a light switch, I come up empty. I reach for my phone and stop myself. Maybe she'll open up in the dark in a way she can't to my face.

"Would you please talk to me?" I ask. "What's up with you?" *I miss you.*

"Nothing is up with me. I just . . ." The silence stretches between us, but I won't fill it. I want to hear the words she's trapped on her tongue. The truth that's waiting there but that she's decided not to trust me with.

"Savannah." My voice sounds rough. The need I've felt for weeks tangles with the syllables of her name. I give up on finding a light and instead search for her in the darkness. I find her hips and pull her back flush with my front. Her sigh is a surrender as she leans her head against my chest.

"I have totally screwed up your life," she says.

The idea is so ridiculous that I don't catch the

shocked cough of laughter that springs from my throat. "How do you figure?"

"You lost your car because of me, and I'll never be able to pay you back. You can't even have a girl over because I'm there. You can't even bring a woman home."

"Savvy," I growl, tightening my grip on her hips. "Do you really think I give a shit about the money? Do you think I *want* any woman that isn't you?" I slide one hand up to her belly, snaking my fingers under her shirt until they come into contact with the soft skin there. I splay my fingers, and my thumb brushes the underside of her breast. She gasps but doesn't pull away.

"Don't you?" she asks, and I'm so fixated on the feel of her skin beneath my palm that it takes me a beat to realize what she's asking.

"No." Offering the truth makes me feel raw. "I don't want anyone else. All I can think about is you."

Her hand finds mine under her shirt. "Why? I'm just this mess you have to clean up."

"Why?" I dip my face into the cradle of her shoulder and run my nose up the side of her neck. "I can't stop thinking about you." Her hand squeezes mine. "You haunt my dreams. You're the reason I wake up hard every morning and the reason I rush home every night."

"Then why don't you touch me?"

I squeeze my eyes shut. I can't answer that question. I stay away from her because I'm ashamed of how I pulled her in. I stay away because I know she deserves better. I stay away because, up until recently, my need for control was greater than my need for *her*.

But that's changed.

"You think you're the screw-up?" I rasp. "You think *you're* the mess, but it's me."

She guides my hand over her breast, and I groan at the feel of her beaded nipple under my palm. "Touch me," she says. "Please. I want you."

"You've been drinking." My lips skim the side of her neck. She smells like fucking heaven. "You don't know what you want right now."

"I've known for a long time that I want you." The words are low but so sure they send blood pumping to my dick. "I like the way you look at me," she says. "I've wanted you to look at me since that first morning at your place. Did everything I could to get those eyes of yours on me."

I circle her nipple before pinching it through her tank and am rewarded with a groan of approval.

"No one's ever looked at me the way you do," she says breathlessly.

I chuckle. "I find that hard to believe, Savvy. You're fucking beautiful. It's impossible to miss." And in those little tank tops and panties she parades around in, I haven't missed a thing.

"No. I mean . . . like I'm more. Men have looked at me and wanted me before. I know they look at me and . . ." She's silent a beat. "It's stupid."

"I don't think so." I scrape my teeth over the shell of her ear. "Tell me."

"It's one thing to be wanted by someone who's attracted to your body. It's quite another to be wanted by someone who's . . ."

I wait, impatient for the words but too hungry for the truth to rush her.

"Someone who gobbles up every little bit of you that you give. Like it's a gift." She leans her head to the side, giving my mouth access to her neck. I gently suck the tender spot beneath her ear before releasing and waiting for more. "I don't mean physically. I mean . . ."

"I know what you mean. And you're right. I can't get enough of you. Of all of you."

She arches into my touch as I stroke her nipple with my thumb.

"I'm not usually home in the mornings," I admit, because she deserves the words too.

She shivers under my touch. "What are you talking about? You're home every morning."

"That first morning was a fluke. I usually change at the gym, but I realized I forgot my dress clothes for my meeting with my advisor. Then you were standing in my closet in a T-shirt and a thong, and I couldn't breathe."

"I remember that," she says, spinning around and looping her arms behind my neck. "I'm sure it wasn't anything you haven't seen before."

I huff out a laugh. She doesn't understand. It's something she does to me. "The second morning I came home early, I didn't even have an excuse. I felt like a fucking idiot. But there you were. In another T-shirt and another pair of panties that showed me the curve of your ass." I grip one hip and squeeze. "All I wanted was to bend you over and sink my teeth into it. That's the first thing I noticed about you when we met—this fine fucking ass." I squeeze the fleshy globes and groan at the feel of her in my hands. "At first I couldn't decide if you were trying to fuck with my head or if you were completely oblivious to what you were doing to me."

"I wasn't oblivious. I liked the way you looked at me," she says. Then, more softly, she says, "Tell me you thought about me."

I love that she doesn't doubt it. This isn't a request for reassurance; it's a request for the *words.* "Every fucking day. Every morning when I'd watch you make coffee in nothing but a thin shirt and a skimpy pair of panties and every night when I'd imagine you sleeping in my bed. I've wanted you from the beginning, and I only slipped that once. Only let myself cross my own lines that one time."

"And you pushed me away the next morning."

"I had to." I lean my forehead against hers as my fingers work the button on her jeans then the zipper. "I'm afraid to take more."

She gasps as I slide my hand inside her panties. "What are you afraid of?"

She's wet, and the feel of her on my fingers is intoxicating. "This."

"Why?"

"Because if I'm willing to fuck up my whole schedule just to get my eyes on you every morning, what will I fuck up to get a chance to do this every day?"

"What if you didn't have to fuck up anything? What if you could have me *and* everything you wanted?"

It's not possible, but it doesn't matter because I'm not sure there's anything I want more than her.

SAVVY

Oliver's hand's between my legs, his mouth at my neck. I'm lost to the pleasure of him. The pleasure of this moment.

"Let me take you home," he says in my ear, even as his fingers continue to play and torment and push me toward the edge faster than I knew I could go. "Jesus, Savvy. I need you in my bed again. I need all of you." He plunges a finger inside me, and I gasp.

"Here. I want you here." I fumble with the button on his jeans, and he spins me around, pressing me against the door.

His teeth scrape across my bare shoulder. "What do you do to me? I'm not fucking you in a utility room."

I free him from his briefs. He's hard and heavy in my palm, harder with each stroke of my fist. "What if I ask nicely?"

"*Christ.*" He shoves my jeans and panties from my hips in one rough movement. I shimmy out of them, kicking them to the side. "You're sure?"

"Please." His fingers are gone, and my sex pulses with the loss. "Now."

All I know is need. I need *him.* His grip is rough as he

lifts me off the ground and holds me between the door and his hard body. And when he drives into me—

"Oliver . . ." *It's good. So good.* "Yes."

"Savvy. Fuck, Savvy."

I wrap my legs around his waist and my arms around his neck. His mouth claims mine, and my body squeezes around him. I tangle my fingers in his hair as he pumps into me.

"You feel so good. Too good." He buries his face in the crook in my neck, his short beard abrading the sensitive skin there. "I've wanted this too long. Thought about it too many times . . ."

He slows his thrusts. Is he trying to hold on? I want him to let go.

I tug on his hair. "Don't stop."

"I've got you, sweetheart." He releases one thigh and snakes his hand between our bodies, finding my clit again. Stroking. Circling. Teasing. Stroking again. At first, it's too much. I'm spread open and sensitive. But his touch is intoxicating, and once I have it, I want more. *More.*

His thrusts are shallow, his breathing is uneven, and I know he's holding back. Trying to bring me to the brink first, and I'm so close. I'm *right there.*

"Harder," I breathe against his ear. "Oliver, just take me."

"Savvy . . ." He comes unleashed. His hips jerk unevenly then in long, deep thrusts that threaten to break the door. I love it and meet him stroke for stroke, biting his neck to keep from crying out as my body clenches in its final release.

He presses deep, following right behind with a shudder I feel in my core.

When his breathing slows, he guides my legs to the ground, but he doesn't pull out or release me right away. He holds my face in both hands and kisses me more tenderly than I've ever known him to do anything. "You wreck me in the best way," he murmurs against my lips.

I smile. "Now you can take me home."

He nips my bottom lip then slowly withdraws, only to freeze when he steps away. "Savvy?"

It's so dark in here. I wish I could see his face. I need to know if it matches the panic in his voice. *Don't pull away. Don't shut me out.* "What's wrong?"

"Shit." He takes another step back. I feel it more than see it. "Baby, I wasn't wearing protection."

My jaw drops. I'm never careless about this. Even when Chuck begged to have me without a condom, I refused. Maybe I didn't trust him even then. "It's okay," I say, trying to convince myself as much as him. "It's . . ." Is it okay? The last few weeks have been so crazy, I'm not sure how long it's been since my last period. "It should be okay."

"I'm sorry. Shit. I'm so sorry. If you get pregnant . . ."

"Oliver, it's not your fault. I forgot too."

He shoves my jeans at me. "Get dressed. I want to get you home."

I blindly pull my jeans on, not bothering with the underwear in the dark. I can feel his panic as if it's sharpened the air in the room, but just when I'm convinced he's angry, convinced he's going to pull away and shut me out again, he draws me into his arms and presses a kiss to the top of my head.

"I'll take care of you. In whatever way you need, I'll do it. You have my word."

I melt completely and half expect to slide out of his arms and into a puddle on the floor. Hard-ass Oliver promising to care for me might be the sweetest thing I've ever experienced.

CHAPTER TWENTY-NINE

OLIVER

As we leave the party, I hold Savvy's hand so tightly I'm afraid I might hurt her. But I need to touch her, and once we're in the car, I keep her hand in mine the whole way home and all the way up to my loft.

Only once I shut the door behind us do I let myself fully process what I've done. What I've risked—made *her* risk.

She bites her bottom lip and studies me. "It'll be okay," she says, inching closer. She touches my face with a tenderness I don't deserve. "I promise it'll be okay."

Of course she would try to reassure *me* in this moment when I'm the one who could walk away. When I'm the one who could've just screwed up her whole life. I grab her hand and press a kiss to the inside of her palm. "I'm so sorry."

Worry lines wrinkle her brow. "I had a full workup at the student clinic after I left Chuck, and I haven't been with anyone since. I don't have any STIs. Do you know . . ." She cringes.

"I had a workup first week of the semester." I swallow hard. "Everything was good."

"And since then? I know you go out a lot. Is there any chance that since then . . .?"

It blows my mind that she thinks I could've slept with anyone else since meeting her. That anyone but her could appeal to me when I know she's in my bed. "The last time I was intimate with anyone but you, you walked in on it."

Her eyes widen. "Wait—before classes started? How is that possible?"

I grunt. "Same way it's possible for you." I knew I wasn't risking her health, so I hadn't even considered that angle, but I'm glad we have it covered. I'm afraid to ask about the other part, but I have to. "Are you on birth control of any kind?"

She stares at the floor and shakes her head. "Chuck thought it was probably what was making me hold on to the extra weight, so I got off it months ago."

If I weren't so fixated on the potential consequences of that choice, I would hunt his ass down for the things he made her think about herself. "He is such a piece of trash, Savvy."

She takes another step closer and puts her hand on my chest. "I realize that now."

I wrap my arms around her and pull her against me

until she rests her cheek over my heart. "I meant what I said. I'll give you anything you need. If you end up pregnant, I'll stand by any decision you make. And I'll support you in every way I can."

I'm not my father. I would never walk away from my child.

But this is the second time I've let this happen, and that means I'm more like him than I thought.

"Oliver?" she whispers.

"Yeah?" My voice is rough. As if I'm already weighed down by the consequences of tonight's choices.

"Let's not borrow trouble, okay? Let's assume everything is fine until we know otherwise."

I kiss the top of her head. "Anything you need."

Part Eleven

PRESENT DAY

CHAPTER THIRTY

SAVVY

There's a scenic pullover not far from my apartment in Orchid Valley that I discovered not long after moving here. It's on a bluff that overlooks Lake Blackledge and all the lovely homes nestled into the trees around it.

I came here a lot when I first arrived in town. I was still trying to figure out who I was, trying to make sense of my life. Ever since, it's been the place I go when the chaos in my mind feels like too much and I need to clear my head to make a decision.

Today, I'm here because I'm about to face Alec's family as his *fiancée* for the first time, and my nerves are getting the best of me. It was bad enough to play this part when I knew Alec's connection to Oliver, but doing it now that I know Charles was Rose and Alec's father? Now that I know Cheryl was Charles's wife?

I sit on the hood of my car and stare out over the lake, forcing myself to take three deep, measured breaths. The wind whips through my loose hair and clouds overhead darken with each passing minute, matching my somber mood.

Two days. Two events. A rehearsal dinner and a wedding, and then I'll be home free.

I haven't talked to Alec since the flight back from L.A. We've exchanged texts twice. The first time he was checking to make sure I was home safely, and the second he asked if I was sure I wanted to go through with this weekend.

I said yes. I didn't tell him that I received an email from Mrs. McCoy, CEO of The Rage.

It was so lovely to meet you and your fiancé, Alec, at dinner last weekend. You are a lovely couple, and we were most excited about what your beauty paired with Alec's business expertise could mean for your success with The Rage.

We'd like to invite the two of you to our little vineyard for a weekend this summer to really dig into what your program would look like, what The Rage could do for you, and what you could offer The Rage. My assistant will be in touch with potential dates so we can find a weekend that works for everyone.

My *beauty.* That's what she thinks would make me successful in a partnership with them. And Alec's business expertise, as if I have none.

The idea of asking Alec to do anything more for me after last weekend was already making me sick, but it turns out that I don't need to ask him at all. I don't have the kind of reach I want to teach women about strength training, but I can build that. And if I don't? At least I'll never have to deliver my message on someone else's terms.

I replied, declining the invitation and thanking her for her time. Pressing *send* left me equal parts relieved and sad. I've been dreaming of this opportunity for years. I suppose the grief that comes with letting it go shouldn't take me by surprise.

Thunder rolls in the distance, and I take a few more deep breaths of the fresh mountain air, mentally preparing myself to meet Alec's family.

Tonight's rehearsal dinner is at Bella's Café, and I chose a black, strapless sheath dress for the occasion. It's elegant without calling any attention to itself, but if I stand out here any longer, it'll be ruined.

I climb back in my car, slide my key into the ignition, and turn it, but the car doesn't start.

"Shit."

Again. *Nothing.*

So much for my promise to not be late. There's no way I can make it on time now. I should've let Alec pick me up, but I told him I'd meet him there, knowing I'd need the time to collect myself.

I give my car once last chance. "Don't let me down."

Nothing.

"Shit."

I don't know much about cars, but I know enough to know mine is a grade-A POS. I just don't care enough to put my limited funds toward the thing that gets me from my apartment to work. If it clicks but doesn't start, I think that means the starter is out. Or is it the battery?

Shit, shit, shit.

I don't remember. Not that it matters. It's not like I have either of those parts handy—or like I would know what to do with them if I did.

I grab my phone and call Alec.

"Alec's phone, this is Rose!" a perky voice answers.

"Rose! I'm so sorry. Is Alec available?"

"He's at The Patio helping Jared tear down the arbor we set up for the ceremony. We're afraid it won't survive the storm."

"So he doesn't have his phone?" Okay. Dumb question.

"He forgot it, but I can call Jared and get him a message."

I cringe. "I'm at the scenic pull-off on Hunter Drive—he'll know where it is. Can you let him know my car won't start and I need a ride?"

"No problem at all. Are you okay?"

Thunder booms again—louder now—and shakes the car. "Yeah. I'm in my car. I'll be fine until he can get here."

"I don't like you being out there," Rose says. "We've been watching the weather, and it says these are ideal conditions for a tornado."

"I'm fine. This time of year, any storm comes with a warning like that. Just the local news making drama so we tune in."

A flash of lightning illuminates the cloud-covered sky.

"Someone will be there as soon as possible," Rose says. "I'm on it."

She hangs up before I can beg her not to send anyone but Alec. If I have to sit next to her mother on the drive downtown, I might shrivel under the weight of Cheryl's judging stare.

Less than ten minutes later, a black Explorer with tinted windows pulls into the spot beside me at the overlook and honks its horn.

I get out of my car and quickly open the passenger door of the Explorer, only to freeze at the sight of the dark-headed man waiting in the driver's seat.

My breath catches, and my mouth goes dry at the sight of Oliver. He's dressed in pressed black slacks and a white button-up shirt and tie. He's loosened the tie and unbuttoned the top button, and rolled the crisp white sleeves to his elbows to expose muscular forearms and a tree-of-life tattoo. He's a far cry from the rough, dangerous-looking guy I knew in college, but the rebel-in-a-suit-and-tie vibe works on him.

"Oliver."

"You're about to get soaked. Climb on in."

I can't breathe. This mountain road suddenly feels far too small. Too private. It's too dangerous to be alone in a car with the man who still owns my heart.

While part of me wants to tell him to get the fuck out of here, to insist that I can take care of myself, the logical part of my brain knows that if I refuse a ride with Oliver, Rose will know something's wrong.

I swallow. "Why are you here?"

"Rose was worried you were going to get swept away in the storm. I was just pulling into town, so she sent me to rescue you."

"You're going to take me to the rehearsal dinner?"

His gaze rakes over me. "I'll take you anywhere you want to go."

His words send warning bells blaring in my head, but I force out a thank you and climb into the SUV. After buckling my seatbelt, I straighten and find him leaning closer—too close—and examining my car with a sardonic twist to his lips.

"What?" I snap.

"I'm surprised my brother lets his woman drive around in something so unreliable." He says the last word like it means *dangerous*.

I stiffen. "It's not Alec's job to buy me anything."

He looks me over one more time before moving from my personal bubble. "Isn't it his job to take care of you? You're his fiancée. Doesn't making sure you're safe come with the territory?"

"I don't need to be taken care of."

"Still as stubborn as ever, I see." He smoothly backs out of the parking spot and turns onto Hunter Drive. "Did you wear that for my brother?" he asks, unapologetically sweeping his eyes over me again before he shifts them back to the road. "Or did you wear it for me?"

"You're an asshole."

His chuckle is deep and raspy. Warmth wiggles low in

my belly. "I never claimed otherwise, but it's good to see you've finally caught up."

I stare at his profile—the hard line of his jaw, the coolness in his eyes. "You knew Charles would want to set me up with Alec. Did you plan on sending me on dates with him and then letting him find out we were sleeping together? Is that how you get off? Taking everything you can from the guy who stole your father away before he could walk?"

His expression goes cold. Guarded. "I didn't take anything from Alec."

"You took Portentia."

His grip tightens on the steering wheel. "Don't bring her into this."

He's quiet the rest of the way to town.

By the time he parks in the lot behind the restaurant, the rain has slowed to a light drizzle.

Oliver cuts the engine and reaches for his door.

"Why are you here?" I blurt before he can open it.

His jaw twitches. "My sister wanted me to be at her wedding."

I nod. "But is that why you agreed to come?"

He scans my face, his expression somber. "How do you want me to answer that question, Savvy? What are you hoping to hear?"

"The truth."

Oliver's gaze dips to my mouth. "The truth is I still don't know if being here is a mistake. The *truth* is that I can't stand the idea of watching him touch you. Dance with you. Hearing him talk about his future with you. I can't stand thinking about you in his bed."

I swallow hard. His voice sounds too husky. Like he's trying to hold back anger or tears or both.

"It's bad enough," he continues, "that every time I close my eyes I remember how you looked, standing in his house in nothing but *his* shirt after a night in his bed. I'm making myself fucking crazy, and coming here is the worst kind of masochism, because I know it will make this ache in my chest so much worse."

I lick my lips, and power zips through me at the way his eyes darken as he watches the movement. "Then why come?"

He pulls his gaze from my mouth and brings it to my hand. The ring. "Because I *am* an asshole, and if you're going to spend your life with him, I want you to have to face me first. To remember *us* first."

"Oliver . . ." I want to tell him the truth, but I made Alec a promise, and what good would it do, really?

"I thought about it," he says, softer now. "I thought about just stepping back and letting Alec give you the life you deserve. I have no doubt he would. And he fits in your world, right? He's, like, the best friend of your best friend's husband? How fucking perfect." His sneer falls away and he shakes his head. "But I can't, Savvy. I fucking can't do that. Not when . . ." Taking my hand, he skims his fingers over my palm before pressing it to his chest. "Tell me you don't feel that. Tell me you feel nothing when we touch. Tell me it's all gone for you. Because if you do, maybe I'll believe that someday it will go away for me too."

I want to tell him what he needs to hear, but the truth is that touching Oliver, even after all these years, makes me feel alive. Makes me feel like my heart's stretching her arms and standing upright after a long sleep. I want to lie, but I'm too weak to form the words. "It doesn't matter."

His eyes shift back and forth between mine. "I never stopped loving you."

"Don't," I rasp. "You never loved me. Don't pull that shit now."

"You know I did. And you felt the same, or you wouldn't have run the way you did."

I squeeze my eyes shut. Walking away from Oliver was one of the hardest things I've ever done, but telling myself he never really loved me carried me through it. Telling myself there was a reason he never said those words was the only thing that kept me from calling him when I woke up in the middle of the night and reached for him before remembering.

Rewriting that history means tearing myself open again.

I squeeze my eyes shut, and when I open them, he's leaned in closer. So close I can feel his heat.

"I'm sorry I couldn't walk away. You deserve better." He slowly lowers his mouth to mine, and I close my eyes, too weak to resist the soft brush of his lips. Who knows if I'll ever see him again after this weekend? I'll let this be the goodbye we never got.

He cups my face, and his lips are as gentle as I remember them. His kiss is intoxicating and a reminder of all the kisses I once naïvely believed we had before us. It's warmth and safety.

He angles to deepen the kiss, but I pull back before he can, shaking my head. All those feelings are lies. Oliver and I crashed and burned, and it's no use pretending otherwise. "I can't do this with you."

"So it's him, then?" he asks.

I hang my head. *It's no one.* "We should get inside."

OLIVER

"Oliver! You rescued Savvy!" Rose squeals when we step into the Italian restaurant's party room. "Thank you!"

Alec snaps his attention toward us from across the room, his gaze angry when it meets mine and then morphing to hunger and lust when it lands on Savannah.

At least I've finally earned the loathing my brother feels for me. I can't regret that kiss, though. Can't regret telling her how I feel. Even if I should.

Savvy gives my sister a brief smile before making a beeline through the room. *To Alec.* Will she tell him about the kiss? Will she think about it tonight when he holds her in bed?

I pull Rose into a hug. "It wasn't a problem." I kiss the top of her head before releasing her. "How's the wedding prep going?"

She groans. "Cruella de Vil is doing her usual. Nothing's good enough; nothing's classy enough. Every choice I made has been declared either *trite* or *overdone*, or in the case of my cake topper, both trite *and* overdone."

"Wow. Who would've seen that coming?"

"Right? I pretended to fight for a few things, but I made my peace with her hijacking my wedding a long time ago." She sighs and scans the room and the dozen or so guests she invited to dinner. "If Dad were here, he'd never let her take over my day."

"He'd totally let you control the details," I say wryly, standing by her side as we look at the guests scattered out in the room, "as long as he got to choose the groom."

"Ugh. You're right, you're right. Mom is the lesser evil." She cuts her gaze to me. "Don't hate me, but I wish he were here to walk me down the aisle at this stupid wedding anyway."

I take her hand and squeeze it. "I'd never hate you for that. The old man had his moments."

She takes a glass of champagne from a passing server, then snaps around to stare at me. "Holy shit! I'm so focused on me I didn't even ask about the car ride." Her whisper is so loud, I glance around to make sure no one is paying attention to our conversation, but they're all happily enjoying the open bar. "Did you tell her?"

"I don't know what you're talking about."

She slaps my arm. "Stop it! I'm dying here."

Across the room, Savvy stands next to Alec at a small cocktail table. He catches me staring at him and slides his arm around her waist, pulling her into his side.

"I'm *waiting*," my sister says.

I tear my gaze off them. I've had my heart pummeled enough for tonight. "I told her," I say so low she has to lean in to hear me.

"And . . . ?"

"And then I kissed her."

"You dirty dog!" she shouts.

Her mother gapes at her from across the room then gives her a pointed look.

Rose turns to face me, giving her back to the room, and I know without looking that her mom is glaring holes into her back. "*That's behavior unbecoming of a hostess, Rose. You greet* each *guest; don't let one person gobble up your time*."

"You're pissing off the dragon," I warn her.

"So what? She won't be mad long. She's too busy being angry with Alec."

"Oh? And here I thought her golden boy could do no wrong."

"That was before he put a ring on Savvy's finger. She's *big mad* about that."

I scoff. "Seriously? Why?"

Rose rolls her eyes. "You know Mom. She wants her children to marry into a dynasty. Like wealth and connections come with blood."

I cough out a laugh. Then a whole string of laughter spills from my lips.

"What?"

"She hasn't figured it out. That's priceless." Savvy was always so insecure about her family not having any money. She never understood that for these people, the name and the clout will always means more. Charles's mother was "new money" and always trying to prove herself, and Cheryl's the same.

"Figured *what* out?"

"Savvy *Downing,* Peony. From *the* Downings."

"The old department store? The one Grandma loved?"

"That's the one." I shake my head. "I'm surprised Alec didn't tell her just so she'd let him marry the woman he loves."

Rose folds her arms and turns to look at the couple in question. His arm is still around her, but neither looks comfortable. If I hadn't seen her half-naked in his family room last weekend, I wouldn't believe they were a real couple.

"Oliver, I honestly don't think he knows."

"No way. They're *engaged.* How could he not know?"

"Yeah, well, like I said before," she says, turning back to me, "pretty weird relationship. Back to the *kiss.* I don't condone this, but I need details. Did she kiss you back? Is she breaking it off with Alec?"

She *definitely* kissed me back, but Rose doesn't need that level of info. "She said it's him."

Rose frowns. "*It's him?* That's what she said?"

"She pushed me away, Rose."

"Well, yeah. That's why you were supposed to have a mature conversation with her, not confess your love and then kiss her like she isn't wearing another man's ring."

I glance toward them again. Alec doesn't have his arm

around her anymore, and they both look more comfortable. "But you say Alec doesn't even know who her parents are?"

"If he knew, why would he keep it from Mom?"

"There's absolutely no reason." I watch Savvy and Alec for a while longer then shake my head. "No reason at all."

Part Twelve

EIGHT YEARS AGO

CHAPTER THIRTY-ONE

SAVVY

For two weeks, I've gotten to see a side of Oliver I once only suspected was there. A side that makes me happy and lustful and hopeful. A side that makes me anxious to get home every night—and so distracted once I'm there that I had to go back to doing my homework in the library just so I could focus. Which worked okay until a library study session evolved into dirty text exchanges that had him hunting me down in the stacks, holding his hand over my mouth so no one would hear my moans as he drove me over the edge.

Since that first night in the utility closet, we haven't been able to keep our hands off each other, but we've been diligent about protection, and while I think the possibility of an unplanned pregnancy hits some deep emotional wound for him, he hasn't opened up about it.

When I get home from my shift at The Naked Bean on Friday, I find Oliver in the bathroom, scowling at the mirror as he straightens his tie.

I give a low whistle as I saunter in. "Damn. Someone cleans up nice."

His scowl wavers for a beat as he cuts his eyes to me then looks back to the mirror. "I hate this shit," he mutters, but something about the look on his face as he takes himself in makes me think he hates what he sees more than the tie.

I step between him and the mirror and hoist myself up on the counter. "Where are you going?"

His face softens as he meets my eyes. "Just a family obligation I can't get out of."

"What family?" I frown. I sound like a heartless ass. "Your sister?"

"And brother and father and stepmother. Hell."

"I didn't think you talked to any of them." And I didn't know any of them lived close by.

He doesn't seem to take offense to my gaffe. He lifts one hand to my face and strokes my cheek gently with his knuckles. "Family only in the strictest definition of the word. These people don't really count."

"But they matter enough that you're all messed up about seeing them." In for a penny, in for a pound, I guess.

"That's how I know they're not real family. They fuck with my head."

I pull him down by his tie and suck his bottom lip between my teeth. "Take me with you, then," I whisper against his lips. "I'll protect you from your big, bad relatives. I won't let them fuck with you."

He groans against my mouth then kisses me hard. "Can't."

I try not to flinch, and fail. "Yeah. These are the fancy kind of family you don't take your bought-and-paid-for girlfriend to see. I get it."

He grips my hips and tugs me to the edge of the counter. I have to wrap my legs around his waist so I don't fall. "Don't tell yourself bullshit stories."

We both know it's not bullshit—at least not completely.

He kisses his way down the side of my neck and snakes a hand up my shirt to cup my breast. "Maybe I'll just stay here with you instead." He scrapes his teeth across my collarbone. His thumb dances over my nipple. Teasing. Promising. "Maybe I'll fuck you right here."

Those words flip something in both of us, and the undeniable need flares back to life.

In a frenzy, I reach for the belt on his pants, and he peels off my shorts.

And he fucks me against the counter just like he promised.

And after, when he straightens his tie before kissing me goodbye and heading out to see his family, I let myself cry. He promises to give me anything, but I don't know if he'll ever give me the only thing I really want. *All of him.*

~

I'm practically skipping when I get home from work on Saturday. My shift dragged on forever, and all I could think about was Oliver being home when I got back and having all day today and Sunday home with him.

It hurt that he didn't want me to meet his family, but after a good night's sleep I decided fighting that particular battle wouldn't be worth ruining the few weeks we have left together.

I unlock the door and push inside. The TV is on, which is weird. Oliver almost never watches TV alone, but maybe we'll do a movie together tonight.

He's sprawled out on the couch, scowling at his phone, seeming oblivious to the TV screen in front of him.

I drop my purse on the counter and take a seat next to him. "Hey, you. I was hoping to see you this morning, but you must've snuck out before I woke up."

He doesn't look at me—just scowls at his phone and scrolls. "You didn't miss me. I stayed in the city."

I flinch. "How was dinner?"

"Only slightly more miserable than I anticipated." He jabs at something on his screen.

These walls of his are high and impenetrable, and having him throw them at me is more painful than anything I encountered with Chuck. Maybe because I never really cared for Chuck the way I care for Oliver.

"Oliver . . ." I swallow hard. "Right now, you're

making me feel like you don't want me here, and if that's the case, I can leave, but if it's not, I wish you'd look at me."

He blinks up at me as if he's been shaken from a dream, then drops his phone and pulls me into his arms. "Fuck. I'm sorry."

I curl into his chest. The words *It's okay* sit on my tongue, but I trap them there and swallow them down. "Thank you," I whisper.

He toys with my hair, his expression softening. "These people are poison, and I feel off for days after I've had to be around them."

"Your father?" I ask.

"Yeah. And his wife and their son." His voice is rough, and I can tell every syllable is hard for him. He doesn't like talking about this. "My sister is the only one I can tolerate. Somehow she turned out decent despite them."

I twist and settle my head in his lap so I can look up at him. "Can you answer a question for me?"

"I can try." He traces along my jaw and across my cheekbones, as if he's trying to memorize the contours of my face.

"Why do you hate them so much?"

His beautiful gray eyes turn sad. "When I was young, I hated my father for abandoning my mother. I was too proud to hate him for abandoning *me*, but I saw how hard it was for her to raise me on her own, to be alone. And then when she died, I hated him for making me move in with him and his perfect fucking family. He wanted me to slide right into their world as if I'd been there all along, but *they* didn't want me there. His wife and son resented my very existence and made sure I knew it. My little sister was the only bright spot in the whole shitty ordeal."

"How long did you live with them?"

"Two long years." He sighs and settles a hand on my stomach, stroking lightly with his thumb. "I wanted to move out before then, to get emancipated, but my father had the money, and if I wanted him to pay for college, I had to live with them until I graduated from high school."

"He didn't see how they treated you?"

"He didn't care." His lips press into a thin line. "There's nothing my father loves more than keeping his children on a tight leash, and I am certainly no exception." He waves a hand, indicating the loft. "But, hey, at least I get to live like a rich brat in exchange for not having freedom, right?"

"The MBA was his choice too?" I take his hand from my stomach and thread our fingers together. "I thought you wanted this degree."

"I wanted an MBA so I could be a sports agent. He wanted me to have an MBA so I could work for him. I played along, figuring I'd wait until I landed an internship with an agency before I broached the subject with him. I was an idiot to think he'd let me make a decision like that on my own."

I squeeze his hand tighter. "You told him at dinner, didn't you? About the internship?"

His gaze goes distant. He's resisting the instinct to put up those walls. I feel it. But he nods. "It didn't go well." He huffs out a breath. "I didn't even make it to the main course before I stormed out of the restaurant. My sister tracked me down, and we drank too much as we lamented a life of servitude. That's why I didn't come home. It wasn't safe to drive." He scans my face. "I'm sorry I didn't text. Sorry if I made you worry."

"Sister." My chest goes warm. "You never call her *half* like you do with your brother."

He sighs. "Sorry. I guess technically she is my half-sister."

I shake my head. "Don't apologize. I'm glad you have *someone* that's truly family."

He huffs out a soft laugh and almost smiles. "Yeah. I'd claim her."

"Peony?" I ask, thinking of the woman I've been so jealous of all this time.

"Yeah." He meets my gaze and lets his smile free. It's so damn good to see. "I think you'd like her. I know she'd like you."

"That's a pretty name. I don't think I've ever heard it before."

He snorts. "It's a nickname. Her name is Rose, but I was a teenage punk when I moved in and liked to pretend I couldn't remember her name, so I called her Peony, and she was so immune to my efforts to antagonize her that it stuck."

I like imagining teenage Oliver, lonely and angry, trying to antagonize his new sister and being met with laughter and acceptance. I can't help but love her for that.

"Can I meet her? Next time we're in the city?"

His smile slowly slides away. "You know what scares me about you?"

"I'm not scary." I sit up, repositioning myself so I'm straddling his lap and our eyes are level. "Certainly not to someone like you."

He tucks a lock of hair behind my ear. "You fucking terrify me."

"Because I might be pregnant?" It's the first time I've said the word since the night we had unprotected sex, and when it hits the air, I half expect him to flinch, but he doesn't.

"You terrify me because if you're *not* pregnant, I'm going to have to come up with another excuse to keep you."

"Oliver—"

He presses his thumb to my lips before I can say more. "When you lose every good thing in your life, you stop wanting the good things at all. Knowing what's coming hurts too much. You terrify me because you make me want to risk losing something good again."

My heart cracks right down the middle for the tough guy who isn't so tough on the inside.

I cup his rough, stubbled jaw in both hands and hold his gaze. "You won't lose me."

He wraps his big hands gently around each wrist then turns his face from side to side to press a kiss into each of my palms. "It would serve me right if I did."

Leaning forward, I sweep my lips across his. "I love you," I whisper.

He spins me around so I'm lying on the couch and he's over me, his hands sliding under my shirt while his mouth claims mine. His kisses are deep and sweet and heartbreaking. I know he's saying with his mouth and body what he's too scared to say with his words.

CHAPTER THIRTY-TWO

SAVVY

Tuesday night after I finish my shift at The Naked Bean, I find Oliver in the kitchen, making me dinner.

I inhale deeply through my nose. "It smells amazing in here." I slide my arms around his waist and snuggle into his chest. "What is that?"

His hands go to my back and sweep down to my ass. "Freshly baked bread and lasagna."

I've had boyfriends who told me they loved me ten times a day and boyfriends who said it once or twice ever. In the three days since I told Oliver I love him, he hasn't said it back even once, but I've never *felt* so loved in any other relationship. He's made love to me every night and held me while I slept. He's made me breakfast and stolen kisses right there in the gym during every workout. And he's watched me. Whether I'm cooking or studying or screwing around on my phone, he seems to like nothing more than to look at me. Sometimes it's like he thinks I might disappear.

"That sounds so good." I smile up at him. "If you keep feeding me like this, you aren't going to be able to pick me up anymore."

He dips down, bringing his mouth to my ear. "Then I'll get stronger." Pulling back, he narrows his eyes at me. "You aren't still worrying about that shit, are you?"

I shrug. "I like getting stronger, and I like the way my body's changing, but it's scary. I've had a lifetime of being told to watch my weight. It's hard to make that go away in a few months. Properly fueling myself without the guilt is going to take time and practice."

He playfully smacks my ass. "Then I'll have to keep cooking for you."

I melt. *I love you.* But if he's going to show me with actions instead of words, I'm going to do the same. "I put in my request for this weekend."

"What's this weekend?"

I draw back so I can look up at him. "I called Coast to Coast Equities and Investments and found out Charles is going to be back in town on Friday. I'm going to go all 'damsel in distress' and get your treasure chest back?"

"No." He presses his hand between my shoulder blades and pulls me against him. "No, I changed my mind. I don't want you involved in that. I'll find another way."

I close my eyes and breathe him in. He always smells so good. The scent of his aftershave will probably forever make me feel safe and happy. "I don't mind."

"Well, I do. It's too risky, and I don't want you tangled up in the middle of it."

I frown. "I thought you said he was looking for a wife for his son."

He huffs out a laugh and loosens his hold on me. "And you think I want to risk his son getting anywhere near you?"

"What is he, some kind of creep?"

Oliver's jaw tightens. "No. He's a golden child. Everything you're looking for in your Prince Charming."

I bite back a smile, but it breaks free. "Oliver, are you jealous of some rich kid?"

"The point isn't that I'm jealous. It's that I don't want a reason to be. I don't want you involved in any of this."

"You didn't seem to care before."

He shrugs. "Aren't I entitled to change my mind?"

"You're trying to protect me," I say softly. "After all you did to make this happen—to get your hands on whatever this guy has—you're going to let it go because you want to protect me."

"Call it what you want."

"Do you always play the hero?"

His eyes go cold. "No, Savvy. I play the villain. And you'll be better off as soon as you stop forgetting that."

Bullshit. "Fine, Oliver. You're a selfish asshole who takes what he wants. So why stop now? Let me finish this. You don't even have to tell me what's in the chest."

"Drop it, Savannah."

"So he *doesn't* have something of yours?"

"That's not what I said. I don't want you involved. Plans changed."

"Okay. What's the new plan?"

He steps back and drops his hands to his side. "The new plan is to enjoy every second I can with you before I have to move and let you go."

I swallow hard. Long distance would suck, but we could make it work. If we both wanted it. "What if you didn't have to let me go?"

"Then I'd know for sure this was all a dream."

I want to push—to tell him it's not a dream and he can have me as long as he wants me—but instead I slide my hands behind his neck and kiss him, willing him with my body and my mouth to give this a real chance.

CHAPTER THIRTY-THREE

SAVVY

My period is late. Only two days, but late enough that I think about it a lot—think about what will happen if I tell Oliver, think about how scared I am that a pregnancy would change things between us, worry that a pregnancy might mean never knowing if he chose me for me or for the baby. Worried that no pregnancy might mean I really have to let him go when he leaves for his internship.

I skipped classes this morning and took the train to New York. Oliver teases me about wanting a hero, but something tells me that he needs one, that no one since his mom has been that for him. I can do this one thing for Oliver—get the box from Charles and get out of there. He thinks it's too much to ask, and that's exactly why I want to do it.

I dial the number scribbled on the business card, and my stomach twists as I wait for Charles to answer.

He doesn't. The call goes to voicemail.

"Charles . . ." My voice shakes, authentic nerves working to my advantage. "Um. I'm sorry. I didn't know who else to call. I'm in the city for the weekend, and I think my ex is following me. My friend is working late tonight, and I'm afraid if I stay at her place, he'll find me." I swallow audibly. "I'm sorry. You don't even know me. This isn't your problem. I just don't know who else to call. Thank you."

I end the call and pace my hotel room, checking my phone every thirty seconds to make sure I haven't missed a call back.

Eleven minutes later, my phone rings.

"Hello?"

"Savannah?" Charles sounds concerned. Fatherly. "Where are you? I can send my driver for you."

"I'm so sorry about this. I'm probably overreacting, but I keep seeing him, and then even when I don't see him, I feel like someone's watching me."

"Where are you?" he asks again.

"I'm at the Saks outlet," I say. It's just across the street from my hotel.

"My driver's in a black Explorer. He can be there in fifteen minutes."

"Thank you, Charles. So much."

"Don't mention it. I'm happy to look out for a special young girl like you, Savannah."

I hang up the call and swing my large tote-style purse over my shoulder before rushing to the elevator.

In fifteen minutes, a black SUV pulls up outside of Saks. Charles climbs out, dressed in a suit and tie like he came straight from his office, and holds the door for me.

"You didn't have to come," I say.

"I was concerned." He motions for me to take a seat in the back then climbs in after me.

Honestly, I was hoping he might not be with me when I went to his apartment, but I'm going to do this for Oliver the hard way or the easy way. "Well, thank you again."

His gaze dips to my hands. "You're shaking."

Indeed I am. I've made some questionable choices in my life, but I've never outright stolen from someone. What is Oliver's relationship to Charles? Why does Charles have something of Oliver's? What will I find in that chest, and what will Charles do if he catches me taking it? I have so many unanswered questions that we pull up to the big building on Park before I'm ready.

"Let's get you upstairs," Charles says, a gentle hand between my shoulder blades.

I let him lead me past the doorman and into the building. In the elevator, I stare at my hands clutching my purse in front of me. It feels awkward and unnatural. As if I'm holding a sign that says, *I'm going to steal from you.*

"Do you want to call the authorities?" Charles asks. "Is he dangerous?"

I shake my head. "They told me there's nothing they

can do until he actually hurts me or breaks a law. And anyway, I know he has to leave the city tonight. He'll lose his football scholarship if he's not at their team meeting in the morning."

Charles sighs, mutters something about "young men these days," then guides me into his apartment.

The place is massive, made bright and airy with tall ceilings and big windows. I cringe to imagine what an apartment this size costs in Manhattan—and this isn't even his primary residence.

"Unfortunately, my housekeeper is gone until morning," Charles says. "But I can order in some food if you're hungry?"

I shake my head. "I'm too worked up to eat."

He waves toward the giant sofa in the living area. "Please, have a seat. It's rather serendipitous that you called. I had planned to reach out to you through your academic advisor. I wanted to talk to you about something."

My stomach feels like it's turning inside out as I lower myself onto the soft cushions. What have I gotten myself into? "What's that?"

He takes a seat on the opposite end of the sofa and scans me. It's not sexual but assessing. "I know this might seem an odd thing to say, given how those your age seem to meet your romantic partners these days—on the apps and everything—but I have a son I would like to see with a good match, and from the first moment I saw you, I felt something."

I raise my brows. "Something like what?"

"Call it intuition—call it a sixth sense. I saw you and immediately thought you could be my daughter someday."

I cock my head to the side, studying him. "And how does your son feel about you selecting his future wife?"

He chuckles. "Trust me, he would not take kindly to it. And yet I can't help myself." He sighs. "I haven't been a very good father, Savannah. I've been more absent than present—letting my business take me away from my children when I should've used the flexibility I gained from my successes to make time for them. And my son . . ." He presses his hand to his chest. "I've made so many mistakes with him. I know it's too late to be the father he needed, but I hope I can play a part in giving him the family he deserves."

My heart squeezes. Whatever horrible thing he's done in the past, this man is sincere now. "That's really sweet." *And now I have to steal from him.* "How can you be so sure he'd be interested in me?"

"Like I said. Intuition." He winks at me. "I'd hoped that I could get to know you better, Savannah, that I could make a better plan before introducing you to my son, but unfortunately, my time is limited."

All the guilt and doubt I felt leading up to this moment doubles with that word. "Limited?"

"Lung cancer," he says. "When I was in my twenties, I thought I was invincible and smoked like a chimney. By the time I quit, it was too late. I've had two lobes of my left lung removed, and when a new spot appeared, I chose not to do anything about it. I wanted to spend my last days preparing everything for my family rather than vomiting my guts up from chemo."

Does Oliver realize Charles is dying? "But if the chemotherapy could buy you a few more years . . ."

"We all die eventually, and I've made peace with my time coming very soon." He coughs into his elbow. "Though judging by my last visit to my doctor, it may be sooner than any of us expected." He pulls an envelope from the inside pocket of his suit coat and hands it to me. It's unique. Sage in color, with *Coast to Coast Equities and Investments* watermarked on the back flap. "I hope you'll find a way to connect with my son, one way or another, once I'm gone."

I frown. "You're not going to introduce me to him?"

He coughs again, lightly. "If I do that, I'll ruin your chance before you get started." Closing his eyes, he takes a long, deep breath. "I need to get back to my office to put a few more things in order, but please make yourself at home. You can let yourself out when you're ready."

"Thank you," I say weakly.

He nods and leaves with a soft click of the door, and I'm left staring at the blank envelope in my hands. I could leave now and Oliver would never know I was here. He'd never know I chickened out when I was so close to what he wanted. Or I could stay and finish what I've started. I'm not stealing from a dying man. I'm retrieving Oliver's belongings and returning them to him.

I glance toward the hall where Charles disappeared and decide to explore the hall that branches off the other side of the living space. The first doorway is open to a tidy office furnished with a solid wood desk and matching bookshelves.

The ache in my gut intensifies, and that telltale sticky heat blossoms between my legs.

I rush to the bathroom across the hall and find exactly what I expected: I've started my period. I clean up, grateful that I had the foresight to put supplies in this big-ass purse, then wash my hands before texting Oliver.

Savvy: I got my period.

There's a weird twinge of disappointment in my heart. It's ridiculous, and I know I should be glad, but I didn't hate the idea of having Oliver's baby. Worried that my disappointment will be obvious from that text and scare him away, I quickly send another.

Savvy: What a relief!

I stare at my phone for a minute, wishing he'd text back right away. When he doesn't, I resume my exploration of Charles's apartment.

Next to the bathroom and across from the office is a bedroom. The king-size bed is dressed with a fluffy white duvet, and the windows are draped in matching sheers. The second my gaze lands on the decorative chest on the dresser, my stomach drops to the floor.

I pull my phone from my purse and check for messages from Oliver. There's a notification for my email, letting me know my econ professor sent a link to some videos she'd like us to watch before class. But nothing from Oliver. I don't know what I want him to say.

Thanks for letting me know.

Cool.

Great news.

No, that's not what I'm looking for, and it's not fair. I want *You would've looked beautiful carrying my baby.* Or *Someday, when we're both ready, we'll do it right.*

He was right. I've been reading too many romance novels. This is real life, where there's nothing romantic about getting your twenty-one-year-old girlfriend pregnant.

I swallow hard before opening the chest. Inside there are maybe half a dozen large manilla envelopes so full they're bursting at the seams.

With a knot in my gut, I open my purse and fill it with the contents of the chest.

I made it back in town just in time for my Friday night shift at The Naked Bean. I didn't even have time to run home and drop off this giant purse and all its secret-treasure envelopes for Oliver, so it's weighing me down as I haul ass out of there after close.

I look up to the dark, moonless sky and groan at the sound of icy rain hitting the trees.

I should wait inside and call Oliver. He'd pick me up

if I asked, but I want to get home and set all this stuff out for him. I want to surprise him. *Look, I did something scary for you. See? You deserve love too. See? I'm not going anywhere.*

A little sleet never hurt anyone, so I decide to walk as planned and turn to lock up.

"You blocked my number."

I freeze at the sound of that familiar voice behind me. I make myself take a breath and turn the lock much more calmly than I feel before palming my keys.

I can already tell how close he is, even before I turn around and look into his dark eyes. Chuck looks exhausted, as if he's been training hard and partying harder. But at least he's not drunk. "What do you want?" I ask.

"I want to talk to you. Jesus. I fucking did everything for you, and you disappeared from my life."

I shake my head. Intellectually, it's easy to see how I could've fallen in with Chuck. How his sweet words and whirlwind love-bombing would sweep me off my feet when my self-esteem was so nonexistent. But I still hate myself for it. It's beyond embarrassing that I fell for his shit. "You lost that fight on purpose—after convincing Nathan to bet more on it than he had. Why would I talk to you after that?"

He jams his hands into his pockets. "I have a problem, okay? I just needed a little extra cash to cover my own gambling debts, and I knew your family had money, so—"

"But they *don't*. My family hasn't had money for decades."

His nostrils flare. "They have that fancy fucking house. And I've seen the car your dad drives."

That "fancy house" is mortgaged to the max and that car was my grandfather's prized possession, but Chuck doesn't know that and doesn't deserve any explanation. "I don't have time for this. I need to get home."

"Home? Is that what you think it is?"

I adjust my purse on my shoulder and walk away, putting distance between us as fast as possible. I've been learning self-defense, but I don't want to use it.

"Time to get home and get on your knees for Oliver?"

I spin around, anger pumping hot in my veins. "Why are you being such a dick?"

"Everyone knows he bought you like a fucking whore, so you can stop pretending he's your boyfriend."

"I never said he was my boyfriend." My voice is shaking. "But for the record, I would get on my knees for Oliver every day of the week before I ever let you touch me again. At least he gives a shit about me and isn't using me because he thinks my family is rich."

"Nah, he doesn't need your family's money," he says, jogging to catch up with me. "He has plenty of his own. So much that he'd rather buy a piece of ass than have to bother with romance and shit."

I roll my eyes and keep walking. "Whatever. Tell yourself whatever you want."

"You're so fucking naïve, Savannah. How do you think he knew to show up and save you that night?" He smirks. "You think he just walks around paying people's debts?"

I have no doubt about how it looks from the outside, but I know the truth, and that's good enough. Oliver helped me because he needed whatever it is I'm carrying in this purse. And because he hates Chuck and wanted to stick one to him.

"You were so quick to call me out for throwing that fight," Chuck says, his steps quick behind me and his voice coming closer, "but did you ever stop to ask yourself who would pay me to do that? Did you ever ask yourself who would have enough money that I'd be willing to risk Nathan's ass?"

I stop walking. It's like my mind can't handle processing his words at the same time as putting one foot in front of the other. My hand tightens around the strap of my purse. "What are you saying?"

"Rhett paid me ten grand to throw the fight. He gave me fat cash to make you the damsel in distress, trying to save her brother. But joke's on him because I don't want anything to do with your used-up cunt."

He storms away, and I'm so unsteady that his ugly words don't even sting. *Oliver is the one who paid off Chuck. Oliver put my brother in danger, and Oliver crafted this whole situation to get me under his roof and doing his bidding.*

I know it's true as surely as I know the icy rain coating the sidewalk is real.

Part Thirteen

PRESENT DAY

CHAPTER THIRTY-FOUR

ALEC

"Do you want me to call a tow for your car?" I ask Savvy when I drive her home from the rehearsal dinner. We made it through the night. Barely. But it's over now. One more event to go, and then I plan to avoid family gatherings like the plague for as long as possible.

"Nah," Savvy says. She has her arms wrapped around herself, rubbing her shoulders like she's cold. "I already called Smithy. He has a friend who took it in to the shop for me."

I nod and turn up the heat instead of offering her my jacket. She doesn't want me to take care of her, and considering everything else, I'm not sure why that's so hard to swallow. "So, I wanted to ask you about something Rose said to me tonight."

"What's that?"

I bite my lip. There's no way I played it cool. Rose has to be suspicious about me and Savvy now, and I hate that. Almost as much as I hate lying to her at all. "She said that you're a department store Downing."

Savvy stiffens then sighs. "Yeah. That was my grandpa's thing."

I cough out a laugh. "Your grandpa's *thing*. Do you realize that my mother would've never treated you like she has if you'd told me that? She would've fawned all over you from the start."

"Just like Charles," she mutters. "What is *up* with you people? Do you have a fetish for families with failed dynasties or what?"

I pull into her apartment complex and park the car before turning in my seat to face her. She's staring out the window, her cheeks flushed from tonight's bottomless glass of wine. "Savvy? What do you mean, *Just like Charles*? Did you meet my dad? Did Oliver actually introduce you to him?"

Her face goes slack, and she puts her hand to her mouth. "Shit." She shakes her head. "Shit, Alec, I've had too much to drink. Let's not talk about this."

I stare at her, and relief and confusion flood me all at once. "You're the blonde who he had in his place with him that day," I say. "Aren't you?"

She worries her bottom lip between her teeth. "Alec . . ."

"Why would you keep that from me?" My chest aches. How much more has she kept from me?

"I didn't want you to know I was there because I didn't want you to know I stole from him."

I shake my head. "That doesn't make sense. What could my father've had that you . . ." I scrape a hand over my jaw. "Oliver sent you, didn't he?"

"It was initially his idea, but then he called the whole thing off, and I went through with it anyway. I thought Charles was just some random rich guy. I didn't know he was Oliver's father," she says. "What did I take?"

"I don't know. My mom was the one who knew there was anything missing at all, and she wouldn't talk about what was in that chest. How do *you* not know, though?"

"I didn't look. The chest was full of stuffed, oversized manilla envelopes. I didn't tell you before because I believe whatever I took belonged to Oliver. He might've lied to me about other things, but I don't think he lied about this."

"Well I know that part of the story now, so why don't you start at the beginning?"

SAVVY

I never meant to tell Alec everything, and maybe if I hadn't had so much wine I would've been able to find a way around it, but once the story is out, I feel lighter. I told him about the clothes, the martinis, about how I truly liked his father and hated taking anything from him.

Alec's staring out the windshield at nothing. "You saw him the day he died and he was giving you my number?"

"I think he wanted to do right by you," I say.

"Do you still have it? The envelope with my contact info in it?"

"No. I dropped it into the big purse with everything else and left it with Oliver."

"My father picked you for me." Slowly, Alec turns in his seat and meets my eyes. I feel like he hasn't really looked me in the eye since that morning Oliver walked into his kitchen and dropped the bomb about our past.

"Alec, I'm sorry. I didn't—"

He shakes his head. "It doesn't matter. Regardless of what Oliver's motivations were, my father picked you for me and then fate still brought us together that night in Vegas. Doesn't that mean anything to you?"

I open my mouth, then snap it shut. Finally, I find words that are neither cruel nor misleading. "I can see why it might seem that way to you. But I . . ." I have to look away. "I don't think this is fate, Alec. I don't think fate would want me to hurt you like I have, and like I no doubt would if we really tried to make this work."

His face goes colder than I've ever seen it. "Yeah. I guess not."

I'm ruining everything. "I should go inside. There's nowhere good this conversation can go." I swallow hard. "I'm sorry."

"Please stop saying that."

"It's true. I hate this."

"My father *picked you for me* eight years ago, and I find

out now, and you want me to treat it like it means nothing."

I slap the dashboard. "Well, he picked Portentia for you too, didn't he? Do you still think *that* means something?"

I was wrong. *Now* his face is colder than I've ever seen it. "You're right," he rasps. "You should go inside. Nothing good can come of this conversation."

CHAPTER THIRTY-FIVE

SAVVY

"Why the sad face, boo?" Stella asks, leaning in my bedroom doorway on Saturday afternoon.

I'm sitting at the small vanity at the foot of my bed, and when I study myself in the mirror, I know it's going to take some heavy-duty concealer to hide the bags under my eyes. "I didn't sleep well last night." I grab my cosmetic bag and get to work.

"Hot dreams of a certain tall, dark, and handsome businessman?"

I scoff. Because she's right—only not in the way she means. I dreamed of Oliver. Of his mouth on mine and his breath in my ear. I dreamed of us back in Crossport, making out on the couch in his loft, and I dreamed of him here in Orchid Valley, stripping me bare in the middle of Smithy's bar while my friends looked on with judgment in their eyes.

"What about Alec?" Dream Brinley asked. "Alec has been nothing but good to you. His dad picked you *for him!"*

I woke up feeling anxious and more tired than I felt when I climbed into bed, but I pulled myself to the kitchen for coffee, mentally repeating my new mantra. *One more day. One more day.*

"Savvy, don't stress," Stella says. "You're hot as fuck, and Alec isn't going to be able to keep his hands off you. And once he sees what you're wearing underneath . . ." She nods toward the black strapless bra peeking out from my dress and whistles low.

I shoot her a look and adjust the top, making a mental note to apply some garment tape before I go. "That wasn't my intention."

"You're not even a little tempted to turn this fake dating ruse into the real thing?" Stella's one of those people who's almost always smiling and almost never serious, but the amusement falls away when she meets my gaze. "You know you can trust me if you ever want to talk about what this is all about, right?"

I *could* trust her. The problem is, I've spent so many years believing Oliver fooled me into everything that I never trusted anyone with the story. But after yesterday . . .

"I never stopped loving you."

My stomach flips, and I take a deep breath to steady myself. "There's nothing to talk about," I tell Stella. "Alec is a nice guy, but we're better off as friends."

She hums, and the doorbell rings. "Expecting someone?"

I glance at my watch. "That's probably the guy Rose was sending over to do my hair."

"She's sending you a personal hairdresser?"

I shrug. "Rich people thing, I guess. Would you let him in on your way out?"

"Sure." She takes me by the shoulders and presses a kiss to my forehead. "You deserve happiness too," she whispers, then she pulls away.

"Thanks, Stella." I close my eyes and focus on my breathing as I listen to the click of her heels as she goes to the door.

"She's in her room," I hear Stella saying. "Down the hall. First door on the right."

I grab the engagement ring from its spot inside my vanity and hurriedly slide it on. It's not like the hairdresser is going to tell Rose that I wasn't wearing it, but I don't want to risk forgetting it.

The guy's reply is a husky rumble so low I can hardly make it out, but it's followed by the sound of the front door closing and heavy steps moving my way.

I take a deep breath and roll back my shoulders, then turn to the door to thank the stylist for coming, but all the words fizzle away when I see the man who haunted my dreams last night and so many nights before.

Oliver surveys me—from the hair I have piled in a sloppy bun on top of my head to the swell of my breasts, all the way down to where the short hem of the fitted dress grazes my thighs. His gaze is like a hot caress as it skates over my bare legs and takes the slow journey back up.

When he meets my eyes, he tucks his hands into his pockets. "And to think I once didn't believe it was possible for you to be any more beautiful," he says, his voice a low rumble. "Time has proven me wrong."

"What are you doing here?" It's a marvel that I was able to get the words out when I don't even feel attached to my body. I'm somewhere else—hovering between this moment and one eight years ago when I waited for him in an outfit not unlike this one. When I let him peel it off me, let him run his mouth over every inch of exposed skin, let him break me apart and then put me back together again.

"I visited my brother this morning—at his hotel." He scans my bedroom, the unmade bed, last night's cotton PJs rumpled in the corner, and the romance novel on my bedside table. "You still have a thing for romance heroes, huh? I wonder how well my brother fits the bill."

"They're books. They're entertaining. Don't read so much into it."

He scans my space one more time. "Interesting that you don't have your fiancé staying here with you."

"What's your point, Oliver?"

"Just making an observation." He steps leisurely toward me. This close, I can see his dark stubble—already breaking through from this morning's shave. This close, I can feel his heat. "Look at you," he murmurs.

Oliver is in my apartment. In my bedroom.

I'm too mesmerized by his gentle touch on my shoulder to put distance between us.

His callused fingers are rough against my skin, and I'm so dizzy with the longing and heartache from the past and present pulling me in two different directions that I have to close my eyes.

"Fucking look at you," he whispers. His fingers skim across my collarbone then dip down to ghost over the swell of my breast. "Tell me you missed me. Fucking lie to me if you have to. I've missed you. So goddamned much."

"Oliver," I rasp. Maybe it's been eight years, but I know this man well enough to know he'd stop if I asked. He'd leave if I asked. But I *have* missed him. More than I even realized. Every time he touches me, it feels like being reunited with a lost piece of my heart. "You aren't supposed to be here."

"I'm supposed to be wherever the fuck I want to be. And right now . . ." He dips his head, and when he speaks again, every word hums against my ear. "Right now I want to be right here."

I'm trembling. This is unfair. I wasn't prepared. This is three times now that I've had to face him without warning, and I'm so unsteady.

"I will spend the entire night thinking about getting you out of this dress and what I'm going to do when you come to me after the reception. I can't decide if I want to unzip it myself so my hands are ready for all this beautiful skin when the dress falls away or if I want you to do it for me while I sit back and watch."

"You're delusional."

"Am I? Are you going to pretend you haven't been thinking about it? About us? About what it would be like to be in my bed again?"

"Why are you doing this?" I ask, even as I sway toward him. "To punish me?"

He nips at my ear. "Do you need to be punished for something, Savannah?" Those warm fingers trail down my back, between my shoulder blades, and dance along the length of the zipper. I half expect him to unzip me now, but he doesn't. "Like lying to me? Lying to Alec's whole family?"

"I don't know what you're talking about."

He hums. His palm flattens on my low back before shifting to my hip, the touch both tender and sensual. My body buzzes. "You always were a terrible liar."

I open my eyes, step back, and lift my chin. "Unlike you. *You* were always good at it."

His smile is so sad. "I never wanted to hurt you. I always believed I could walk away, but even after all this time . . ."

"Why are you here? What do you want?"

"What about what *you* want?" His gaze travels to my thighs and then back up, as if he can see right through the black fabric of my dress. "Have you given much thought to what you want?"

"What I want doesn't concern you."

"You're wrong about that. It's always concerned me. From the first night we met, there was nothing that concerned me more than giving you what you wanted."

"There you go, rewriting history again. You wanted to take something from Chuck and get your things back from Charles. *That* was why you paid my debt. *That* was why you took me in."

"That was what I told myself. That was what I wanted to believe. Your name was just the excuse I needed to get you close. I wanted you close from the moment I fed you for the first time." His knuckles graze my stomach. Up and back down with only the barest contact. Shivers of pleasure and anticipation race down my spine. "You were the only person who ever thought better of me. The only one who believed there was any kindness in this bitter heart. And I ruined that, didn't I? Now I'm standing here wondering if I can ever convince you to see that side of me again."

I still see it. I know who you are. But I bite back the words. "You're too late for that."

"Are you planning to feed me more of that bullshit about you and Alec being madly in love?" He drops his hand, staring unblinkingly into my eyes. "Because I'm not buying it. Either it's total bullshit and you're both liars, or you're leading him on."

"What's that supposed to mean?"

"He might be in love with you, but you're not in love with him. I've seen you in love. Alec's family might fall for that shit, but I know better."

My stomach flips. I need to get through today for Alec and then talk to him about telling Oliver the truth—decide if I even want Oliver knowing the truth. Maybe I don't need to tell him. He'll figure it out eventually—

when there's no wedding, when Alec and I are never together at family functions.

Oliver's suddenly closer somehow, too close—and the self-preservation part of my brain tells me it's time to put space between us again. But I don't. Because today, when I'm feeling so lonely and sad, when I've seen the best and worst of his family and had to say goodbye to my dreams, I want to stay right here. Close to him.

"Oliver," I whisper. Maybe I'm delirious from lack of sleep or maybe it's because I know exactly how it feels to be that alone in the world, but I place my hand on his chest. His heart pounds beneath my palm. His breath hitches at my touch. I didn't realize—didn't *let* myself realize—how much I missed him. Not just the crazy fun we always had together, but *him.* The way his closeness wrapped me in a warmth I could never understand, the way I never felt alone when he was close.

He wraps his long fingers around my wrist but doesn't move my hand from his chest. Instead, he brushes his thumb across my pulse point. We stare at each other for a long time like that, feeling the beat of each other's heart until they pound in time.

He closes his eyes and touches his forehead to mine, exhaling. "I'm going to kiss you now, Savannah."

I tilt my mouth up to his, and he takes it, sucking my bottom lip between his teeth and biting gently before sliding his tongue against mine. I moan, and he growls into the kiss, angling his head and tugging on my hair.

He tastes like memories and regret. If I were smart,

I'd back away now. If I were smart, I'd push him out the door and forget this happened.

But when it comes to Oliver Rhett, I've always been more foolish than wise.

"Fuck, I missed this mouth," he says, sliding his fingers down between my breasts as his other hand unzips my dress. His mouth is a beat behind his hands. He trails hot, open-mouthed kisses between my breasts and over my stomach.

The dress falls to my feet, and I'm standing there in nothing but a lace bra and matching panties. And my heels.

Oliver's hands roam, cupping my breasts before his mouth trails back up to have a turn. He parts his lips over my nipple, making it pucker through the lace before sucking hard.

I cry out, my hands in his hair. I tug and bring him back up to my mouth. This kiss is softer, but his grip on my hip is anything but. It's a possessive squeeze, a hungry claiming. *You were always mine,* his hands say. *And I was always yours.*

He traces the waistband of my panties with one knuckle, his breath against my lips. "Ever since I saw you in that fucking trench coat, I haven't been able to stop thinking about getting my mouth on you again."

I shiver, lust turning my blood to liquid fire. Every nerve ending is a live wire, waiting for his touch.

He nudges me back until the backs of my thighs hit the vanity. He lifts me onto it by my hips, and I spread my thighs and grab his shirt to pull him closer.

Oliver smiles against my mouth. "You still scream when you come?" he asks. He slides one hand between our bodies and cups me, pressing into my clit with his palm. "Fuck, you're wet. So wet. You've been thinking about this as much as I have."

I don't want to admit it, but to deny it would be an outright lie. I shut him up with a kiss, and with his mouth on mine, he deftly unclasps my bra and slips my panties from my hips.

Without warning, he tears his mouth from mine and drops to his knees. He uses his palm to spread me open and stares for a long beat before licking up the center of me. I clench my thighs, trying to squeeze them together to capture the sensation, but he holds me open as he does it again. His tongue flicks over my clit again and again, and I gasp as pleasure coils tight in me. "Please."

Oliver circles my entrance with two fingers and lifts his head. "Please what?"

I lift my hips, searching for those fingers, for—"More."

He plunges two fingers inside me. My body clenches around them, and I moan. "I could stay here all night and watch you fuck my fingers with that pretty pussy."

"I need . . ." I circle my hips, desperate, hungry. "Oliver."

He grunts in approval and dips his head, his mouth on my clit, curls those fingers, and finds that perfect spot. My hips jerk. My body clenches and releases in a violent wave.

I'm still shaking as he backs away and leads me off

the vanity. He looks me over in nothing but my heels and scrubs a hand over his face. "Shit, Savvy . . ."

The doorbell rings, and it's like I'm snapped from a dream.

I'm supposed to be pretending to be Alec's. This ring on my finger is supposed to be real. And I just let Oliver . . .

"That was a mistake," I say in a rush, and my body and heart scream in protest. The only moment with Oliver that ever felt like a mistake was the one where I walked out on him. But the last thing I want to do is embarrass Alec. I promised. "Oliver, please don't tell anyone. If the family finds out . . ."

"I see." Oliver's face is a mask of indifference, but I see the hurt in his gray eyes. "Still your dirty little secret."

CHAPTER THIRTY-SIX

ALEC

Savvy's distracted and upset on the drive to the wedding, and I'm pretty sure it's not just work-related.

Derek McCoy, the douchey husband of The Rage CEO, contacted me to let me know Savvy turned down an opportunity for a second interview during a weekend away with them at their vineyard. He was disappointed and wanted to be sure I, as her future husband, was aware of the opportunity she was throwing away.

I didn't reply. Mostly because no matter what Savvy's reasons were, letting this guy know that he's a misogynistic piece of shit isn't going to do her any favors in her industry.

When I picked her up from her place to drive to the wedding, she could barely look at me. I keep checking her hand to make sure my ring is still there because I'm so convinced that any minute now, she's going to take it off and tell me she can't pretend anymore.

Sure enough, by the time I park at The Orchid, she's staring at it as if agreeing to this ruse is the biggest mistake she's ever made. "Alec—"

"I know that you turned down the next interview with The Rage."

Her head snaps up. "You do?"

"Yeah." I clear my throat. "I hope it wasn't because of anything I've—"

"No." She shakes her head. "I decided I didn't want to play by their rules. I knew you'd come with me if that was what I wanted, but I realized it wasn't. I don't like the way they run their business, and I don't like the way they make me feel."

I swallow. "If you're sure."

"I am." She gives me a sad smile. "It works out better this way anyway—no more awkward pretending."

I cringe. "I am so sorry about last night. It's no excuse for pushing the way I did, but grief is a funny thing, and it makes us cling to whatever remnants of the person we have left."

"I'm sure it was hard to hear me tell you that when you know how I feel."

I close my eyes. It's how she *doesn't* feel that's the problem. "I just need you to get through tonight. Mom invited Portentia after all, and as ridiculous as it sounds, I don't think I can endure this without you."

"You won't have to," she says, squeezing my hand on

the console.

"Then why do you look so wrecked?"

When she blinks up at me, there are tears in her lashes. "Oliver came over earlier, and . . . things happened."

Why are those words like a knife in the heart? I clench my jaw. "Of course he did."

She puts a hand on my arm. "I didn't tell him that this isn't real, but he suspects. I wonder if maybe keeping the truth from him is worse. After what happened with him and Portentia—"

"You mean after he seduced the woman I planned to marry?"

She flinches. "Maybe it would be better if we told him it's not real. Otherwise, he's walking around thinking I cheated on you with him."

I cough out a dry laugh. "Are you worried he's going to feel guilty? Because trust me, Savvy, Oliver doesn't do guilt. He's conniving and manipulative and—" I smack the steering wheel. The idea of his hands on her makes me want to tear my hair out. "You *know* all this. How could you let him touch you anyway?"

"Because I've missed him for eight years," she blurts. Then, softer, she says, "I'm sorry." She folds her arms, hugging herself tightly. "I want you to choose how we handle this."

I cock my head to the side and study her. "You know his game, right? This doesn't end with him sweeping you off your feet. He steals you away, and then once he ruins *us*, he's gone."

"Alec, there is no *us*. I keep trying to tell you that. There can't be an us."

"Because of him." She doesn't reply. Maybe because it's not a question. "Have you asked yourself where he was all these years if he really wanted you? Have you stopped to wonder if he would've bothered coming to town and being the mysterious outsider if he didn't believe you were my girlfriend?"

She stares at her lap. "Of course I've wondered that."

"This is what he does, Savvy. He was so fucking wounded by the way our father abandoned him when he was a baby—and let me be the first to say that was total shit behavior on my dad's part—but you know who's gotten to pay the price for his bitterness? *I have.* From the moment he swept into our high school and took my fucking place as the starting running back to the moment he got my girl pregnant in college. And after all these years, once I finally think he's living his own life and not just trying to ruin mine, I find out he's the reason you never let us have a chance. And now that he thinks we're *engaged*, he's here. Rescuing you from a broken-down car and showing up at your house before my sister's wedding. He's seducing you when he thinks you're mine, but you better be careful, because the second that ring comes off your finger, he'll lose interest. You'll be nothing to him all over again."

"Thanks for the vote of confidence."

I flinch at the pain in her eyes. "I'm sorry. I'm trying to be honest because I don't want him hurting you."

"So you're saying you want me to keep the ring on

and keep pretending we're getting married. If that's what you want, I'll do it."

"I'm saying that *just once* I want him to think I won."

"That's what this is really about, isn't it? You want to pretend I'm yours so you can shove it in his face. Is that why you were so determined for me to give you another chance? To prove that you can win?"

I feel like I've been slapped. "I want you to give us a chance because I *want you.* Taking something Oliver lost is just the icing on the cake."

She's quiet for a long time, studying me. "For the record, I think you have him all wrong."

"How can you say that when he hurt you like he did? When he *bought* you like he did?"

She digs in her purse and pulls out a tissue before flipping down her mirror. "Because I knew him once. Better than he knew himself—despite all his efforts to keep me at a distance." She wipes at her face, clearing away the smudges of makeup beneath her eyes.

I sigh. Why do women fall for Oliver like this? "I'm right about this. And I hate that you're determined to learn that the hard way."

SAVVY

Rose and Jared's ceremony was short but so sweet. I love the way they look at each other. The way the rest of this day seems unnecessary to them, and they only care about each other.

Unlike the simple elegance of the ceremony, the reception is over the top. We were serenaded by a string quartet while served a five-course meal with wine pairings. Brinley and The Patio staff truly outdid themselves.

Now that the tables are cleared and the toasts are done, couples are swaying around the dance floor, and I find my gaze drifting to Oliver, who's kept himself on the periphery throughout the festivities. He catches my eye before sweeping his gaze over me. *Hungry. Proprietary. Knowing.* I yank my attention away.

Whatever animosity Alec and his mother feel for Oliver, it clearly didn't rub off on Rose. From the moment we walked in the door of the rehearsal dinner last night, they were side by side. She even kept him close at dinner, taking the spot between him and her fiancé. Tonight, she's more distant, but she checks in with him every so often.

I wonder if he realizes she's protecting him? Either way, I can't help but like her even more for it.

"Will you do me a favor?" someone asks behind me.

I turn and see Jared's mother. "What's that?"

"Will you go and get Alec on the dance floor? Cheryl didn't think anyone would dance with so few guests, and I'm desperate to prove her wrong—for Rose's sake, of course."

Of course. We exchange conspiratorial grins, and I nod. "I can do that."

I turn to find Alec chatting with a silver-haired man

at the bar. When he spots me heading his way, he stiffens for a beat before catching himself and winking like we share some sort of sweet secret.

"I don't mean to interrupt your conversation," I say, ducking my head. "I was told to get you and dance."

"I'm always happy to be interrupted by a beautiful woman," the silver-haired man says.

I force a smile, but I'm afraid he can tell I'm gritting my teeth. I can't wait for this night to be over.

"This is Paul, Rose's father-in-law," Alec explains. "He was just telling me about the progress on the renovations of their vacation home in Nice."

"Wow." I try to pretend like I regularly engage in conversations about vacation homes, let alone ones in foreign locales. My grandparents had a second home in Naples, but my father was forced to sell that when I was young and he couldn't pay the taxes.

"You and Alec should take a week or two there once we get it finished. You'd love the South of France."

Dodge and weave discussions of the future. "It must be challenging to handle renovations from so far away."

"Yes, indeed," Paul says. "That's why my wife's been spending so much time there—at least, she was up until the wedding planning made it too overwhelming for her to be away."

"I bet!"

This *world* Alec's from—homes in other countries, elaborate parties. My childhood was all about pretending we had more than we did so that these people with their yachts and European vacation homes would even give my parents the time of day. Bowing and scraping and praying we might pass for wealthy. I left that world for a reason.

A big part of me is glad Alec and I never really had a chance. I'm not sure I could bring myself to go back to it.

You'd go back for Oliver, a little voice in my brain whispers.

Of course, it would be different with Oliver. He's not about climbing social ladders and rubbing elbows with the most important people in the room.

Irrelevant. Oliver and I ended years ago.

"Well, I can leave you two," I say, taking a step back. "Alec and I can dance anytime."

"I'll just be a minute," he says, giving my hand a gentle squeeze. He feels bad about our talk in the car, but I don't. I'm glad I got to stand up for Oliver—even if only in the smallest way.

"I'll keep her company until you're ready," a smooth, deep voice says behind me. *Oliver.*

Shivers dance down my back at the thought of Oliver pulling me into his arms. What we did this afternoon happened so fast that it almost doesn't feel real.

Alec's face goes stony. "I won't be long at all."

But suddenly Alec's mother is at my side. "You *must* get to know Oliver," Cheryl says. "He always has such great stories to tell. Go on, dance."

Oliver's eyes go wide, and I almost laugh. She hasn't said one positive word toward me since I arrived, and now she's encouraging me to dance with Oliver. Oliver, who stole Portentia away from Alec. Oliver, who Alec believes is trying to steal me away from him.

I look to Alec, mentally pleading him to give me an excuse. But he doesn't want to reveal his jealousy or insecurities in front of these people, so he forces a smile. "Don't keep her long."

Oliver takes my hand and nods toward the dance floor. When we step among the other dancing couples, he pulls me loosely into his arms, leaving a respectable distance between us.

I can't risk meeting his eyes. I might forget myself, might lose myself in memories of the days when those eyes represented safety and love. So instead I stare over his shoulder, taking in everything and nothing.

I spot Alec and a graceful blonde stepping around the building and into the darkness together. "I've been thinking about what really happened between you, Alec, and Portentia when you all were in college," I say.

Oliver's hand tightens on my hip before loosening again. "What do you mean, *what really happened*?"

"I mean, I know his side of the story, and I'm curious to know yours."

"Let me guess. He told you I seduced her and got her pregnant right under his nose?"

"Yes, and that she was another casualty in you wanting anything he had."

He's quiet for a long time, and we do a few turns around the floor before he says, "And do you think that's what today was? Me trying to seduce you just so my brother can't marry you?"

I slow my steps and stare at him. "Wasn't it? Isn't that how you paid Chuck back for hurting Rose? Stealing me away from him? You've been out of my life for eight years, and once Alec put a ring on my finger, you were here with your tender kisses and sweet words. Seems pretty convenient."

He stops dancing. "Today was me finally getting to touch the woman who walked away from me eight years ago. Today was me crossing a line because I fucking love you."

"You never said it. All you would've had to do to keep me from walking out that door was say the words, but I'm supposed to believe them now?"

He takes my chin in his hand, turning me to look at him as he scans my face. "I'm not the scared kid I was back then. I believed you'd still walk away, even if you knew, and I didn't think I could survive that, so I never said the words and I let you go. And I have regretted both every day since."

"You just disappeared." The words don't come from my mouth so much as my chest. "You left town without a word to me."

"My father died, and I . . . I was such a mess. I wanted you but didn't think you'd ever be able to forgive me or ever be able to accept me for the imperfect mess I've always been."

"We're *all* imperfect."

"Not you." He tucks a loose lock of hair behind my ear. "You were always perfect for me. If you gave me another chance, I would stick around for every second of it. I would let you shatter my heart if it meant one moment of feeling your love again."

I squeeze my eyes shut. "Why are you doing this now?"

"I'm sorry," he says. "I'm sorry for leaving you. I'm sorry for lying about who Charles was to me." He swallows hard. "I'm sorry for never having the courage to tell you how I feel before now, but for what it's worth, when I came to your apartment, I truly had myself convinced that you two weren't really together. Maybe I was so desperate for this ring to be a lie that I was imagining things, but believe me when I say that my end game has never had anything to do with Alec. This is about *you.* And I hope you'll listen to me when I say, don't marry him if he isn't everything you want. Regardless of how you feel about me."

When I don't answer, he drops his hands, putting distance between us. "I hate that my timing made any part of you think this was about him. I loved you long before you met my brother, and I will love you long after you marry him." His throat bobs as he swallows. "You deserve the hero, Savvy. You always have. And for all my objections, there's nothing that hurts more than knowing I've finally convinced you that hero can't be me."

He steps back, and I watch him walk across the patio and whisper something to his sister. She glances toward me briefly before nodding and hugging him.

I'm aware of every step as he makes his way to the exit, and the rest of the night I catch myself looking for him.

CHAPTER THIRTY-SEVEN

ALEC

"Congratulations, by the way," Portentia says as we walk to a quieter spot at the side of The Orchid. "On the engagement, I mean. She's a very lucky woman to get to spend her life with you."

I'm so sick of this lie. So sick of myself and my old anger and hurt. "We're not really engaged, Portentia."

She stops walking and turns, scanning my face. "What?"

I study her and wonder how long it's been since I let myself really look at her, really look into those brown eyes, really absorb the impact of her beautiful features. Probably not since college. Not since the day I caught Oliver comforting her after their trip to the hospital.

"It seemed easier to pretend Savvy and I were

together than to have my mother push you at me all weekend."

"Wow." She flinches then shakes her head. "But you love her. That's not pretend. I see it in the way you look at her."

I hold her gaze. "Love doesn't always go both ways. No matter how much we want it to."

She tilts her head to the side. "I never stopped loving you, Alec. I loved you through every stupid decision I made."

"But you loved him more?"

"I loved you both," she says softly. "And like an idiot, I tried to have you both."

We should've had this conversation back in college, but I wouldn't hear her out. I was too crushed at the time to consider that maybe we both needed it. "It wasn't your fault. Oliver should have never—"

"It *was.*" Tears well in her eyes. "It was my fault because when I started spending time with Oliver my freshman year, I fell hard for him, but our parents had this idea about you and me getting married, so I made him keep us a secret."

I frown. "I don't understand."

"I was already dating Oliver before I ever went out with you." She stares at her feet. "I told myself it didn't matter because you and I wouldn't have any chemistry and it wouldn't go anywhere. I told myself we'd go on a few dates and that was it."

"You were . . ." I step back as if she's taken a swing at me. "You were with Oliver from the beginning?"

"He and I had been dating for almost six months when I went on that first date with you. I was just trying to appease our parents, but then my dating you made them so happy. I don't think I realized how desperately I'd been craving their approval. So I went on a second date and a third, keeping it from Oliver the whole time. But you were so sweet, and I didn't want to give you up, so I broke up with him. But then I found out I was pregnant and lost the baby and ended up in the hospital. That was the first Oliver even knew I'd been seeing you too. He never did anything wrong."

I close my eyes, trying to rewrite history as I've accepted it for over a decade. "Then why didn't he say so?"

"I imagine for the same reason you haven't let him know that you and Savvy aren't really engaged." She cocks her head to the side. "You stormed in there and made assumptions, and they fit so neatly into the box you'd all been shoving him in since the day you met." She shrugs. "I think it was easier for him to play the villain than to admit I'd broken his heart right alongside yours."

I put a hand on the building, needing to steady myself.

She bites her bottom lip. "At the time, I was rocked by my miscarriage and grateful that he spared me from having to own up to my own deceit. I know it probably doesn't mean much to you now, but for what it's worth, I regret not being honest with you."

"You didn't cheat on me with him. You cheated on him. With *me*." I stare at the woman I once loved more than anything and let the truth hit me. I feel sick. And even sicker that there were moments when I . . . I *suspected.*

She gives a shaky nod, and tears spill down her cheeks. "I thought it was exciting—dating brothers, keeping it from both of you." She swipes under each eye with her knuckle. "I was so stupid."

I close my eyes and tilt my head back, staring at the clear night sky. "You let me blame Oliver. You let Oliver be scorned by *everyone*."

"I know." She clears her throat and draws in a ragged breath. "When I ran into him in L.A. a few years ago, I told him I was ready to come clean, but he said there was no point. He said everyone had already made up their minds about him and revealing the complicated truth of what I did would only bring me more pain. But you've been so angry with him for years, and he never deserved that. I'm the one you should've been angry with. I'm the one who deserved your scorn."

I scrub a hand over my face. I told myself I needed Savvy to wear my ring and pretend to be mine because I wanted to avoid embarrassment, but it wasn't just that. I wanted to hurt him the way I thought he hurt me, and I used Savvy to do it.

Part Fourteen

EIGHT YEARS AGO

CHAPTER THIRTY-EIGHT

OLIVER

I headed to the city yesterday, determined to confront my father again about the internship and giving me back my things, but I got there just in time to see Savvy heading into the building by his side.

I'm not sure what's worse—the possibility that she might learn the truth or the idea of her being introduced to Alec and falling desperately in love. Both options make me feel sick to my stomach. I wish I'd never brought her into this.

Savvy would like Alec. I already know it. What was it Portentia said to me the day she broke off our secret little fling so she could date him? *"The bad-boy thing is hot, Oliver, but women want to be ravished by the bad boy. Alec's the kind of guy we want to marry."*

And even after that, I let everyone think I seduced

her. That I stole her away from Alec. Rose was the only one who ever knew the truth.

When I saw Savvy going into the building with my father, I could see how it would play out. A month after I'm out of here, she'd run into him again, or maybe he'd track her down. He'd sweet-talk her into meeting Alec, and Alec would charm her. He'd be able to give her everything I couldn't. A family. Stability. A relationship she wouldn't have to hide. *Honesty*.

Then they'd get serious, and she'd find out I'm the half-brother. She'd find out I lied and twisted the truth to keep her from seeing what I am to them. And I'd have to see her at every Christmas my father demanded I come home for. I'd have to watch her live happily with Charles's real son. The one who got more than his genetics. The one who got a *dad*.

I have no one to blame but myself, but I already know it would destroy me.

The only stupid thread of hope I had left was dashed by the text she sent me not long after. *I got my period.* And then the one that was the real gut punch, *What a relief!*

Of course she's relieved. Who wouldn't be relieved to find out they weren't tied to me for the rest of their life?

When the door opens, I jump off the couch.

Savvy slams it behind her and drops her big purse on the ground. She glares at me. "What did I steal?" She points to the bag, and tears fill her eyes. "What the fuck is in those envelopes that's worth your car *and* ten grand —and let's not forget *my dignity*."

The disgust on her face is an anvil to my heart.

My phone rings, and I decline the call without looking at the screen.

I swallow hard. "What are you talking about?" I glance to the bag again, and my mouth drops open. "You did it? You got what was in the chest? Everything?"

"Yes. *I stole it.* For you. Because I thought I loved you, and I wanted to do something good for you. Because you're right, you know. I wanted to believe you were the hero, and you've been warning me all this time that you're not. I just didn't peg you for my villain."

Thought I loved.

Thought.

Past tense.

I knew this couldn't last. I'm not the kind of guy who gets to be loved. I'm the mistake. The one they walk away from. "I didn't mean to hurt you," I rasp. It's the only thing I can say without falling to my knees and begging for something I don't deserve. Something that would never work.

My phone rings, and I decline the call again. This time, the name *Peony* catches my eye. Leave it to my little sister to know when my world's falling apart.

"Never mind. I don't *want* to know what's in that bag," Savvy says. Tears spill down her cheeks. "Whatever it is, I hope it was worth it." Her steps echo off the high ceilings as she rushes to the bedroom.

I sink onto the couch, and when she appears again, the big duffel Julie brought her on her first morning here is slung over her shoulder. It's packed so full, it can't even be zipped.

She strides toward me and stops in front of me. I can't bring myself to look her in the eye, so I stare at her feet. If I have to see the loathing on her face, I'll crumble.

"Your key," she says, tossing it onto the couch.

I close my eyes. *Don't go. Please don't go.*

But why beg for a delay to the inevitable?

"You know what's crazy, Oliver?" she asks. "You didn't even have to spend all that money. I would've been your thief for no reason other than you were kind enough to feed a drunk girl pancakes. I guess we both made some stupid mistakes."

I don't answer. I just listen to the sound of her steps heading to the door and then the ding of the elevator beyond.

My phone rings again, and I nearly drop it in my rush to answer. "Savvy?"

"No. Rose," my sister says. "I've been calling."

"What is it?" I snap.

"It's Dad," she says, and I register how wobbly her voice is. "They found him in his New York office. He's . . ." She draws in a ragged breath. "Oliver, he's dead."

SAVVY

"Wait—so you had unprotected sex and he was freaked that you might get pregnant, but neither one of you thought to run to the store for the morning-after pill?"

I cover my mouth with my hand. I'm sitting on the couch in Julie's boyfriend's basement, spilling my guts to my best friend. "It didn't even occur to me," I admit.

"How? How did that not occur to you? Do you *want* a baby before you graduate?"

"No, but . . ." I blow out a long breath. "I guess I was so okay with leaving it to chance, I didn't consider finding a way I wouldn't have to. In that moment, having Oliver's baby didn't seem like it would be a terrible thing." It sounds ridiculous when I say it out loud, and I bury my face in my hands. "Oh my God. I just wasn't thinking."

"Hey." Julie rubs my shoulder. "Sav, it's okay. You're not pregnant. It worked out."

I shake my head, sending tears rolling from my eyes and down my cheeks. "I was an idiot. I would've done anything for him, and he . . ." I swallow hard. "He set me up, Julie." I lift my gaze to meet hers. "He set this all up."

She frowns. "What are you talking about?"

"I've been convinced someone paid Chuck to throw that fight at the beginning of the semester."

She snorts. "Yeah. You and everyone else."

"Well, we were right. Chuck came clean. Oliver paid him to lose that fight. He knew Nathan had bet on Chuck, and Oliver made Chuck an offer he couldn't refuse so he could swoop in and save the day." *So he could buy me. So he could use me.* "Ten grand. That was all it took for Chuck to throw me under the bus."

Julie's brows shoot up. "Holy shit."

"I know. And then I fell for him." I swipe at my tears. "I'm such an idiot."

"No. I mean *holy shit* he gave Chuck ten grand *and* gave up his fancy-ass car all for the chance to get you under his roof?"

I can't bring myself to tell her about New York. About Charles. About becoming a thief. What could possibly be in those envelopes that could be worth all this risk and calculation? "Talk about bought and paid for," I whisper.

She leans back. "I don't know, Sav. Did he ever treat you like you were something he paid for? Like you were an object or you owed him sexual favors?"

I shake my head. "No, but . . ."

She tilts her head, scanning my face. My tears. "But what?"

But I fell in love with him and now my heart is breaking. I fell in love with him and told myself he loved me too. My chest shakes and my tears pick up speed. Julie pulls me into a hug, and I cry into her chest.

It's a week before I have the courage to go to his loft and give him a chance to explain, but when I get there, he's already moved out.

Part Fifteen

PRESENT DAY

CHAPTER THIRTY-NINE

SAVVY

I stick around the reception for the hour after Oliver leaves. I dance with Alec twice and am sure to eat a piece of wedding cake, but then I sneak away to a little alcove of trees by the lake. It's quiet out here, even with music drifting from the party not so far away.

I sit on the cool ground and wrap my arms around my knees, breathing easier as I watch the moon reflect off the water.

"You deserve the hero, Savvy. You always have. And for all my objections, there's nothing that hurts more than knowing I finally convinced you that hero can't be me."

"Mind if I join you?"

I blink up to a tall blonde—the same woman I saw

Alec leaving the reception with. I wave to the spot of dirt beside me. "It's all yours."

"Thanks." Even in heels and a floor-length gown, she's graceful as she lowers to the ground and extends her legs in front of her. She offers me her hand. "I'm Portentia."

Portentia, Alec's ex. Portentia, the first woman who came between the brothers. I swallow. "I'm Savannah. Nice to meet you."

"Same."

The silence, blissful moments before, is now awkward and loaded with potential disaster. What an unlikely pair we are.

"I know a little about how you're feeling right now," she says softly. "Well, that's not quite true, but I know what it's like to have them both love you. And I know what it's like to not want to choose."

I close my eyes and sigh. "I don't know what you mean."

"Alec told me earlier that the engagement isn't real—that he only wants it to be. He also told me you have a history with Oliver, though I would've guessed it anyway. I saw the way you two looked at each other tonight."

"Oh." I'm not quite sure what to say. But then I realize she might be right. She might understand how I feel in a way no one else can. "Did you believe it?" I ask, studying the way the moon's reflection looks like an accordion on the rippling water. "That he loved you?"

"Alec or Oliver?" she asks.

I huff out a dry laugh. "Either, I guess."

"But you're really asking about Oliver," she says.

"Because if this were about Alec, you'd be with him, not sitting out here all alone."

Tears heat my cheeks before I even realize they're coming. "It's been eight years, but I'm still as tangled up over him as I was the day I walked out his door."

"Why did you leave?" she asks, and I know she's not fishing for gossip. Despite the mistakes she made in the past, this woman cares about these men.

I sigh. "It was complicated, but I was angry. Angry about some choices he'd made and some secrets he'd kept. Angry that I would've done *anything* for him, and he couldn't even give me three little words." I close my eyes and let the breeze off the water dry my tears on my cheeks. "When I walked away, I needed him to come after me. I needed to know he *did* want me. And instead, he just left town. That was it. It was over. Until he thinks I'm engaged to Alec, and now? Now I'm supposed to believe he's wanted me all this time? And that it's not just about taking something his brother has?"

She hums. "Interesting."

I glare at her. "What's *interesting*?"

She shrugs. "That line of thought sounds like *Alec* thinking." She huffs. "Well, no. If I'm honest, it sounds like Cheryl thinking. That woman was always in his ear telling him Oliver was going to take what was his. Convinced him that Oliver was out to get him—as if everything Oliver earned wasn't by hard work alone." Her face falls. "And then I made it worse when I cheated on Oliver with Alec."

I pull back. Surely I misheard her. "You mean you cheated on Alec with *Oliver*."

"I suppose I cheated on them both, but I was with Oliver first. No one knew. I knew what my mother and Alec's thought about him, and I was a little embarrassed. He didn't care, though. He loved me regardless of whatever horrible limitations I put on our relationship—and trust me. I was *horrible*."

I feel sick. No wonder Oliver was always trying to convince me he was the villain. He'd had years of being knocked down if he dared to think differently.

"You know the worst part?" she asks. "When Oliver found out, after the miscarriage, how long I'd been dating Alec, that Alec and I had been talking marriage in the future all that time, he didn't even seem surprised. It was a blow, but almost like one he was expecting." She shakes her head. "He'd been put second over and over again. First by his father when Alec was born, and then by that whole family when he was forced to move in. And then by me. Worst of all, by me."

"He hurt me," I whisper, and for the first time I realize it wasn't because he paid Chuck off or because he lied to me. He hurt me when he didn't come after me. He didn't fight for me. But after all he'd been through, how could he have known I wanted him to?

"If it matters, you hurt him too," someone says. I turn and see none other than the bride herself walking up behind us. "For what it's worth, I'd like to lock the two of you in a room for twenty-four hours so you were forced to work through it. I bet you'd both come out of it better. Not to mention together."

The implications of Rose overhearing this conversation click into place for me. I glance at my fake engagement ring and then back to her. "Rose, I . . ."

"Relax. Alec just confessed the whole deal." She pulls up her skirts and takes a spot in the grass.

"Your dress!" I squeal.

She waves me off. "Not my first choice or even my third. Mom picked it out, and I have no intention of keeping it after tonight."

Portentia shifts to angle herself toward Rose. "Can you teach me that?"

"Teach you what?"

"The way you are with your mother. The way you let her do her thing so she can be happy but somehow without ever giving up your own free will."

Rose beams. "I would enjoy that more than you can imagine." She turns her attention to me. "Now, back to Oliver. Let's make a plan to fix you two up, shall we?"

My stomach feels hollow. "I think it's too late for that, Rose."

She narrows her eyes at me. "He has the courage to come to you eight years after you two split and tell you how he feels when he thinks you're marrying his brother, and you don't even have the tits to fight for him a few hours after he lets you go?"

"I just . . ."

"What do you have to lose?" Portentia asks.

Oh hell. "I'm terrified I might lose *him*. All over again."

Rose grins like she already knows she's won. "Imagine how he felt when you showed up on his brother's doorstep and he had to decide whether to contact you or not."

"Should I go now?" I look down at myself. "He liked this on me enough to take it off me once tonight. Maybe we should try for number two?"

Portentia squeals in delight.

Rose wrinkles her nose. "First of all, *what*? Second of all, never mind. I don't want to know. And third—" She takes a breath. "Not tonight. I think he and Alec should settle some things first. Then you take your turn."

"How should I do it?" I ask. My stomach is vibrating with a combination of terror and excitement. I want to beg. *Tell me how to make this work.*

"Well, first you should know that I first heard about you eight years ago when I got to play personal shopper for the pretty girl who was making my ice-cold brother all ooey and gooey inside."

"That was *you*?"

"Personal shopper?" Portentia asks. "Can someone please explain?"

"Let's start at the beginning," Rose says. "It's the only way to come up with a proper plan."

CHAPTER FORTY

OLIVER

I need to get out of town and away from Savvy before I do something reckless and demeaning. Like begging.

But I can't go before talking to my brother, no matter how much I might want to avoid him. He's left me three messages asking me not to leave town without seeing him first.

Is this about me stripping your fiancée bare and putting my mouth all over her? Sure. Be right there.

I haven't fought in a while. In fact, I'm old enough now that it's hard to remember a time when getting the shit beaten out of me was enjoyable on any level. If I'm going to revisit my appreciation for it, there's no time like the present.

Rose told me I'd probably find him at The Orchid,

working with his business partner in the restaurant, and she's right. He looks so fucking official sitting at a small table in his dress shirt and tie, his business partner across from him. Our father would be proud.

The restaurant is buzzing this morning, with all but a couple of tables full of diners eating their breakfasts. With any luck, Alec will only maim me in such a lovely establishment rather than committing outright murder.

Marston looks up from his computer and spots me before Alec does. "Oh, hey." He reaches out a hand. "I'm Marston, Alec's business partner. You're the brother, right?"

I swallow back a nasty reply and nod, accepting his firm handshake. "It's nice to meet you, Marston. I'm Oliver. Half-brother, technically."

"He knows all about you," Alec says, studying me wearily. Wearily but not like he's imagining my insides all over the floor. Okay. That's something. "I'm glad you found me. You're heading back to Monaco today?"

"Tonight," I say, nodding.

Marston's chair rumbles as he shoves away from the table. "Here. Take my seat. I want to go check on my wife anyway." He stands, tucking his laptop under his arm, and gives me one last meaningful nod before turning away. "It's good to meet you, Oliver."

I stare at his seat, unwilling to sit down if Alec doesn't actually want me here. Story of my fucking life, really. It's just that I've finally gotten to the point where I'm not interested in sitting at tables where I'm not wanted.

"Sit," Alec says. "We need to talk. Savvy told me what happened yesterday."

I blink at him. This has to be some sort of trick, but I've fucked up Savvy's life enough, and I'm not falling for it. "I had to tell her how I feel," I say.

He grunts. "And you had to show up at her apartment too? Was getting her naked part of telling her how you *feel*?"

I lower into the chair and scrub a hand over my face. *No fucking way.* "She really told you."

Alec flinches. "She told me enough that I could connect the dots."

"Shit. That's . . . Shit."

"Yeah," Alec says. "No kidding."

"I fucked up." I swallow hard. What was I thinking? It's ironic, considering that's what he's always believed happened with Portentia. Even in my angriest moments, I never would've chosen to deliberately destroy his chance for a happy marriage. I don't want that. Not for him and certainly not for Savvy. "Why are we sitting here? Because if our roles were reversed, I would already have me in a chokehold."

He puffs out a breath. "Don't think I wasn't tempted."

"Can I go first? Before you say anything else?" I swallow the lump in my throat. *Fuck.* Why is this so hard? "I want you to know I won't do anything more to compromise your relationship with Savvy. I've said my piece. I've—" I look toward the picture windows that overlook the patio and the lake beyond, shame heating my cheeks. “I’ve let her know how I feel and probably taken advantage of every unresolved emotion left between us. But she’s wearing *your* ring, and it’s time I accept that. She deserves to be happy, and if you can give her that, then . . . well, I’ll still hate your fucking guts, but I won’t seduce your wife while you’re on business trips or anything like that.”

Alec’s brows shoot up to his hairline. “I’m not sure if I should say thank you or punch you in the face.”

I cough out a laugh. “Maybe both?”

He relaxes. Yeah, this is definitely weird. “Portentia and I had a heart-to-heart last night, and it seems I owe you an apology,” he says. “A big one.”

“The past is in the past.” I scan the restaurant, searching for a server. “Think I could get some coffee?” I ask when I catch the eye of a young woman a table away.

She nods and scurries off.

I lean back in my chair. A few years ago, Portentia said we should tell my family the truth about what happened. I never thought she’d actually do it. “To be clear, she told you—”

“I know she was with you first. I know you let us all believe you’d seduced her when in truth you’d done nothing wrong. I just can’t believe that you let me think something so terrible about you.”

“To be fair, you never asked. You assumed. It was easier to let you continue assuming.”

“You spared her everyone’s judgment.”

“I wanted to think of it that way at first.” I smile at the waitress as she places a mug in front of me and fills it with steaming coffee. "But I'm a lot older now, and I know that was only part of it."

"And what was the rest?"

I hold my brother's gaze longer than I ever have, see the kindness and empathy there that I never wanted to see when I was younger. "I wanted you to hate me for something I didn't do so I had an excuse to hate you in return."

He sits back. "Well. I guess that's good to know."

"But I don't," I say in a rush. "I want to, given that you have somehow won over the woman I love—the woman I've never been able to let go—but I don't. You may be Charles's son, but you are so much better than him. Savvy wouldn't be marrying you if that weren't true."

"I appreciate that," he murmurs, but then he grimaces and shakes his head. "Shit. I can't believe I'm doing this."

I frown. "Sitting here instead of knocking me out? Yeah. Same."

"Savvy and I aren't getting married. It was all pretend. She needed me for a job, and I needed her to get Mom off my back."

Relief is a wave that hits me in the face. If I weren't already sitting, I might fall down. I take a big gulp of my coffee and burn the roof of my mouth. "I was right."

"Say what now?"

"I suspected something, but she denied it and I didn't believe her. That's the only reason I went to her yesterday—the only reason I tried anything. I was so sure you two weren't really together. Between the shit car she drives and you not knowing her family legacy—it just didn't add up." I shake my head. "But then, somehow, she convinced me otherwise."

"She did that for me, Oliver. I asked her—begged her, really—not to tell anyone the truth. Including you—*especially* you."

I drag a hand through my hair. The hope creeping over me is almost as terrifying as walking away. "But last week? That morning she was at the house?"

Alec turns toward the windows and stares out at the lake for so long I think he might be done talking. Finally, he says, "That was exactly what you thought it was. I was so pissed that you showed up when you did because I'd convinced myself I had a chance to make it real. I'd convinced myself that you'd ruined it." He turns back to me, grief pulling at his features. "But Savvy was never all in with me. I wanted to think she was, but she always held back, and once she told me about everything between you two—about how it all unfolded—I realized it was because she's never gotten over you. I wanted something from her that she no longer had to give, and that would've been true whether you showed up that day or not."

I cup my hands around my coffee mug and stare into the dark contents. "Looks like we're both screwed, then. She thinks I only want her because I want to take something from you."

Alec arches a brow. "Then I guess you better find a way to prove her wrong."

"Did she tell you about Dad?" I ask. "About what I asked her to do for me back then?"

He nods somberly. "What was in there? What did you have her take?"

"Remember the day before high school graduation when I destroyed the China cabinet?"

"Classic Oliver moment. Who could forget?"

"Do you remember why?"

He shifts uncomfortably. "I never agreed with him destroying that stuff. I couldn't believe he . . ." His eyes widen. "He *didn't* destroy it? And you got it back?"

"Savvy got it back for me."

"Well, damn. I'm glad. I mean that."

I stare at my coffee. "It only worked because he picked her for you. I knew he would, but there's a small part of me, even now, that can't help but wonder if he was right. If you two could've been good together."

"Does it matter?" Alec asks. "Does it matter who our controlling father planned to match her with? Is that enough to keep you from fighting for her?"

"No," I breathe. "It isn't."

"Oliver, I won't sit here and pretend I wouldn't snatch her up in a heartbeat if she'd have me. But after Portentia's confession last night, I realize that maybe I've never bothered to see you for who you really are. If you're the man who can make Savannah happy, if you're the one she wants, then I won't get in your way."

"And if she doesn't want either of us?"

"Then the race is on, brother," he says, but there's

something sad and resigned in his eyes that belies his words. He's already let her go.

Maybe he can teach me how to do that. I've been lying to myself for years, believing it was just a matter of time before I stopped missing her, telling myself that it was never as good as I remembered it, that I'd exaggerated our connection in my memories.

Now I know better.

"You still flying out tonight?" Alec asks, wiping a few stray crumbs from the table.

"I have to, unfortunately. But I'll see if I can track Savvy down before I go." Track her down and what? Beg her to come with me? Make all the same bold declarations she wasn't swayed by last night? I'll have to figure out something.

"Unfortunately, that won't be possible," Rose says, strolling toward us from the entrance. She drags a chair from an empty table and sits between me and my brother. "She left town early this morning, but I'll be sure to text her and let her know you two managed a civil conversation. She'll be proud, I think."

"Where is she?" I ask, already standing. Maybe it's not too late. Maybe I can catch her at the airport or—

"She has some really awesome ideas on getting heavy weights into women's hands, and Jared's business partner is meeting her in Atlanta to make her an offer before their competitor could."

"That's incredible," Alec says.

"So maybe you could both give her some space while she works that all out, m'kay?"

I narrow my eyes at my sister. "What are you up to, Peony?"

"I was just wondering the same thing," Alec says.

"I'm just saying The Rage will be old news in no time once Diva Fitness gets Savvy on board," Rose says. "Do you have any idea how strong that girl is?"

I grin all out now. "So fucking strong."

CHAPTER FORTY-ONE

SAVVY

I've been staring at Oliver's hotel room door for two minutes, just trying to work up the nerve to knock.

I lift my fist and rap on the door three times, my heart in my throat. On the other side of the door, steps pad lightly toward me, and when he pulls it open, longing takes my gut in its fist and squeezes.

He's barefoot and bare-chested, and the top button of his jeans is undone. In one hand, his knuckles are nearly white where he grips the door, and in the other, he's holding a glass of bourbon. "Savvy. What are you doing here?"

I swallow hard and hoist my shopping bags in the air. "Come on. We don't have much time. I need you to try these on."

He looks me over again. I swear, he can see not only beneath my cotton sundress but inside me. This man has always been able to see me, even when I didn't want him to.

"Can I come in?" I ask when he continues to stare at me.

He shrugs and gestures into the room. The room is no Four Seasons suite—we don't have anything like that in Orchid Valley—but it's neat. Tidy. The king-size bed is draped in the kind of fluffy white duvet that seems to beckon. Or maybe that's just the natural result of being in the same room as Oliver and so close to a bed.

Rose texted from the airport to tell me he'd decided to stay in Orchid Valley another night.

Alec told him the engagement was fake, so Oliver is staying another night, but he thinks you get back in the morning, so tonight is your chance to make your move.

"Should I make you a drink?" he asks.

I nod and watch him pour two fingers of that same amber liquid into a crystal glass.

My fingers brush his as I take it. I drain it in two swallows, hoping it might calm these frayed nerves. It burns going down, but the warmth in my chest leaves me looser. Braver.

"We don't have much time," I say, shoving the shopping bags toward him. "Hopefully it all fits. My personal shopper helped."

He takes the bags and peeks inside them. "Your *personal shopper*? What is this?"

"Listen, the less you know, the better. Just put on the

clothes, walk into the bar down the street, and . . ." I shrug. "Make meaningful eye contact."

He coughs out a laugh. "These clothes are for me?"

I look at my watch. "Yes, but you need to hurry."

He flips the bags upside down, spilling the contents onto his bed before sorting through them. "A T-shirt, a pair of jeans . . ." He lifts a pair of boxer briefs out of the pile. "You know I already have underwear, right?" he asks, and relief floods through me. *He gets it.*

I lean against the wall, trying to resist the urge to get as close as I can to him. I'm feeling reckless. I don't need bourbon to get intoxicated around Oliver. Having his eyes on me was always enough to make me lose my sense. "Yes, but my shopper wanted to make sure you had the right kind. Flash the waistband of some tighty-whities in front of my friends and I'll never hear the end of it."

His serious façade cracks and he chuckles. God, that sound is so nice. "You really want me to wear this stuff?"

I wrinkle my nose. "I actually have no idea if my friends will be there. They're entirely unpredictable when it comes to stuff like that, but I would like you to come have a drink with me." I skim my gaze over his bare chest and nearly groan. "At Smithy's, because we should talk, and I don't trust us to do much talking here."

He smiles. "Yeah? Why's that?"

I fold my arms. "You had me naked and coming within ten minutes last time we were alone in a room together."

His smile stretches broader. "And orgasms are off the table for tonight?"

"I didn't say that. I just said I want to go get a drink. In public. Where we will be forced to keep our hands and mouths to ourselves."

He grabs my wrist and tugs, bringing my body flush with his. He lowers his mouth to my ear. "I don't recall that being in public was much of a deterrent for us in the past."

Now I'm smiling too. Smiling and warm all over, and so hopeful it hurts. I know I came with an adorable plan, but all I can think about is the man in front of me. The feel of his touch, the heat of his skin.

He cups my face, sliding those long fingers into my hair. His thumb finds my bottom lip and rubs it gently. "You know, I've imagined this moment a million times and always promised myself I'd proceed with one question guiding me."

I take his thumb between my teeth and bite it lightly. "What's that?"

"What would Arturo do?" He scoops me into his arms and then plops me on the bed, climbing over me.

I squeal. "Who?"

He nuzzles my neck, muffling a laugh. "Your romance novel hero. I don't want to let you down."

"Ah." I tilt my head a bit so he has better access to the sensitive spot beneath my ear. I change my mind. There's no way I'm letting this man out that door tonight. "The thing about Arturo is that he thinks he's not good enough for our heroine, even when the opposite is so obviously true."

His hands at my hips slide around my waist as he

holds me tight. He touches his forehead to mine. "I've fucking missed you." His breath is ragged. "I didn't want to leave, but I didn't think it mattered. You'd walked away, and I didn't understand how you could possibly come back. I was afraid I didn't deserve you. I'm still afraid."

"Do you *want* me?" I ask.

He finally opens his eyes, and they're so close to mine that I see a whole future for us outlined there. Hopes and dreams he locked away because he didn't think he was worthy. "With every piece of my soul."

"Then I'm yours."

"I will do whatever necessary to prove I can be *your* hero."

"I was onto you that first night," I say, relishing the rough stubble under my fingertips. "The pancakes gave you away."

OLIVER

I've spent eight years just accepting the fact that I was in love with a woman who didn't want me. Just accepting that I'd have to walk around with half my heart for the rest of my life.

Now that she's sleeping in my arms, naked and more beautiful than I remember, I can't help but wonder why I ever thought that was an acceptable way to live.

She rolls to her back and stretches, arms overhead, back arching, nipples taut in the cool air of the hotel room. "We were supposed to talk," she murmurs, rolling toward me.

"If I recall, I talked a lot," I say, grinning. "And you liked it."

She bites back a smile and buries her face in my chest. "That I did."

I comb my fingers through her silky hair. "Come with me to Monaco? I have to fly out tonight, but if you come with me, I promise we can talk about whatever you want while we're there."

She groans. "Monaco? You are so fancy." She lifts onto an elbow and frowns. "And I can't. I have work. Clients who are counting on me, a group fitness program I'm responsible for. I might not sound important, but—"

I put a finger to her lips. "Savvy. It *is* important. It's important to every one of those people you work with, and it's important to you. You don't have to justify it."

She wrinkles her nose. "Sorry. I get defensive."

"I like that you made a career of it. That you never stopped loving your own strength and that you share it with others. You need to know that you don't ever have to justify your passions to me. Just share them, and I'll support you."

"I wish I could go, though. I've seen pictures, and it looks incredible."

"It's gorgeous, and I'll take you someday." I swallow hard. "If you still want to go."

She scans my face, traces my jaw with her fingertips as if my whiskers are secrets she's reading like Braille. "I want to have all the adventures with you."

"Same." I kiss her forehead and wrap my arms around her. "I'm sorry I worked so hard to push you away when all I ever wanted was to have you close."

"I'm sorry I walked away when all I wanted was for you to say you didn't want me to."

I swallow back the thick emotion in my throat. "Where do we start? To make this real, I mean." Then I smile. "What does Arturo do when he realizes he's in love?"

"Can I tell you a secret?" she asks, her voice low. "I don't really care about Arturo. Back when I listened to his book, I spent the whole time thinking about this hot guy I lived with."

"Yeah?" I hook my leg around her and roll us so I'm on top of her and I'm holding her hands over her head. "And what about him then? What would you want him to do next?"

"I'd want him to come back to Orchid Valley as soon as he could. And I'd want him to meet my friends and hang out with me at my favorite bar."

"I can't imagine he'd object to any of that."

"And if I get to shoot these videos with Diva Fitness, maybe I'll visit you in L.A."

"I'd like that. Consider it an open invitation."

She strokes my cheek and sighs. "We should get dressed and head to The Orchid."

I sit up. "I'm sorry. Am I making you late for work?"

She shakes her head. "No, but my best friend wants to meet you before you leave town."

"But no tighty-whities," I deadpan, and she breaks into laughter.

CHAPTER FORTY-TWO

SAVVY

I wasn't looking forward to my first visit to Oliver's place in L.A. I was afraid he'd live in some marble and crystal monstrosity like so many other rich people in this town.

Instead, he brought me to a downtown loft that reminds me so much of his place in Crossport that I felt at home the minute I walked in the door. Which is probably good, since he had me naked two minutes later.

Now we're cuddled up on the couch, him shirtless, me in nothing but his shirt, each with our own book. I keep catching him looking at me instead of the pages in front of him. Not that I mind. I know I do the same.

"It's very distracting when you look at me like that," I tease. "I'm trying to focus on the story."

He grins. "I'm not trying to distract you, but I like the way you look curled up on my couch."

I grin right back. "Funny. I like the way *you* look curled up on *my* couch."

He winks at me. "Good. I like it there."

I put my book down. "Hey, you never told me what Alec needed to talk about when he asked you to meet with him last week."

He coughs out a laugh. "Believe it or not, he wanted to talk to me about Portentia."

"About what happened in college? I thought you'd worked all that out."

"About what's happening now." He puts his own book down and pulls one leg up on the couch so he can face me. "Apparently they've been spending a lot of time together since Rose's wedding."

"His mother must be on Cloud Nine."

"No doubt." He shakes his head, amusement dancing in his eyes. "Alec said he still has feelings for Portentia and wanted to make sure I'd be okay if they started dating."

"Wow. That's . . . I'm surprised. Not that they're dating but that—"

"That he gives a shit what I think? Yeah, same. And to be fair, I think it was more about the gesture than anything. He knows how I feel about you." He studies me, and his expression goes somber. "How I've always felt about you."

Smiling, I lean forward and sweep my lips across his. "So what did you say?"

"I told him Portentia had never stopped loving him, and that I wanted to see her happy. As crazy as it is, I think they might actually have a chance."

I twine my fingers through his and smile. "I'm such a sucker for a second-chance love story."

He grabs my hand and brings it to his lips. "While you're here, I wanted to show you something."

I look around. "What's that?"

"It's in the bedroom. Let me go grab it."

I watch him stroll out of the room, very much enjoying the view of his shirtless back and his strong ass accentuated perfectly by his jeans.

It's been five months since Rose's wedding, and Oliver has spent more time in Orchid Valley than I ever could've expected. It turns out that a sports agent can do a lot of his work from wherever he chooses, so Oliver chooses to do it near me.

But this weekend I needed to come to L.A. to see the Diva studios and meet with "my team" (that's still crazy to me) to flesh out my vision for this program. It's not a live-streaming program like The Rage is, but that might be for the best. Instead of just me on the screen, I'll get to have a whole group working out with me—which means I'll be able to represent a half-dozen of the infinite different ways a fit body can look. That alone might excite me as much as putting heavy weights in women's hands.

Oliver returns with a big purse I recognize from one of the hardest days of my life. The purse I filled with the contents from Charles's chest.

"Oliver," I whisper.

"You deserved to look through all this a long time ago," he says, putting the bag on the couch and taking a seat on the other side of it.

I open it up and lift out the first manilla envelope, glancing at him. "I can open these?"

He nods. "I want you to."

I carefully pull the contents from one manilla envelope and then another. Oliver helps me, grabbing a third and fourth, until they're all empty and everything from inside sits on the couch between us.

My heart aches as I scan the contents. "This is all? This is what you needed me to steal?"

It's not nothing, but it's all so . . . personal. Piles and piles of photos, scrapbooks, and scrapbook pages that were clearly never finished. I flip through the photos, and the ache in my chest intensifies when I realize one stack is entirely from the short months of Oliver's life when his father still lived with them.

The woman in the pictures is stunning, and if I knew her while she was living, I would've seen Oliver in her at first glance. But it's not just her in the photos that breaks my heart. These are pictures of a family. Charles looking at Oliver's mom like she's the light of his life. In other pictures, he's holding a baby Oliver, grinning at him. But the majority of the photos are of Oliver and his mother, and I imagine Charles behind the camera capturing those moments. For a short while, they were a family.

All the other stacks of pictures feature a little boy in

all stages of his life, captured by someone who so obviously adored him.

Beneath the photos there's a stack of three journals, and I immediately remember the first night I met Oliver and how he told me his mother was always journaling.

"You said your father burned these."

He clears his throat. "Yeah. That's what he told me. Imagine my surprise when I found them with all her other things he'd been keeping from me."

I flip through a journal, admiring the loopy script without reading the words. The secrets in here aren't mine to know. "Why did he have them? Shouldn't these have been yours?"

"He said I couldn't be trusted with them, but I think it was just another way to make me do as he demanded."

I frown. "Alec's mother knew this stuff was gone after Charles died." I lift my gaze to meet Oliver's eyes. "Why would she even care?"

He gives me a sad smile. "Cheryl was always so jealous of my mother. I think that's why she hated me so much. But these journals and pictures tell a story much different than the meaningless affair she described to explain away my existence." He places a big hand on the front of a leather-bound journal and strokes it with his thumb. "I think part of me wants to believe that when Charles told me he burned the journals, he wanted her to think it was true so she wouldn't be so set on destroying them herself." He sighs. "Or maybe I'm giving him too much credit."

I squeeze his hand, and we spend the next hour going

through pictures and scrapbook pages. He tells me about each, as well as everything he can remember about his mother. Sometimes he even talks about his father, and I'm grateful when I realize that though their relationship was strained, Oliver has some good moments to remember.

When we're cleaning up and sliding everything back into envelopes, I pick up a stray sage-color business-size envelope with the Coast to Coast Equities and Investments watermark. "You kept this?" I ask.

"Oh. Yeah. I don't know how that ended up with the rest. It's just a random envelope with my info in it." He extends his hand, palm up. "I'll throw it out."

I shake my head and frown at the torn edge. Hope flutters in my heart as I meet his eyes. "*Your* info?"

He narrows his eyes. "You're acting weird. What is it?"

It shouldn't matter. In fact, it doesn't really matter *to me*, but I know it would mean so much to Oliver.

My hands shake as I pull out a small slip of paper. I recognize Charles's blocky script—even all these years later—and bite my bottom lip as I read the note.

Trust my intuition.

Oliver Rhett – Crossport University

Beneath that, he wrote Oliver's number and the address for his loft.

"I don't know why he had my info with this stuff," Oliver says. "I like to think he wanted it all to get back to me if something ever happened to him, but it's strange."

"This wasn't with the other envelopes," I say carefully.

"I dropped it in the bag with everything else, but *this* envelope is one your father gave to me." I hold his gaze. "He told me he thought I'd be the perfect match for his son, and he wanted his son to someday have the family he deserved as a child."

Oliver's eyes go glassy with tears, and he shakes his head. "No. You don't have to—"

"He gave me this envelope and said he wanted me to reach out to his son in a few weeks."

Tears spill over and onto his cheeks. "Alec. He was always looking for the perfect match for *Alec*."

"After everything you told me, I assumed it was Alec too, but Oliver"—I wave the envelope in the air—"this was who he wanted me to contact. He wanted me to be with *you* because he wanted you to be happy, and some instinct of his told him that I could be your family."

Tears slip from the corners of his closed eyes. This strong man. This impenetrable *force*. Crying at a note left eight years ago by a man he claims to hate.

"Do you hate that your manipulative old man wanted me to be with you?"

He swallows, his throat bobbing. "No. I don't hate it at all."

I wrap my arms around him. "I love you."

He slides a hand into my hair and kisses my cheek. "I love you too."

ONE YEAR LATER

OLIVER

Orchid Valley is the perfect retreat.

In fact, I spend more time here than in L.A., so maybe that makes our California place my second home.

Either way, I'm rather fond of this sleepy tourist town. I like the people and mountains. There are plenty of trails to hike and places to visit within a couple hours' drive. But mostly, this is where Savvy is happiest, so it's where I'm happiest. And tonight that's truer than ever.

"Did you bring it?" my sister asks, elbowing me in the side much harder than necessary.

"No, Peony. I forgot the most important part."

"I'm sorry," she mutters, wringing her hands. "I'm nervous."

We're in the backyard of our Orchid Valley home surrounded by Savvy's friends—*our* friends—celebrating the long Labor Day weekend with a cookout and a few beers. And, if I have my way, one big surprise.

Brinley joins us on the patio. "You about ready?" she asks under her breath.

"Just about," I say, grinning at her.

"Hey," Rose says with *another* elbow in my side. "Why didn't she get a snarky reply?"

I roll my eyes and shake my head. "Sorry, sis. I'll try to be more equal-opportunity snark."

"Have you seen the ring?" Rose whispers to Brinley.

"No." Brinley's eyes go wide. "Have you?"

Rose nods like a bobblehead. "It's gorgeous." She holds her hand out, palm up. "Gimme. I want to show Brinley."

"You two can't wait, like, twenty minutes?"

"That's *forever*," Rose whines. "Come on. I want to see it again too!"

I nod toward the outdoor kitchen Kace and Dean helped me install this summer, and we step behind the counter so Savvy won't see anything from where she's standing, chatting to Stella in the backyard. I open the blue velvet box and show them what's inside.

"Oh my God," Brinley whispers, her hand to her chest. "She's going to love it."

"Isn't it *gorg*?" Rose says.

The back door swings open and Smithy walks out. "Hey, all!" he announces. "I brought more beer!" He hoists a six-pack of O'Doul's in the air. Dude makes me laugh. He owns a bar and is always stoned, but he's decided alcohol is the devil's water and has switched to nonalcoholic beer—and not even the good craft kind.

"Hey, Smithy," Brinley says. "Glad you could make it." But her tone says, *I told you not to be late.*

"Shit, man! That ring is gorgeous! Is that for Savvy? About damn time!" He holds a hand in front of his eyes, pretending to be blinded, but everyone else is gaping because Smithy has *one* volume, and now everyone on the lawn knows what tonight's surprise is.

Including Savannah.

I snatch the box back from Brinley, who looks as mortified as Smithy *should* but won't, snap it shut, and tuck it back into my pocket before turning to my girlfriend.

She's staring at me, biting her bottom lip like she's trying not to laugh. A dozen pairs of eyes are trained on us.

I squeeze the back of my neck and stroll down the steps and into the yard. "I guess I'm doing this now," I say when I'm standing in front of her.

"You better," she whispers.

"You gotta get down on one knee, man!" Smithy calls from the porch. "Otherwise it doesn't count, and she gets to cancel the wedding with no notice."

Brinley and Rose both spin around to gawk at him.

"Hey, I don't make the rules," he mutters.

"I wouldn't want you to do that," I tell Savvy, dropping to one knee.

She's smiling so big. "I love you." The stars are out,

but no one will see them with the way that smile lights up the night.

I blow out a breath and try to remember how words work. “Savannah, you are the love of my life.”

“Mine too, dude,” Smithy calls. “You’re gonna have to do better than that!”

I close my eyes for patience.

“Ignore him and continue, please,” Savvy says, offering me her left hand.

I squeeze her fingers in mine. “Sometimes I feel like I’ve been lonely since the day my mother died, but I’ve never been lonely a single day I spent with you. I’m told I can be a little grumpy”—Rose cackles from the porch—“but that I’m better when you’re around. And I’m no hero, but I feel like one when I’m with you.”

“Oliver,” Savvy whispers.

“Which is all to say that I am better with you near me, and life is better with you in it.” I pull the ring box from my pocket and open it. “If you marry me, I’ll do everything I can to make sure your life is better with me in it too.”

She drops to the ground and wraps her arms around my neck. “It already is,” she says before kissing me.

I pull the ring from the box and slide it on her finger.

“Clever girl,” Smithy says, coming closer. “If you never say yes, you aren’t locked in.”

She snorts. “Who invited you anyway, Smithy?”

“You know,” I say, sliding my arms around her waist, “he has a point. You never really answered the question.”

She grins up at me. "Yes, I will marry you. As long as Smithy doesn't get to make the rules for the wedding."

"Your loss," he mutters. "I have some killer ideas."

He starts going on about something with parakeets and heavy metal, but I tune him out and focus on my fiancée.

We're both still on our knees, but I pull her in closer without bothering to stand. When I whisper in her ear, I make sure only she can hear. Because it's early and we're not ready for our friends to know yet. "And what do I have to do to talk you into marrying me before the baby comes?" I ask.

She hums. "I can probably come up with a few ideas."

"So, short engagement?" I ask.

She holds my face in both hands and kisses me hard. "I'd marry you tonight." She doesn't bother to keep her voice down this time.

"Nope!" Rose calls. "You want a real wedding. With flowers and shit. Trust me on this."

Savvy shrugs and meets my eyes again. "How quickly can we pull together flowers and shit?"

I sweep my lips over hers. Once. Twice. Damn, this woman makes me happy. "I'll start making calls in the morning."

THE END

Thank you for reading *Every Chance with You*, the fourth book in The Orchid Valley series. To receive an email when I release a new book, please sign up for my newsletter: lexiryan.com/signup

I hope you enjoyed this book and will consider leaving a review. Thank you for reading. It's an honor!

OTHER BOOKS BY LEXI RYAN

Orchid Valley

Every Little Piece of Me (Brinley and Marston's story, includes their prequel novella)

Every Sweet Regret (Stella and Kace's story)

Every Time I Fall (Abbi and Dean's book)

Every Chance with You (Savvy's story)

The Boys of Jackson Harbor

The Wrong Kind of Love (Ethan's story)

Straight Up Love (Jake's story)

Dirty, Reckless Love (Levi's story)

Wrapped in Love (Brayden's story)

Crazy for Your Love (Carter's story)

If It's Only Love (Shay's story)

Not Without Your Love (Colton's story)

The Blackhawk Boys

Spinning Out (Arrow's story)

Rushing In (Chris's story)

Going Under (Sebastian's story)

Falling Hard (Keegan's story)

In Too Deep (Mason's story)

LOVE UNBOUND: Four series, one small town, lots of happy endings

Splintered Hearts (A Love Unbound Series)

Unbreak Me (Maggie's story)

Stolen Wishes: A Wish I May Prequel Novella (Will and Cally's prequel)

Wish I May (Will and Cally's novel)

Or read them together in the omnibus edition, *Splintered Hearts: The New Hope Trilogy*

Here and Now (A Love Unbound Series)

Lost in Me (Hanna's story begins)

Fall to You (Hanna's story continues)

All for This (Hanna's story concludes)

Or read them together in the omnibus edition, *Here and Now: The Complete Series*

Reckless and Real (A Love Unbound Series)

Something Reckless (Liz and Sam's story begins)

Something Real (Liz and Sam's story concludes)

Or read them together in the omnibus edition, *Reckless and Real: The Complete Series*

Mended Hearts (A Love Unbound Series)

Playing with Fire (Nix's story)

Holding Her Close (Janelle and Cade's story)

Hot Contemporary Romance

Text Appeal

Accidental Sex Goddess

Decadence Creek (Short and Sexy Romance)

Just One Night

Just the Way You Are

These Hollow Vows Duology (Sexy, Action-Packed YA Fantasy)

These Hollow Vows

These Twisted Bonds

CPSIA information can be obtained
at www.ICGtesting.com
Printed in the USA
LVHW080217271022
731700LV00012B/965